Midnight Memory Lane

WHAT NOW

By

Donna Anderson

Gotham Books

30 N Gould St.
Ste. 20820, Sheridan, WY 82801
https://gothambooksinc.com/

Phone: 1 (307) 464-7800

Published by Gotham Books (July 1, 2024)

ISBN: 978-1-0881-7294-0 (H)
ISBN: 978-1-0881-5091-7 (P)
ISBN: 978-1-0881-7290-2 (E)

Because of the dynamic nature of the Internet, any web addresses or links contained in this book may have changed since publication and may no longer be valid.

The views expressed in this work are solely those of the author and do not necessarily reflect the views of the publisher, and the publisher hereby disclaims any responsibility for them.

FOREWORD

Jeannette had still not figured out where her life had gone wrong. Her memories of half of her life had shown her what she had learned through life lessons, but she was not finished with her journey.

She met Robert on a plane and played checkers for three hours during a flight to Chicago. He kept her mind occupied so she did not have to think about why she was heading to Chicago; her friend Jerry had died, and she was going to his funeral. When she got there an attorney met her in Jerry's office to inform Jeannette about his will. He left her *Windy City Publishing and Recording Company*, lock, stock, barrel, and building. It was all hers.

Overnight she was thrown into a CEO position of a major business with no college or formal training of any kind on how to run a successful business. Jeannette was a natural and used basic instincts and common sense. The business thrived under her command.

Robert lived in the same city as Jeannette, Clark City. It was by chance they met on the plane. He is an attorney and was flying to the corporate office in Chicago on business. By the time the plane landed, they had become friends. He asked Jeannette if she would have dinner with him when they were both back in Clark City. She accepted.

Jeannette's ex-husband Jeff lost his business. She received a phone call from Jeff before she left for Chicago announcing he moved to Clark City and wanted to have dinner as a family. She turned him down flat and told him to leave her alone.

Is Jeff ever going to be out of her life? Is Robert going to be in Jeannette's life? How will she run a company in Chicago when her home is in Clark City?

What Now?

Contents

1

Stepping off the plane, there to greet Jeannette were her two favorite people, Sean and Tyler. "My boys! I have missed you so much!" She threw her arms around both of them and held on tight. "I am back in Oregon!"

"I am so glad you are home! It just isn't right when you aren't here," Tyler said.

"Well, I'm here now. Sean, did you get registered for college?" Jeannette asked.

"I did. I had plenty of money. I need to pick up my books next week and then I am ready. Will you be able to help me pay for the books I need? One book is $125.00! It's ridiculous!"

"That is a lot for one book. But we won't have a problem with paying for whatever you need. I will explain on the way home. Let's get my bags and go home," Jeannette said.

She explained everything to the boys; how much she and her company is worth, how much she was getting paid, an apartment, and commuting to Chicago. By the time they got home, she was tired of her own voice. Sean and Tyler were stunned by all the information and had not said a word the entire drive home.

"So let me get this straight. At this point, every other week you are going to spend a week in Chicago. You will have an apartment there too?" Sean asked.

"Right now, that is correct. It could change in the future, but for now, this is what I came up with so I can be with you boys and run the company. If you have a better idea, I'm all ears," Jeannette said.

"Well, I don't like it! I don't like you being gone!" Tyler erupted.

"Tyler! I'm trying to make a difficult situation; one we can live with. Do you want to move back to Chicago? Is that what you want? If that's the case, we need to discuss it, all three of us," Jeannette said, looking directly at Tyler.

"No, I don't want to move back to Chicago. I love Oregon. I want you here, in Oregon," Tyler said with a bit of a pout.

"It's a lot to wrap your head around, I know. Believe me. It has been tough for me too. Let's give this a try and see how it goes, for now. If it doesn't work, then we will work on another solution. Don't pout! It is not a good look for you," Jeannette told Tyler.

It suddenly occurred to Sean, "Mom! We're rich!" Sean shouted.

Jeannette let out a big laugh and said, "Well, yes and no. The company is rich. I own the company, and I am getting paid quite a bit, plus extras, so I guess you could say we are rich."

"Wow! This is awesome! Can I get a new car? Maybe a sports car?" Sean asked excitedly.

"No, you are not getting a new car. The one you have right now is fine. I will buy new tires for your car, and I can help pay for your college," Jeannette said.

It was vital for her to keep them grounded and not let them become spoiled rich kids that think they can have anything they want.

"Will you help pay for my college too? Tyler asked.

"Of course! Why wouldn't I?" Jeannette asked.

"Well, you might run out of money," Tyler said sadly.

"Oh, honey!" Jeannette stopped and had to laugh. "I won't run out of money! You should know by now I have always managed to take care of whatever you two needed. I am not about to stop now. Silly boy."

That eased Tyler's mind and put a smile on his face.

"Sean was mean to me when you were gone."

"Sean? Do you have something to tell me?" Jeannette asked.

"Oh, Tyler! I was not! I told you to get your homework done before you went out with your friends just like Mom does. Knock it off!" Sean said with irritation.

"Okay, I see we have some things to discuss this week. Let's not do it now. I'll fix us something to eat, and you guys can tell me all about your week."

The rest of the day and into the evening was filled with laughter, details of the weeks' events, who did what, who was dating who, and everyday things Jeannette would have known about if she had been at home. At midnight, the three were talked out and ready for bed. Jeannette gave each of her boys a big hug and kiss before they went to their rooms for a much-needed rest.

In the morning, things were normal. Jeannette fixed a big breakfast, and the boys got up as soon as the smell of bacon wafted into their rooms.

"Now, this is normal. I like getting up to the smell of bacon. I am glad you are home, Mom," Tyler said.

"I'm glad to be home. Although I was getting used to having room service," Jeannette told him.

"You had room service? You could order whatever you wanted?" Tyler asked.

"Yep! It was nice," Jeannette said with a sigh.

"Wow! That would be so cool. Pick up the phone and get whatever you want," Tyler said. "Hey, Sean! Mom had room service in Chicago! Wouldn't that be cool?"

"Isn't it kind of like what Mom does for us? The only difference is she usually picks what we have for meals," Sean said.

"Oh, I guess you're right. I didn't think about it like that," Tyler frowned and looked at his plate.

"Tyler, don't frown," Jeannette said. "Since I got home, you have been acting like a little boy. Act your age. I know you haven't been happy with me, but it's been good for all of us to have some time away from each other. You will have more responsibilities, which will serve you well when you leave home."

"It's just such a big change. I will try to get used to it. I promise," Tyler said.

"I need to get some grocery shopping done today. Will you come with me and help with carrying the bags?" Jeannette asked Tyler.

"Sure, Mom," Tyler answered.

"Sean, what are your plans?" Jeannette asked.

"I am working until four then I'll come home and shower. I'm taking Patty for a burger this evening."

"So how are things with you and Patty?"

"Fine," was all Sean had to say.

Things were in normal mode for Jeannette and the boys. Windy City was running smoothly, and Bridgett was compiling a list of apartments for Jeannette to see next week. She was delighted with the world in general, until Wednesday. There was a knock on her door. Jeff was standing on the other side. The happy look on her face faded to a frown.

"What are you doing here, Jeff?" Jeannette asked blandly.

"I hear you own a big company," Jeff said sarcastically.

"Yes, I do. What does that have to do with anything?"

"You don't know how to run a business! It should be my business! How did you get it anyway? Did you sleep with Jerry?" Jeff accused, raising his voice.

"No! Of course, not! Jerry was my boss, and we were friends! That's all! For crying out loud, Jeff! My life is none of your business!" Jeannette yelled and tried to shut the door.

"You owe me, little missy. You owe me for supporting you all those years and taking care of you!" Jeff said, sounding evil.

"You have lost your mind! You didn't support me! I supported you through two failed businesses and anything else you did!" Jeannette yelled in disbelief.

"You didn't support me and my businesses! That's why they failed! It was your fault, not mine!" Jeff accused.

"This conversation is ridiculous and a waste of time," Jeannette said and stomped on his foot that was holding the door open. He let out a yell of pain, and she slammed the door in his face.

"I'm going to make sure Tyler has to come live with me! You are a terrible mother leaving him home for a week at a time while you go off and play! I will make you pay, Jeannette!" Jeff yelled as he left. "You will be sorry, you ugly fleabag!"

Jeannette locked the door and leaned against it. What was she going to do? Robert. "I'll call Robert and ask him what I can do, legally, about Jeff. He can't take Tyler! I won't let him!"

She called Robert's office and left a message with his receptionist to call her. He called as soon as the message reached his hand.

"Jeannette! You must be in Clark City," Robert said.

"Yes, I am. I have to go back to Chicago Sunday. I called because I need some legal advice. Can you help me? I hate to ask, but I didn't know who else to turn to. You are the only attorney I know in town."

"That's what I do, Jeannette, and I will do my best to help. What's the problem?" Robert asked.

She explained the situation in detail.

"So, what would you suggest?" she asked.

"This can be rectified, Jeannette, legally. But what I am going to do is refer you to another attorney in my office."

"Why? You don't want to help me? Forget that I asked. I apologize for calling," Jeannette said, feeling embarrassed she had just told him her situation. "I won't bother you again, Robert."

"Jeannette! That's not it at all! Don't hang up. I want you to see Mr. Baker because he specializes in this kind of case. But the main reason is, if you are my client, then I cannot date you, and I would really like to see you," Robert explained, quickly, before she hung up.

"Oh," Jeannette said surprised. "That would be nice. I want to see you too."

"Listen. I am going to go over this with Mr. Baker and have him call you to set up an appointment. Is that acceptable?" Robert asked.

"Yes. It is fine."

"Now, business is finished, would you like to have dinner with me tonight?"

"That would be nice. Yes, I would like to have dinner," Jeannette said without much thought. It just spilled out of her mouth.

"Is six-thirty alright with you?" Robert asked.

"That would be fine," Jeannette said and gave him her address.

"I am looking forward to seeing you. Bye," Robert said and hung up.

She replaced the receiver and sat down hard on the nearest chair. She thought, "What have I done? A date? I have a date? I called for legal advice and ended up with a date. Life really can change in a moment. If Jeff hadn't come over, I would not have called Robert. I forgot to call him when I got back to Clark City. Maybe this is the man God has sent for me? Okay, now you are getting ahead of yourself. This is not the time to start a relationship! Oh, good grief! You're dreaming!"

She kept her mind busy the rest of the day cleaning the apartment and talking to *Windy City.* In between calls and domestic chores, she thought about how she was going to tell Sean and Tyler she was going on a date. They had never seen her with another man before. Life was, without a doubt, changing.

When the boys arrived home, she screwed up her courage and began the conversation.

"Sean, Tyler, I need to talk to you for a minute. I wanted to let you know I . . . I have a dinner date tonight. His name is Robert, and he is an attorney. He will be here at six-thirty to pick me up. Are you two okay with that?"

There was a brief pause of silence. "Of course, it's alright, Mom!" Sean said with approval.

"It's okay with me. I wondered if you were ever going on a date. It's about time!" Tyler said.

"Really? I was scared to tell you guys. I didn't know how you would feel about it. I am so relieved," she said, letting out a breath of air.

Jeannette explained how she had met Robert on the plane and the reason she had called him earlier in the day.

"I don't want you two to worry about the situation with your dad. I will handle it."

"Will I have to live with Dad?" Tyler asked.

"No. You are old enough to make that decision. It was just a bluff. Jeff is trying to hurt me, and he knows the way to do it, is by using you and Sean to get to me. Put it out of your mind. It is not going to happen, Tyler. He will never take you from me."

"Are you sure?" Tyler asked with a worried voice.

"I am positive, Tyler. Now just as a precaution, anything we say in this house, about what we are doing, stays between us. You don't tell your friends or anybody. Understand? We don't want anything getting back to your dad," Jeannette explained. "Now, I need to change clothes for my dinner date. Oh, Lord. I just said dinner date." She shook her head as she went to her room.

"Hey, Tyler. Trust Mom. She has never let us down. Besides, you must be the special one. Dad only said you. Nothing was said about me." The thought brought a smile to Tyler's face.

"Yea, I'm special," Tyler said and strutted around the room.

"Don't let it go to your head, little brother," Sean said, rolling his eyes.

Robert knocked on the door at six-thirty sharp. Jeannette opened the door. She was looking at the most handsome man in the world, and he was there for her. He stood six-foot-two, dark hair with just a hint of gray at the temples. His facial features exuded all man, with a muscular physique and broad shoulders. He was wearing blue jeans, a light blue cotton shirt, and a dark blue sport jacket. When he smiled, it covered his whole face, and his eyes squinted ever so slightly. He didn't take his eyes off Jeannette standing in the doorway.

"Hi, Robert," she said with a huge smile to match his.

"You look beautiful, Jeannette."

Jeannette had a hard time picking out just the right thing to wear for her dinner date. After several attempts, she chose a simple light blue dress with a matching shrug. It was perfect. They were both wearing blue.

"Please, come in. I want to introduce you to my boys."

Introductions were made to her judgmental-looking boys. After all, this was someone they didn't know and wanted to make sure Robert was going to treat their mother with the respect she deserved. He picked up on that right away and handled it nicely to put them at ease.

Robert took Jeannette to Blackberry's, which was one of the most beautiful restaurants in Clark City. They each ordered the same meal, sautéed shrimp, which was the favorite meal for both of them. Throughout dinner, their conversation never lagged. It was as if they had known each other for years. It was comfortable.

After dinner, as Robert opened the car door for her, he said, "I have wanted and waited to do this all evening."

He took her in his arms and gave her the most passionate kiss she had ever experienced. It was so gentle but held so much passion. Her skin hummed with excitement.

"I hope that wasn't too forward of me," he said and took one step back.

"No, it wasn't forward. I enjoyed it very much. Would you mind doing it one more time, please?"

"My pleasure," Robert obliged and took her in his arms.

He drove around town not wanting their date to end. He showed her where his office was located, where he lived, and any place he could think of to stretch out more time with Jeannette.

"Well, here we are, back at your apartment," Robert said.

"Already?" Jeannette almost moaned. He opened the door for her.

As he walked her to the door, he said, "I enjoyed spending this evening with you, Jeannette. I would like to see you again."

"I would like it very much," she said and put her key in the lock.

Robert put his hand on hers and gently turned her to face him. Once more, he took her in his arms and kissed her. She felt sensations she had never felt before. Jeannette leaned into the kiss and let herself enjoy the taste of a real man, named Robert.

He held her close, drinking in the sweet smell of perfume mixed with a beautiful woman.

"I don't want to say goodnight to you, Jeannette. You have stirred up feelings in me that I would like nothing more than to act on. No woman has ever made me feel this way. What are you doing to me? I could kiss you all night long if you let me."

"Right now, I think I would like it very much, but I have two sons inside who might not approve. Besides, it has been years since I have been with a man. I'm not sure I remember how. You make me nervous. This is the first time I have given any thought about wanting to be intimate with a man."

"One day, Jeannette, I assure you, it will happen. I can wait until you are ready. Can I see you tomorrow? Lunch, maybe?" Robert asked.

"I would like that very much, Robert."

"I don't know what it is, but when you say my name, it gives me goosebumps. What are you doing to me?" Robert questioned.

Robert stood inches from her mouth and couldn't resist tasting her one more time. His kiss wasn't as gentle this time. It was mixed with passion and hunger. To her surprise, Jeannette's entire body responded, leaving her breathless when he took a step back.

Robert asked, "Is one o'clock at the Blue Bucket a good time? It is just down the block from my office."

After she had regained her composure, she managed to say, "Whatever it is I am doing to you, I think you might be doing the same to me, too." Jeannette let out a stabilizing breath and said, "I will meet you there," and turned the key in the lock. The door opened, and she stepped inside. As she watched Robert walk away, she thought, *"What a man! Those jeans he is wearing sure shows his cute butt."* The thought made her blush. She shut the door and leaned against it.

"Mom? Did you have a nice time? Was he a gentleman? Where did you go?" Sean asked.

"Slow down, slow down. Yes, I had a nice time. Yes, Robert was a gentleman. We went to Blackberry's and ate shrimp."

"You're smiling. It must have gone well."

"Yes, it did. I am meeting Robert for lunch tomorrow. I didn't wake you, did I?" Jeannette asked.

"No, I couldn't sleep until I knew you were home. I don't know about this dating stuff, Mom," Sean said.

Jeannette giggled and then said, "Now you see how I feel when you are out. It seems the tables have turned," she said with a grin. "It's late. Go back to bed. I'll lock up. Goodnight, honey," she said and kissed him on the cheek.

Trying to sleep was impossible. Jeannette couldn't get Robert's face out of her mind. The touch of his lips still lingered on hers along with an unusual tingling sensation. She could still smell a musky scent he had left on her as he held her close. His touch had stirred something inside her she never knew existed. *"Is this what I have been missing out on all these years? Do other people feel this? Or is it just me? It can't be! Maybe it was just that I hadn't kissed anyone in years. I didn't experience this with Jeff. Maybe I didn't love him? Maybe he couldn't kiss me this way because he didn't love me? Too many maybes,"* she thought and closed her eyes.

The next day, one o'clock could not come fast enough. Jeannette was on the phone most of the morning with *Windy City* giving Bridgett instructions about meetings to set up, clear some time on her schedule to look at the apartments and general things that needed to be happening at the office.

"Will you have Greg give me a call when he can? I want an update on the new singles. Make sure you call David to pick me up at the Airport on Sunday. He needs to know what time my plane gets in. Yes, I received my ticket yesterday. I'm glad you booked it for early morning. Please do that each time. Instead of having Greg call me, I will call him. I am going to be out for a while today. Is there anything else? Okay. I will talk to you later, Bridgett. Bye," Jeannette instructed.

She looked at the clock, "Eleven-thirty? That's it? Oh, good grief. I guess I can get changed and maybe then I can take care of a few errands before lunch."

At one o'clock, Jeannette pulled up in front of the restaurant. Perfect timing. Robert arrived just in time to open her car door and take her hand. Jeannette thought, *"Here he is. Just as handsome, the same musky scent, and making my body hum with excitement from his touch. Is this real? Am I dreaming? He is wonderful."*

"I am so glad to see you! I see you remembered how to get here," Robert said.

"Remembered?" Jeannette said, looking puzzled.

"Last night, after dinner, we drove by here. I pointed it out," Robert told her.

"You did? I don't remember. Guess my mind was distracted with other thoughts," she said, slightly embarrassed with a blush.

"May I kiss you right here, right now?" Robert asked, standing so close, there was barely an inch between them.

"I wish you would," Jeannette said.

He leaned in and gently touched her lips. Just as he did, a horn honked at them, and some guy yelled out his window, "Way to go, man!" Robert spun around and shot a dirty look at the driver as he sped away.

"Let's get out of the street. We don't need an audience. I will get another kiss from you before I go back to the office."

"Promise? I will let you," Jeannette said, looking into his brown eyes that were making her knees weak.

"You can count on it," Robert said and placed his hand on the small of her back. His touch sent chills down her spine, making her shiver, slightly. "Are you cold? Do you need a sweater?"

Jeannette let out a little giggle and said, "No, but thank you for asking."

She was thankful for a voice, which seemed to come from nowhere, "Hello, Robert. I have your table ready. Please, follow me."

They were taken to a very intimate corner table. The waiter handed them each a menu and said, "Enjoy your lunch," and left them alone.

"Robert, I shivered because I felt your hand on my back. That is what your touch does to me. I probably shouldn't tell you all this, but I want you to know how I feel about you." Jeannette couldn't stop herself from talking, "I didn't get any sleep last night thinking about you and your kisses. You have awakened something inside me I didn't know existed. My skin feels like electricity is dancing across it. My lips tingle when they meet yours. My mind goes blank when you look at me. The only thought I can form at that time is, just kiss me! I want to feel your touch on my skin!" She suddenly stopped. "Oh, Robert! I'm so sorry! I didn't mean to say all that! It just came out! I don't want to make you feel uncomfortable. I . . . I couldn't stop! Now I'm uncomfortable."

"Jeannette. Calm down. I am not uncomfortable. The things you just told me are music to my ears. I feel the same way about you." He reached across the table and took her hand, brought it to his lips, without taking his eyes off her, and kissed it. Her shiver was uncontrollable. "You have no idea what it does to a man when he can make a woman shiver. It is intoxicating. It's special, and to my knowledge, rare. It makes me want to—"

A waitress made an appearance at their table, "Can I bring you something to drink?" she asked.

Jeannette said, "I'll have iced tea, please." Robert ordered the same.

"I can take your order if you are ready," the waitress said.

"Oh, I haven't looked at the menu!" Jeannette said, glancing at the menu and suddenly forgetting how to read.

"Just bring us two Cobb salads with dressing on the side," Robert said, rescuing Jeannette. The waitress took the menus and left the table.

"Thank you. How did you know to order me a salad?"

Robert responded very sure of himself, "Because I like salad, so I know you do. So far, we have ended up ordering the same thing, so it just made sense. Was I wrong?"

"No, you were not wrong," Jeannette said with a small frown. "Please, next time, ask me, first? I am not upset with you. Please get that out of your mind. I have deep scars from my ex-husband. He told me what I liked and what to do. I wasn't allowed to make a decision or do anything without his permission. When he left me, after all the years of him drilling into me I was stupid and ugly, it sunk in and I believed him. It has been difficult for me to make decisions in fear of being wrong or stupid. I didn't even know what I liked to eat. Everything I cooked was what he wanted. After he left me, when the boys asked me what was for dinner, I had to ask them what they wanted, because I had no idea what to fix. It took me a long time to build up my self-esteem, and now, I have confidence in myself, and I will not let anyone take it away. I don't mean you are trying to take it from me. I want you to know what kind of a relationship I have come from. If this is a deal-breaker, then let me know now, please," Jeannette explained.

"You had told me a few things about your ex not being a good man when you called about needing an attorney, but I had no idea how bad he treated you. I am so sorry. I will never treat you that way, Jeannette. You are an exceptional person who I want to spend more time with. I'm glad you told me. You can tell me anything," Robert said with great empathy.

"I am embarrassed about what I told you," she said as her face turned red and looked down at the table.

"There is no reason to be embarrassed. I want to know everything about you," Robert said, reached for her other hand, and gave it a reassuring squeeze.

Jeannette looked up. Her eyes met his. She felt like someone just hit her with a bat. She was in love with Robert. In her mind, she was freaking out. *"Oh, God! I am in love with him! I can't be! No! What do I do? I can't tell him. Not now, anyway. It's too soon. Can love happen this quickly? Am I sure? Oh, Lord! My heart is pounding. I can barely breathe."*

"If you will let me, I want to take care of you. I will never let Jeff hurt you again! I want to smash my fist into his face for treating you that way!" Robert said.

"Robert, it's over, and I am fine. I survived, and it made me the woman I am today, the woman that attracted you. You might not have been interested in me or given me a second glance before now. I wasn't ready to let any man into my life until I met you on the plane. It's amazing how God works. I truly believe he put us together."

"I believe it too, Jeannette," Robert said and kissed her hand. He lingered just long enough to see the goosebumps rise on her arm. It pleased him immeasurably that he had that effect on her. He raised his head to see her looking at him with a tear running down her cheek.

"Did I say something wrong?" He wiped away her tear with his thumb.

"No. You said everything right. You have touched my heart, Robert."

The waitress appeared again out of nowhere, "Two lovely Cobb salads for a lovely couple. Can I get you anything else?"

"No, thank you. The salad looks delicious. Jeannette, do you want anything else?" Robert asked.

He was doing precisely as Jeannette had asked, "No, thank you," she said to the waitress, then turned to Robert and said, "Thank you, Robert."

Their conversation through the rest of lunch was lighthearted, making them both laugh from time to time. Robert and Jeannette shared experiences and beliefs only to discover how much alike they were.

Jeannette looked at her watch. "Robert! It's two-thirty! Don't you have a meeting right now?"

"Damn it! I do! I don't want to leave you again. Can I see you tonight?"

"I'm sorry, no. I need to spend some time with my boys. I am leaving again on Sunday for Chicago. How about tomorrow night? They usually have dates on Friday nights. I am meeting with Mr. Baker in an hour, so I will see you then."

"Great!" Robert said hurriedly.

"Go! Don't be late!" Jeannette said as she watched him leave. She sat a little longer and sipped her iced tea while her imagination ran wild with thoughts of Robert. A voice jolted her back to reality.

"So, this is the man that is your sex buddy? Should have known you would find some high and mighty guy who thinks he's better than everyone else," Jeff hissed, looming over her.

Her automatic response was to jump up and push away quickly.

"Get away from me! You can't tell me who I can see! You gave up the right a long time ago!" she said in a loud whisper. She didn't want to make a scene in the restaurant. She picked up her purse and stood to leave.

Jeff grabbed her arm tightly to hold her where she was.

So, no one else could hear, he whispered in her ear, "Listen here, little missy. I will tell you anything I want. You are going to pay me what I want, or you will be very sorry." He threw her arm, pointed his finger at her as a warning, and left.

Her legs went limp, and the color drained from her face. She sat back down, trying to regain strength in her legs so she could walk out of the restaurant without anyone noticing how shook up she was.

The waitress had seen what happened and brought a glass of water to Jeannette.

"Are you okay? Do you want me to call someone?" She asked.

"No. Thank you. I want to sit for a minute if that's all right?" Jeannette said and took the glass of water.

"Take your time. You really look pale. Come with me. It's quiet in the bar right now, and the chairs are comfortable. My name is Peggy. What's yours?"

"Jeannette."

"The man you were with earlier, Robert, is a very nice guy. He has come in a lot. Always has a smile and something nice to say. Here we are. You need whiskey. Water is just not going to cut it. I'll be right back. Hey, Ed, give me two fingers, on the rocks of the top shelf. Thanks."

Jeannette took the glass gratefully. "That's better, thank you, Peggy."

"The other guy, the one who upset you, has come in here before. When he does, the bartender keeps a close eye on him. He's a mean drunk. Do you know him, or was it a random thing he picked you out?"

"Unfortunately, I know him," Jeannette confessed.

"Well, that sucks!" Peggy said.

Jeannette let out a small giggle and said, "Yes, it does suck. Thank you for your kindness. I hope he didn't cause a problem in the restaurant. What time is it? Why am I asking? I have a watch.

Oh! I have to go! I have an appointment in ten minutes!" Jeannette said and swallowed the rest of her whiskey.

"Good luck, Jeannette! Come back sometime!" Peggy said. She watched Jeannette give her a wave then disappear out the door.

Still flustered, but trying to act like she wasn't, Jeannette walked to the receptionist. "Hello. I have an appointment with Mr. Baker. My name is Jeannette."

"Hello, Jeannette. Mr. Baker said to send you in as soon as you arrived. I will show you to his office. Mr. Baker, this is Jeannette."

"Please come in. Robert has told me all about you. Have a seat and tell me how I can help."

There was a light knock at the door of Mr. Baker's office. Robert poked his head in and said, "Would it be all right if I sit in on this?"

"Jeannette, do you have any objections?" Mr. Baker asked.

"No. I would like it if Robert did," Jeannette said. Robert took a seat next to her.

"Let's start from the beginning, Jeannette," Mr. Baker began.

"How far back do you want to go?" she asked.

"Let's start with your marriage to Jeff. Have I got his name right?" Mr. Baker asked.

"Yes. His name is Jeff." She turned to Robert and asked, "Are you sure you want to hear this? It might change your mind about me."

"I am positive I want to hear this, and nothing will make me change my mind about you," Robert said with a reassuring smile.

Mr. Baker stopped her after thirty minutes. "I am sorry to interrupt you. Has Jeff ever put his hands on you?"

"He came very close in the past. But he hadn't until . . ." She looked at Robert nervously. "Until today."

"Today? Why didn't tell me!" Robert raised his voice and leaned toward her.

"After you left the restaurant, I stayed and finished my iced tea. I didn't see Jeff until he walked up to my table," Jeannette began. She recounted the whole thing, even about Peggy.

"Let me see your arm where he grabbed you!" Robert insisted.

"I don't think it's anything," Jeannette said, pulling her sleeve up. She was wrong. The bruising had already begun. A handprint was visible. "Oh, I guess he did squeeze a little harder than I thought."

Mr. Baker buzzed for his secretary. "I need you to type up a restraining order immediately. I have the information you need. Then call Judge Hill. Tell him I am sending it right over for his signature."

"Right away, Mr. Baker," the receptionist said.

Jeannette could tell it was taking a lot of restraint on Robert's part not to run out, find Jeff, and lay him out. His face was turning slightly red.

"Robert, I'm okay."

"Please go on, Jeannette," Mr. Baker said.

After another thirty minutes, she finished her story. All three sat in silence.

"That's quite a story, Jeannette. Is there anything else you want to add?"

"I don't think so. I hit the main highlights. Can you help me? I want him to stay away from my boys and me. I think he has lost his mind, or he is so blind with jealousy toward me he can't see straight. Whatever the case may be, I think he is getting violent," Jeannette said.

"Mr. Baker, I have the restraining order ready for your signature," the receptionist's voice came over the intercom.

"Bring it in." Mr. Baker signed it, then had Jeannette sign it. He gave instructions to get it to Judge Hill immediately.

"Oh, he's not going to take this well," Jeannette said. "When will he be served?"

"After the judge signs it, it will be sent over to the police department. An officer will be dispatched to find and serve him right away. It won't take long. I would suggest you keep all your doors locked whenever you are home. Be aware of your surroundings. Don't have tunnel vision. We want to keep you safe," Mr. Baker said.

"Thank you for your help — one more thing before I go. I am leaving for Chicago on Sunday for a week. Do you think my boys will be safe by themselves?"

"His beef is with you, not your boys. I think they will be fine, but to make sure, I will call the chief and ask to have the officers on duty keep an eye on your neighborhood. Tell your sons to keep the doors locked," Mr. Baker advised.

"Thank you, Mr. Baker. I will," Jeannette said.

"I'll walk you out, Jeannette," Robert said.

"Now, you know my story. Have I run you off? Are you having second thoughts about being involved with me? If you are, tell me now. Don't string me along, Robert," Jeannette said very seriously looking into his eyes.

"No second thoughts. Just the opposite. You are an amazing woman to have gone through all you did and turned out to be the most wonderful woman I have ever known. You are strong, smart, independent, caring, and a warm-hearted person," Robert told her.

"Thank you, Robert, but I don't see myself with your eyes. I am simply a woman who has done what she had to do to survive and feed her children. I don't pretend to be someone I am not. What you see is who I am. Maybe you should think about it? I'll bet when I leave Mr. Baker is going to give you the advice to stay away from me and not get involved. I wouldn't blame him if—"

Without a thought, Robert took her in his arms and crushed his lips to hers. "Stop talking. I won't listen to you talk that way about yourself," he said when he pulled out of the kiss.

Jeannette's eyes were as big as dollars. She gasped in shock. "Robert, do you realize you just kissed me in front of your receptionist?"

"I don't care who saw me! I am proud of you, and I want people to know how I feel about you. Will you let me take you and your sons to dinner tonight? I can get to know them, they can rake me over the coals, and you will be safe."

"Let me ask Sean and Tyler if they have to work tonight and I will call you."

Robert walked her to her car and opened the door for her, then bent down to kiss her one more time. He watched her drive away and thought, *"If I ever run into Jeff, I swear I will hurt him! Nobody hurts someone I love! Wait a minute. Someone, I love? I love*

Jeannette! I'm going to marry that woman." He put his hands in his pockets and walked back into his office, where Mr. Baker was waiting for him.

"That's quite a woman. She has come a long way, no thanks to her ex-husband. You are in love with her. It is written all over your face. It's about time you found a good woman," Mr. Baker said with a big smile. "I approve."

Robert let out a breath of air and shook his head. "I just came to the realization, I love her. We have just started dating. How is it possible for me to feel this way about her this fast?"

"Robert, if you can figure out life, love, and women, please explain it to every other living male on the planet and me. We could use the help." They both laughed. "This calls for a drink. I have a bottle in my office. Have you told her you love her?" Mr. Baker asked.

"No. I just figured it out myself a few minutes ago. I don't want to scare Jeannette off. She's been through a lot, and she has a lot on her plate right now."

"A blind man could see she feels the same way about you. The perfect time will present itself. Don't let her slip away. You will regret it for the rest of your life." They clinked glasses and downed a shot of whiskey.

As soon as Sean and Tyler got home, Jeannette sat them down to tell them about the events of the day.

"Jeff is not to come around here at all. If he does, call 911. An officer will be here right away. Neither one of you has anything to worry about. I promise. I am the one he has a problem with. He is a jealous, vindictive man who thinks I owe him something. Chances are you won't see him at all."

"If I see him, I am going to deck him!" Sean said.

"No, you are not!" Jeannette said with authority.

"Mom, he can't just go around threatening you! He needs a rap in the mouth! I can do it! I am bigger than he is, and it wouldn't take but one hit and he'll be on the ground!" Sean said with anger.

"No! Sean, no. He would probably try to have you arrested for assault. Just stay away from him. That's it, Sean! I mean it!" Jeannette said with demand.

"Mom, I'm sorry Dad treats you this way. You don't deserve it," Tyler added to the conversation.

"Tyler, you, Sean, or me have no control over what another person does. It is not your fault or your fight. I'm a big girl, and I will handle it. Please don't take responsibility for the actions of your father. Do not let him make you feel guilty about anything! He manipulates everyone to get what he wants and takes no responsibility for his actions. Do you understand?" Jeannette asked.

"Yes. But what if Dad calls?" Tyler asked.

"Hang up. You don't need to listen to anything Jeff has to say. It's okay to hang up. Are we clear?" Jeannette asked.

"Yes, ma'am. Wow. I've got permission to be rude! Hot dog!" Tyler shouted.

"Oh, good grief," Jeannette said and thinking she has just opened a can of worms that might not be pleasant. "On a lighter subject, Robert wants to take all three of us to dinner this evening, if you are agreeable. Are either of you scheduled to work tonight?" They both shook their heads. "Would you like to go to dinner? I am not going to force either of you to go if you don't want to. What do you think?"

"I say, yes. I want to know the guy who is dating my mom," Sean said.

"I'm in. I agree with Sean. I want to check this guy out too," Tyler agreed.

"Great! I will call him and let him know. We can take two cars. Robert will pick me up. You boys can drive my car in case we want to stay longer and have a glass of wine. Sound like a plan?" They both agreed, and Jeannette called Robert immediately.

"We have reservations at seven. We are going to Blackberry's, so dress appropriately," Jeannette said, only to get a look of 'what do you mean' from both Sean and Tyler. "Nice. Dress nice. Not a suit and tie nice, dress slacks and a button-up shirt. No T-shirts."

Jeannette fussed around the house to calm her nerves. She cleaned the kitchen, checked in with *Windy City*, ironed a few blouses, and finally got dressed for dinner.

The four of them were seated at Blackberry's by a big picture window with a great view of the mountains in the distance. Jeannette beamed with pride at her handsome boys across the table. She believed she had done an excellent job raising them.

There were a lot of subjects discussed during dinner, such as sports, school, each other's interests, where Robert went to college and law school, events coming up, and finally, Robert dating Jeannette.

"I know I have been under the microscope tonight. Did I pass? Do I have your approval to date your mother? I will always treat her with the utmost respect. She is a very special person," Robert said, looking at Jeannette beaming with love.

"Well, I don't know. How about you, Tyler? What do you think?" Sean asked.

"My vote is yes!" Tyler said with a broad smile directed at Jeannette.

"So, I have the deciding vote, huh?" Sean said with his arms crossed on his chest. "Let's see. He is a good dresser, has nice hair, his personality is okay, he chose a good restaurant, but the real kicker is, he treats mom with the respect she deserves. I vote yes too."

"Well, that was interesting, Sean. I am glad you both approve of Robert because I had decided I was going to see him anyway," Jeannette said with a straight face. It caused a look of surprise from across the table. Jeannette broke into a laugh at their reaction. "Oh, that was fun! I'm just kidding. I knew you boys would like Robert but thank you for your seal of approval. It does mean a lot to me." She turned to Robert and smiled with love in her eyes.

"Tyler, I think it's time for us to excuse ourselves," Sean said as he stood up. "Goodnight, Mom. Enjoy the rest of your evening. I won't wait up this time. You are in good hands." He bent and kissed Jeannette on the cheek. Tyler did the same.

"You have two outstanding young men. You have taught them well. It's plain to see they adore you," Robert said.

"Thank you. I am very proud of my boys. It's hard for me to be away from Sean and Tyler, but I also think it is good for all three of us. I have always been home for them. Now they have more responsibilities to get used to. So far, so good," Jeannette said.

"Let's order a bottle of wine." He motioned for the waiter and ordered a bottle of cabernet. Then he went on to tell her his story.

"I need to tell you a few things about me. I was married once before. My ex-wife lives in Texas with our three daughters. We divorced because she was sleeping around with other men. When

I found out about her exploits, I left her. The girls thought they should stay with their mother at the time. Long story short, my daughters are grown. Two of them have been married, divorced, and remarried. The third has never married. Two of them have given me a total of three grandchildren." Jeannette gave him a surprised look. "Yes, I am a grandfather. I carry their pictures in my wallet. Would you like to see them?" Jeannette nodded. "Two boys and a girl. Aren't they sweet? I don't get the opportunity to see them very often. But when I do, I spoil them!" Robert beamed when he talked about them. "My being a grandfather is all right with you? In your words; is it a deal-breaker? If it is, tell me now."

"Are you kidding? Of course not! Now if you served time in prison that would be a deal-breaker. But these sweet faces I am looking at makes me want to pick them up and kiss them all over their sweet little faces," Jeannette said.

"I am so glad to hear that! Whew. I was nervous about telling you I am a grandfather," Robert said, wiping his forehead.

"I am looking forward to being a grandmother someday. I never had grandparents to speak of, so I have no example to follow. I believe in loving them as much as humanly possible, teaching them what I can, and did I say love them?" Jeannette grinned.

"I am glad to hear it, because I am flying them here to meet you after you get back from Chicago."

Jeannette swallowed hard. "Meet me? Robert, are you sure? Do you think we should slow down a little? It is so fast. We have just started dating. What if they don't like me? Have they met anyone else you have dated?"

"Slow down. I just met your sons. I want you to meet my daughters. No, I have never introduced them to someone I was dating because it has been a rare occasion when I took a woman out. I don't usually go on a second date because I am not interested. No, I don't think we should slow down. I want you, Jeannette, like no other woman. I didn't love my ex-wife. I thought I did. I was young. It seemed like the right thing to do at the time. Thanks to a client in Chicago, and a plane ride, I have discovered what love is. I love you, Jeannette."

"Oh, Robert. Are you sure?" Jeannette asked.

"I have never been surer about anything," Robert said, lifting her hand to his mouth for a gentle kiss.

"I love you too. Oh my god! I love you too! I'm shaking. Look what you do to me!" Jeannette said. She lovingly placed her hand on the side of his face and gave him a kiss that poured out love. It was a very light and gentle kiss and came from deep within her heart. It sent explosions of feelings through both of them. "Oh, my goodness. I need to catch my breath." She started to pull away, but Robert took her hand and brought her back to him.

"I want to make love to you. That's all I have been able to think about. It's interfering with my work, sleep, my appetite, and everything in between," Robert said, holding her as close as he could in a public place.

Jeannette swallowed hard. Her mind was racing with possible excuses not to be intimate with Robert. None of them were acceptable. The truth was, she wanted to.

"Robert, I want you to make love to me. Right now. Will you take me home with you?" Poured out of her mouth.

He could feel her shaking. "Jeannette. If you don't want to, just say so. I am not going to force you into anything you don't want to do. You are shaking. We can wait."

"No! I don't want to wait anymore! I am very nervous but at the same time, excited. I have never had tingling in places that are tingling. I am sure. I want you. I want to feel your skin next to mine. I want to feel the weight of your body. I—"

"Stop! I can't take it anymore! I don't want to explode! Especially in a restaurant. Woman, you know how to drive a man crazy. We need to leave right now!"

"I drive you crazy?" Jeannette said, honestly surprised. "I wasn't trying to. I was just telling you what I am feeling."

"Well, it worked! Let's go!" Robert said hastily.

"It has never taken this long to get home!" Robert complained.

"It is okay, Robert. I am not going anywhere, except to your bed," Jeannette said as she leaned over and nibbled on his ear.

"You are driving me out of my mind! Thank God, we are finally here!" He jumped out of the car, and hurriedly opened her door. He took her by the hand to lead her to his door. His nerves had gotten to him. He couldn't get his key in the lock. He yelled, "Come on, you, stupid lock!" in frustration. Jeannette muffled her mouth to hold in a snicker. He was finally successful with the lock. He still had hold of her hand and almost yanked her inside.

"Robert! You've got me! I'm here. Slow down and kiss me. We only get one first time. It is a night we will always remember, so let's make it memorable."

"I don't know if I can slow down," he said, breathing hard. "I want you so much I am thinking about taking you right here on the living room floor! Come on!" He spun her around, picked her up, and took her to the bedroom.

"Robert, kiss me," Jeannette said softly.

He gladly obliged her request. It wasn't a gentle kiss. There were so many feelings and emotions running through both of them, their heads were spinning.

"Jeannette, are you sure about this?"

"I have never been surer about anything in my life. Be patient with me, please. It has been years since I have been with a man. I want to apologize ahead of time if I don't satisfy you," she said worriedly.

"All you have to do is look at me. Right now, that is all it will take!"

She started unbuttoning his shirt, slowly, until the hair on his chest was plainly visible. She ran her hands all over his chest, sending more shockwaves through him. When his eyes rolled back in his head in pleasure, she unbuttoned the last two buttons and freed him from his shirt.

"My turn," Robert said, his voice shaking. "I want your bare breasts against me." He followed her example of one button at a time. As her bare skin emerged, he kissed each inch, giving her goosebumps. "You are shivering. Are you cold?" He knew the answer but wanted to hear her say she wanted him.

"What? Oh, no. I'm not cold. You are making me hot! I can't stand it!" Jeannette whispered through broken breaths.

Nothing was more erotic to him than hearing Jeannette whisper her desire for him. "I am going to drive you just as crazy with desire as I am. Oh god! Your beautiful breasts, I have wanted to touch them, hold them, and kiss them since the day we met on the plane."

He cupped her breasts in his hands and kissed each one as if they were made of porcelain. He went back to her mouth and ravished her with kisses of pure pleasure.

Jeannette was flying so high with passion she didn't notice she was utterly naked until Robert picked her up and laid her on the bed.

"Where are you going?" she asked Robert.

"Nowhere, my love. I need to take my pants off."

"Let me."

She rolled to the side of the bed and unbuttoned his pants while kissing his stomach and the skin that had just been revealed. She slowly pulled his zipper down, one inch at a time and always kissing his bare skin. Her hands slid down his hips and freed his rock-hard manhood from the thin fabric that shielded it from her and released the throbbing muscle. Jeannette lay back on the bed with her arms stretched out to Robert, ready for him to take her.

"My god, Jeannette! What are you doing to me? I can't wait any longer! I am going to make you mine, completely mine, right now!" he said as he slowly lowered himself over her.

"Take me. I am all yours."

Never had she experienced such intense sensations. She let out a moan, and Robert covered her mouth with his to capture her pleasure. It sent pure passion through him knowing she wanted him.

Later . . .

They laid tangled in each other's legs and arms, trying to catch their breath. Jeannette moved ever so slightly, and Robert held tighter. He was not going to let her go anywhere. She was his.

"Where do you think you are going?" Robert asked.

"Nowhere. I wanted to see if my body was capable of movement. I am embarrassed to ask, but did I do alright?"

He let out a laugh that came from down deep.

"Oh, honey, I don't think it's possible to do any better than you did! It was wonderful. I felt sensations with you I can't explain. I want you next to me every minute of the day from now on. I want to protect you, love you, make love to you, and make you happy."

"That's going to be difficult as far as being next to me. I don't know how we can manage it from Chicago," she said with a grin when he started to pout. "I felt things I couldn't explain either. I love you and want to be loved by you, and if it is possible, make love to you every single day. Your happiness is important to me, Robert."

"Are you happy, Jeannette? I mean truly happy right now?"

"I can say with all honesty. I am truly happy right now lying with you, hearing your heartbeat, and knowing it is beating for me," Jeannette said.

He caressed her arm that was wrapped around his chest. She flinched. He looked at her arm. The bruises were very evident where Jeff had grabbed her.

"Sorry, I didn't realize my arm was that sore," Jeannette said.

"I would like to kill him!" Robert said with a mean grin. "He is never going to hurt you again! You are mine now. I dare him to mess with what's mine!"

"Okay, tiger. I feel very secure in your arms. I know you will protect me. I don't have the words to begin to explain how wonderful it makes me feel." She kissed his chest and ran her hand back and forth across his chest. "I hate to say this since I am not sure I can walk, but I need you to take me home. I can't stay the night. This is not something I want to explain to my sons just yet."

"Just a little longer, please?" Robert begged.

"You don't have to beg, honey. I need a few more minutes too." It made Robert chuckle with pride. "So many things have happened to me in three weeks. My friend died and left me a company and made me rich, my ex-husband assaulted me, and I fell in love with a wonderful and handsome man named Robert."

He tightened his hold on her. "What time does your plane leave on Sunday?"

"Early, 6:00 a.m. It puts me in Chicago about three their time, I think. David will pick me up at the airport and take me to the hotel."

Robert raised his head and said, "David? Who's David? Should I be jealous?"

"No!" Jeannette giggled. "He is my driver."

"Well, aren't you the big shot! You have a driver," Robert teased.

Jeannette couldn't help but laugh. "He is a very polite young man who is married. I am getting an apartment this week. My secretary, Bridgett, has several for me to look at. When you come to Chicago, you can stay with me."

"And David can drive us around?" Robert asked.

"Sure. David won't mind another person in the car." Jeannette teased. "I hate to bring this up again, sweetie, but I really should be getting home."

Robert let out a groan. "Are you sure you can't stay? I would make you breakfast in the morning and serve it to you in bed."

"It sounds tempting, but I can't." She rolled out of bed, stood naked with her hands on her hips, and looked at his body sprawled across the bed. She walked around to his side and kissed his back. "Come on, Tiger. You need to put some clothes on. You can't take me home in the buff."

He rolled over to look at Jeannette. There was moonlight streaming in through the window onto her naked form.

"You are beautiful. So beautiful, it makes me ache for your touch. The moonlight shining on your skin is so sensuous it makes me want you again." He stood and took her in his arms, pulling her as close as possible. "I love how your skin feels against mine. Every one of your curves fits perfectly against me."

"You say such beautiful things to me. I don't want to leave. We will do this again, soon," Jeannette said with certainty.

"Do you promise? How about now?" Robert asked and made Jeannette giggle. "It won't take long."

"No. Now put some pants on. Next time I will drive my car, and you won't have to get up."

"I don't think I like that idea. This way, I can keep you as long as I want and have my way with you."

"Silly man. What does your schedule look like for tomorrow?"

"I don't know. I still don't have enough blood flow to my brain to remember. I hope by morning to have a fully functioning brain once again. But right now, I'm lucky to know how to zip my pants," Robert said with a little bit of a whine.

"Are you complaining?" Jeannette asked.

"No, ma'am! It has been the most wonderful night of my life." He moved to her and placed his hands on her hips. He looked into her eyes and said, "I love you. I don't know how it is possible to fall in love this fast, but I have with every ounce of my being. I am yours completely. You have my heart, Jeannette."

"And you, Robert, have my heart. I have never truly given my heart to anyone. I know you will be gentle with it and never hurt me. I can trust you. This is something that I have only said to you. Trust does not come easily to me. Right here, right now, you hold my heart in your hands. I love you with every ounce of my being." Jeannette professed. Robert bent and kissed her with love.

2

The next morning, she hummed a tune in the kitchen while she made breakfast. "It's nice to hear you singing. You are happy," Sean said.

"I am son."

"Robert seems to be a good man. You like him a lot, don't you?" Sean questioned.

She stopped what she was doing and sat with Sean at the table. "I do. I think very highly of him. Is it a problem?"

"No. Not with me. Maybe. It is new. I have never seen you with a man before, other than Dad. It's, I guess, different. If he makes you happy, then it is what I want for you. You deserve to be happy, Mom," Sean said.

Jeannette knew he meant it. She could feel it. Tears welled up in her eyes, and she said, "Sean, it means the world to me to hear you say that. It's a new experience for all of us, but it is important to me you boys are okay with me having a relationship with Robert. I know a lot of things have changed in our lives in just a few short weeks, and we are adapting. But my love for you and Tyler will never diminish or change. The love of a mother's heart only grows stronger. You, boys, are my number one priority."

"I'm glad you found Robert, but if he hurts you, I will hurt him!" Sean declared.

"Simmer down. Robert won't," Jeannette said and rose from the table. "Is your brother up?"

"I think I heard him."

"Tyler! Come eat breakfast, or you will be late for school!" Jeannette yelled from the kitchen.

"I'm coming!" Tyler yelled as he walked toward the kitchen. "Geez. I'm here. Give me a break."

"Tyler, what's up with you? Did you sleep all right? Are you sick?" Jeannette asked.

"I slept fine, and no, I'm not sick. I don't like all these changes! I know I will be graduating soon and going on to college like Sean. But I'm not ready for you to be gone all the time! Now you have a boyfriend, you are going to forget all about Sean and me!" Tyler confessed.

"Tyler! What's wrong with you! Don't you think Mom deserves to be happy? Grow up!" Sean shouted.

"Sean! Knock it off! Tyler, you don't want me to see Robert?" Jeannette asked with concern.

"Yes. No. I mean, I don't know. I guess I'm afraid you will forget about me," Tyler said, looking down at the table.

"Oh, Tyler. How in the world could I ever forget about you? You and your brother are my number one priority. That will never change. I love both of you to the moon and back. I haven't been interested in having a relationship with anyone until now. I wasn't looking for Robert. It just happened. We met on the plane, and it has grown from there. Don't you think Robert is a good man?" Jeannette asked.

Tyler hung his head feeling guilty about what had spilled out of his mouth.

"I'm sorry, Mom. Yes, I think Robert is a good man. I know you are going to want to spend time with him, and I won't see much of you. That is what really upsets me. You have always been here if I needed you. Now you will be off with Robert, travel to Chicago, and Sean and I are left here alone."

"Sounds like I have spoiled you," Jeannette said with a grin. "Tyler, I will always be here for you. Robert makes me happy. He makes me feel good about myself, and he treats me like a queen. I will make sure I am here for you as much as humanly possible, but on occasion, I will be with Robert. As far as Chicago goes, well, I shouldn't have to address it. My company is in Chicago. Whenever there is a break in school, like Thanksgiving, Christmas, or spring break, I will fly both of you to Chicago to stay there with me. I am getting an apartment next week."

"Promise?" Tyler asked.

"Absolutely, my tender-hearted son. I promise. I love you," Jeannette said and put a smile on Tyler's face.

"Man! You really are spoiled!" Sean said to Tyler.

"Shut up, Sean!" Tyler yelled.

"Hey! Enough! Is this how you guys treat each other while I'm gone? Because this is unacceptable!" Jeannette said with her hands on her hips.

"No, we don't act like this. It just bugs me when Tyler acts like a baby," Sean said.

"Sean, apologize to your brother!" Jeannette said sternly.

"Sorry," Sean said.

"Thank you. Please finish your breakfast, both of you. Sean, do you have the early shift?"

"Yep. As soon as I eat, I'm off. What day are you leaving for Chicago?"

"Sunday. Each time I fly to the big city, it will be on Sunday, bright and early. When I come home, I will fly back on Saturday. That's the plan anyway," Jeannette said. "What are you boys doing this evening? Dates?"

"Yea, I am taking Patty to the movies. Do you think you could make dinner for us before we go? Shake chick?" Sean asked.

"I would be happy to make shake chick for dinner. I'm glad you gave me a heads up. I need to go grocery shopping today to fill the cupboards. I don't want you guys to starve. What about you, Tyler?" Jeannette asked.

"Could I have some of my friends over too?" Tyler asked.

"Sure. We'll make it a movie night. How many? I have to make sure I make enough chicken."

"Um, six? Is that too many?"

"That's fine. Now, would you mind if I ask Robert to dinner?" Jeannette asked.

Sean and Tyler looked at each other, shrugged their shoulders, and in unison said, "Okay."

As soon as the boys were out the door, the phone rang. It was Robert. "Good morning. Sleep well?"

"I tried, but I kept replaying the events from earlier in the evening," Jeannette said with a smile.

"Events?" Robert asked.

"You are going to make me say it, aren't you? I kept thinking about you and me, naked, making love, and how it felt. Oh, Lord. I am going to stop right there!"

"Why stop, honey? I'm enjoying it," Robert said with a little chuckle.

"Whew. I just got a little warm," Jeannette said and fanned herself. "I'm glad you called. I wanted to invite you to dinner at my apartment this evening. Sean is bringing his girlfriend, and Tyler is having six of his friends over. So, you might want to think before you answer. I am warning you. It will be a zoo!"

"Oh, all the little animals in their natural habitat, huh? It sounds like fun. What is on the menu?" Robert asked.

"Don't laugh, but my boys' favorite dinner is what we call shake chick. When they were little, they stood on chairs and helped me cook. I put flour and spices in a paper bag for each one, dropped in a few pieces of chicken, and had them shake the bag to coat the chicken. Thus, the name shake chick."

Robert laughed out loud, "That's great! Can I help? You can teach me to shake. I'll bring a bottle of wine. What time?" Robert asked.

"Is six, okay? If you could be here a little earlier, it would be great. I will put you to work," Jeannette told him.

"I will be there as soon as I can this evening. Good-bye, my love."

"Bye," Jeannette said and hung up the phone. She felt like a schoolgirl, happy, giddy, and unable to concentrate. The grocery store seemed like a whole new world. She couldn't pick up anything without thinking about Robert. It took her twice as long as usual.

On her way home with her bounty, she thought, "Robert, what have you done to me? My stomach is full of butterflies, and you are constantly on my mind. Is this what love is like? How am I going to balance my boys, Robert, and Chicago? One day at a time. One day at a time is all I can do. Tonight, is going to be interesting to see how Robert handles all the hubbub." She pictured Robert in shock standing in the middle of all the chaos and giggled.

It was five o'clock and time to start preparing for the on-slot. Jeannette was humming again in the kitchen when the doorbell rang. There was Robert.

"You are early! Come in!"

"Are the boys at home?" She shook her head. "Good. I can't wait any longer. He scooped her up in his arms and kissed her in the doorway. "You taste so good."

"I think we should close the door. Don't you?" Jeannette asked.

"I don't care if the world sees. I love you, and I am proud of it!" Robert proclaimed.

"I would like to keep our kisses intimate, for now," Jeannette said.

"Anything you say." He freed one hand and shut the door, but never took his eyes off Jeannette. "You smell good. How about I take you to bed right now and ravish you blind before all the kids get here?"

"Down, boy. There's not enough time. It won't be long before they invade us. Come on. I will get you an apron."

"Apron? Do I have to wear an apron? Really?" Robert asked.

"In my kitchen, yes. It's going to get messy," Jeannette said.

By six-fifteen, there were teenagers everywhere. A few more than Tyler had expected. She anticipated for more and was prepared. All in all, there ended up to be nineteen for dinner. Everyone was shaking chicken, including Robert. What a sight! Flour was flying everywhere. A couple of the paper bags broke open from shaking too hard, which sent flour, spices, and chicken flying. Jeannette ducked just in time. A drumstick almost hit her in the head.

"Okay! We have flying chicken! Time to call it done! Give me your bags and get washed up while I start cooking! You might want to go outside and dust off a little. Some of you have quite a bit of flour on you," Jeannette instructed.

She was laughing at the mess they made. It seemed everyone was having fun. She turned to Robert to see how he faired through the flying chicken. He was leaning against the counter, drinking a glass of wine and observing all the activity with a smile and shaking his head.

"Does this happen often?" Robert asked.

"No. But when it does, we have fun. I enjoy having the kids here. I know where they are, what they are doing, who they are doing it with, and it's a safe environment. I believe it is important to have somewhere for these teenagers to feel comfortable to be themselves. They can talk to me about anything, and we always end up laughing about something. By the way, it's movie night. Sean and Patty are leaving for the movies after dinner, but the rest of them are staying to watch a movie. I don't know what they have picked out yet." She stopped when she saw Robert's face. He was looking at her with his eyes wide open. "Oh, dear! Did I scare you? Are you going to leave?"

"No. Don't be silly. I am not going anywhere. I have been watching you with these kids. You are truly a good person. They respect you. I am going to have to be careful. If I do something wrong, they might attack me!" His smile was one of caring. "Why don't you come a little closer and I can show you how attractive this man thinks you are?" Robert said, tempting her.

"Robert, not now. Please, honey. Give the boys a little time to get used to seeing us together before you kiss me in front of them, okay? I want to kiss you really bad too. Be patient? Please?"

He moaned and said, "Oh, okay. But as soon as I get you alone, look out, lady!"

"I can hardly wait," she said and put a spatula in Robert's hand. "But for now, I need you to watch the potatoes. Don't let them burn." She turned to attend to the chicken.

He came up behind her and gently kissed the back of her neck and then moved slightly to the side. "See? No one saw me kiss the cook."

The gentle kiss sent shivers down her spine. It pleased Robert immensely to see her shiver from his touch.

"Oh, God, Robert. How am I supposed to cook?" she said quietly. Her eyelids fluttered, and her breath caught. "I'm not going to tell you what feelings I am experiencing right now because I would be too embarrassed. What you do to me is . . . is criminal. Lord!"

Robert smiled and was so pleased with himself. He could melt her with one kiss. She made him feel entirely male.

"Jeannette," he whispered. "I want to make love to you."

"Oh, my sweet Lord. I can't concentrate on the chicken." Jeannette wiped her forehead and leaned against the stove. "Robert! I want you so bad. My knees are weak. We have a houseful of teenagers on the other side of the wall who are expecting dinner. Let's get dinner out of the way, and maybe we can sneak out for a while?" She suggested. He whined a little but agreed.

After dinner, the kids all knew the routine: clear the dishes, take them to the kitchen and pick up any mess they had made. It impressed Robert how she had taught them to respect her home. But in all actuality, they respected her, loved her, and would probably do anything she asked of them. Seeing her in this way with all these young people only made Robert adore her more. He didn't think it was possible to love a person as much as he does Jeannette. Every day was a surprise and an adventure with her.

Sean left with Patty, and the rest of the herd had settled in front of the TV watching some action adventure and had them watching intensely. Robert and Jeannette had cleaned most of the kitchen when she said, "Leave the rest. I will mop up the rest in the morning. Let's go for a walk." She leaned down and whispered in Tyler's ear so she wouldn't disturb anyone, "We are going for a walk. Be back in a bit." Tyler glanced at her and nodded his head.

They left, quietly, and stepped into a cool moonlit evening. Robert took her hand as they walked down the sidewalk. "I finally have you all to myself," he said and kissed the top of her head. "Did you know you have flour in your hair?"

She let out a laugh and said, "After all the flour that was flying, I'm sure I do! You didn't find any chicken in there, did you? It's okay. I don't mind the flour. They had fun, and so did I. These are times they will remember and maybe pass on to their children. I will guarantee you; I will teach my grandchildren how to make shake chick!"

"Let me know when you do, so I can keep my distance," he said, smiling down at her.

"Deal. On another subject, I am going to miss you so much this next week! Chicago is a long way from Clark City. What am I going to do? We just found each other, and now I have to leave. Guess we are going to be talking a lot on the phone," she said.

"Oh, I almost forgot to tell you! I might have to come to Chicago on Wednesday. Corporate has a case they might have me handle. I won't know until Monday."

She squealed with excitement and pulled his face down to kiss him. "That's great! You can stay with me! That is, if you want to. I doubt I will have my apartment set up by then, but I will have a hotel room and room service."

"Well, I don't know. I'm going to be busy, but I think I can fit you in."

She stopped dead in her tracks. "Robert, do you not want to stay with me? Was this evening more than you want?"

"Oh, sweetheart, nothing could be further from the truth. I was teasing you. Nothing could keep me away from you! I want to make love to you all night long. If I should fall asleep, I want to wake up with you next to me. That's where you should be every morning." He took her in his arms and kissed her under the streetlight.

"Why hasn't some woman caught you before now? You are one in a million," Jeannette said as he held her close and swayed slightly.

"Because I didn't want anyone else. I hadn't met a woman who interested me until you came along. I was a goner the first time I looked into your eyes."

"Robert, you know just what to say. I love you."

He kissed her one more time and drew it out as long as she would let him. "I think we should be getting back. The movie should be close to the end."

"If we have to," he said with a pout.

She bumped up against him with her sore arm and flinched.

"Ouch. Sorry."

"Your arm? Let me see it." He gently pulled her sleeve up to reveal black-and-blue markings of a hand. Even in the darkness, he could see how bad they were. "Oh, Jeannette. These are awful! We are taking pictures of them tonight. He is not going to get away with this! I want to kill him!" He kissed her bruises, wishing it would heal them.

"Robert, my arm will heal. I didn't mean to flinch. I had not even noticed it hurt. He won't hurt me again. I have you, Mr. Baker, and the police are watching out for me." Just at that moment, a police cruiser drove by. "That was timing. See?"

"I would feel better if I were with you, 24-7," Robert told her.

"Well, sweetie, we know it is not possible, so we will have to make the best of it. There's my home. Back to the group." She smiled and kissed his hand holding hers.

The credits were rolling on the TV as they came through the door. Zach yelled, "Hey, Jeannette. How about some guitar music?"

"Oh, tonight?" Jeannette asked, surprised.

"You play the guitar? Or are you putting on some guitar music?" Robert asked.

Her face turned red with embarrassment. "Yes, I do play. A little."

"Don't let her lie to you, Robert! She has two songs on two albums she wrote and performed them on the albums," Zach said with pride.

"You better give your audience what they want. I'd like to hear you play," Robert encouraged.

"Tyler, is it all right with you?"

"Yep! Get it out, Mom!"

"I will be right back. Have a seat." She came back with a worn guitar that had seen better days, but it was hers, and she loved it. "Okay. What am I playing?"

"How about the song on the first album?" Zach suggested. "She wrote this!" he said with pride.

She started to play and sing. Robert's jaw dropped. "It's no wonder she owns a recording and publishing company," he thought with amazement. "This song came from the depths of a broken heart. It's haunting but beautiful." It touched him so profoundly a tear rolled down his cheek. He quickly wiped it away before anyone noticed.

When she finished, she turned to Robert. "Well? What did you think?"

"I am speechless! You didn't tell me you play, let alone you write music. How long have you been doing this?"

"I picked up the guitar when I was in high school and started to play. It just seemed natural. I had written some poems, so I put them to music with my guitar. That's it," Jeannette explained.

"That's it, you say. I would say pretty miraculous." He was still in shock.

"It's just something I do. I sold this song and one more. It gave me enough money to move us to Oregon. The royalties from the albums are giving me an income, so I didn't have to find a job right away," Jeannette said.

"Play the other one!" Zach yelled.

"Aren't you tired of that one? You all have the album," she said.

"Hearing it on an album is not as good as hearing it live. Please play and sing it for us?" Zach begged.

"Okay, but then it's time for all of you to hit the trail. Deal?" Jeannette asked.

They all yelled in unison, "DEAL!"

It took Robert by surprise. One more thing she had taught this group.

She started tapping her foot and then the guitar. It was a happy tune with an excellent beat. Every teenager was tapping and singing along. She hit the last chord, and everyone applauded. "Hey!" she shouted and threw her arm in the air and laughed. Again, Robert was in a state of shock.

"Are you okay, Robert?" She giggled. "What did you think of that one?"

"I loved it!" he gasped. "My god, Jeannette! You have so much talent!"

"Thank you. Okay, people, we had a deal. I hope you all had a good time and plenty to eat. Drive safely."

"Mom, we're going to go to the bowling alley for a while and have something to drink. I won't be late. You were great," Tyler said and kissed her on the cheek and walked out the door.

"Thank you. Have fun!" Jeannette said. They were finally alone. The silence was deafening after all the teenagers had left. It was a loud, fun filled evening.

"Well, this is my life. Are you still not considering running away? I wouldn't blame you if you did. A lot was going on tonight."

"Jeannette, I love your life, and I love you. The only place I will run to is your bedroom. I have never had a more fun evening, and with teenagers no less." Robert shook his head in disbelief. "You showed me several different sides of you tonight, and I loved every one of them."

"I'm glad to hear I didn't scare you off. You know, you can kiss me now. We are alone."

"You read my mind," he said and kissed her with heated passion. "I want you. Please? I don't think I can hold myself back."

"Honey, we can't. Not here. Why don't I leave the boys a note saying we went for a glass of wine? We can have that wine at your place. Do you get my drift?"

"Brilliant! Get the paper! I'll start the car!" He hurried out the door, leaving Jeannette giggling and pleased to know she makes a man like Robert want her.

Boys,

Robert and I went for a glass of wine. Don't wait up. See you in the morning.

Love, Mom

It was another fantastic night with Robert. He made love to her with so much passion and gentleness she got a lump in her throat lying next to him.

"Sweetheart, are you shaking?" Robert asked.

"It's because you have touched me so deeply, I can't help but shake. I don't want you to leave me. It scares me to think it could be a possibility." Her voice cracked.

"Don't cry. You are safe in my arms. I will never leave you. You are all mine." He kissed the top of her head and tasted flour. "You need to take a shower. I just kissed flour again," he said and smacked his lips.

It made Jeannette laugh. "Yes, I need a shower. Tomorrow, I have a big job ahead of me cleaning up the rest of the mess in my kitchen."

"Need some help? I can come over," Robert suggested.

"Let me get back to you tomorrow about it. I need some time with Sean and Tyler before I leave on Sunday. Speaking of which, you need to take me home, again."

"Damn it! You didn't drive your car."

"Nope. You were in too much of a rush. It is hard for me to believe I can have this effect on a man."

"Woman, you don't give yourself enough credit. You know exactly what to do to me to drive me crazy, and I love it!"

"It warms my heart to hear you say things so sweet to me. But now I am going to drive you crazy in another way. Take me home. Did that do it?"

"Nailed it! Alright. Alright. Don't nag. Next time you are driving your car," Robert told her.

"My sweet, sleepy man, I will."

He walked her to her door and gave her one more kiss. "I will call you tomorrow, Jeannette. Sleep tight. I know I will."

Saturday morning, she was up early, knowing it was going to take some work to clean up after last night. It took her almost three hours to get the kitchen back to normal and all the dusting done. But she didn't mind. She smiled and hummed the entire time. She had just finished when Tyler came into the kitchen.

"Morning. Is breakfast ready?" Tyler asked and yawned.

"Not quite. Sit down and talk to me while I cook. What time did you get in?" Jeannette asked.

"I think about midnight. I read your note."

Good, you found it. Did you enjoy last night with the chicken and all?" Jeannette asked.

He let out a laugh and said, "Yea. It was fun. We all had fun. Thanks for doing that."

"It was my pleasure. I had fun right along with you. I'm not sure what Robert thought of it, but he said he had fun. I just got the kitchen cleaned up before you walked in."

"Robert likes you. I saw him looking at you all evening. Mom? I'm okay with him liking you. But I'm still working on the Chicago thing. I'm not completely sold on it yet," Tyler told her.

"You have come a long way since yesterday. Why the change?" she asked.

"My friends and I were talking about you and Robert. They liked him. They thought he was cool. Then they teased me about how he looked at you. We may be young, but we aren't dumb."

Jeannette laughed. "He is fond of me, and I feel the same way, for now, anyway. I don't know what the future holds for us, but I can tell you I am enjoying the ride. I am going to see Robert for a couple of hours this afternoon. Don't worry. I will be home for dinner to be with you two before I take off again."

Tyler smiled.

Robert asked Jeannette if he could take her to the airport on Sunday morning. First, she asked the boys if they were okay with it. They were. They sounded grateful they didn't have to get up so early. Jeannette said her good-byes to Sean and Tyler before going to bed.

It seemed her head just hit the pillow, and it was time to get up. Robert would be here to pick her up in an hour. She was ready and waiting when he pulled up. Bags in hand, she walked to the car.

He took her bags and set them on the ground so he could kiss her. He wanted nothing in between them.

"Good morning. I missed you. Your scent is still on my pillow, so I hugged it all night pretending it was you."

"That's sweet. I missed you too, but I was so tired I was out as soon as my head hit my pillow. I did have a couple of dreams about you."

"Did you make me happy?" Robert asked, picking up the bags.

"Oh, I made you very happy," Jeannette said with a slightly evil smile.

"You are doing it to me again, woman! Don't do this now. We can't do anything about it. Damn it! I don't want you to go!" he said as he slid behind the wheel.

"I have to. I have a company to run. I will call you as soon as I get to my hotel, I promise. Let's keep our fingers crossed that corporate wants you in Chicago this week."

They chatted all the way to the airport, making the trip go by quickly. Robert dropped her off and watched her disappear into the terminal. His heart was aching. *"God! I have got to pull myself together! I am acting like an idiot! I am going to marry that woman!"* He drove back to Clark City, planning how and when he would ask her to marry him. *"It can't be too soon. She might say no. But if I don't ask her right away, I might lose her. Good God man! You are tied in knots! A woman you just met a few weeks ago and have only been dating for a short time, you believe you are in love with, and you want to marry. Whew. It sounds crazy. Maybe I'm crazy? Until I figure that out, I will proceed with my plan to ask her."* He talked to himself all the way home, trying to make some kind of sense of this whirlwind romance.

"That was such a magical time. My Robert was such a romantic. It was difficult trying to be together, but we managed. Love always finds a way."

"The bad time then, was having to deal with Jeff. It seemed I was never going to be rid of him. I have learned the things we do when we are young, we pay for when we get older. Whether it's abusing our body with too many sporting injuries or marrying the wrong person, there is always a price to pay. In my opinion, I was paying dearly for choosing the wrong mate. Jeff was my way out at the time, but to my dismay, it quickly turned into a disaster."

"I was so nervous about the restraining order and what he might do. I can still feel the bruises he left on my arm that day. If he left any injuries before then, I have blocked it out of my mind, and I don't remember. It's possible he did, which would have explained some of my fear I had of him."

"Over the years, I have learned even though he didn't put his hands on me, it doesn't mean he wasn't abusive. Abuse is control, hurtful words, and blatant disrespect. Bingo! In the earlier years, I thought it was okay to settle for verbal abuse (which I didn't recognize as abuse at the time) because he wasn't physically hurting me. The scars he left on the inside that can't be seen are something I have to deal with every day of my life."

3

David was waiting at the Airport in Chicago for Jeannette with the car door open and a smile on his face.

"Hello, Jeannette. Nice to have you back." He shut the door and took his place behind the wheel.

"It's nice to see you too, David. Did Bridgett tell you what hotel I am staying at? At the moment I don't remember," Jeannette said and shook her head.

"The same one you stayed at a week ago." He looked in the rearview mirror and saw Jeannette blushing with embarrassment. "Is everything okay with you? You seem different. Please forgive me. I don't mean to pry."

"You are not prying. If I don't want you to know, I will tell you it's none of your business. A lot of things happened to me last week. Some good, some not so good. The good? I met a wonderful man with a nice smile, David. I see by your smile, that pleases you. The bad? Well, I will keep that to myself. I haven't been in a relationship since my divorce, quite a few years back. I wasn't looking. Then Robert walked into my life." She stopped and shook her head. "Okay, that's probably too much information. Sorry." She paused again and looked up to see David still smiling in the mirror at her. "I can't wipe this silly grin off my face, and I need to be a professional when I walk into the office tomorrow. Oh, good grief!" She began to laugh. She was happy.

"It is nice to see you this way. Love becomes you," David commented.

"I didn't say I was in love, David."

"You didn't have to. It is written all over your face," David said teasingly.

"Well, to be honest, you hit the nail on the head! I have fallen for him. That reminds me. He might be flying in on Wednesday. He has business here in Chicago. If he does, I will probably call you to pick him up and take him where he needs to go."

"Yes, ma'am. Just call. Here we are at the hotel." David handed her bags to the doorman and turned to Jeannette to say, "What time shall I pick you up in the morning?"

"Seven. I need to go in early. Thank you, David."

"I will see you at seven. It's nice to see you happy." He tipped his hat and drove off.

Before she settled in, she had phone calls to make. The first was to Sean and Tyler. Everything was excellent on the home front. Then she called Robert. He sounded relieved she had made it safely but also sad because they were so far away from each other. Their conversation lasted almost an hour. She made sure he had phone numbers and addresses where she could be reached before she hung up.

Now for the task to settle in and read all the faxes Bridgett had sent her on Saturday informing her of appointments and general information about what transpired the previous week. Each time she tried concentrating on work, Robert's face popped into her mind. "This is ridiculous!" She thought. "I have got to concentrate!"

She battled with herself for a couple of hours until she threw her hands in the air and yelled, "I give up! I have got to get out of here for a while!" She called for David to pick her up. He came right away.

"Thank you for coming so quickly, David. I just needed to get out for a while, so I thought I could do a little shopping and then get a bite to eat. I want to go to the little boutique I went to when I was in town a week ago, please."

"Yes, ma'am."

Jeannette needed to update her wardrobe with a few suits. It was important for her to look professional even though she didn't feel like she was. Her professional clothes she will hang in her new apartment. It would cut down on her baggage a lot. She had no need for professional type of clothing in Clark City. She also purchased a few items that were a common type of wearables, and one very sexy nighty. The last of her purchases were two lovely dresses in case of a business dinner or if Robert comes to town and takes her to dinner. Next stop, dinner.

David took her bags and stowed them in the trunk. "Where to, Jeannette?" he asked.

"I am open to suggestions for a good place to eat. Nothing fancy. Someplace with good food where I can feel comfortable eating alone."

"I have the perfect place. My wife and I like to eat there."

"Okay, let's go. I am starving," Jeannette declared.

David was right about the restaurant. The food was excellent, it was cozy, and the service was wonderful. I wonder if Robert knows about this place, she thought. Everything was revolving around Robert.

Jeannette was hoping her shopping trip would help put Robert to the back of her mind. She was wrong. He was becoming more important by the hour. I wonder if he's thinking as much about me as I am of him.

"You were right about the restaurant," Jeannette told David when he picked her up. "Good choice. I got you and your wife a piece of cheesecake. I hope you like that kind of dessert. Let's head back to the hotel, please. I'm done."

"Thank you, Jeannette! This is a first. It is a very nice surprise. We love cheesecake!" David said and shook his head.

"You are very welcome. Please take me back to the hotel, and I won't bother you for the rest of the night."

She puttered around the hotel room, hanging up her new clothes, ironing a few things, and unpacking. After her tasks were completed, she sat down at a small table and started going over business matters. That lasted for an hour. The phone rang. It was Robert.

"Hello, love. How is your evening?" Robert asked.

"Well, it could be better. You see, I have this man on my mind and I can't seem to shake him off. He's driving me crazy! A good crazy," Jeannette responded. "How are you?"

"Oh, fine, I guess. I am missing you. All I can think about is you. I refuse to change the sheets and pillowcases on my bed and lose your scent. I have been hugging one of the pillows that smells the most like you while watching TV. It is just nuts! Now I have embarrassed myself!"

Jeannette giggled and said, "I wish I had something with your scent. But to smell you, all I have to do is close my eyes. That's what I am doing right now. I smell a musky man. Changing the subject before I am too far gone, you will know sometime tomorrow about coming to Chicago? Correct?"

"Yes. I should know around ten Clark City time," Robert told her.

"I have told my driver, David, you might be coming. If you do, I will have him pick you up — no need for taxis. I had him take me to a little boutique today to buy some new business clothes. All I could think about was if you would like this or that? Of course, I picked what I thought you would like, especially a little red number," Jeannette told him.

"Oh, Lord. Don't start my engine, woman! We are too far apart! Jeannette, please don't tell me if you bought something sexy. I couldn't take it," Robert said, almost moaning.

"Okay. I won't tell you. How am I supposed to get any work done or sleep, with you on my mind? We are acting like school kids! I must confess I kind of like it," Jeannette said with a slight giggle.

"Just so you know, I am having the same problem. It's late in Chicago, so I had better say goodnight. I will call you in the morning. I love you," Robert said and hung up.

She sat looking out a very large picture window at the stars and dreamt of two wonderful evenings she spent with Robert. She crawled into bed sometime after midnight and hoped for sleep.

She walked into her office the next morning before anyone had arrived and strolled through the building getting a more familiar feeling of her company. It seemed like months since she had been there. On her desk, Bridgett had left her meeting schedule for the week. On Tuesday, she had blocked out three hours to tour the apartments she had picked out. On Wednesday, Clay was scheduled to see her. It made her smile. She set her schedule aside for the time being. She dug into paperwork needing her attention and was thoroughly engrossed when Bridgett walked in.

"Jeannette! You scared me! I didn't expect you yet," Bridgett gasped.

"If it's any consolation, you scared me too," Jeannette said all the while smiling. "It's good to see you. What do you have for me?"

"Nothing until ten. I was going to make your coffee, and I brought in the newspaper. I saved the article about you in the Sunday edition. Nice picture and so was the article. I was a little concerned. Sometimes the newspaper can be real stinkers. I think you will like what they had to say. Is there anything you need?" Bridgett asked.

"Thank you for the picture and article and yes. I need to talk to Greg about the new singles we are going to release."

"I will buzz him right away," Bridgett said and slipped quietly out of the office.

Greg came immediately to Jeannette's office. "Jeannette! So good to see you! You look wonderful!" he said and hugged her. "It looks like Clark City agreed with you."

"Something like that. Now, fill me in on the new singles," Jeannette said. They went over each one with a fine-tooth comb. "It all looks great. You have done a wonderful job, Greg. I would like to hear them. Are they ready?"

"All cued up," Greg said.

"Good! Let's have a listen!" Jeannette said.

She sat quietly and listened without a word, in the sound booth. It made Greg a little uneasy.

"Nice job. Really nice job, Greg. The artists are talented, and of course, you make them stand out. I do have two suggestions of tweaking one of the songs," Jeannette said. She went on to explain in great detail what she thought would make it a better sound. By the time they finished, they both thought it was a masterpiece.

It was time for her ten o'clock meeting.

She was thankful for all the distractions. It helped keep her mind off Robert. But what Jeannette did not realize, she had not stopped smiling. She always smiled before, but in a friendly way, not in a loving way.

After her meeting, Bridgett knocked on her door and entered Jeannette's office. "Jeannette, while you were in your meeting, a man by the name of Robert called you. No message."

"Did he leave his phone number?" Jeannette asked.

"Yes, he did, but he said you had it," Bridgett said and looked puzzled.

"Would you get him on the phone for me, please?"

"Robert, please hold for Jeannette. Robert is on line one."

"Thank you, Bridgett. Robert! I'm sorry I couldn't take your call earlier. Have you heard from corporate?"

"That is why I called. I will arrive in Chicago at one, meet with corporate, and be done by five. Does my invitation still stand for staying with you?"

"Yes! A thousand times, yes!" Jeannette squealed with excitement. "I will have David pick you up at O'Hare unless corporate is sending a car for you."

"This time, they are sending someone to the airport to get me," Robert said.

"Well, then I will send David to corporate at five to retrieve you and bring you here to my office. I will show you around. I can hardly wait!" Jeannette said and wanted to clap her hands together like an excited young child.

"Jeannette, there's a disturbance in the waiting area. I will call you back later. Bye." Robert hung up.

Her face went pale. Her instinct, or knowing, told her it was Jeff. "Oh, Lord, no!" Her mind said over and over. "Robert don't kill him! Don't kill him! He's not worth it!" she said while she held her face in her hands. It was torture waiting for him to call back. Her concentration was lost, so she paced.

Finally, after a grueling thirty minutes, Bridgett buzzed, "Jeannette, I have Robert on line one for you."

"Robert! What happened? I know it was Jeff. What did he do?" Jeannette asked impatiently.

"We took care of it, and yes, it was Jeff. He's a real piece of work. He was yelling and ranting about the restraining order and how it was all lies. I had Mr. Baker show him the pictures of the bruising on your arm while I stared him down. I was hoping he would take a swing at me, but he didn't. We told Jeff he was lucky to only be getting the restraining order. If he kept it up, we would charge him with assault! Our receptionist had called the police when he started raising his voice. They arrived pretty fast."

Robert took a breath and went on with his story.

"A big six-foot four-inch police officer said, sir, you are going to have to leave the premises. We will escort you out. If you do not leave, we will arrest you and take you to jail. It's up to you. What's it going to be?" Robert recalled.

"Arrest me? For what?" Jeff yelled.

"For one thing, disturbance and disorderly conduct. If you do not comply, we will charge you with resisting. By the smell wafting from your mouth, we might throw in drunkenness with the disorderly. What's it going to be?" the officer asked.

"You lawyers have this all tied up in a pretty little package, don't you?" Jeff yelled. "I know you are screwing Jeannette! She's bad in bed, isn't she?"

"That's enough, sir! Let's go!" the officer said as he and his partner took either of Jeff's arms and escorted him out.

"Jeff wasn't very bright," Robert went on. "As soon as they got him outside, he started fighting with them. He was arrested. It took every bit of restraint in me not to take a punch at him!"

"Oh, Robert. I am so sorry for the trouble he is causing you." Tears began to fall onto Jeannette's desk. "Why can't he leave me alone, and everyone associated with me, alone? He is going to cause trouble for me until the day I die!"

"Don't worry about him. Between the police, me, and Mr. Baker, he is going to be out of everyone's life for quite a while. Jeannette, I will make sure he doesn't hurt you or cause you any more trouble. I promise. He's going away."

"I wish you were here right now. I need you to hold me."

"I will be there in forty-eight hours, and I won't let you go!" Robert said, trying to comfort her. "You are in the safest place you can be right now. Over two thousand miles away. He can't get to you."

"You are right. Jeff can't get to me. I wonder if he is going to call Sean or Tyler and try to con them into paying his bail. I'll call home and leave a message for them to call me so I can explain all this mess and tell them not to bail him out! Thank you, Robert. I don't know what I would do without you. I love you. I will call you tonight. Bye."

Jeannette felt a sense of relief. He was in jail because of himself. She had nothing to do with it. Karma can be a cruel beast if you cross her. He is finally starting to reap some of what he has sowed.

She called home when she knew, at least, Tyler would be home. She told him all about what happened at Robert's office. She also told him, if his father calls and wants either one of them to bail him out, they are absolutely not to do it!

"You didn't cause him to go to jail, and you are not responsible for him. He will try to manipulate you. Hang up. Do not listen to him. Again, hang up."

"This is awful. My dad is in jail. If my friends find out, they might not want to be around me anymore," Tyler said.

"Tyler, chances are they won't know about this. But if they do, I don't believe they will shun you. They are a good group. They know you for who you are, and you are nothing like him. Chin up and do not take on the guilt of your father."

"Sean just got home. Do you want to talk to him?" Tyler asked.

"Put him on." Jeannette instructed.

She proceeded to tell him all about what his father had done, and Jeff was sitting in jail. She gave him the same instructions to leave him there. By any means, they were not to bail him out.

"The sperm donor did it this time, didn't he? Don't worry, Mom. He can rot in jail for all I care. He is not worth a red cent," Sean said.

"Sean! Language! Even though you don't think very highly of him, he is still your father. Remember what I told you. Help your brother. He has a tender heart, and Jeff knows it. He will try to play him. Tell him not to answer the phone at all. Let the machine answer. I will call tonight. I love you. Bye."

"Tyler, don't answer the phone. Mom told me to tell you to let the machine get it," Sean yelled down the hall. He went into Tyler's room to check on him. "Hey. How's it going?" Tyler looked up at him and shrugged his shoulders. "Yea, it's a tough spot Dad put us in. I don't know about you, but I am humiliated to call him my father."

"Me too," Tyler agreed. "I'm worried my friends will find out about him. I don't know what I will do if that happens."

"How would they find out? Put his picture on the front page of the newspaper and tell the world he is our father? Ha! He's not that important. He has not been around us, so no one associates him with us. Chin up! He's the one who has to pay for his stupidity, not us. Got it?"

"Got it. Thanks, Sean. You are the next best thing to have Mom here," Tyler told him.

"Thanks, little brother. Now that is a compliment. I'm proud of Mom. Well, I have to go back to work. Just came home for a jacket. I should be home around ten. Later!" Sean said and waved his arm in the air.

"Later," Tyler responded.

Tyler finished his homework and watched a little TV. When Jeannette called, he listened when the machine answered just like he was instructed. He was relieved to hear her voice and immediately picked up.

"How's my handsome son tonight?" Jeannette asked with a happy sound in her voice.

"I'm fine. I finished my homework. Dad hasn't called."

"Good. You sound better, Tyler."

"Yea, Sean and I talked. I'm good," Tyler said.

The rest of the conversation was chit-chatting about what happened at school, who said what, and possible tests coming up. Talking to Jeannette, as he did when she was home, really helped calm him before bed.

"Leave a note for Sean and let him know I called. If he needs me, both of you have my numbers. It doesn't matter how late. It's okay to call me. I love you, sweet boy. Call me at the office when you get home from school tomorrow. Goodnight."

Jeff didn't try to contact either of the boys, to Jeannette's surprise. She thanked God for answering her prayers.

4

It was Wednesday morning at last. Robert should be on a plane right now headed for Chicago.

"Bridgett, did you call David about picking up Robert at five?"

"Yes, ma'am. Do you need anything?"

"Not right now. Thank you, Bridgett."

"Just a quick reminder, Jeannette, Clay is coming in at four."

"Oh, good. I forgot. Thanks. Would you please come into my office for a minute?"

She knocked lightly before entering. "What can I do for you?" Bridgett asked.

"Can we talk girl to girl and not a boss to a secretary for a few minutes?" Jeannette asked.

"Sure. I'm all ears," Bridgett said and sat in a chair.

"Have you ever been in love? I mean crazy silly act like a teenager in love?"

Bridgett let out a laugh. "Sorry. We have all noticed something different about you, but nobody wanted to ask you about it. You are in love. That is wonderful! To answer your question, yes, I believe I have been in love, but it didn't feel like what you just described, so I don't think it was real love. We broke up after a year. It sounds like yours is the real deal. Is it Robert, the man who has called several times?"

"Yes. It's that obvious? I thought I was hiding it pretty well. Of course, I can't wipe this silly grin off my face, so it was probably a dead giveaway. He is wonderful. He treats me like a queen, and he is going to be here tonight! I am so nervous!"

"Just be your sweet self and relax. Does Robert feel the same way about you?" Bridgett asked.

"Yes. Robert told me he loved me. I feel secure and protected when I am with him. I will introduce you to him when he arrives. David is going to bring him here so I can show my man off." Jeannette giggled. "Thanks for listening. I needed to vent before I exploded. Okay, back to work. Do I have a meeting with advertising this week?"

"Thursday at eleven," Bridgett said, pointing to her calendar.

"Good. Thank you, Bridgett. When Robert arrives, let me know immediately." Bridgett nodded her head and gave her a wink on her way out.

The next thing she knew, Clay was walking into her office. They discussed anything and everything, business and personal. Although she didn't offer any information about Robert or being in love. That, she kept to herself, for now. They went to the sound booth to discuss another album with Greg.

"I hope you don't mind, but I asked The Band to come here to play some songs we are thinking about for the new album. You can give us a listen and your opinion," Clay said.

"It is fine with me, Clay," Jeannette said. "Greg? It's your sound booth. What do you think?"

"I say, where are they? Let's do this!"

"Perfect timing boys," Clay said as his band walked through the door. "It's a go. Let's get set up. We would love it if you sat in with us, Jeannette. I know you can pick right up on it. What do you say?"

"My guitar…"

"Is right here where Jerry left it," Greg said.

A lump welled up in her throat. When she regained her speech, she said, "You heard the man, Greg! Let's do this!"

Clay counted down a four-beat. The drums picked it up, and they were off. Clay was right. She picked it up easily. It was a fun tune that made you tap your toe and want to dance. Laughter broke out as soon as the song ended. She and the band were having a wonderful time. Of course, Greg was taping everything.

"One more, Jeannette," Clay pleaded.

"One more and I have to go. Greg? Do you have time?"

"I am all ears! Do it!" Greg said.

It was another toe-tapper. A war of guitars began between Jeannette and Clay. Halfway through, Bridgett brought Robert to the sound booth. He watched and tapped his foot along with the beat. He couldn't help but smile. There was the love of his life in a war of guitars and winning. He beamed with pride that she was his.

They erupted in laughter once more at the end of the song.

"Jeannette won, Clay! She took you down!" one of the band members shouted.

"Always a pleasure to have you sit in, Jeannette. One of these days I will win," Clay said.

"No, you won't! Thanks, Clay. It's been a long time. It was fun. Let's do it again sometime," Jeannette said.

"I am going to hold you to it," Clay said.

"Jeannette, there is a gentleman here to see you," Greg said from the booth.

"Excuse me, gentlemen." Jeannette hurried out of the sound room and straight to Robert. "You made it! Bridgett, Greg, this is Robert. Greg runs the sound booth, and Bridgett keeps me on schedule."

"You were great! It looked like you were having a lot of fun," Robert said, smiling from ear to ear.

"This is the band I played and sang a song with on their albums. I want to introduce you to Clay. He's the leader of The Band and my friend." She then took Robert by the hand and led him into the sound room. "Clay, Band, I would like you to meet someone very special to me. This is Robert. Robert, meet Clay and The Band."

They shook hands. "Nice to meet you, Robert. Someone special, huh?" Clay said, giving him a cautious look. "This is our girl, so be careful with her."

"I will take excellent care of her," Robert promised and looked at Jeannette with love. "Are you ready to go?" he asked Jeannette.

"Let me put my guitar away first, and then I am all yours. Excuse us. Greg and Bridgett, make sure everything is locked up. I will see you in the morning."

Robert took her by the hand as they walked to her office. "Can I kiss you?" Robert asked quietly.

"In my office," she said and pointed to a door. As soon as the door shut, Robert had her in his arms and giving her an I-missed-you kiss. "Oh god, you make my knees weak!" she gasped.

"That's the idea. David is waiting for us, and I want to get you out of those clothes! Let's go!"

The trip to the hotel was only ten blocks, but it seemed like one hundred.

"Thank you, David. Will you pick me up at eight-thirty tomorrow morning, please?"

"Yes, ma'am. Have a good evening."

Robert took the key from Jeannette's hand because she was shaking so hard, she could not get it into the lock.

"Easy, Jeannette. There's no reason to be nervous. I am here to pleasure you, not hurt you."

She looked into Robert's eyes and fell lost in love. Before he could push the door open, she threw her arms around him and kissed him hungrily.

"I'm nervous, I'm scared, I'm excited, and I think I want you more than any person has ever wanted another!" Jeannette declared.

"Move over, because I am right there with you! Why don't we go inside before we are arrested for what I want to do to you?" Robert said and pushed the door open.

Every time they made love, it was more magical than the time before. How was it possible? Neither cared.

As they lay in each other's arms, Jeannette knew this is where she wanted to spend the rest of her life—tucked securely by

Robert's side, knowing his heart was beating only for her. Her heart was so full of love she thought it would burst at any second.

"Sweetheart?" Robert said, groggily. "I need food and fluids if you want me to keep this up. I am not complaining by any means. I have worked up an appetite."

"I will call room service. Do you want a steak and a baked potato?" Jeannette asked.

"Oh, baby, you know what I like. Tell them to hurry before I faint from starvation," Robert said, letting his arm flop on the bed as she rolled away.

Jeannette giggled and placed the call. She stood by the side of the bed and watched Robert. He had fallen asleep, and only his chest had movement from breathing. She thought, "He is so handsome, and he loves me! He could have any woman he wanted, but he chose me! How could someone like him love someone like me? He is refined, kind, caring, has a sense of humor, lots of muscles, and I can turn him on. Wow! I am living a dream, and I never want to wake up!"

She stepped out of the bedroom and called home to check on the boys. All was well and eased her mind.

Room service arrived. She wheeled it into the bedroom where Robert still lay, sleeping, and content. Jeannette kissed him gently on his cheek and then his ear.

"Sweetheart, your steak is here. Can you wake up to eat? Or will I have to feed you?"

He opened one eye and said, "I think you are going to have to feed me. I have no strength. You took it all."

"My poor baby, I guess you will just have to waste away while I eat, unless . . ." She ran her hand down his chest and to his stomach, and he shivered with goosebumps.

"I'm awake and ready to go!" He grabbed her and pulled her to the bed. She laughed with delight.

"Just because you are awake does not mean you are ready to go, stud. Let's eat first," Jeannette said, and Robert moaned as he sat up.

"How far away is this food? Do I have to walk very far?" he said, his eyes barely open.

She pushed the cart to him, "No walking required. You can eat in bed."

The rest of the night was filled with laughter and love.

David picked both Robert and Jeannette up at eight-thirty as planned. She was the first to be delivered to Windy City, and then he dropped Robert at corporate. They both looked tired but happy.

"Bridgett, I need the prices on the apartments I toured. Thank you. Don't leave. I will have a decision on an apartment right away. Have a seat. Okay. This one. It has a view of the city, an office and three bedrooms. The price is right also. Would you call and tell the agent I will take it? I will call my accountant and have him send a check over immediately. I want to hang my clothes there before I leave on Saturday. My schedule tomorrow looks pretty packed until three. I am going to leave at four, so I can pick out some furniture and a bed. I will have them call you when it is going to be delivered so you can let them in. I am also going to need four sets of keys. Okay, I think that's it. Thank you, Bridgett."

"Can I get you some coffee?"

"Do I look like I need it?" Jeannette said as she yawned. "I think I had better have a cup, maybe two."

Now that Robert was in Chicago, it gave her a sense of security and calmness. She took comfort in the thought she could be in his arms in a matter of minutes.

The next two days consisted of business, pleasure, and furniture shopping. It only took Jeannette two hours to pick out what she wanted. If it wasn't on sale, then it was not hers. She managed to negotiate an even better deal with the store manager than the sale price listed. Robert watched in awe.

"Where did you learn to negotiate like that? You would have made a good lawyer."

"When you have nothing and every penny counts, you learn by doing. I will never stop negotiating for a better deal. If you haven't noticed, I am frugal."

"Is there anything you can't do?" Robert asked.

"No. I have learned, if I want to do something, I can. I couldn't afford classes on things I wanted to do, so I would save up to buy a book and teach myself. There is macramé, crocheting, painting, guitar, and cooking for some examples. The guitar was more natural. I learned chords from books. How I play is all me — my style. I even wrote a little play in the eighth grade. My class performed it, just in our classroom — no big deal. In my young years, I daydreamed a lot to escape my real life. I was miserable. I didn't have the greatest childhood. It taught me, if I want to be a good mother, I need to do the exact opposite of how I was treated," Jeannette explained.

"You could have ended up being a bitter woman. You have experienced a lot of ugly in your short life. It's time for the good things, and I am here to show them to you. There will be no more ugly, I promise," Robert said and kissed her hand.

They flew home together holding hands for hours even as they dozed off during the flight. A flight attendant had to wake them before they landed.

"I had Bridgett call Sean and Tyler to tell them you were picking me up so they wouldn't know we were in Chicago together. I'm not ready to tell them yet."

"Whatever you say, sweetheart. My daughters will be here Thursday. I thought we could all have dinner Thursday evening."

"Okay. Sean and Tyler also?" Jeannette asked.

"Yes. The whole family."

Her smile turned to a worried look. "What if they don't like me? Oh, God, Robert! Then it would be all over between us! I couldn't bear it!"

"Calm down. This is not an audition. Just like you did with Sean and Tyler, you wanted us to meet so you could ask their opinion of me. You wanted approval. In my case, I don't want or need their approval. I want them to meet you because you are the one, I love."

"You know what to say to make me feel better," Jeannette said. "Well, we are back home in Clark City and a much slower pace."

"Will I see you tonight?" Robert asked with pleading eyes.

"No, sweetie. I need to spend time at home with my boys. Tomorrow. Lunch at the Blue Bucket?"

"I don't like this, being away from you, especially sleeping alone. Your place is tucked under my right arm and snuggled into my chest," Robert said with a slight whine in his voice.

"That is my favorite spot, but we are back home and have to face reality. For now, I am not comfortable telling the boys I have slept with you. Please, be patient with me? I will tell them. This romance has been so fast I don't want the boys to think badly of their mother. That I hop in bed with a man who takes me to dinner."

"That's silly. You are human and a desirable woman. They would never look at you disapprovingly! I know they are concerned about the amount of time you spend with me. It takes time away from them. They have never had to share you until now. I understand all about it. But I hope someday soon you will tell them. I need my hands on you."

"Okay, okay. I will find the right time to tell Sean and Tyler. We will find some time this week to be alone, I promise. I love you. Will you help me with my bags?" Jeannette asked. He walked her to her door and gave her a kiss goodbye. As soon as she shut the door, she yelled, "Boys! I'm home!"

Tyler was the first to greet her with a big hug. Sean came out of his room with his work clothes on and hugged her also.

"You two are a sight for sore eyes! I have missed you! Tyler, I think you grew some more this last week!"

"Ah, Mom. I'm no taller. Monday you need to go to school with me. It's about graduation and what we need to order," Tyler said.

"No problem. I'll be there. Sean, what's bothering you? Something up? Tell me," Jeannette asked.

"I saw you kiss Robert when he dropped you off. I'm not sure about this. It's different. I know you deserve to have someone in your life. But you are my mom. That is what makes this different."

"Sean, life changes. Things change. People change. The one thing that will never change is my unconditional love for you and your brother. I will always be available for whatever you and Tyler need. That is a promise. But it bothers you I kissed Robert?"

"It's going to take a little time to get used to the idea of you being with a man. I guess I'm jealous. I don't want another man to take you from me," Sean said, looking guilty he told her how he felt.

"No one is taking me away from you or Tyler. I am very fond of Robert, and he feels the same about me, so you are going to have to accept it, or not accept it. Your choice. Now, on another related subject, Robert has three daughters. They are coming to town to visit him, and he wants to introduce us to them. So, if you two will, please, make sure you have Thursday evening off? I want to show my handsome sons off."

"Are they our age? Pretty? Single?" Sean anxiously asked.

"No. Robert's daughters are a little older. Two of them have children, have been married, divorced, and remarried. The youngest has not been married and has no children. Mind your manners," Jeannette instructed.

"If the younger one is single and pretty . . . It's not as if they are related to us," Sean pointed out.

"Nice argument, Sean. Remember Patty? The blond you see almost every day?" Jeannette asked.

"Who?" Sean said with a big smile.

"Sean, get a grip on your hormones!" Jeannette said. "What are you grinning at, young man?" she asked Tyler.

"Watching you and Sean is funny. He is a head taller than you, and you have to look up to point your finger at him. It's just funny," Tyler said. "I like Robert, and it is okay with me if you see him, but he can't take up too much of your time, or he's gone!"

"Pretty tough talk, Tyler. I almost believed you. Okay, it's settled. I am going to see Robert, and we are having dinner with him and his daughters on Thursday. Will you help me with my bags?"

She made a home-cooked meal that evening, and they caught up on all the details of the week. Jeannette told them about her new apartment and described it in detail.

"We can start making plans to be in Chicago for Thanksgiving if you want. If Clark City is your choice, then it is fine with me. I need your decision in a couple of weeks to get reservations booked on the plane. So don't dilly dally?"

The week flew by. It was Thursday before Jeannette took a breath. Things were busy at Windy City, and she spent a lot of time on the phone, the fax machine and her computer. Thankfully it kept her mind busy and not on dinner later in the evening.

"Sean, Tyler, we need to go. Our reservations are in twenty minutes. I don't want to be late," Jeannette shouted. "My, you two clean up nice. How do I look? Does this dress look okay?"

"You look beautiful, but does it need to be so low-cut?" Sean asked.

"It's not that low! I am not showing anything! The girls you two hang out with show a lot more!" Jeannette protested.

"They are a lot younger than you!" Sean said.

"Thanks a lot! I'm not going to argue with you. This is what I am wearing. Let's go! Sean, you drive." She flipped the keys to him. "Remember your manners."

Robert and his daughters had just arrived at the restaurant and were waiting to be seated when Jeannette, Sean, and Tyler walked in the door. Her face lit up, seeing Robert standing there looking so handsome. She walked up to him and said, "Kiss me?"

"Really? Here? Now? In front—" She covered his mouth with hers for an unexpected kiss. "Well, that was nice and unexpected. You can do it anytime. You look gorgeous." They saw no one but each other until the waiter interrupted.

"Your table is ready. Please follow me."

Being a gentleman, Robert held Jeannette's chair for her. Sean and Tyler followed suit for his daughters. Upon sitting, they ordered drinks, and it was time for Robert to make introductions.

"I would like to introduce Shelly, Pam, and Susan. Girls, this is Sean, Tyler, and Jeannette." He lingered on Jeannette and kissed her hand.

She leaned in so no one could hear and whispered to Robert, "When you kiss my hand, I melt." He gave a little chuckle and sat back.

"It is very nice to meet you, ladies. Your father has told me a lot about the three of you," Jeannette said and started the conversation off.

It was a pleasant evening. The conversation never stopped among the five younger ones. It gave Jeannette and Robert time to look dreamily at each other and hold hands.

"What do you say we send the kids home and we have a bottle of wine after dinner?" Robert suggested.

"Sounds wonderful. By the way, I had a talk with the boys about us. We are good to go. Well, Sean is a little squirmy about it, but he will get used to it."

"Do you want to stay with me tonight?" Robert said, excitedly.

"I think you need to spend some time with your girls. They just got here. Why didn't the little ones come to dinner? I would love to meet them."

"You will. I didn't want to overwhelm you any more than I already have. The little ones are going to love you." Everyone at the table and the entire restaurant saw the love the couple shared.

"Would all of you young people mind if Jeannette and I stayed and had a bottle of wine? We aren't trying to rush you off, but . . ." They all nodded and stood.

One by one the girls told Jeannette it was nice to meet her. Pam went so far as to lean down and whisper, "It's obvious Dad loves you. I have never seen him this happy before. You are good for him." Jeannette teared up a little.

Susan said, "Dad, you have a grill, don't you? Why don't we have a barbeque tomorrow in the backyard and invite them all over? Jeannette can meet the little people we call our kids."

"Boys? Do you have plans?" Jeannette asked. Each shook their heads. "We would love to. I will bring a couple of side dishes if you want to supply the meat," Jeannette offered.

"It's a date," Susan said.

Finally, the two lovebirds were left alone. They went into the bar and sat at a secluded corner table and shared a bottle of wine. It was a perfect evening.

The next day, the barbeque was full of chaos and laughter. The little ones played with Jeannette like they had known her all their lives. Robert watched them play as he tended the grill. He thought, "She has made me love her even more than I did yesterday. How is it possible? My grandkids love her. She is so gentle and loving toward them. How did I find her? Thank you, God, for sending her into my life. I don't know how I ever lived before Jeannette." It was Robert's turn to tear up with a full heart.

"Dad, are you crying?" Susan asked.

"Nope. It's just smoke from the grill," Robert lied.

"I'm sure it is," Susan said with a smile. "You picked a good one. She is wonderful with the kids, and it's quite obvious you are head over heels in love with her. I would bet my house she feels the same about you. When are you going to pop the question?" Susan asked.

Robert's mouth dropped, and so did the spatula he had in his hand. "Susan! You have always been one to see through people. For your information, I want to ask her very soon. But it can't be too soon. I don't want to scare her off. We haven't known each other very long. I fell in love with her the first time our eyes met. I want to spend every moment with her. When I am away from her, all I can think about is her. It's ridiculous, I know, a grown man acting like this."

Susan stood on her toes and kissed Robert on the cheek. "It's not ridiculous. It's wonderful. I dream of having someone love me as much as you love Jeannette. Don't wait too long and let her get away."

"Sunday, she has to go to Chicago for a week. She goes there every other week. Before you ask, she owns a company there. Last week we were both in Chicago, and we spent three wonderful nights together. When we got back, and I dropped her off at her place, I felt like my heart had been ripped from my chest. I didn't like it at all. I think when she gets back from Chicago this next time I will ask her, but it has to be perfect, so I have to come up with how to ask and, of course, purchase a ring."

"You got this," Susan said and walked away.

While Jeannette was in Chicago, it was the worst week of Robert's life. He hated being without her, but it gave him time to buy a ring and plan how to ask her.

Jeannette settled into her apartment in Chicago. It was much more comfortable than staying in a hotel had been. The only thing she missed was room service. Several nights during the week, she had dinner meetings with radio representatives, advertising people, and a photographer, so she didn't have to cook. Jeannette enjoyed going out to dinner. She was not able to do that for most of her life. It made her feel extravagant.

Friday evening came, and she was exhausted. She wanted to sleep but found it almost impossible without being tucked under Robert's secure and robust arm. She began to think, "I fly back home tomorrow, to my Robert. I hope he hasn't lost interest in me. That's just stupid, Jeannette! You have talked to him several times a day for the last week! You know he loves you! Don't let those old insecurities raise their ugly head! You are better than this!"

Robert met her at the airport. She ran into his arms and didn't care what people said or who saw them. He greeted her with the same hunger.

"You feel so good. I want to take you right here in the airport!" Robert whispered in her ear.

Jeannette giggled as she blushed. "Take me home, big boy. We'll see if we can carve out some time tonight," she said.

"You bet we are! I have waited a week! I'm almost ready to erupt!" Robert said.

Sean and Tyler greeted her at the door and said hello to Robert. Jeannette looked a little surprised that they were cordial to one another. This was an improvement! Before Robert left, Sean announced he wouldn't be home this evening, and Tyler was going out with his friends for a while.

"So, Mom, if you want to spend some time with Robert, you are free to," Tyler announced.

"Well. Thanks. Robert, do you want to take me to dinner since my boys have better things to do?" Jeannette asked while thinking this was odd.

"Absolutely! Thanks, boys. Don't wait up. We have some catching up to do. Jeannette, I'm going to take you someplace special. Dinner and dancing. I will pick you up at seven if that's alright?"

"I will be ready."

She picked out a rose-colored dress that was long and form-fitting. It was simple but eye-catching. The neck was scooped low and showed off her ample breasts. She chose a simple pearl necklace with matching earrings and bracelet. It was just enough to finish her ensemble without overpowering the look.

When Jeannette opened the door to greet Robert, his jaw dropped. "You are gorgeous! I think I lost the feeling in my legs. I have lost blood flow to my head! Can we skip dinner and get you out of that dress instead?"

"Listen, you promised me dinner, buddy, and I am holding you to it! But after dinner . . . We'll see what happens. Sweetheart,

I think you are starting to drool," she teased. It was just the reaction she was after. "Are those flowers for me?"

"Huh? Oh, yes. Sorry. Blood loss," Robert said to a giggling Jeannette.

"Come in while I put them in water. The flowers are beautiful. Thank you. Did—" Robert spun Jeannette around and crushed her mouth with his. She responded in kind.

"Don't you think we should eat dinner first? You are going to need your strength for later," Jeannette said, nipping at his lower lip.

"Woman, you are killing me! You planned this, didn't you? You like to see me squirm."

"I love I can get this reaction from you, yes. I never dreamed I could excite a man. Especially a man like you."

"A man like me?" Robert questioned, puzzled.

"You are a respected member of the community, a professional with impeccable manners, a college education, and oh so handsome. No one like you has ever given me a second look. I keep pinching myself. You love me and are interested in me as a woman and sexually. I'm afraid I will wake up one day and find I have dreamt the whole thing."

"Jeannette, I need to send out thank-you cards to every man alive for letting me, have you. They don't know what they passed up. Thank you for being part of my life and showing me what love is," Robert said, leaning against her.

She could feel a bulge rising and proving to her he meant what he said.

"I think we should probably go to dinner before it's too late." Robert took her by the hand and led her out the door.

They pulled up in front of a very fancy restaurant. A doorman opened Jeannette's door to help her out of the car. Robert tossed his keys to a valet. As they entered, there was a huge chandelier overhead, large bouquets on either side, soft music playing, dim lighting, and the most romantic atmosphere she had ever felt. Every color of the spectrum was in various bouquets displayed everywhere she looked. The aroma was intoxicating.

"This is the most beautiful place I have ever seen! I didn't know it existed. Am I dressed all right for this fine dining establishment?" she asked.

"Sweetheart, the flowers pale next to you," Robert said and raised her hand to his lips.

"You know what that does to me," she said, and her eyes rolled slightly.

"Sir. It would be my pleasure to show you and the lady to your table," the waiter said and held his arm out for Jeannette to take. "Madam?" Jeannette glanced at Robert for guidance. He gave her a quick nod, and she took the arm of the waiter that was offered.

He took them to the dining room, where heads turned and made Jeannette feel self-conscious. They arrived at a private dining room with a table set for two. The room had decorations in purple, lavender, and pink with a crystal chandelier hung over the table. She counted six bouquets placed around the room. The table setting had gold-colored utensils, delicate China with a gold rim, and matching crystal. Linens in deep purple covered the table, adding a stunning look of richness. The beauty took Jeannette's breath away. After seating Jeannette, the waiter silently left the room.

"Robert, this is the most beautiful and stunning room I have ever been in! Did you notice people were staring at us as we walked through the dining area? Are you sure I am dressed appropriate?"

"Yes. Those people were looking at your beauty. I'm serious, Jeannette. Please don't talk negatively about yourself. You don't see what others see and what I see. I love every inch of you."

The waiter reappeared with a bottle of wine for Robert's approval. He gave the waiter a nod. The waiter poured two glasses of wine before slipping out silently.

"There is something I have been waiting and wanting to ask you for two weeks. But first I want to tell you Sean, Tyler, and I got together to talk about our relationship. Yours and mine. To my relief, they approved of us. My daughters love you. Their children adore you. My love for you grows every single day. I don't know how it is possible, but it's true. I have asked myself countless times how I can love you more. You have shown me real love. You are the love of my life. I don't want to live another day of my life without knowing you are completely mine."

He got down on one knee and opened a small box to reveal a three-carat diamond ring with purple amethysts on either side for accent.

"Jeannette, will you take me as your husband? I promise to love you for the rest of my life. I will protect you and make sure you want for nothing. Will you marry me?"

She couldn't make a sound. Tears ran freely from her eyes. She dropped to her knees and threw her arms around Robert.

"Is that a yes?" Robert asked. She nodded and held onto him tighter.

"Shall we see if the ring fits?" He placed the ring on her finger. It was a perfect fit. "A perfect fit for my perfect love."

Her voice found its way back after a few quiet moments.

"My sweet, wonderful man. The ring is absolutely gorgeous. I love you so much! I promise to love you to the moon and back for the rest of my life. God has sent you to me, and I will thank him every day of my life for you. I will be proud to be your wife."

"I want you to know, I asked the boys for permission to marry you. They gave me their blessing. My daughters wanted to know why I was taking so long in asking you. I planned to ask, but I was dragging my feet because I thought it might scare you off," Robert told her.

"You can't scare me off. There is no way you are going to get rid of me! I am yours for life."

After dinner and a little dancing, Robert took his fiancé home and made gentle, passionate love to her. This time he did not have to drive her home. She securely laid under his right arm for the rest of the night. It was a night the couple would never forget.

5

The wedding was planned for the spring, but an exact date had not been decided on. Jeannette needed to find the perfect place for the wedding. So far, she has come up with nothing. When Robert would ask her if she found what she was looking for, she had to answer with, "No. I will know it when I see it. I have it pictured in my mind. I promise you, I will find it!"

During the weeks she spent in Clark City, most of her time was scouring real estate listings, newspapers, and calling caterers to ask if they knew of such a place. She would describe it to each one in great detail.

One day she got a call back from a real estate agent. "I think I might know where the place is that you have described. I can take you there this afternoon if you have time."

"That would be great! I can meet you at your office at about two. What was your name again?" Jeannette asked.

"Shirley. Do you know where my office is?"

"I do. I will see you shortly, Shirley, and thank you," Jeannette said and squealed with excitement as she hung up the phone.

It was a bit of a drive outside of town and into the country. All the way there, Shirley talked about the house and how beautiful it was. The two women finally pulled up to a house that had the look of a castle. It was all stone with turrets and bay windows but still had a warm, inviting feel to it. The lawn was lush, thick green, and manicured flawlessly.

"This is it! The place that I pictured! What does it look like in the back?" Jeannette's mind was racing with pictures of how it would look on her wedding day.

The back of the house was even better than the front. There was a huge patio which spanned the length of the house. At one end was a massive stone fireplace with a complete outdoor kitchen and a grilling area. Trees encircled both front and back yards, making the area secluded and comfortable. A short sidewalk made of stone led to a seating area where plush furniture surrounded a large fire pit for those cool romantic evenings.

"Shirley, would the owners be willing to rent it to us for our wedding and reception?" Jeannette asked, worried they would refuse her.

"I don't know, but I will certainly ask. The house is part of an estate. The children don't want to be here. It is not because of bad memories, it is the opposite. This was a happy place. It hurts too much to come back here. Their parents, who lived here for thirty years, were so much in love, when their father died, their mother lost the will to go on. She passed away three weeks later. It's a sad story. So far, they have not found the right buyer. They told me they would know them when they met them. It had to be the right people, or they won't sell," Shirley explained.

"How soon can you contact them?" Jeannette asked.

"I will give them a call as soon as we get back to the office."

Shirley hung the phone up after talking with the sellers of Jeannette's perfect venue for her wedding.

"Don't keep me in suspense, Shirley! What did they say?"

"They want to meet you and your beau before they give you an answer. If you are free this evening, we could all meet and have dinner at the Blue Bucket," Shirley suggested.

"I will check with Robert and give you a call as soon as I talk to him."

Jeannette rushed out of Shirley's office and went straight to Robert's office. He was with a client, so she had to wait thirty minutes until she could talk to him. She started making lists. When she finally got to speak to Robert, she spoke so fast he couldn't understand what she was trying to say. He sat her in a chair and told her to take a deep breath. After doing so, she explained about the castle-looking house and dinner tonight. Robert was free.

Jeannette called Shirley right away and said, "Shirley, set up dinner. We can meet them tonight."

Jeannette skipped around Robert's office, giggling. "Wait till you see this place, Robert. You are going to fall in love with it just as I did. I know it! It's the perfect place!"

Robert shook his head and watched her bound around the room. "If your staff at *Windy City* could see you now. Their CEO has turned into a happy child." He let out a laugh and grabbed her around her waist to pull her close. "I want you to be happy like this all the time."

"I am, and it's all because of you. I have found my *happy,* with you." She kissed him and said, "Okay, big boy, I have some things to do. I will see you at the Blue Bucket tonight."

She spent the rest of the afternoon on the phone with *Windy City* and gave instructions to Bridgett, "Could you, when you have time, do a little research for a good bridal gown shop? I think I will purchase my gown in Chicago. You know my taste and how frugal I am. I won't wear a used one! I probably did not need to say it, but I was thinking it. Okay. Have we covered everything? Great. See you on Monday."

Jeannette and Robert were a little early for dinner because she couldn't sit still with excitement. She spotted the real estate agent as soon as she walked in. Another couple followed close behind. Jeannette assumed they were the owners of her perfect place.

Shirley made introductions, "Jeannette and Robert, I would like you to meet Sharon and Dennis, owners of their parents' home we visited today." Robert and Dennis shook hands.

"It is very nice to meet you," Robert said. "Please, sit. I have to confess, I wasn't able to visit your home today, but my fiancé did, and she is in love with it. If it makes her happy, then I am all for it. Did Shirley discuss possibly renting it to us for our wedding in the spring?"

"Yes, she did," Dennis said. "Quite honestly, we have never given any thought about renting it. The house and grounds were exceptional to our parents. It was their wish to sell it to a couple who would love it as much as they did. A 'special' couple who are in love as much as they were. So far, we have not found that couple."

"I can understand your reluctance. I assure you we would respect the home and grounds. Why don't we have dinner and get to know each other better and leave this business talk on the table for now?" Robert suggested.

"I agree," Dennis said.

It turned out Dennis and Sharon had a lot in common with Jeannette and Robert. By the end of the evening, they were laughing and joking.

"I am going to have to excuse myself," Shirley said. "I have some paperwork at the office which needs my attention before I call it a night. Thank you for the dinner and great conversation. Dennis and Sharon, give me a call. Goodnight."

After Shirley was gone, Dennis brought up business. "Robert, did Shirley tell you or Jeannette what the asking price is on the property?"

Robert turned to Jeannette, and she answered, "No. She didn't. I know it will be high, and well worth every penny of the asking price. I have had a picture in my mind of the place I call 'the perfect place' to marry the love of my life," she said and placed her hand on the side of his cheek in a loving gesture then turned back to Dennis. "Your house is the exact match to my picture. We decided to take a chance and ask to rent it. All you could do was say no."

"Well, Sharon and I are going to have to discuss it. I'm glad Shirley left. She's a nice lady, but I wanted to talk to you without her present. I am more comfortable talking to both of you one-on-one. Tell you what. Sharon, if you agree, we can talk about this and give them an answer next week," Dennis said, turning to his sister.

"I would like to take them on a tour of the house first," Sharon began. "I know it will be hard for us, but I want them to get the feel of the place and see if they still want to use it. If we decide to rent it to you. Is that agreeable to you, Dennis?"

"I think it is an excellent idea. Do you have some time tomorrow to do a walk-through with us?" Dennis asked Jeannette and Robert.

"Honey, how does your schedule look for tomorrow?" Jeannette asked.

"My last appointment is at two, so I will be free at about three. We can meet you there at three-thirty if it is okay."

"Perfect," Dennis said, stood, and shook Robert's hand. "It was great to visit with you this evening and thank you for a delightful dinner. We will see you tomorrow."

Robert looked at Jeannette and said, "Do you remember how to get there?"

"Oh, God! I hope so!" she exclaimed with a worried look. Robert chuckled and kissed her on the cheek.

The next day Jeannette and Robert headed out to meet Sharon and Dennis as soon as Robert finished with his client. Jeannette wanted to make sure she remembered how to get to her perfect place. They only took one wrong turn but managed to arrive just before the owners.

"Well, what do you think, sweetheart?" Jeannette asked. "Isn't it the most gorgeous place you have ever seen? It's so quiet and peaceful."

"You were right. It is gorgeous, and what makes it perfect is you," Robert said and took her in his arms and kissed her. "I can't keep my hands off you! I can hardly wait until we are married. Unless you would consider moving in with me?"

"No! You know how I feel about living together. I have told my boys time and again if you love someone enough to want to live with them, make a commitment, and marry them. It's too easy to walk out and end the relationship if you live together. With marriage, you think twice and work a little harder to mend the relationship, especially if there are children involved. In my opinion, it is backward to live with someone and then get married. I would not be a very good example for my boys, to go against what I have taught them. So, no, I will not move in with you until we are married," Jeannette explained.

"I had to try. I love waking up in the morning with you cuddled up to me. I don't like waiting, but I will," Robert promised.

Sharon and Dennis arrived to see Jeannette and Robert in each other's arms. The love they were witnessing put a smile on their face.

"Are we interrupting?" Dennis said teasingly.

"Matter of fact you are, but we will get over it," Robert teased back and made Jeannette blush.

Sharon and Jeannette led the way to the front door where Sharon turned the key and opened the door.

"It might be a little dusty. No one has been inside for several months. We have a gardener who tends to the grounds," Sharon said.

Jeannette stood in awe. "It is magnificent!"

It had cathedral ceilings, an enormous fireplace, the walls surrounding it were varnished cedar, oversized windows, two bay windows, and a marble-topped bar. The atmosphere was cozy and yet elegant. She closed her eyes to imagine what it would be like to live here. She got a jolt of love that could have only come from the couple who had lived here. Jeannette's knees buckled, and her eyes flew wide open. She reached out to Sharon to steady her and get her breath back.

"Jeannette? Are you okay?"

"I just felt an extreme wave of love like never before. It took my breath away."

"That was my parents," Sharon told her with a sniff. "Would you like to see the bedrooms? There are six, not including the master bedroom. Our parents always opened their home to friends and relatives, so it was important for them to have extra rooms and bathrooms," Sharon explained.

Robert and Dennis talked about the structure, design, plumbing, where the electrical box is, and whatever men discuss.

The four ended the tour on the patio in the backyard. Sharon and Jeannette stood quietly without saying a word, hugging each other, and quietly crying.

"Ladies, what is going on?" Dennis asked.

Robert rushed to Jeannette's side and asked, "Honey, what in the world is wrong? Have you changed your mind about having our wedding here? What? Tell me."

"No. It's not that. As we walked through the house, I could feel the love this couple shared. It overwhelmed me. I assume Sharon is crying because she has so many memories here?" Sharon shook her head, yes.

Robert took Jeannette in his arms and comforted her.

"I knew you were sensitive, but I didn't know the extent. Don't cry. Their love must have been wonderful to have this effect on you."

Dennis held a tissue out for his sister and one for Jeannette. He looked at Sharon and gave a slight nod and a wink.

"I'm sorry about the tears. I couldn't help it. Their love was so strong. I hope you will forgive me?" Jeannette asked.

"Have you noticed you are not the only one crying? Don't give it another thought. Now you have had the grand tour, are you still interested?" Dennis asked.

Jeannette looked at Robert, and he gave her a smile of approval. "Absolutely. The spirit of love is everywhere. There is no other place on earth I could imagine marrying the man who holds my heart."

"Well, we will talk about it and give you an answer next week as we said last night," Dennis promised.

Robert handed him one of his business cards as they left. In the car, Jeannette leaned her head back to rest it on the headrest.

"Robert, could you feel the love in that house?"

"Not like you did. But I liked the house and the grounds. I didn't find anything I didn't like. We will have to wait until next week for their answer."

"I'll be in Chicago. As soon as Dennis calls, you will call me, right?"

"Of course, honey. I know you have your heart set on this place, so I will do everything I can to convince them to rent it to us."

"I love you, Robert. I want us to share the same kind of love their parents did. Complete and unconditional."

"I believe we already do."

Jeannette left for Chicago, as usual, on Sunday. Robert said good-bye to her at the airport, as usual. He hated those good-byes. He couldn't protect her when she was so far away.

Jeannette's only difference in the usual business at Windy City was Bridgett found three bridal stores for her to check out.

"Bridgett, would you call David and have him pick me up in an hour? I am going to take a little time and check out those bridal stores. Would you have the addresses ready when he arrives? Thank you," Jeannette said over the intercom.

In Clark City, it was business as usual until Robert got a phone call from Dennis. "Hello, Dennis. It's good to hear from you. Have you and your sister made a decision?"

"That's why I am calling you. We talked at length. I'm sorry, but we have decided against renting our parents' home," Dennis said.

"Can I possibly change your mind? Could I offer you more money? Is there anything at all I can do? Jeannette has her heart set on having the wedding there. Give me a price," Robert said, almost begging.

"We don't want to rent it, Robert. It doesn't matter how much you offer us. We are not interested in the money. Our parents left us financially well off. Please, hear me out. We want you and Jeannette to buy the property. We are prepared to make you an outstanding offer to buy the house. Shirley was not happy about it and tried to talk us out of it."

"Buy it? We hadn't considered purchasing it. We are going to need a bigger place. What is your price?" Robert asked, cautiously.

"Let me begin by telling you we had it appraised at just under one million, and that is the price we are asking," Dennis said. Robert almost dropped the phone. "But it is not the price we want to offer you. We know our parents would have liked you and would want you to have it. We watched both of you together and how sensitive Jeannette is. Together, you reminded us of our parents. We want to offer it to you for one-hundred-thousand and an invitation to your wedding."

Robert was stunned. "Would you repeat the price? I don't think I heard you correctly."

"You heard me correctly, Robert. One-hundred-thousand dollars," Dennis repeated.

"I would be an idiot if I didn't take you up on your offer! We'll take it! How soon can Shirley get the papers drawn up? I will write you a check right now!"

"I have already told her to start the process. We knew you would say yes. I warn you, Shirley is not happy with our price. She did her best to talk us out of it, so she might be a little out of sorts when you see her."

Robert could hear Dennis grin through the phone.

"Dennis, how can I ever thank you? Your offer has made us the happiest couple in the world! I can't wait to tell Jeannette! She is going to be astounded! Better yet, I'm going to call her and tell her we get the house. She will assume we will be renting it. When we know when the closing will be, I will get her to the mortgage company with the excuse we have to sign some documents stating we are responsible for any damage."

"You are a sneaky guy, Robert. I like it. Neither Sharon nor I will say a word. Just remember we want an invitation to the wedding."

"Shoot, I'll send a limo for you and Sharon!" Robert said and made Dennis laugh. "Shirley will be in touch with you about closing. Bye."

An extremely loud "Yahoo!" came from Robert's office and had Mr. Baker rushing to see what the noise was all about.

"Robert? Are you having a breakdown? Should I call an ambulance? Or Jeannette?" Mr. Baker asked with genuine concern.

"You will not believe the deal I just made! It's going to make your head spin right along with mine!" Robert said excitedly and proceeded to tell Mr. Baker the whole story and the offer.

Mr. Baker's jaw dropped, and he plopped down on the nearest chair.

"You are the luckiest son-of-a-bitch I know! First, you find a wonderful woman who adores you, and now this. Amazing. Break out the good stuff. I need a drink."

"I want to keep it a secret about buying it for now. I want to surprise Jeannette. Maybe she will move the wedding date closer? A winter wedding. Okay, I have to call Jeannette!"

Mr. Baker walked out, shaking his head, and told the receptionist Robert was okay. It was nothing to worry about. He just got overly excited about some good news.

"Hello, Bridgett, this is Robert. Is Jeannette available?"

"I am sorry. Jeannette is out of the office. She should be back in about an hour. Do you want to leave a message?" Bridgett asked.

"Have her call me when she gets a minute. Thank you."

Robert paced until Jeannette called.

"Hi, sweetheart. Dennis called. We get the house!" There was total silence on the other end and a loud thump. "Hello? Jeannette? Are you there?"

He heard her fumbling with the receiver before he heard her speak, "Yes, I'm here. What did you say?"

"We get the house! How about we move up the date and have a winter wedding?"

"Whoa! Hold on. We get the house? Really? Oh my god, Robert! It's a dream come true!" She burst into tears. After she had calmed herself enough to talk, she said, "What was the second thing you said?"

"Let's move the wedding up and make it a winter wedding. Then I won't have to wait so long to have you all to myself. Isn't that a brilliant idea? Oh, and Sharon and Dennis want to be invited to the wedding."

"Move it up? Well, I might be able to pull it off. Maybe the weekend following Thanksgiving? It will not be winter, but there will be a chill in the air, and we can light the fire pit and fireplace. The one inside too," Jeannette suggested with excitement.

"You realize it is about four and a half weeks away, right?" Robert asked.

"Yes. I want to be your wife as soon as possible, now you have secured the perfect place I can start making arrangements from here. Oh, Robert, you have made me so happy! I can't wait to start our life together. I love you. Bye."

She pushed a button for Bridgett to come into her office. "Yes, Jeannette?"

"Bridgett, I need to ask you to do some things for me that are not part of your job description. Robert and I have set a date for the wedding. It will be the Saturday after Thanksgiving. It doesn't leave a lot of time to pull this together. I have a list of vendors I need you to call for me in Clark City. Set up appointments with each one for Monday. Call Judy and see if she can go with me on Thursday at four to check out wedding gowns. I will send David to pick her up."

"Anything else?" she asked with a grin.

"Oh! One more thing. Get Clay on the phone for me."

"May I say one thing?" Bridgett asked.

"Of course, Bridgett!"

"Congratulations! I am so happy for you! You are going to be a beautiful bride," Bridgett squealed.

"Thank you." Jeannette rose from her desk and hugged Bridgett.

Shopping with Judy was always a lot of fun. They laughed at some of the dresses and styles after having a couple glasses of wine. At that point, everything was a little funny. The laughter stopped when she saw the dress.

"Oh my," Jeannette gasped. "It is perfect in every way. It is off-white, the color I wanted. It has pearls, lace, and sequins. A V-neckline not too low cut, and a train about six feet long. Perfect! What size is it? Judy! It's my size!"

"Try it on! I'll help you get into it."

Moments later, she was standing in front of the mirror, admiring how the dress looked on her. "What do you think, Judy? Is this the dress?"

"It is! It's perfect! The search is over!" Judy announced.

"How much does the tag say?" Jeannette asked.

"Oh, you are not going to like it. It says a thousand dollars!"

"What? No! I can't justify paying so much for a dress! Would you ask one of the clerks to come in?" Jeannette asked Judy.

"May I help you?" The clerk asked.

"Is this the correct price?"

"No, sorry, it isn't. Today we have a half-off sale. If you purchase it today, the price is five hundred."

Jeannette could not get "I'll take it" out fast enough. "I think it needs a couple of inches taken off at the hem. Do you take care of alterations also?"

"Yes. When do you need this dress?"

"I need it shipped to Oregon in two weeks. Can you do that?"

"Yes, we can. I will send in one of our seamstresses to take measurements while I make out a sales receipt."

The clerk left the fitting room, and Jeannette let out a squeal! "Judy, it's all coming together! I am getting married! I never thought I would ever say that again. I'm getting married!"

After the seamstress was finished, Jeannette got dressed, paid the salesperson, and gave her the address for shipping. The two friends had dinner and a bottle of wine at a beautiful, quaint restaurant. They told stories and laughed until they were exhausted.

"Judy, do you want to stay at my apartment tonight or shall I have David take you home?"

"I should go home. My husband is going to wonder where I am as it is. Maybe next time?"

"Anytime, my old friend. Thank you for helping me with my gown. I had so much fun. Are you feeling a little tipsy? I am. Thank God David is driving!" They managed to walk out of the restaurant like ladies and got into the awaiting car.

The next morning Jeannette had a slight headache and was a bit tired. *"I guess I might have had a little too much wine,"* she thought as she dressed for work. *"A couple of aspirin and a cup of coffee will help."*

Her day was finally complete at eight o'clock in the evening. After arriving at her apartment, she packed her bag, took a hot bath, and crawled into bed. She dreamt of her knight in shining armor and the magical wedding they would have at the perfect place.

The next day, she stepped off the plane to see her Robert waiting for her, and to her surprise, Sean and Tyler were with him.

"All my boys together! How did I get so lucky?" She hugged the boys and kissed them on the cheek. Robert got a hug, and a kiss on the mouth, along with a whispered, "I love you."

"I thought we should get more acquainted with each other since we are going to be a family in a few weeks," Robert explained.

"That is a great idea. Have you boys seen the house we are having the wedding at?" They shook their heads no. "Maybe after lunch, we can take a drive and show it to you," Jeannette suggested.

"You read my mind, Jeannette. How about the Blue Bucket for lunch?" It had become their favorite place to eat.

After lunch, they drove to the wedding site. They walked all around the outside while Jeannette explained where all the decorations will be hung and where she and Robert would stand during the ceremony.

"That reminds me. We need to pick a day this week I can get Sean and Tyler together for a tux measurement," Jeannette said.

"You want us to wear tuxedos?" Sean asked.

"Absolutely! I want my handsome boys to look their best. Do you have a best man, Robert?"

"Mr. Baker agreed to stand up with me."

"Perfect. I need to call Shelly, Pam, and Susan to talk about bridesmaids' dresses."

"Jeannette don't put so much stress on yourself. The day is going to be perfect, and I am sure you are going to look gorgeous. So, take a breath," Robert said with concern.

"I have a lot done already. Tomorrow is a leisure day. Monday is busy."

As they drove back to Jeannette's apartment, Robert asked, "What do you have planned for Thursday?"

"Right now, nothing. What do you have in mind?"

"Well, we have a couple of documents needing signed for Dennis and Sharon stating we are responsible for any damages. They would like to meet at about one o'clock on Thursday. Is it okay with you?"

"Sure." Sean and Tyler looked at each other and snickered. "All right, you two. What's so funny? Did I miss out on a joke?"

"Nope. We were laughing about what happened to one of Tyler's friends. It's nothing," Sean said.

Robert shot a look at Sean in the rearview mirror. It was an unspoken 'don't-blow-it' look. He had told the boys about buying the house and swore them to secrecy.

"Well, boys, since we moved the wedding to the Saturday after Thanksgiving, we won't be spending the holiday in Chicago. Are you agreeable with that?"

"Sure. No big deal," Sean said.

Tyler chimed in with, "Yep. No big deal."

With keeping *Windy City* on track, the release of the new singles, and meeting with vendors for the wedding, the week flew by. Thursday was upon her before she knew it.

The phone rang, "Hi, honey. Oh, I'm glad you reminded me! I will jump in the shower and meet you at your office. I love you too. Bye."

When Jeannette arrived at Robert's office, he was acting a little antsy. Jeannette thought, *"Something's up. He's not acting like himself."*

She took his hand and said, "Honey, is everything alright? You're not quite yourself. Are you having second thoughts about marrying me?"

"Absolutely not! I have a lot on my mind. I love you with all my being. Let's sign those papers. Shall we?" Robert said, smiling, and put his arm around her waist.

"There's Sharon and Dennis! Oh, Sharon, I am so excited you decided to let us use your gorgeous estate. I don't know how we can ever thank you," Jeannette said and hugged her.

"It is our pleasure. We know it's what our parents would want. Let's go inside," Sharon said.

Robert and Dennis walked behind the ladies trying to have a private conversation. "So, were you able to keep this quiet?" Dennis asked.

"Believe me. It has been tough. I almost blew it a couple of times. I wanted to tell her countless times to see her face. But I held my tongue. Whew," Robert told him.

"Well, I'm impressed you kept the secret this long. I wouldn't have been able to. It won't be long now," Dennis said, opening the door to the mortgage office.

"Hello. You must be here for the closing. My name is Rose. I will be handling all your documents. I have everything ready for you in the room on your left."

Jeannette looked bewildered. "I think you have us confused with someone else. We are not here for a closing."

"Sweetheart, let's go have a seat at the table she has set up, and Dennis will explain what is happening."

Dennis explained what he and Sharon had discussed, the conclusion they came to, and the offer they made to Robert.

"He wanted to surprise you. We are here to make the estate all yours and Robert's. You are buying it. The estate will be your home."

Jeannette turned pale and became light-headed. Her mouth opened, but no sound came out. She looked back and forth from Robert to Sharon to Dennis, totally shocked. Then the tears started. She sat on Robert's lap and cried into his shoulder.

"Does this mean you are happy about this?" Robert asked. She shook her head, yes. "Well, maybe we should sign the papers and make it official?" She pulled her head from his shoulder and kissed his cheek. "Sweetheart, I think you should sit in the other chair."

She stood and threw her arms around Sharon and then Dennis. She was unable to form words coherently.

"The house belonged to you the day you stepped inside, Jeannette. It is our pleasure to sell it to you," Sharon said. "Let's get this show on the road."

After an hour of signing their name, at least, a hundred times, Rose handed the swollen-eyed Jeannette and the beaming Robert the keys to their new home.

"It's ours!" Robert declared. "Dennis, Sharon, will you join us for a celebratory drink?"

"I wish I could, but I have to be somewhere in fifteen minutes," Sharon said.

"I have someplace I need to be also, or I would join you. Don't forget to send us an invitation to the wedding!" Dennis said as he walked off.

"There is not a better man on the planet, and I am marrying him. How did I get so lucky? I had no clue we were buying the estate. We are homeowners! Well, you have a house, but this is my first!" Jeannette declared.

"I have already put my house up for sale. Since you won't live with me until we are married, I thought you could move into the estate and I will stay where I am until it sells or we are married, whichever comes first. What do you think?"

"Oh, Robert, this is so wonderful."

Jeannette gathered boxes from the grocery store that evening and started to pack. It was amazing how much she had packed before she had to leave for Chicago on Sunday. Jeannette left instructions for Sean and Tyler to pack what they could before Jeannette got back. She planned to move in next Sunday. If she were living there for a couple of weeks before the wedding, it would help a lot when it came to decorating and preparing for the big day.

When she arrived at her apartment in Chicago, she made her usual calls to the boys and Robert. Her next call was to Judy to tell her the exciting news. While she was talking to Judy, it occurred to her the invitations needed to be sent out, ASAP.

"Holy crap, Judy! Can you help me address about two hundred invitations tomorrow evening? You can spend the night with me at my apartment. I'll order dinner in, and we can have some wine. We can make it a two-person pajama party."

"I will talk to my hubby to see if we have anything going on and call you right back!" Judy said. She called back a couple of minutes later with good news. The plan was set, a sleepover at Jeannette's apartment.

The fun Jeannette and Judy shared that night was as if they were teenagers all over again and having a real pajama party. They ate pizza, drank wine, laughed, and at the last count, addressed 225 wedding invitations.

"Do I know that many people? Oh, yeah, part of those are Robert's," Jeannette said, and Judy burst out laughing, which made Jeannette laugh. "Finally done. I'm too tired to get up off the floor. If there were a blanket and pillow handy, I'd sleep right here. Oh, crap! Come on, Judy, I'll help you up if you help me?"

"Deal. I think. Give me a minute. I have to get the blood flowing to make my legs work," Judy said, and they burst into laughter once again.

"Well, crap! We're not getting anywhere!" Jeannette said. "Okay, one more try! Up!" This time, the two were successful in standing. "Now we are standing, but who is going to pick up the box of invitations?" Laughter ensued once again. "Forget it! We'll pick it up in the morning. I'm hitting the sack. You can sleep in Tyler's room. First door on the left. Goodnight." They hugged each other and crawled into bed.

6

Saturday came around fast. She had been working long hours during the day and making sure everything was in place for the wedding in the evening. It was time to go home to Oregon. Jeannette always got a burst of energy when she saw Robert waiting at the airport to greet her.

"Oh, Robert, tomorrow I am moving into the home of my dreams! I am still having a hard time believing it is ours! We are going to have to make love in every room to truly make it ours!" Jeannette exclaimed.

"That is going to be quite a job, but I am willing to give up my evening and start the process tonight! It will be a sacrifice, but I'm willing to do it," Robert teased.

Jeannette giggled and said, "Don't you think the first time we make love in our home should be on our wedding night?"

"Are you kidding me? Do I have to wait that long? Oh, hell, no!" Robert shouted.

Jeannette couldn't help but laugh.

"Why are you insisting on torturing me? I already have to wait a week to see you. Now this? I could explode!"

Jeannette burst out laughing. Then said, "Okay, my sweet, horny man. I won't make you wait. I better pick up a case of energy drinks. We might have to start christening our home tonight."

"Now that is more like it! How about right now?" Robert said, excitedly.

"First, I need to go home and see the boys. Then we can grab the boxes I already packed and take them with us. Just hold on for a few more hours."

"Fine," he said pouting. Jeannette smiled and kissed him on the cheek and nibbled on his ear.

"Jeannette! You are looking for trouble!" he warned. She stopped.

Sean and Tyler were just as excited as Jeannette to move. They had always lived in an apartment. Now, finally, a real home.

"When do we get to stay there, Mom?"

"Let's shoot for tomorrow night as long as you packed as I told you to do. If you and Tyler get a few of your friends to help us, it will go fast. Then we will definitely be sleeping there tomorrow night. But tonight, Robert and I are going to take a few boxes and spend some time alone in our new home."

"Deal!" both boys shouted in unison.

That night, they made the house their home. A fire blazed in the fireplace, soft music played, and dozens of candles lit the room. It was a night Jeannette was consumed by the love of Robert. She gave herself entirely to him as she had never done before. The love that lingered in their home somehow made their love for each other bigger, stronger, and sweeter. It was a night of passion like no other.

"If this is what it is going to be like after we are married and you let me live here, I am going to have to get in shape. This might kill me! But I will love every second of it," Robert said and held her tight as she snuggled under his arm.

Moving day had arrived, and there were teenagers everywhere carrying boxes, teasing one another, showing off but generally getting the job done. Sean and Tyler had not taken any of their friends to see where they were going to live. As they drove up to the circular driveway, their friends gasped. Wow was the general census.

"Oh my god, man!" Zach exclaimed. "This is your new house?"

"Isn't it a beauty? On Thanksgiving, maybe you can come over, and we can play some touch football? There is plenty of space," Tyler suggested.

The first order of business was to take everyone on a grand tour. The only word said and repeated every few seconds was, "Wow."

Zach punched Tyler in the shoulder and said, "Are you going to be one of the spoiled rich brats now you are living in grand style?"

"Ouch! No! Mom will see to it. You know how she is. Things will stay the same only out here. Hey, Mom!" Tyler yelled across the room. "I'm hungry! Anything to eat?"

"It should be here any minute. I ordered pizza and soda to be delivered," Jeannette said and looked out the window. "Speaking of which, the pizza just pulled up. Why don't some of you help the pizza guy? I ordered a lot."

"Fifteen pizzas and drinks for Jeannette," the delivery man said. "Nice house."

"Thank you. Here's your money plus a tip," Jeannette said when she paid him. The delivery man was looking at their house and making her uncomfortable. "Is there anything else, young man?"

"Huh? Oh, no. Thanks."

"You must have other deliveries to make, so I'm sure you need to be on your way," Jeannette suggested. "Robert? Could you see this young man out, please?"

"Let me show you the door," Robert said and took him by the arm. He understood why she asked him to show this guy out. His gawking made him feel like this guy was casing their house. "Thanks for the delivery. We won't need your services again," he said and shut the door in his face.

After all the boxes were unloaded, every last piece of pizza was consumed by the herd of teenagers. Jeannette stood in the middle of the room and announced, "Thank you so much for all your help. Now my work begins. Why don't you explore the grounds? There's room for a football game, and there's a basketball hoop on the side if you didn't notice before. If you don't understand what I am getting at, I will say it plainly. Thank you but go outside. I have unpacking to do."

They moaned from full stomachs but managed to get up and walk outside. Robert came up behind Jeannette, wrapped his arms around her, and whispered in her ear, "You know how to be a boss! It's a turn on!"

She turned to face him and patted him on the cheek. "Honey, I have a lot to do, and all those kids are still here. Why don't you spend the night?"

"Really? You're serious?"

"Yes, I am deadly serious," Jeannette said, looking him straight in the eyes. "I want you here tonight. But there's a catch,"

Robert sighed at the thought of a catch. "You have to help me unpack the boxes in the kitchen. We are going to want coffee in the morning, so we need to find the coffee pot."

"Is that all? I'm on it!" Robert said and hurried to the kitchen.

The next two weeks were chaotic and consumed with wedding preparations. The week of Thanksgiving she spent Sunday through Tuesday at *Windy City* preparing for some time off after the wedding. She took a red eye home so she could start preparing their first Thanksgiving dinner together. Robert's daughters and their families were scheduled to arrive Wednesday afternoon. Since Jeannette was preparing a feast for the holiday, Robert made reservations at the Blue Bucket on Wednesday evening for all the family to eat dinner together.

Lately, Robert had spent more nights with Jeannette than not. It just didn't feel like home if they weren't together. But he wasn't officially moving in until after the wedding according to Jeannette.

Their home was filled with joy, food, and fun on Thanksgiving. The laughter from little ones and older ones made it feel like a home. It was a wonderful family time with controlled chaos.

The next day was the wedding preparation day. Robert's daughters pitched in and helped hang decorations and things Jeannette couldn't get to. Robert and the girl's husbands did whatever was instructed and then sat on the patio with a beer.

Jeannette walked out to the patio, looking exhausted. "So, this is where you are. Dare I ask if you guys were hiding from us?" They looked innocently at one another and shrugged their shoulders. "Uh-huh. Honey, could you go to the deli and get a bunch of sandwiches for everyone? I'm exhausted. I don't want to cook."

Robert stood, took her in his arms, and said, "Sweetheart, I have already taken care of that. I called the deli an hour ago. I sent the boys to pick up the sandwiches. They will be back shortly."

"You wonderful man. Gentlemen, take lessons, and learn how you treat a woman." She kissed him and disappeared into the house. A few minutes later she reappeared with women and children in tow. "Ladies put the fold-out table over there. Kids put plates, napkins, and utensils on the table. Let's move more chairs over here. Perfect. Now, let's relax and wait for the food to get here."

"Gentlemen, that's how you take charge. That's my woman," Robert bragged.

Long about 9:00 p.m. Jeannette said good-bye to the love of her life. "Tomorrow you are marrying me, big boy. Don't be late! I will miss sleeping next to you tonight."

"I will be on time. I promise. My bed will be cold without you. I love you. I will see you at the altar," Robert promised and kissed Jeannette one last time as a single man.

The ceremony took place just after dusk. Thousands of tiny lights had been strung to light up the grounds. Tables covered with white and purple linens were set up to seat four hundred guests. The florist made small bouquets for each table and larger ones around the grounds. Lilies, carnations, roses, and baby's breath in purple, lavender, and white were in each one. The arch the bride and groom stood under, was decorated with lavender and white flowers that had tiny white lights peeking through.

The caterer was prepared and ready to serve. It was 'go' time.

The music began. Robert and Mr. Baker took their place by the minister. Shelly, Pam, and Susan walked down the aisle in long lavender dresses and carried a single lily. Robert's three grandchildren came next, dropping flower petals and carrying two pillows with a wedding ring tied on each. The wedding march started. It was the cue for everyone to stand. Jeannette appeared with Sean and Tyler on either side, escorting her down the aisle. At the sight of Jeannette in her wedding gown, it took Robert's breath away. He got a little weak in the knees. Mr. Baker quickly steadied him.

"Who gives this woman to be married to this man?" the minister asked.

In unison, Sean and Tyler said, "We do." They turned, kissed their mother on the cheek, and joined Robert and Mr. Baker.

Jeannette and Robert had written their vows of love to one another. They were both in tears before the minister said, "You may now kiss your bride." At the end of the ceremony, there wasn't a dry eye in the audience. They had all been touched by the love the newlyweds shared.

The entire day was magical. Everything had gone as planned. Now it was time to introduce Robert to Warren and Rebecca. She found them standing with Sean and Tyler attempting a conversation over a piece of pie.

"Robert, I would like to introduce Rebecca and Warren. These are my parents. Robert is my husband," Jeannette said with a pained smile. Out of the corner of her eye, she was watching Sean and Tyler. They were slowly moving away, so they didn't have to attempt talking anymore with their grandparents.

"It is nice to meet you. Jeannette is an amazing woman," Robert told them and shook Warren's hand. Warren's eyebrows went up at the description of his daughter, and Rebecca smiled. "You live in Stokes Landing? I have not been there. One of these days, I am going to have my wife take me there and show me your town." Robert told them.

"Where are you from, Robert?" Warren asked.

"Chicago, but I have made Clark City my home."

"That is quite a house you have. How much did it set you back?" Warren asked.

"The price isn't important, Warren," Robert said, getting a little irritated. "I bought it for Jeannette as a gift. I want to make her happy."

"Well, it's going to take a lot of work to keep her happy. You knew she was married before?" Warren asked.

"I am well aware of her past. I am also acquainted with her childhood family life. Is that something you would like to discuss? Her childhood past?" Robert was thoroughly irritated with Warren and was prepared to take him down a notch or two.

"Robert, it's time to cut the cake, honey," Jeannette said and tugged at Robert's arm.

"Maybe some other time we can pick up this conversation again? I would like to discuss it with you," Robert said with an evil smile Jeannette had never seen before. "Yeah, let's cut the cake," Robert said, staring down Warren.

As the new couple made their way to the cake, Rebecca was whispering something to Warren. Neither looked happy. But of course, it was their normal look. Jeannette shrugged it off. If they didn't want to be here, they could leave anytime. It wouldn't hurt her feelings.

The cake was cut and served when a familiar voice came booming from the speakers.

"Ladies and gentlemen, my name is Clay, and this is The Band. Say hello, Band."

They threw their hands in the air and yelled, "Hello!"

"Jeannette and Robert had no idea we were coming today. Surprise! I have known Jeannette for a lot of years. There was always one thing missing in her life. It was Robert. She is sweet, caring, kind, generous, a good person to work for, and damn if she isn't talented! Maybe we can convince her to play a song with us later. We couldn't let you get married without us playing for your first dance as a married couple. So, Jeannette and Robert, this is for you. The dance floor is yours."

The dance floor cleared when the newlyweds stepped into the middle. They danced to a sweet tune from the Big Band era. Jeannette felt like she was flying. Her feet didn't touch the floor as Robert swept her around the dance floor with grace. When the song ended, the crowd erupted into applause. Robert kissed his bride in the middle of the dance floor with passion.

As they walked off the floor, it hit Jeannette, honeymoon! "Robert! I didn't plan a honeymoon! That is the only thing I forgot! Oh, no!"

"Calm down. The honeymoon was my job. The limo will be here in an hour to pick us up," Robert said.

"Where are we going? How long are we going to be gone?"

"First of all, we are going to change out of these clothes. Then we are going to the airport. We can sleep on the plane. It will take roughly fourteen hours to get to Ireland. I am going to have you all to myself for ten days."

"Ireland? Oh, this is too much!" Jeannette exclaimed.

"We are staying in a castle I have rented, complete with servants. You won't have to lift a finger. It sits at the top of a hill overlooking the ocean," he explained.

"How did I ever get a man like you? I love you, husband of mine. I love calling you my husband," she said.

They changed out of their wedding attire and into something more comfortable to travel in. Jeannette and Robert reappeared at the reception to say their good-byes. Clay had a request.

"I see the happy couple is about to leave. Jeannette, will you play one song with us? Just one?" The crowd applauded. She looked at Robert, and he gave her a nod.

She took her place next to Clay as he counted them down. She followed his lead. It was the second song she had sold him. Some of the guests danced, some clapped, and others tapped their feet. Everyone had a smile, except Warren. He just watched. The song ended, and Jeannette took the microphone. She thanked everyone for coming and said good-bye. Robert swept her off her feet and placed her in the limo. They were off.

"Oh, Robert! What about all the cleanup? Returning the tuxes?"

"I want you to relax. I have taken care of everything. My girls are staying until Wednesday to make sure everything is cleaned up and taken back. The boys have grocery money and extra money for whatever they do for fun. See? No worries," he said to his new bride and stroked her cheek. "You did a wonderful job putting a wedding together in four and a half weeks! It turned out beautifully. You were gorgeous. You glowed. I lost feeling in my legs when I saw you, and Mr. Baker had to steady me."

Jeannette laughed and settled back into the seat under Robert's right arm, next to his heart.

That was the happiest time of my life. I married the love of my life, all our friends were there, and we went on a dream honeymoon. Life was perfect. That certainly did not turn my life to crap!

Looking back, I think I have learned these life lessons from experience, to this point in my life:

1.   I had to make peace with my past so it wouldn't play havoc with my present.

2.   It doesn't matter what other people think of me. That is their business. It doesn't concern me.

3.   Given time, I can heal from almost anything.

4.   My happiness is up to me, no one else.

5.   Never compare my life with someone else's life. Don't judge others. I have no idea what they have been through or are going through. Their life's journey is not the same as mine.

It is nice to remember the good times in my life, but it doesn't tell me where everything went wrong. I would much rather stay with this beautiful and magical time in my life. But I have to move on.

7

Ireland was the most beautiful and romantic place in the world. They left the castle a few times to explore some of the nearby towns and sights, but most of their time was spent laying on lounge chairs on a patio watching the waves crashing against the rocks. Robert always held her close to him. Neither noticed the chill in the air. It was warm and comfortable in each other's arms.

When their time was at an end in Ireland, and it was time to leave, they discussed staying longer, but quickly snapped out of the dream and back to the present. They knew they had to go home. There were responsibilities that awaited them in Clark City and Chicago.

"Are you all packed, sweetheart?" Robert asked.

"Unfortunately, I am. Staying in this castle, in Ireland, was another dream of mine you made come true. It was so wonderful; I don't have the words to describe what it meant to me. We bought a mansion, our wedding was made of a fairy tale, and then Ireland. Since I can't express it in words, I hope you can feel how thankful I am God sent you to me. I love you so much," Jeannette said before they left the castle.

"I love you with all my heart. There has never been anyone before you I have truly loved. You are my only and my last love," Robert said as they traveled to the airport.

The flight home seemed to go faster than the flight to Ireland. At the airport in Oregon, Sean and Tyler were waiting for Robert and Jeannette. She was the first to spot her boys. She waved and jumped up and down to get their attention. It was embarrassing for teenagers to be associated with what looked like to be a slightly unbalanced woman. They gave her a quick wave and hoped she would stop drawing attention to them.

"My boys! It is so good to see you! Tell me everything that has happened while we were gone," Jeannette said excitedly.

"Well, I'm not sure where to start. Lots of things have happened. Let's catch up in the car. We need to get your bags," Sean said.

The drive home was full of chatter. Some about Ireland, some about the teenage group, and some was about Sean's experiences in college.

"Did my girls get everything taken care of after the wedding?" Robert asked.

"Yes, they did. Our new sisters made some meals for us, some I'm not sure what it was. But we ate it, and it tasted pretty good. Pam makes delicious chili. I think it was Susan who made the unique dishes. We had fun playing with our new nephews and niece," Sean said.

"You haven't mentioned Shelly. Did she do anything?" Robert asked and looked in the rearview mirror at Sean. He and his brother shared a look before Sean answered.

"Shelly didn't leave. She is still here, at our house. She said she thought she should stay and take care of us. We told her it wasn't necessary, but she insisted."

"She didn't leave? I gave her a round-trip ticket to make sure she went home. She is still at our house?" Robert asked, hoping he heard wrong and sped up a little.

"Robert, what's wrong?" Jeannette asked.

"I don't trust Shelly. I love her, but I don't trust her alone in our home. She has had some issues in the past. But she has been doing fine and seemed to be on the straight and narrow," Robert explained.

"She seems okay," Sean added and looked at Tyler and whispered, "Your turn."

"There's one thing I think I should tell you," Tyler paused and cleared his throat. "She asked Zach if he knew where she could score some pot. He told her, no, and then he told me what she asked him. Zach doesn't think too highly of her. I'm sorry, Robert. Shelly is my new sister, and I know you love her, but she really embarrassed me with my friends."

"Thank you for telling me, Tyler. I will take care of this as soon as we get home. Is everything in the house intact? What I mean is, have you noticed anything missing?" Robert asked.

"No. Everything seems fine," Sean reported.

They pulled up to their beautiful home and Shelly was standing at the front door ready to greet them.

"Surprise, Daddy! I decided I liked Oregon and I am going to stay! I made your favorite sandwich," she said and hooked her arm through his.

"Shelly, I want to talk to you! Let's talk on the patio. Jeannette, I want you there with me," Robert said and shrugged Shelly's arm away and took Jeannette's hand.

On the patio, Robert began, "Number one, you don't just decide you are going to stay in our home without asking us first! Number two, you think you are going to live with us? No way! You are a grown woman. If you are going to stay in Clark City, you will get a job and an apartment! You will not sponge off us!

Number three, what do you have to say about asking Zach about drugs?" Robert shouted. His face was red with anger and was directed solely at Shelly.

Shelly snickered and said, "Oh, Dad. It was no big deal. It was only pot. Pot is not drugs."

"It is a drug! I will not have drugs of any kind in our house! If I find any drugs, pot included, at all, you are gone! I mean on a plane back to Texas! I will personally put you on the plane!"

"You don't mean that. You are just tired from your trip. I'm your daughter, and you love me. You know you do. You're not going to kick me out," Shelly said, smiling the entire time, then reached out to Robert's arm thinking it would calm him. Jeannette wasn't sure what to do or say, if anything, so she stood by Robert's side and stared at Shelly.

"First thing tomorrow, you are hitting the street and looking for a job! Are we clear? And if I hear a whisper about you and drugs, including pot, you are on a plane! We will not have you in our town shaming us and ruining the respect we have built in the community! If you think I'm joking, just try me!" Robert shouted. Jeannette thought she might have seen fire shoot from Robert's eyes at one point. He was furious. "Honey, do you have anything to add?" He asked Jeannette not taking his eyes off Shelly.

"I agree with you one hundred percent, Robert. I have never had to deal with drugs before, and I am not about to start now. There is no information I find out about you that I will not share with Robert," she told Shelly. "We are a team and in agreement. I suggest you do what he told you to do," Jeannette said.

"That reminds me. You had a round-trip ticket from Texas. What did you do with the return ticket?" Robert asked Shelly.

"Since I decided to stay, I cashed it in," Shelly answered.

"Where's the money?" Robert asked.

"I spent it."

"On what, Shelly?" Robert questioned intently.

"Stuff I needed. Toiletries and things."

"Uh, huh. Sure, you did," Robert said all the while thinking she spent it on pot.

Robert rubbed his face with both hands then took Jeannette's hand, led her inside, and left Shelly standing alone on the patio.

"Oh, sweetheart, I am so sorry about coming home to . . . to her. Of all my daughters, she had to be the one to stay. She hasn't changed. She's still a pot-smoking freeloader! I promise I will get her out of our home."

"Sweetheart, as long as we stand together, this will work out. You had no idea she was going to do this. It's not your fault," Jeannette said, trying to comfort him.

"It may not be my fault, but she's, my daughter. I will deal with her. When I leave for work in the morning, she will be in the car with me so she can look for a job. I don't want her here if I am not. I don't trust her! If she asks to borrow any of our cars—yours, Sean's, or Tyler's—the answer is a resounding no! Boys, will you come in here for a minute, please? Listen, if Shelly asks to borrow money or your car, the answer is no! I mean it! DO NOT GIVE HER THE KEYS TO YOUR CAR! She is not a responsible person and will probably wreck it or do something to it. Just tell her no."

Sean and Tyler both said, "Got it" in unison.

"Has Shelly been a problem while we were away? Did she make you feel uncomfortable, besides the pot thing?" Robert asked.

"No. Shelly has been nice to us. The only thing she asked from us was if she could use some of the money you left us. I think it was forty dollars. We thought it would be okay since she is your daughter. So, I gave it to her," Tyler confessed.

"Tyler, you didn't know. It's okay. If she asks for money again, your answer is no! Give her nothing! Does she know where the extra money is? Did she see where you got it from?" Robert questioned with concern.

"No, I don't think so. She was talking to Sean when I got it for her."

"Okay, just to be safe I am going to grab what is left and put it somewhere else. I will let you two know later where the new place is," Robert informed them.

"Okay," Tyler said, almost timidly.

"I'm sorry, Tyler. You too, Sean. I'm upset with Shelly, and I am taking it out on the both of you. I am really, very sorry. It won't happen again. I promise. Thanks for telling me. I needed to know. I wish Shelly were more like you guys," Robert said, gave them a hug, and turned to leave the room. Jeannette started to go with him, but he asked to have some time alone. Jeannette understood even though it hurt her not to be able to comfort him.

Jeannette hugged Sean and Tyler tightly and said, "Thank you for being such good sons. I look at you two, and I know I have done something right in my life. I love you both." She gave them each a kiss on their cheek before letting them go.

"We love you too. If we hear anything more about Shelly, we will let you know, Mom. This sucks. We were happy until she came along," Sean said.

"Shelly does not dictate if we are happy or not. Do not let her drag you down to her negativity and her issues! Just keep on being yourselves. Robert is going to see to it she leaves. It just might take a little while," Jeannette explained.

"Mom, I don't want my friends here if she's here! It was humiliating for Zach and me. The rest of the group overheard her, and it was an awkward silence. Shelly laughed and thought it was no big deal. But it was! None of us smoke pot! It wasn't long after that, my friends all left. But not before giving me that sorry look of pity," Tyler complained.

"I am sorry Shelly put you through that, but your friends are okay with you, aren't they?"

"Yea," Tyler said.

"See? They knew it had nothing to do with you. They are sorry she put you in such an awful predicament. As soon as she's gone, you can have them all over for a pizza and movie night."

"Okay, Mom," Tyler said, still not happy.

"This pot thing freaked out little brother," Sean said.

"Believe me. It has freaked us all out!" Jeannette said. "Just keep your eyes open, okay?" Sean shook his head and walked away.

That evening was more than awkwardly uncomfortable. Everyone didn't know what to say, which made for a tense, quiet evening. Robert would not go to bed until he knew Shelly was in bed for the night. It was the first night since the wedding Robert and Jeannette had not made love. They said goodnight and tried to sleep on either side of the bed. Shelly had succeeded in disrupting their happy dream home.

Things were tense while Shelly stayed with them. She managed to get a job at a restaurant after Robert vouched for her. He didn't want to, but it was the only way she was going to get a job.

"I vouched for you, Shelly. Don't make me sorry for doing that! My word and reputation in this community are on the line. Don't screw it up!" Robert threatened Shelly.

To help out, Jeannette started looking into low-income housing for Shelly. Shirley, the real estate agent who introduced their home to her, found an opening at a complex in town and was within walking distance of her job. She called Robert right away.

"Hi, honey. I called Shirley the other day and asked her to help me find a low-income apartment for Shelly. She found one within walking distance of the restaurant! She needs to fill out an application right away before they give it to someone else," Jeannette told Robert.

"That's great, sweetheart. I was hoping Shelly would do it on her own. She's too comfortable at our house to want to. Can you pick up the application? I will sit her down and make her fill it out!"

"I am on my way!" Jeannette told him.

She was in Robert's office with the application in hand, within twenty minutes of hanging up the phone. "You aren't anxious for Shelly to leave, are you?" Robert asked with a chuckle.

"I think we are all anxious. I want my Robert back. The one I married. He smiled, held my hand, and was always loving on me. He wasn't stressed like you are. I will do anything I can to get him back."

Robert rose and walked around his desk to Jeannette. He took her in his arms and held her.

"I'm sorry I have neglected you. I didn't mean to. You're right. I have been stressed with Shelly here. When are you going to Chicago?"

"That's another reason why I wanted to talk to you. I need to leave tomorrow. There are some new clients I need to meet and talk to about a contract. I knew I was going to have to go soon, but I was putting it off for as long as I could. I don't want to leave you here with Shelly to deal with alone. We work together," Jeannette said sadly.

"She's my daughter. I will deal with her. I don't have any problem with your boys. As a matter of fact, I enjoy having them around. We have guy time when you are gone."

"Oh! I see how it is! You enjoy me being in Chicago," Jeannette teased.

"No, honey! That's not what I meant!" Robert protested.

Jeannette laughed and said, "Sweetheart, I was kidding. I know you hate my having to spend time in Chicago. My company is there. If you want me with you all the time, we either move back to Chicago, or I sell the company. Neither one of those options works for me."

"I would never be so selfish as to ask you to sell the company you love or move back to Chicago. I love our home here, so I will live with you going back and forth. I will take any time you give me," Robert said.

"Maybe corporate will want you in Chicago for something, and then we can have a working second honeymoon. I know it is out of the question for now. But it is something to think about for the future," Jeannette encouraged. "What time does Shelly get off?"

"In ten minutes. I am going to take this application to Shelly personally and watch her fill it out. Then I am going to take her to turn it in. There is no putting it off!" Robert said, putting his jacket on.

"We still have some of my furniture in storage. We can give it to Shelly so she has no excuse of needing to have some before she can move in," Jeannette offered.

"Great idea! I love you. See you tonight," Robert said and hurried out the door to catch Shelly.

Jeannette made lasagna for dinner planning to have leftovers for her family to eat while she was in Chicago. Robert broke the silence at dinner and started the conversation.

"So, Shelly, tell everyone your news."

"What news?" she said, not looking happy.

"Your apartment news," Robert said without looking up from his plate. Sean and Tyler stopped eating and looked at Shelly.

"Oh, that news. Dad helped me find an apartment. They said I could move in immediately, but I don't think I can," Shelly said.

"What are you talking about? I told you we have furniture to give you! What's your excuse now?" Robert asked, almost throwing his fork on the plate.

"I don't have any way of getting around, no dishes, or any groceries. I think I better stay here until I can get those things."

"Oh, the hell you will! We will supply your dishes and groceries. There is nothing wrong with your legs. They will get you where you need to go. Sean and Tyler, will you help me move her in tomorrow after she gets off work and you guys get home from school? It won't take us long," Robert asked.

"Sure, we'll help," Sean said, and Tyler shook his head in agreement.

"It's settled. You are moving tomorrow! No excuses. Pack your things tonight after dinner. We will take them with us in the morning," Robert ordered.

"You sure know how to make a girl feel wanted, Dad," Shelly said with sass in her voice.

"Shelly! You have done this yourself! I want our home back, and you need to be in one of your own!" Robert threw his napkin down and shoved away from the table.

After the dishes were done, Jeannette found Robert sitting by the fire pit watching the flames as they danced in the cold night air. Without saying a word, she sat next to him and held his hand. No words were necessary. He understood she felt terrible for him and only wanted to comfort.

They sat for a while, and Robert said, "I apologize for the outburst at dinner. She frustrates the hell out of me! She tries to manipulate me, or anybody for that matter, to get what she wants. I won't fall for her crap! There was a time when I did fall for it. I will never again be in her web of manipulation. It pisses me off she still tries to do it to me! Why can't she be like Sean and Tyler?"

"Because Shelly is who she has made herself to be. She has chosen this path. No one chose it for her. You didn't, and I venture to guess her mother didn't expect her to turn out like this. The only one to blame is Shelly. It was her choice. She wants everything given to her. She sees how we live in this beautiful place, and she thinks since you are her father, she is entitled to live here as my boys do."

"I know everything you are saying is true, but she's my daughter, and I feel responsible. I wasn't around Shelly very much when she was growing up. Maybe if I had been, she would have turned out differently," Robert said, leaning forward with his elbows on his knees.

"You can't think like this! Shelly is a grown woman and is capable of making her own choices, no matter if they are good or bad. She knows the difference between good and bad. You cannot blame yourself for the actions of another adult. Maybe this will be the shove she needs to turn her life around. In my heart, I believe you are doing the right thing, honey," Jeannette said.

"I wish you weren't leaving in the morning. It will be the first time we won't be together since we got married. I always feel incomplete when you are not with me."

"I feel the same way, Robert. I will be home on Saturday. By then, Shelly will be in her apartment, and our home will be back to normal. Just remember to get the key from her," Jeannette said as a second thought.

"Humph. I will. Do you mind if I spend a little more time out here before bed?"

"You take all the time you need. I love you," Jeannette said and kissed him on the cheek.

The next morning, Sean took Jeannette to the airport so Robert could make sure Shelly was moved entirely out of their house.

"It's nice to spend a little time with my boy. Thank you for taking me this morning."

"It's nice to be out of there right now. I would never have thought Robert would have a daughter like her. I didn't see it at first. I don't want people to associate me as her brother," Sean said.

"If anyone asks, tell them she is your stepsister. At this point, I don't think anyone will pay attention to who she is related to. Most of the people who attended the wedding were from out of town. Don't worry. After Robert gets her moved, you will have a better outlook. You guys can have your guy time back," Jeannette said with a smile.

"I have to admit. We do have some good guy time. Too bad Dad couldn't have been like Robert. Here we are, Mom. You are off again. Love you," Sean said as Jeannette kissed him good-bye.

It only took Robert, Sean, and Tyler about two hours to get everything moved in for Shelly. Robert had taken his lunch hour to purchase kitchen items and some basic groceries. She was set.

"Maybe I should stay to take care of you boys until Jeannette gets back?" Shelly asked, still trying to manipulate Robert.

"No! We are fine. We get along just fine. You have unpacking to do. Boys, let's go," Robert said with authority. They left Shelly standing in the doorway of her new apartment not looking happy about how this was working out for her.

Jeannette called home after she spent several hours at *Windy City*. Robert and her boys sounded like their old selves, relaxed and happy, eating leftover lasagna. It was music to her ears. Things were back to normal, and she was in Chicago. It was good for Sean and Tyler to have some guy time with Robert. He would have made a wonderful father for them, growing up. Why couldn't she have found him instead of Jeff? She knew the answer, but she asked anyway. The answer: *"We were two different people then. We needed time to develop into who we are today."* She answered her own question. Regret was not an emotion she wanted to give any energy to, so she put it out of her mind.

The week went by quickly. Jeannette had a lot of work to catch up on at *Windy City* and spent long hours doing so. The new clients Greg brought in had a great sound and Jeannette was happy to offer each of them a contract. She signed them before she flew back to Oregon. Greg had done a good job while she was gone. She thought, *"Maybe at some point, I could have him manage the company for me. Then I would only have to spend one week each month in Chicago. But that's down the road for now."*

Robert was waiting for her at the airport. She ran into his arms. "The man I married is back!" Robert picked her up and spun her around.

"Yes, I am. How about you and I have dinner at the Blue Bucket tonight?" Robert asked.

"It's a date. What about the boys?" she asked.

"They have dates. So, it's just you and me, baby."

"That sounds wonderful."

It felt so good getting back to some normalcy. Robert and Jeannette were having dinner at their favorite restaurant and enjoying each other's company. After dinner, they went into the bar for a glass of wine. A disturbance of some kind drew their attention. It was Shelly. She was drunk and loud. The bartender was trying to calm her down. He cut her off from being served, and she was not happy about it.

Robert's face went from smiling and happy to embarrassment and fury. He looked at Jeannette and shook his head.

"I'm okay, Robert. Do what you have to. I will help," Jeannette promised.

Together they walked to the bar. Jeannette talked to the bartender about Shelly and paid her tab she had run up while

Robert took her by the arm and walked her outside despite Shelly's loud objections. Shelly succeeded in turning every head in the bar to her attention.

Outside, Robert jerked Shelly around to face him. "What the hell are you doing? Is that how a responsible adult acts? You promised me you were going to turn your life around! Instead, you have just humiliated me and made yourself into a rude joke!"

"Lighten up. I came in to have a drink. I can't drink at the restaurant I work at, so I came here. It's a nice place. You come here, so why can't I? I'm not drunk! I've only had a couple of beers. What's the big deal . . . Dad?" Shelly said, slurring her words almost beyond understanding.

Jeannette handed Robert the receipt from the bar tab she had just paid. One look at the total of sixty dollars and Robert blew up.

"A couple of beers?" he seethed through his teeth.

"Robert," Jeannette said, trying to get his attention. "Robert, let's get her in the car and take her to her apartment. We don't need to do this in the street."

"Get in the car, now!" He put her in the front seat so they both could keep an eye on her. "What the hell is wrong with you, Shelly? You drank sixty dollars' worth of alcohol! That's not a couple of beers! I am furious and ashamed of you!"

Robert continued to yell at Shelly until they reached her apartment. Again, he took her by the arm and escorted her inside. Jeannette followed close behind.

"We are staying until I know she has passed out for the night! Will you help her get ready for bed? I will help you get her into bed once you get pajamas on her."

Jeannette had never wrestled with a drunk before but was finally successful. "Okay, Robert! I need your help!" Jeannette said from the bedroom. "I'm going to have bruises tomorrow," she said under her breath.

"You took my daddy away from me. Now he doesn't like me! This is your fault! You goodie, goodie bimbo! You think you are better than me! Well, you're not! I don't know why he married you! You're no good! Your dad told me you're no good!" Shelly yelled in a drunken stupor.

"Shut up, Shelly!" Robert yelled, then lowered his voice to an evil whisper to say, "Shut up! You don't know her! I don't want you to know her! Now you are going to shut the hell up and go to sleep!" He pushed her back onto her pillow. He then took Jeannette by the hand and led her into the kitchen. "Honey, I am so sorry. She is drunk. She didn't know what she was saying."

Jeannette had a tear forming in her eyes when she said, "She is drunk, but Shelly knew exactly what she was saying. There's always some truth in what a drunk says. They have lost their inhibitions, and they say what they are thinking. You know that's true. What she said hurt. I know I shouldn't take it to heart considering who is saying it. But I can't help it. My father would say something like that. I have no doubt."

"I hate her for hurting you like this!" Robert said.

"Honey, I will get over it. I know you are furious with her, but she's still part of you. She will never make me stop loving you. Why don't you check on her and see if she's out for the count so we can go home?" He peeked in on her. She was sleeping.

"Let's go home," Robert said.

The ride home was silent. Neither knew what to say.

As they laid in bed, Robert turned to Jeannette and asked, "Are you sorry you married me?"

She, in turn, faced him and said, "I am not sorry for marrying the love of my life. You are my heart. Just because she is the way she is, does not make me regret marrying you for one second."

"I couldn't bear losing you." He pulled her close. She felt a teardrop on her cheek.

"Oh, sweetheart, please don't worry. I am here to stay. You can't get rid of me! Remember our vows? For better or worse? I take those seriously. It might be the worst part right now, but we will get through it, and back to the better part real soon. We are in this together!"

"I love you so much! I don't deserve you," Robert said with a slightly shaky voice.

"Stop it right now! We deserve each other! We are good for each other! Shelly will not come between us! Am I clear?" Jeannette asked sternly.

"Yes, ma'am, you are quite clear. Thank you. Tomorrow I am going to tell Shelly to move back to Texas. I don't want her here."

"I will stand beside you with whatever you want to do," she said and snuggled up to his side, under his arm, and against his chest. They slept without moving from each other's embrace.

After breakfast, Robert went to see Shelly. It took pounding on her door to wake her. When she came to the door, he could tell she had a horrible hangover, which made him smile a bit. He knew her head was pounding and the noise he had made amplified it one hundred times.

"So, you're up!" he said, trying to sound cheery. He knew it would piss Shelly off. "Got a headache? Good! You deserve it after last night!"

"Morning to you too, Dad. Come in," Shelly said in a whisper.

"I don't want you here anymore. You need to move back to Texas. I will not have you causing trouble between Jeannette and me. What will it take to get you to leave?"

"I'm not leaving. I like it here, and I have made some friends who like me. I'm going to stay," Shelly said, tipping her chin in the air.

"It doesn't matter to you that I don't want you here, does it? Do you remember what you said to Jeannette last night?" Robert asked.

"Um, something about her dad?" Shelly said, trying to remember.

"Yes! I take it you visited with her parents at the wedding. You hurt her. I will not stand by and let anyone hurt her! Do you understand?" Robert yelled.

"I met her ex-husband last night. We got cozy. He told me what a liar she is," Shelly told Robert.

Robert crossed the room so fast Shelly didn't have time to blink. "Say that one more time and you will be picking yourself up off the floor! He's the liar and a drunk! You don't know the real story! Why am I arguing with a drunk?" Robert questioned and stepped away from her.

"Really? How about it was her fault both of his businesses failed? She took money out of his till and broke him!" Shelly said and managed to raise her voice a little.

"Shelly, I'm warning you! She had nothing to do with his failures! If that were true, then why has her multi-million dollar business not failed? Why is it getting more successful every day? If I find out you are spreading these lies, so help me . . ."

"What? What are you going to do? Nothing, because I can charge you with assault. What would that do to your reputation? That's what I thought. Alright, I screwed up! It's not easy staying on a straight and narrow path. I will try harder. I promise. Tell Jeannette I'm sorry for what I said."

"I'm not telling her anything. I don't believe you, but I'm going to give you one more chance. Keep it together, or I will personally put you on a plane and escort you back to Texas! I mean it, Shelly! No drinking, no drugs, and no bad-mouthing my wife! Got it?"

"Got it, Dad," Shelly answered with a sarcastic attitude.

Robert left, slamming the door, knowing it would send pain through Shelly's head from the loud noise.

Over the next week or so, Shelly behaved herself. Things were quiet, and Robert and Jeannette had their happy home back. It was almost Christmas. Jeannette had decorated everything inside and out of their beautiful home. It was her favorite time of year. The Christmas tree stood eight feet tall. It was placed in front of a huge window facing the driveway at the front of the house. It was the first thing seen when arriving. It was a white tree, decorated with purple lights, gold-and-purple bows, butterflies, and birds. There were a few decorations different from her theme, but they were special ones to her. They were ornaments Sean and Tyler had made growing up. Those would always be hung on the tree. Robert was in awe when he saw the finished product. He told her it looked like something out of a magazine. She was giddy with pleasure.

When Jeannette was home, she liked to bake holiday goodies. Not just for her family, but for friends, Robert's office, their favorite waitresses, the mailman, and anyone she could think of who had treated them well throughout the year. Jeannette even took a plate of goodies to Shelly.

The last time Jeannette was in Chicago before Christmas, in her apartment, she assembled a small tree for a table, a few decorations were strategically placed around her apartment, and the evenings were spent baking and making candy. Trays of goodies were in each room at *Windy City* made by Jeannette. She made David a big basket filled with sweets, cheeses, crackers, and a nice bottle of wine, then attached a card with a one hundred dollar bill tucked inside.

She flew home three days before Christmas and finished the last of the gift shopping. Jeannette and Robert invited Mr. and Mrs. Baker, a few close friends, some business associates, and Shelly for a Christmas Eve feast. It was their first Christmas as husband and wife celebrating the holidays in their new home, so Jeannette wanted to make it a special event.

Robert and Jeannette sat in front of the fireplace, sipping a glass of wine the night before the feast. He asked, "So what's on the menu for dinner tomorrow night?"

"Before dinner, we are having hors-d'oeuvres made by the deli. I have too much to do to make those. Moving on to dinner: prime rib, turkey, dressing, mashed potatoes and gravy, sweet potatoes, green beans, fruit salad, a vegetable platter, and to finish it off, homemade rolls. For dessert, pumpkin pie and pecan pie. How does that sound?" Jeannette asked.

"I think I had better unbutton my pants right now. My middle grew just hearing the menu. It sounds wonderful. What time should our guests arrive?"

"Probably around 6:30 p.m. We will eat between seven and seven-thirty. By the way, have you heard from Shelly?"

"Not a word. Shelly has been quiet. Don't say anything. I don't want to break the spell," Robert said.

"Someone is going to have to pick her up. She doesn't have a car. Do you want me to have one of the boys pick her up?"

"No, I should. I will call Shelly tomorrow and tell her to be ready at 5:30 p.m.," Robert said, not sounding happy at the prospect. "Let's go to bed. It is going to be busy tomorrow, and I want some attention tonight," he said with a grin.

"You little devil you," Jeannette laughed. "Okay, big boy. I don't want you to feel neglected."

At 6:00 a.m. the oven was heating and the mixer humming with pumpkin pie batter. Robert woke up to the smell of coffee and pie.

"What wonderful aromas to wake up to," he said, coming up behind Jeannette and putting his arms around her waist.

"How about some breakfast? As soon as these pies are in the oven, I will make you some French toast and bacon. Does that sound good? Coffee is ready."

"I would rather nibble on your neck for an appetizer," he said, burying his face in her neck. It tickled and made her laugh and squirm. "Oh, baby, I like it when you squirm."

"You are a bad man! I am trying to make pies. Maybe later if I get a lot done. Have a cup of coffee for now." Robert groaned and poured himself a cup of coffee. "Why don't you sit here at the counter and talk to me while I cook? I like the company."

"Sure. I love looking at a beautiful woman in the morning. So how many will there be for dinner? Fifteen?"

"I think that was the count I had. Although Tyler asked if he could invite a couple of friends, and Sean is bringing Patty. So probably about twenty. That's the count I am planning for."

"Wow! That's a lot! I will help you."

"I was hoping you would. I have a twenty-pound bird I would like you to stuff," Jeannette said.

"You want me to do what? I have never done that before. It sounds gross," he said, curling up his lip.

Jeannette laughed and then said, "It's not that bad. I will talk you through it. One other thing. Would you pick up the order at the deli? They are closing early, so someone needs to be there by 1:30 p.m."

"How about we send Tyler? Sean might want to, and then he could pick up Patty early. I will ask them when they get up. I have to pick up Shelly and don't want to make two trips to town. I have to remember to call her in a few hours."

Once the boys got a whiff of French toast, they were up and sitting at the counter with fork and knife in hand ready to be served. The day had begun with happiness and laughter. God willing, it would end the same way.

"Merry Christmas, Shelly!" Jeannette shouted when Shelly walked through the front door. "Hang up your coat in the closet by the door. I could use some help if you are willing."

"I guess," Shelly said indifferently. "What time are your guests supposed to be here?"

"About 6:30 p.m. I think there will be about twenty of us."

"Make that twenty-one. I invited a friend. I told him how to get here and to be here around six. You have enough food, right?" Shelly informed Jeannette.

"Oh. I wasn't aware you were bringing someone. Robert? Did you know Shelly invited a friend for dinner?" Jeannette asked.

"No! Shelly, that's rude of you not to ask before you bring a guest!" Robert said with a raised voice.

"I know the boys have friends who are coming, so it was only fair I had a friend also," was Shelly's response with a shrug of her shoulders.

"First of all, the boys ASKED if they could bring a friend! Shelly, you and your friend, had better be on your best behavior this evening. I have some important people coming who are beneficial to my firm. You had better not embarrass me or this will be the last time you will be invited to anything in this house!" Robert threatened.

"Whatever, Dad. Hey, that bottle of wine is open, mind if I have a glass?" Shelly said and reached for the bottle.

"Um, not right now. It needs time to breathe. It's for our guests," Jeannette said nicely.

"I am a guest!" Robert shot Shelly a warning look. "Fine, I will wait until later," Shelly said. There was the sound of a car horn honking coming from the driveway. "There's my friend! I told him to honk when he got here."

"Hey, Bill!" Shelly shouted, standing in the open doorway. "You made it!"

"Shelly! Shut the door! If you are going to greet him, go on out and shut the door!" Robert thundered.

Jeannette could see Robert was getting irritated, so she bent over him as he sat on the couch and kissed the top of his head.

"Sweetheart, it's only one evening. Try and be patient with her." Robert looked up and nodded his head in agreement.

"Wow! What a fancy place! I didn't know we were going to rub elbows with the rich! You look good, Shelly," Bill said, walking to the door.

"You clean up pretty good yourself, Bill. Come in. Let me introduce you to my dad, Robert, his wife Jeannette, her sons, Sean and Tyler. I didn't catch your name, young lady."

"It is Patty. She is my girlfriend," Sean said.

"Oh, and that's Patty. Everyone, this is Bill," Shelly said.

Robert decided to be polite and shake his hand. He stood to offer his hand, but Shelly intercepted the gesture and took Bill's arm and said, "Come on, Bill, let's shoot some pool," and off they went without a handshake.

Robert shot a dirty look at Shelly and said under his breath, "And so it begins. I hate her."

The couple was anything but quiet playing pool. Bill could be heard saying, "Hey, got any beer? We can't shoot pool without beer." Shelly went to the refrigerator and took out two beers. Robert shot her a warning look, but she defiantly, kept on walking.

The next to arrive were three of Tyler's friends. "Robert, do you mind if we start a fire in the fire pit?" Tyler asked.

"That's fine. It's all ready to be lit," Robert said.

"How about some hot chocolate while you sit by the fire?" Jeannette asked. "You go on out and get the fire going, and I will bring the mugs of chocolate to you in a minute."

"Sounds good. Thanks, Mom," Tyler said. Sean and Patty went along with them. Shelly and her friend were irritating Sean with their obnoxious, loud voices.

"Honey, will you help me take the hot chocolate out to the kids?" Jeannette could see Robert was almost ready to yell at Shelly, so she tried to defuse his temper by enlisting his help. It worked.

After serving the hot chocolate, the doorbell rang. The guests had started to arrive. Jeannette took a deep breath and opened the door.

"Merry Christmas! Come in. I will take your coats. Robert will pour you a drink. Well, it seems everyone has arrived at the same time! Come in! Please make yourself at home. Robert is pouring drinks."

"Oh, Jeannette! Your tree is breathtaking! Did you decorate it?" Mrs. Baker asked.

"Thank you. Yes, I decorated it. Robert wasn't sure how it was going to look with purple decorations. That isn't a typical Christmas color, but after I finished, he liked it."

"Oh! You good for nothing, jerk!" Shelly shouted from the other room. "I can't believe you made that shot!" By now, Shelly and Bill had drunk about three beers each and were starting to feel pretty good.

Robert excused himself and quickly made his way to the room where the pool table was located.

He pulled Shelly aside and said, "What the hell are you doing? This is not a pool hall! You will not act like this in our home! Our guests have arrived, and you will not be shouting while they are here. Lay off the beer. If you can't act properly, you and Bill can leave!"

"Geez, Dad. We're just having fun. Lighten up. Have a glass of that fancy wine. It's a party, isn't it?" Shelly said.

"I'm warning you, Shelly and Bill! Keep your voices down!" Robert warned.

"He's a real buzzkill," Bill said to Shelly. Robert heard him but didn't bother to turn around.

"Sorry about that. The game got a little exciting in the other room. I hope you are all hungry. Jeannette has been cooking all day. She has made a feast fit for a king," Robert said proudly and made her blush. The party had begun.

Together, Robert and Jeannette made a perfect couple and a great host and hostess. It was time to serve dinner. Robert called the teenagers in, and Jeannette told Shelly and Bill it was time to eat. She noticed twelve empty beer bottles sitting around the room. Her stomach did a quick flip-flop. This wasn't good. She said a silent prayer on her way to the kitchen, *"Heavenly Father, please keep Shelly's tongue in check and give my husband patience in dealing with her. Let this dinner be peaceful and pleasant. Amen."*

The dinner table was set with china they received as a wedding gift. The crystal was Robert's grandmothers', and the silverware was a new purchase. The tablecloth was white lace over deep purple felt, and the centerpiece included pine boughs and four short fat candles. It looked beautiful.

Mrs. Baker commented, "Jeannette, you are amazing. So creative. The table is stunning. Where did you learn to do this?"

"I get a picture in my head what I want something to look like, and then I create it. No lessons required," she explained.

The turkey and prime rib sat on a smaller table next to the dining table where Robert could carve. Dinner was family style, so the side dishes were passed around while the carving was being done. The platters of meat were quite large, so Jeannette served each person from them. She was proud of her sons and their friends. They acted like they had done this all their lives. Their manners were wonderful. Shelly and Bill, on the other hand, couldn't hold a fork right and were somewhat sloppy with their food. But they were better than Jeannette had anticipated after all the beer they consumed. Then Bill opened his mouth that was full of food.

"There are some pretty nice cars in the driveway. You all must make pretty good money. How much money do you make? How do you make your money, and where can I get a job?" Bill spit out with a stupid grin on his face and chewing with his mouth open. All conversations stopped.

"Bill, our guests are not required to tell you what they do for a living, least of all tell you about their income," Robert said as politely as he could when what he wanted to do was grab him by the throat and throw him out! "These are our friends, and we don't care what they do for a living."

"Geez, I was only trying to make conversation. Got any more beer?" Bill asked and stuffed his mouth with more food.

"I'll get you one," Shelly said and got up from the table.

Jeannette excused herself and followed her to the refrigerator. "Shelly, I don't think that's a good idea. How about coffee?"

"Coffee? What kind of party is this? You drink alcohol at a party, not coffee," Shelly protested.

"I think you and Bill have had enough beer. How about iced tea? A coke?" Jeannette suggested.

"Hell no! We want a beer!" Shelly shouted and got Robert's attention.

Robert excused himself and went to the kitchen. Jeannette was trying to quiet down Shelly and give her more options for drinks.

"Beer. Can't you understand? Read my lips, beer," Shelly said and almost lost her balance.

"I warned you, Shelly! You and Bill are leaving right now! You are embarrassing us! Including all of the teenagers are embarrassed! Didn't your mother teach you anything?" Robert said through clenched teeth.

"At least let us finish our dinner. We'll have a glass of iced tea. How's that, Daddy?" Shelly said sarcastically.

"I will let you finish your dinner, and then you and Bill will excuse yourself and leave. You will not stay for dessert! Got it? Did I make myself clear? Tell me what you are going to do."

"Eat dinner, excuse ourselves, and leave. No dessert," Shelly repeated.

Jeannette said, "Robert, I will take care of the iced tea and help Shelly take it to Bill. Why don't you join our guests?"

He glared at Shelly and went back to the table and joined the conversation. Shelly and Jeannette came out with two glasses of iced tea and sat one in front of Bill.

"What's this?" Bill asked.

"It's iced tea. We are out of beer. My apologies, Bill. I failed to get enough. I promise to have more on hand next time," Jeannette said, hoping Shelly would keep her mouth shut.

"Well, okay. Iced tea isn't bad," Bill said and seemed content with the tea.

From the other end of the table, Robert sent a look to Jeannette that said: "thank you."

Dinner was almost over, and the men were groaning over how much they ate. Jeannette suggested, "Why don't we sit by the fireplace in the other room? We can have coffee in there. For dessert, there is a pumpkin or pecan pie, which I will serve later."

Shelly couldn't leave well enough alone. She announced, "Did you all know I am Robert's daughter? Yep. I am from Texas. I came for the wedding and stayed because I liked it here so much. But I embarrass Daddy. Jeannette, you are from Stokes Landing. Is that correct? She and I have daddy issues. Her dad hates her."

Jeannette's mouth dropped open, and her face turned pale. Robert pushed away from the table and said, "Ladies and gentlemen, would you care to go into the other room for coffee while I take care of this? Thank you."

Sean took the lead and showed the guests into the other room. When the last person had left the dining room, Robert's face turned to fury. He quickly went to Shelly and Bill.

"Get your coats and get the hell out! Bill, never come back to this house again! How dare you say such a thing about Jeannette? Shelly, you will never be allowed to have alcohol in this house again, and that's IF I let you come back! Get your asses out, now!" Jeannette handed them their coats. They left without a word.

"Damn her! I knew better than to have her here! I am so sorry, honey," Robert said and tried to put his arms around Jeannette.

"Robert, if you hug me, I will cry. I don't want to cry right now. We have guests. I will make coffee. Why don't you join everyone in the other room? We can talk later." She turned and walked away.

His heart ached for her. He wanted to comfort her and protect her from the world and Shelly. He was doing a piss-poor job of it so far.

Sean had done an excellent job of entertaining the adults while Robert was throwing out the "trash." He gave them some background information on the estate and treated them with a few card tricks he knew until Robert joined them.

"Coffee will be in shortly," Robert announced.

"Robert, your wife plays the guitar beautifully. Do you think she might play for us this evening?" Mr. Baker asked.

"Oh, I don't know. We will have to ask Jeannette. Here she is now. Honey, Mr. Baker, asked if you would play your guitar for them?" Robert asked.

"Well, I hadn't planned on it, but I don't see why not."

"Here's your guitar, Mom. I was hoping you would play," Sean said as he handed her the instrument.

She played a few Christmas songs and thought that would be it. She had a request for something she had written. She agreed to do one. It was the first one she sold to Clay. It fit her mood. When she had finished, there was not a sound. It was uncomfortable for her, so she immediately played an upbeat Christmas carol and had them all join in singing with her. Spirits were lifted.

"Is anyone ready for pie?" Jeannette asked. Several nodded their heads. "Teenagers, follow me," Jeannette said, and they disappeared into the kitchen. She had hot chocolate made for them and put a scoop of ice cream on their pie. "This is my way of thanking you for coming tonight."

Unexpectedly, each one hugged her and thanked her for a lovely evening. It brought Jeannette to tears. "Oh, you guys. Now, look. You have made me cry. How can I go out there like this?"

"We can take it out for you," Tyler said. They all picked up plates with pie on them and a tray to serve the awaiting guests. Jeannette followed a few minutes later with a carafe full of fresh coffee.

Not long after dessert, people started saying their good-byes and thanks. Jeannette handed their coats to them as they left.

"Merry Christmas, everyone! Drive carefully!"

She and Robert stood in the doorway arm-in-arm and waved goodbye. When the door was shut, and the house became quiet, he wrapped his arms around his wife. She broke into tears and sobbed into his shoulder.

"Honey, I . . ."

"Robert, there is nothing to say. You didn't hurt me, Shelly did. You are not responsible for what she says. I'm sorry for the tears. I've known all my life that he hated me. The feeling was mutual. But as I grow older, I get more tender-hearted, and it hurts to know he is still saying these things about me. It hurts. I try not to speak of him because it would only be negative. What good would it do anybody? None. She caught me off guard with her statement, and it hit home," Jeannette explained.

"If I could take it all back from her, I would. You handled it with grace. I have to hand it to you with the beer problem. What you said to Bill was perfect. It mellowed him out right away. It was awesome to watch you work," Robert said.

She chuckled a bit and then said, "When the kids and I were in the kitchen, each one hugged me and thanked me for this evening. I know it was because they felt bad for me for what Shelly said. They didn't come out and say it, but I knew. It made me cry. That's why they served the pie so I could pull myself together. They are good kids, all of them. I am so proud of the young men my boys have become. I did something right."

"You have done a lot of things right, sweetheart. You have accomplished so much in your short life. Try to keep that in mind?" Robert suggested.

"I try, but to do that, I have to remember the bad times and how it led me to be whom I am today. Sometimes that is not the best medicine. I am a work in progress, and I am so glad you love me anyway. I love you, Robert. Thank you for being by my side."

"Let's leave the cleanup for tomorrow. I know it will be Christmas, but I will help you. I'll bet the boys will help you too. We can open presents, have breakfast, and then clean up. Let's go to bed. You are exhausted." He led her to the bedroom.

No matter how tired she was from the day before, it was Christmas morning, and she was up early ready to open gifts. Her enthusiasm did not spread through the household. They slept. She made coffee and banged dishes hoping to wake them. When 10:00 a.m. rolled around, she had had it!

Knocking on Sean and Tyler's bedroom doors, she said, "Wake up! It's Christmas! Let's open presents! Get up!" She woke Robert differently. She bent and nibbled on his ear then whispered, "Wake up, sweet man. It's Christmas. I have coffee ready. Let's open presents! Wake up!"

He rolled over and opened one eye. "Already? We just went to bed. What time is it?" She showed him a clock. "Oh, ten, huh? A.m. or p.m.?"

"A.m. Silly man. Come on. Coffee is ready. I just woke up the boys."

He got up, slowly, and put his sweatpants and t-shirt on for comfort, then staggered into the kitchen, yawning. Sean and Tyler matched yawn for yawn.

"How do you do this, Mom? Work and cook like crazy and still want to get up at the crack of dawn to open presents? You're nuts," Sean said, rubbing his eyes.

She laughed at Sean. "My poor little tired guy." Sean was not little. He was six-foot-three-inches tall, and Jeannette had to reach up to pat him on the cheek. "You know I have always loved the holidays. I have an extra shot of energy when it comes to this season. Christmases, when I was young, were not always the best of times. I vowed my children would always have a good holiday."

"You have succeeded in making this one special, by waking me up," Sean said with a teasing unhappy look. "Okay, we're up. Let's do this."

"I have hot chocolate and coffee. Want a cup?" She asked all three. They showed great enthusiasm for the hot drinks.

Jeannette took on the part of Santa and handed out gifts. The boys got snow ski gear. Robert got a pinky ring with a black onyx stone in the middle and twenty-two small diamonds surrounding it. Jeannette received a diamond ring made up of three rows of diamonds. It was a Christmas to remember, their first together.

There was one gift left under the tree. Jeannette didn't want to leave Shelly out. She is family.

"You missed a gift, honey," Robert said and picked it up to read the tag. "Shelly? You're kidding! You got her a gift? Why on God's green earth did you do that?"

"I thought about it while I was shopping. Despite all of Shelly's shortcomings, she is family and your child. I didn't want to leave her out," Jeannette explained.

"Even though she has been horrible to you, you still bought her a gift?" Robert asked, astonished.

"In a nutshell, yes. I am going to drive into town this afternoon and give it to her."

"You are not going alone! I will go with you!" Robert said, sternly.

"Tyler and I will ride along with you too," Sean volunteered.

"What a wonderful support group! I love you all. Let's have some breakfast. It's more like brunch, you sleepy bunch!"

That afternoon Shelly opened her door to see Robert, Sean, Tyler, and Jeannette standing with a gift in Jeannette's hands labeled for Shelly. She was shocked.

"Uh, Merry Christmas. I didn't expect any of you to drop by."

"We had a gift for you and wanted to deliver it. Can we come in? We won't stay but a few minutes," Jeannette asked Shelly with a smile. "We also brought you some leftovers from dinner. I thought you might like some turkey for sandwiches."

"That was very, uh, thoughtful. Thank you. Come in. Let me move stuff off the couch so you can sit," Shelly said, scurrying around picking things up and throwing them in her bedroom. "There you go. Have a seat."

They sat, and Jeannette said, smiling, "Open your present. That's what we are here for."

She tore into it excitedly. This was her only gift. She would have had nothing if it weren't for Jeannette's big heart.

"Oh, it's a gorgeous sweater! I have never had something this soft! I love it!"

"There's a card too," Jeannette said.

Shelly opened it and found a one-hundred-dollar bill inside. Jeannette signed the card with 'love.' It brought her to tears.

Robert had not said one word. He only observed. If it had been up to him, she would have had nothing. He didn't like the idea of Jeannette giving her a gift, especially after last night's performance.

Jeannette stood and hugged Shelly.

Shelly said, "After the hurt and embarrassment I have caused you, you still gave me this gift? I don't know what to say. I expected nothing."

"It's the kind of gift that when received unexpectedly, means the most. You are family. I was not going to leave you out. It is given with love. If you want to give us a gift, stop the drinking and drugs. That would be the best gift of all," Jeannette told her.

"As of right now, I am turning my life around." She walked to the kitchen, took the beer out of the refrigerator, and handed it to Robert. "Take it, Dad. I don't want it."

Robert stood and looked Shelly in the eyes. He said, "This is a good gesture, but it's going to take more than this to convince me. You are going to have to prove it every day."

"I promise I will. I love you, Dad!" She hugged Robert, and tears fell down her cheek.

A noise came from the bedroom.

"Oh, Robert, we need to go. Shelly, you should have told us you had company. Merry Christmas. Enjoy your day," Jeannette said on their way out the door.

"Thank you. Merry Christmas to you too, Jeannette!"

On the drive home, they talked about how surprised they were at Shelly's reaction.

"This gesture might have finally gotten through to her," Robert said.

"I hope so. Shelly seems so lost. What happened to her growing up?"

"It's a long story. I will try to condense it as much as I can. Shelly's mother and I fought a lot in front of our three girls. I don't know why I married her in the first place. That's not true. I married her because she was pregnant with Pam. I was raised to do the right thing. My mother was totally against our marriage. She knew what kind of woman she was. But I did it anyway. I wasn't home very much. I was going to college and then law school and working nights to support my growing family. My wife was unhappy. We were poor and struggling, yet she did nothing to help. So we would argue. I would threaten to leave her, but she always managed to get pregnant. So I stayed. After law school, I was hired at a small law firm to get my feet wet as an intern. Normally the interns were there only for education and no pay. I received a small wage. I think because the attorney who hired me felt bad for me. Whatever the case, I was glad to get the wage, and I worked hard to prove myself an asset to the firm. After a year, I passed the Bar and I was hired as a full-time attorney. I started making pretty good money for the first time, but I still didn't want to be home with her. I spent as many hours at the office as possible. When I went home, all she did was nag and complain. We would end up fighting."

"About six months after I was working as a full time lawyer, I received a phone call telling me my wife had been finding comfort from a lot of other men. Bluntly, she was cheating on me. I went home that night, packed my bags, and left her and my girls. We divorced soon after. I stayed away. I didn't see much of the girls because their mother wouldn't let me be alone with them. I wasn't allowed to take them anywhere, either. She did it out of spite to hurt me. She was a horrible example of a mother."

"She got into smoking pot and drinking a lot. As the girls got older and started dating, when the young men came to pick them up, she blatantly flirted with them, which embarrassed the girls. Then came the buying of pot. She taught them how to get it and who was selling it. Then she taught them to smoke it. She always had alcohol around, so naturally, teenagers are going to sneak alcohol and try it. Shelly was the worst. She liked alcohol and pot, and how it made her feel, drunk or high, sometimes both, she liked it."

"Shelly became promiscuous and hung around with kids that all they did was smoke pot. She dropped out of high school and has never gotten a diploma or a GED. Her sisters did not take the same path. They could have, for the example they had but chose a better life. When the girls got older and were on their own, we spent time together and developed a relationship. We were not close, but it was a relationship. Shelly always blamed me for her unhappiness. It's her nature, like her mother, to blame others and bear no responsibility for what she does. Shelly is a lot like her mother and has a lot of her traits. Well, that is the long and short of it."

"That explains a lot. She is a narcissist." Jeannette said. Sean and Tyler did not say a word. "So Shelly tries to make you feel guilty for leaving her with her mother and everything she had to endure with her mother?" Robert nodded his head. "Honey, guilt can be a powerful emotion. You have to try not to let her make you feel guilty. It was a tough situation, and you had to make a choice. She had a choice also. You are not to blame for those decisions. Pam and Susan turned out pretty good. Shelly could have. Again, it was her choice, not yours or anybody else. After watching her reaction today, I believe there is still hope," Jeannette said.

"Time will tell. I would never have made the gesture you did. Thank you," Robert said.

The day after Christmas, Robert, Jeannette, Sean, and Tyler got on a plane for Chicago. They would celebrate 1997 in Chicago. Jeannette had year-end things to wrap up at *Windy City*, so it only made sense. Robert needed to go to corporate and wrap up a few year-end deals also. They stayed in Jeannette's new apartment. The boys had not seen it yet and were in awe of the view of Chicago from the living room.

On January 2, Robert, Sean, and Tyler flew back to Clark City. Jeannette stayed in Chicago to work. It had snowed in Oregon, so the boys were invited on a ski trip with their friends. They were excited to try out their new equipment.

Jeannette's company was busy, busy, and busy. It was getting an excellent reputation in the music world. Jeannette's name was getting more well-known all the time. She was known not only as a smart businesswoman but as a talented artist. Her employees loved her, and her clients thought very highly of her. She treated everyone with kindness and respect.

Corporate was very pleased with Robert's work. He had doubled the clientele over the last year. They rewarded him with a substantial raise. Best of all, Shelly had not caused any trouble. Everything was quiet with her. Life was good.

It was a shock we were so fortunate to be offered our beautiful home for such a fantastic price. It never occurred to me I would someday be a homeowner. The older couple who lived there had to have been very special. I can still feel their presence surrounding us. It is a comforting presence of love and protection. I know they were watching over us at our wedding. I could feel them.

Our wedding was so beautiful. It was a dream wedding of any bride. I got to live out my fairy-tale wedding and honeymoon.

Getting to know Robert's daughters was great. They were a big help at the wedding. I became a grandmother that day to the cutest and sweetest children ever. They even called me grandma. My heart swelled with happiness. It was a magical day in my life. However, I was oblivious to what Shelly's character really was. That day also marked the beginning of some terrible times that involved Shelly.

Our first Christmas was a rough one. When Shelly announced in front of all those people my father hated me, it was like being stabbed in the heart. I knew he did, but I had never heard it said out loud. What made it worse, my father told Shelly he had always hated me, and Shelly used it to hurt me. I believe she was taking shots at me because she was jealous of the attention Robert gave me and not her. That was not the only reason for her jealousy. Her father spent quality time with Sean and Tyler and the time should have been her quality time, not theirs.

Our time together would get more difficult because of Shelly. She let that green-eyed monster of jealousy get the better of her and take it out on, usually, me.

Now the remembering gets darker, but I need to push on to put all the pieces together that is my life.

8

Life went on with the daily and weekly routine. Robert and Shelly were actually getting along, and her drinking had almost stopped, as far as Robert and Jeannette knew. They had not heard any bad rumors or adverse reports concerning her.

Jeannette was still traveling back and forth to Chicago to run her business. David was still driving her around, and she felt more at home in her apartment.

The months were flying by, and it was almost graduation day for Tyler. He was not like Sean. He was nervous about going to college. He planned on going to the community college like Sean, but he had no direction for what it was he wanted to do. Unlike Sean, it weighed on Tyler's mind. He had always been sensitive and a worrier. Jeannette and Robert encouraged him not to worry. He would know just what was right for him when the time came. But for now, they wanted him to enjoy his teenage years and be a kid.

Sean had almost completed his first year of college and was looking forward to one more year until he would get his associate's degree. He was already thinking about where he would go after graduating. First, Sean would have to decide what he wanted to study, but it didn't worry him. He took life as it came.

Graduation day was here. Jeannette got teary-eyed anytime she thought about her baby graduating. They had come a long way since he was born. It was hard to believe how much had changed in their lives. Even though Jeannette and Robert could give them anything they wanted, they didn't. Sean and Tyler still had jobs.

She wanted to make sure they stayed grounded, remembered where they came from, and not to expect something for nothing. They had chores to do, such as clean the bathroom, take out the garbage, clean their rooms, keep the fire pit cleaned out, do their laundry, clear the dishes off the table after dinner, and do some of the yard work. The boys managed to do all these things and still got good grades. Both boys graduated with honors, which made Jeannette a proud mama and Robert a proud stepdad.

They had a graduation party at their home, but not just for Tyler. He and his friends wanted to combine their separate parties into one big one. Tyler had the most prominent place, so naturally, it was held at the estate.

The adults watched these best friends have a great time taking silly pictures, laughing, and teasing one another. There must have been over three hundred people who attended throughout the day. That evening at the high school there was an all-night party for the graduates. Thirty adults chaperoned the party. There was zero tolerance for alcohol or tobacco. There were activities and games throughout the night with prizes to be won. The awards were all about preparing for college. There was a microwave oven, bedsheets, things to decorate a dorm room with, gift cards, and numerous other prizes.

Tyler came home the next morning with an ice chest stuffed full of things he had won—including the ice chest. He slept most of the day but got up in the evening and told them all about the party and the silly things they did.

At the end of listening to Tyler's exploits from the night before, Robert had something he wanted to tell the family.

"I have been thinking about something for quite a while and thought I would run it by you boys. Your mother and I are so proud of you two for your grades and all your help. We wanted to do something special. We have come up with an idea you might like. How about we put in a pool in the backyard?"

Sean and Tyler jumped in the air and started dancing around the room. Tyler stopped dead in his tracks and asked, "This isn't a joke, is it?"

"No, Tyler. It is not a joke. We have been talking about it for a while and wanted to surprise you guys. We break ground next week," Robert announced.

"I have got to call the guys! A pool! Wow!" Tyler shouted. "We can have pool parties with girls in bikinis!" Tyler was wide awake after hearing the news about a pool.

"I think they approve of our decision, Jeannette. What do you think?"

She sat on Robert's lap with her arm around his neck. She kissed him on the cheek and said, "They approve, and so do I. I am going to have to shop for a sexy swimsuit."

"Don't make it too sexy. We might not get any swimming done," Robert replied.

The first scoop of dirt came out of the ground on Tuesday. Tyler and Sean spent a lot of time watching the pool take shape. Each evening Tyler would call Jeannette in Chicago and give her updates on how it was coming along.

On Saturday, Robert picked up Jeannette at the airport. "I have something for you," Robert said on the way home. "It's called a cell phone. It's a portable phone you can talk on no matter where you are and call anyone you want."

"I heard something about these things. Can I call any phone, like a home or the office? Or does it have to be to another cell phone?"

"You can call any phone. If you are shopping and I need to reach you right away, I can call your cell phone and get you. You need to carry it with you all the time. I think I will like this cute little phone. It might be a good idea to get the boys one too. Then we can reach them wherever they are all the time," Robert explained.

"Okay. Let's do that. How's the pool coming?" Jeannette asked.

"Moving right along. There's a possibility it might be completed at the end of next week."

"Oh, so you and the boys can christen it and have fun while I'm in Chicago? Not fair," Jeannette pouted.

"We will be thinking about you the whole time, honey," Robert said, smiling.

"I'll bet."

"On another subject, Shelly seems to be doing well. I had lunch with her this week. She is applying for a different job. She wants out of the restaurant. It's at a manufacturing plant at the edge of town. You know the one I'm talking about?" Jeannette nodded. "Well, she needs transportation to get her there. She asked me if she could borrow enough money for a car and she would pay us back. I don't think it is a good idea. I didn't give her an answer. I told her we would talk about it and we would make the decision together. Thoughts?" Robert asked.

"I'm on the fence about it. Do you think Shelly has changed? If we do this, it won't be a new car, but it also won't be a Junker either. Why don't we have her over for lunch tomorrow at our house? We can visit with her and see how different she acts. But she cannot bring Bill or any other friend. Just her. We need to make that clear," Jeannette sternly said.

"I think that's a good idea. I will call Shelly when we get home," Robert said.

"Let me call. I can use this handy little phone!" She dialed Shelly. "It's ringing, Robert! I can hear it ringing! Hi Shelly, this is Jeannette. You will never believe what I am using to call you on. I am using a little phone and calling from the car! Robert got me a cell phone. It's a portable phone! Well, the real reason I called, we would like to invite you to lunch at our house tomorrow at about one o'clock. Yes, one of us will pick you up. It is lunch with you. Not you and a friend. Do you understand? Good. Okay, we will see you tomorrow. Bye." She pushed a button to end the call. "Okay, honey, lunch tomorrow. I like this phone," Jeannette said, turning it over in her hands.

For lunch, Jeannette made homemade rolls for French dip sandwiches and tossed a salad together. It wasn't a fancy lunch at all, but tasty. Sean and Tyler were not excited about Shelly coming to their house, but they would mind their manners unless Shelly decided to be a loudmouth like she was at Christmas. If that happens, they were prepared to defend their mother.

Robert drove to town and retrieved Shelly. When she arrived, Jeannette noticed she looked pretty good. Her face had color, her hair looked styled, and she did not have alcohol on her breath. Three good signs. But it was too early to tell if she was doing better.

"Good to see you, Shelly. It's been a while. You look good. What have you been doing?"

"I have been working a lot of hours trying to get ahead. I haven't gone out much. If I do, it's to a movie or dinner. I rarely go to a bar. I did go to one last weekend, but I drank iced tea and got teased a lot. It was okay. I didn't mind. Did Dad tell you I have applied for another job?"

"Yes, he did. Tell me about it," Jeannette inquired.

"Well, it pays a lot better than what I am earning right now. I would have benefits, including health insurance. I would work four ten-hour shifts a week. I don't know what days or nights I will be working if they hire me."

"It sounds like a good job for you. You asked for a loan to buy a car to get you to and from work. What kind of car are you looking for?" Jeannette asked.

"Yes, I did. These sandwiches taste great," Shelly said. "Just a car that is good on gas, reliable, and not very expensive."

"Have you tried to get a loan from a bank?" Robert asked.

"No. I wouldn't qualify. I think I make enough money, but my credit isn't good. I had some problems with bills in Texas."

"I see. How much could you afford to pay each month?" Robert asked.

"About $150.00," Shelly said with a mouthful of food.

"I can see you have given this a lot of thought. What if you don't get the job? Can you still afford the same amount?" Jeannette asked.

"No. Probably $100.00."

"Do you have a budget you follow? Or have you made one?" Jeannette asked.

"No. I don't know-how. I guessed by what I spend I could squeeze that much out."

"Shelly, how in the world do you pay your bills when you don't know if you have enough money?" Robert asked. "I am sure if you ask Jeannette, she will help you make a budget. If we even consider loaning you the money for a car, you have to make a budget and stick to it."

"Jeannette, will you help me with a budget?" Shelly asked.

"I would be happy to help you. We can do it right after lunch if you have the time. This way, you will know what you can afford."

"Okay, I guess I can stay that long. It won't take long, right?" Shelly asked, wanting to get it done and over.

"It shouldn't. Remember, you have to be truthful about your expenses and income. If you are not, then a budget means nothing," Jeannette warned.

"Can we start now? I have eaten enough."

"Yes. Let's go into the office. I have some ledger paper in there," Jeannette suggested.

After forty-five minutes had passed, the two emerged from the office with a piece of ledger paper in Shelly's hand. She was not looking thrilled.

"How did it go, ladies?" Robert asked. Jeannette shook her head negatively.

Shelly said, "Well, I'm not sure. It was an eye-opener. I can't afford a car if I stay at the restaurant. If I get the job at the warehouse, I could afford a car, but I would make too much money to keep my low-income apartment. Now I'm perplexed. What do I do?" Shelly asked.

"Unfortunately, I can't give you an answer. You have to make that decision yourself. It is part of being an adult, making hard decisions. You are in your mid-thirties, Shelly. It's time to step up. Are you ready for me to take you home?" Robert asked.

"I guess. Hey, what are you doing in the backyard?" Shelly asked, noticing the yard was torn up.

"We are putting in a pool," Jeannette answered.

"Cool, I can use it to exercise and get a tan! When is it supposed to be done?" Shelly asked.

"Possibly at the end of the week," Robert told her and not looking happy she was inviting herself to swim. "Okay, let's take you home."

Later that day, Robert and Jeannette sat down to discuss Shelly and a car. "So how did her budget look?" Robert asked.

"Not good, and that's if she is truthful. I don't think she has any idea how much her bills are or how much she spends. I'm not sure if she's paying her bills. Honestly, I don't see how she can pay her bills with what she makes," Jeannette said. "If she gets the other job, she could probably afford a car, but she would have to move. I suggested Shelly get a roommate to split the rent. She would be financially better off if she did. Shelly wasn't receptive to such an idea. She doesn't want a roommate. My suggestion is let's see if she sticks to the budget we worked on and see if she gets the new job. We can decide then according to what she has done."

"I agree. I will have lunch with Shelly at the end of the week and see how it's going," Robert said.

"So, is Shelly going to be coming out here to swim?" Tyler asked.

"Probably. Occasionally. Please try to have some patience with her? Shelly has been doing a lot better lately. We need to show her some support," Jeannette said.

"Okay, but I'd rather she wasn't here when I have a pool party with my friends here. She will try to flirt with them. She's too old for them, and they don't like it," Tyler complained.

"Flirt with them? Since when?" Robert asked.

"Since always! Whenever she is around them. It started at the wedding."

"Why didn't you tell us?" Jeannette asked.

"How was I supposed to tell you and Robert his daughter was hitting on my friends at your wedding? No way was I going to spoil your day! It has gotten worse since then. I'm sorry for saying this, but it's gross, and my friends don't like it. If they know she will be here, they probably won't come to swim," Tyler said.

"I'll take care of this," Robert said sternly. "It will stop, I assure you. Don't let it worry you. If your friends ask if she will be here, tell them I have taken care of her, and she will leave them alone."

"Thanks, Robert. I feel guilty for telling on her. I couldn't take it anymore!" Tyler apologized.

"Son, I never want you to be afraid to tell me anything. You can be open with me, without fear. I promise. I will always listen to what you have to say," Robert reassured him. "Don't hold things in. I need to know whether it's bad or good. Okay?"

"Okay," Tyler said. He looked like the weight of the world was lifted off his shoulders. "Do we have any ice cream?"

"Yes. I picked some up this morning. Your favorite, chocolate swirl" Jeannette said.

Tyler left the room almost skipping and singing a made-up song: "Ice cream, ice cream, I love you my ice cream! I am screaming for my ice cream! You are so beautiful, my ice cream!"

Jeannette and Robert laughed at him as he danced around the kitchen with a bowl of ice cream in his hands.

Sean and Tyler were working more hours now that school was out, so it was always a surprise at how much work had been done on the pool when they got home. On Friday, it was very close to being done, but they ran into a snag with the gas line to the pump. The natural gas company was called but would not be able to fix it until Wednesday. After the problem was taken care of, they will finish the work by the following Friday, according to the construction foreman.

Tyler moaned as he told Jeannette over the phone. "Almost another week! It's so hot! I wish it were finished right now!"

"Patience, Tyler, patience. The pool has a lot of parts, and we want it done right. Besides, it means I will be home to christen it with you. So, it's good for me, but not so much for you," Jeannette said teasingly.

"Aw, Mom, that's not nice!"

"Maybe not, but I got a laugh out of it! Listen, I need to get back to work. I will talk to you tonight. I love you. Bye."

It was torture waiting for the last touches the pool had to have before it was complete. Alas, Friday evening the chemicals were put in and then the bad news. They couldn't swim until Saturday. The chlorine level was too high. It needed to dissipate overnight.

Robert told Jeannette the news, so she had Bridgett change her plane ticket to a red eye so she could be home in time for the first swim.

"Mom! You are home early!" Tyler said after waking to the smell of bacon cooking.

"Did you honestly think I was going to miss the first swim in the pool? Ha!" Jeannette said.

"Some of the guys are coming over this afternoon to swim. Robert said it was alright," Tyler announced.

"That's fine with me. It will be fun. We can cook some burgers on the grill, so you boys don't starve," Jeannette suggested.

"I already thought of that, honey. I picked up hamburger, buns, chips, and soda yesterday after I had lunch with Shelly," Robert said.

"Great minds think alike," Jeannette said and kissed Robert.

"You two are like one person," Tyler told them.

"That's a great compliment, son. Thank you," Robert said. To him, it meant he and Jeannette were in sync. They thought alike and anticipated what the other would do.

The day seemed to drag on. They waited for Sean to get off work at two o'clock before they got into the pool. They all needed to be there for the first swim. Sean hurried home, changed, and charged out the back door.

"Hold on, Sean!" Robert yelled. "We are going to do this all together. Grab hands, and on the count of three, everybody jump. One, two, three!" All four hit the water at the same time, creating a huge splash. One by one, their heads popped out of the water with a shout of joy.

Jeannette and Robert floated around holding hands while the boys tried making the biggest splash with a cannonball jump off the side. After an hour of fun in the water, Tyler's friends started arriving. Jeannette and Robert got out and let them have the pool. They sat in lawn chairs under an umbrella watching the fun.

"This was a great idea. The boys are having so much fun, and I loved floating around with you," Jeannette said, taking Robert's hand.

"I enjoyed it too, but your swimsuit is giving me other ideas. We could go inside. They would never miss us."

"Later, big boy. We have burgers to make," Jeannette reminded him. "How did lunch with Shelly go?"

"It was okay. I had a talk with Shelly about flirting with Tyler's friends. Of course, she denied it, at first. I told her to knock it off. I don't think she will be doing it anymore. It looks like we have one more car pulling up. Oh Lord, Shelly's here! Who brought her?" Robert asked.

"Hi, Dad," Shelly yelled across the yard and waving. She had a towel in her hand and some guy following her. "You said it was christening day, so here I am, and this is Austin. He drove me out here."

"Hello, Austin," Robert said, looking quite surprised since he didn't invite her or Austin.

"Let's get in the pool, Austin!" Shelly yelled and headed for the pool.

"Honey, did you invite her?" Jeannette turned and asked Robert.

"NO! I DID NOT! I wanted this day to be this family and a few of the boys' friends! Damn it! And what the hell is she wearing? She doesn't have the figure to wear a tiny bikini!"

"It is a little small. Well, we can't un-invite Shelly. Technically, Shelly is family. She's here, and she's brought a friend. He will keep her occupied, and she will stay away from the teenage boys. Let's see how it goes. Now, about those burgers," Jeannette said.

The smell of sizzling meat caught the attention of the swimmers.

"Hey! Are the burgers done?" Sean yelled.

"By the time you walk over here and grab a towel, they will be!" Robert shouted back. "Come on, everyone, step up and get a burger!"

The swimmers did not have to be told twice. The first ones in line were Shelly and Austin. Robert served them but did not look happy about it. Shelly avoided looking at Robert. She must have known he wasn't pleased with her.

Austin disappeared for a minute and came back with a six-pack of beer. He sat it between him and Shelly but not before cracking one open and handing it to Shelly. Robert heard it, and his head snapped around to see her take a pull from the bottle of beer. His face turned red with anger.

Jeannette saw the look on Robert's face. She put a hand on his arm and said, "Honey, it is okay. Let's give her a little space and see what happens. It will tell us how well she is or is not doing. Don't let it spoil our day."

Robert did not say a word. He went back to serving burgers all the while watching Shelly.

"Relax. She isn't causing any trouble with the teenagers," Jeannette told Robert after a few minutes. "Come on. Let's eat one of these yummy-looking masterpieces you cooked."

After her second beer, Shelly refused any more, and Robert let out a big breath of air. "Okay, you were right," Robert said to Jeannette. "But I am still going to keep an eye on her." She could see he was finally able to relax a bit. "Hey! Cannonball contest!" Robert shouted and ran for the pool with ten teenagers following him. "Jeannette! Who won?" he shouted.

"Zach had the biggest splash!" Jeannette yelled. "But your form was the best!"

"Look out! Here I come," Austin yelled. He hit the water right next to Robert, sending a wave that covered him completely. When Austin came up for air, he yelled, "Now that was a cannonball! How was it, Shelly?"

"You definitely won it hands down, baby! Whew!" Shelly shouted.

Jeannette sat by Shelly and said, "Shelly, why didn't you tell us you were coming and bringing a friend? How many times have we told you about this? You need to ask."

"When I talked to Dad yesterday, he said the pool was done, and he was going to christen it with the first swim on Saturday with a family swim. I'm family."

"You should have told us you were coming and bringing Austin," Jeannette said.

"I knew the boys would have their friends here, so why couldn't I have a friend? It's only fair," Shelly said and shrugged her shoulders. It was the same old argument.

"Well, that may be true. The difference is, they ask, and we know who and how many will be here. Next time, please let us know ahead of time you plan to be here with a friend. We have asked you before, several times. I would have been embarrassed if we didn't have enough burgers to serve your friend. By the way, I noticed you only had two beers and turned down the third. I'm proud of you. It is a big step in the right direction," Jeannette said.

"Thank you. I am trying. Have you and Dad talked any more about that loan?"

"We will discuss it tomorrow. I was in Chicago all week. Would you mind helping me take some of these dishes inside?" Jeannette asked.

"I would, but I don't want to leave Austin out here by himself. Here I come, baby!" Shelly shouted and left Jeannette, staring at her in disbelief.

She shook her head and gathered leftovers from the table. On her second trip to the kitchen, Robert helped her with a tray of items.

"You should have asked Shelly to help you," Robert commented.

"I did. Shelly wanted to get back to Austin. It's okay. Don't worry about it," Jeannette said, trying to make light of the situation.

"It is not right! She should offer to help! She's got a lot of lazy in her, and I don't like it!" Robert said.

"I know you don't. Shelly will have to learn we are not here to serve her. Shelly thinks she should be able to do everything the boys do. She knew they would have friends here, and she thought it was only fair for her to have one. You know that same old argument? It was only fair," Jeannette informed him.

"That's total crap! She doesn't do anything here! But she thinks she should have all the privileges. Nope. I won't have it!" Robert said, getting upset.

"She also asked me about the loan if we had discussed it. I told her we would tomorrow. The one good thing she showed us today, is she has cut way back on the beer. I told her I was proud of her, and it was a step in the right direction. I think it surprised her. I am going to make more of an effort to be friends with her, starting this week. I think she needs a friend."

"Are you sure about this? I don't want to see you get hurt again. I might have to kill her if she does," Robert threatened.

"I think those days are over. I will take Shelly to lunch and do a little shopping on her day off this week. We'll make it a girls' day. Maybe get a manicure. I'll talk to her before she leaves and ask if she is interested."

"You don't have to do this, Jeannette. I know she's my daughter, but she is trouble," Robert warned.

"Sweetheart, I know I don't have to. I want to. She needs some guidance. Maybe I can help."

"I love you," Robert said and kissed Jeannette.

Surprisingly enough, the rest of the day went well. In the evening they made a fire in the fire pit and roasted marshmallows. Shelly and Austin were the first to leave. Austin wanted more beer, and Jeannette informed him there wasn't any. That was all it took to send them on their way.

The next day Jeannette had promised Shelly, she and Robert would discuss the loan. So, the discussion began.

"I am reluctant to do this. I know she is doing better, but will she be responsible and pay us back?" Robert questioned.

"That is the sixty-four-thousand-dollar question. There is no way we can answer it unless we give her the loan. Why don't we bite the bullet and give her the benefit of the doubt?" Jeannette suggested.

"You think we should?" Jeannette shook her head yes and put her hand on his arm. "Alright, but I am not going to give her the cash and trust her to buy a car. I am going to help her pick one out and hand the money directly to the owner. I am going to hold the title until she pays us back."

"Sir, you drive a hard bargain, but I agree. I talked to her about having a girls' day. Shelly said she would like to, so Wednesday we are going to lunch and do a little shopping."

"Okay. Call me after you drop Shelly off. I want to know how it went. Right now, I am going to give her a call about the loan," Robert said.

Shelly agreed. Robert would start looking tomorrow at a few car lots to get an idea of what was available. He was going to make sure it was a decent car and not something that one of her friends wanted to sell her.

Wednesday's lunch at the Blue Bucket was pleasant. They talked and were getting along really well until Shelly waved at someone across the room. Jeannette turned to see who it was. Jeff. It took everything Jeannette had in her to control the urge to scream at Shelly. It was a slap in the face to Jeannette, that she had made friends with her ex-husband.

"How do you know Jeff?" she asked, trying to hold her voice level.

"Oh, I met him a while back when I was with my friends. I see him from time to time, and we visit. He's a nice guy," Shelly said.

Now Jeannette wanted to strangle her and Jeff. He kept his distance from the two, but he stared at them with an evil grin, like he had been successful with infiltrating enemy lines. She put her hands on her lap so Shelly could not see them shake. It wasn't fear like it used to be. It was anger. Shelly knew precisely what she was doing. Luckily, Robert called her on her cell phone. He asked them to meet him at a car lot. Jeannette was happy to end the lunch.

Robert had found a car he thought would be good for her. It was a small compact that got excellent gas mileage. It was light blue, no dents, ten years old with low mileage. The previous owner had taken outstanding care of it.

When the girls arrived at the car lot, Robert could tell something was bothering Jeannette, but she didn't want to talk about it right then.

"What do you think about this one, Shelly?"

"It's okay. Not very sporty, is it? It's on the small side. How much is it?" Shelly asked.

"The asking price is four thousand dollars," the salesman said. "Let's go for a ride, shall we? You can drive so you can get the feel of her."

"I will ride along with you," Robert said.

"Please, will you take her home after the test drive?" Jeannette asked.

"Of course, honey. Is everything alright?"

"We can talk about it later," she said and kissed him on the cheek.

The deal was struck, and Shelly had a car. Robert had drawn up a contract between him and Shelly and had her sign it. He kept his name on the title until Shelly paid off the contract. Maybe it wasn't her dream car, but it was transportation, and beggars can't be choosey.

"Your first payment to us is due on the fifteenth of next month. Here is a copy of our agreement, which tells you when the payment is due and how much, in case you forget," Robert explained.

"Boy, you want to make sure I am going to pay you back," Shelly said snidely. "I don't know why you are insisting I pay you back anyway. You're rich. You can afford to give me the car. Sean and Tyler have cars I bet you paid for," Shelly said with sarcasm.

Robert's face turned red immediately and he jumped to his feet.

"Not that it is any of your business, but THEY earned the money, THEY paid for their cars, and THEY have jobs that pay for gas, maintenance, and insurance. We DO NOT HAND THEM ANYTHING! Jeannette has taught them to work for what they want. You are NOTHING like them! You want everything handed to you, the easy way! It's high time you learned to be a responsible adult and EARN the money for what you want!" Robert snapped back inches from her face.

"All right, Dad. I got it. Here's your signed contract. Can I go now?" Shelly said with her hands on her hips.

"Yes. Go!" Robert said with impatience. "Wait a minute! What happened at lunch with you and Jeannette?" He demanded an answer.

"Nothing. We had a nice lunch. I saw a guy I knew and waved at him. That's all. No big deal," Shelly said with a cat-that-ate-the mouse grin.

"Does this guy have a name?" Robert asked.

"Jeff. I believe he is Jeannette's ex-husband," Shelly said, again with an evil smile.

"Really? How did you meet him?" Robert asked her.

"Remember? I told you a while back. I met him at a bar when I was with my friends a while ago."

"And you knew he was her ex?" Robert asked with amazement.

"Yes. What's the big deal? They aren't married anymore. He's a nice guy," Shelly said, not seeing anything wrong with her actions or attitude.

"You really don't get it do you?" Robert asked loudly. Shelly shook her head and shrugged her shoulders. Again, Robert was in her face shouting, "You have no idea what he did to her! Now you are all chummy with him. It is a betrayal of her and me!"

"Lighten up, Dad. We're friends. I can be friends with whoever I want. Besides, she was the one that caused his businesses to fail. She has lied to you," Shelly said as if she had the real truth about Jeannette.

"How dare you! If she caused his LITTLE and I do mean, LITTLE businesses, to fail then why is she so successful in owning and operating a multi-million-dollar business of her own? Don't be stupid! Think about it!" He rubbed his face in frustration and said, "I don't know why I am standing here arguing with you about this, again! I have argued this before with you! We're done, Shelly. Go! Get out of here!" Robert pointed to the door.

Robert sat at his desk in his office quietly for quite a while, trying to calm himself before going home to Jeannette. He decided to work for another hour to get his mind off his daughter. That didn't work at all. He needed to hold Jeannette and make sure she was okay.

When he arrived home, he found his love sitting by the pool, staring at the water. He sat next to her, took her hand, kissed it, and said, "A penny for your thoughts."

She chuckled and said, "My thoughts aren't worth a penny. You must have had a talk with Shelly about lunch."

"I did, yes. I yelled at Shelly. It seems like that's all I ever do. She is so jealous of you and the boys, and I don't know how to combat it. She told me I was rich and should give her the car like I did the boys. Before you say anything, I put her in her place. I am so sorry she has made friends with Jeff. I believe she did it on purpose. She's evil. I am ashamed to call her my daughter."

"Thank you for defending me. You shouldn't have to. I should have been the one to jump Shelly, but I couldn't in the restaurant. I know that is what Jeff was hoping for, to see me lose it. He stared at us with a cat-that-ate-the-mouse grin, and she had an evil little smile looking back at him. Shelly knew it was upsetting me, even though I held myself together. Having a friendship with Jeff is like a big slap in my face. I felt betrayed. Maybe that's wrong to want loyalty or support from my family and extended family. Lord knows I never had any support growing up. That's probably where all this emotion stems from." She paused to look at Robert and then said, "I was grateful for your call. It was perfect timing, and it gave us a reason to leave. I don't think I will have lunch with her again in the near future. I don't understand why she insists on hurting me. I have only been nice to her, and I will continue to do so out of respect for you."

He took her hand, brought it to his lips, and gave her hand a soft kiss. "If you can figure Shelly out, then please, explain her to me. She is filled with jealousy, and I know it. But the rest is just .

. . Well, evil. I don't know where she got it. I wish she would move back to Texas and leave us in peace! Things were so nice and peaceful before she arrived."

"In my heart, I think she thinks she is entitled to what you and I have, material-wise. Shelly is all about material things and money. She is going to do her best to get as much as she can. I would lay money on it," Jeannette said.

"I think you are right." He paused for a moment. "Honey, I am afraid she will come between us the longer she lives in Clark City."

Jeannette looked at Robert and said, "We have to be a united front. We have to fight her, not each other. We are strongest together. I will never stop loving you. You are my knight in shining armor who showed me what real love is. We will get through this, together and we will not let her come between us."

He kissed her, and they sat by the pool, silently, until the sun went down.

The next day, Shelly called Robert as if nothing had happened. She was happy and excited to tell him she got the job. She starts in two weeks. He kept the call short, congratulated her, and hung up. It amazed him how she could act as if nothing happened. How could she continually hurt others and live with herself? It was a mystery how she liked herself.

Shelly drove to the estate on the day her first payment was due and handed Robert the money. She was all smiles and pretty proud of herself.

"Thank you, Shelly. Keep it up," Robert said.

"Would you like to stay for dinner since you drove all the way out here? There is plenty," Jeannette asked with a smile.

"What are you having?" Shelly asked.

"Spaghetti and meatballs," Jeannette answered.

"Shelly," Robert said and shook his head yes.

"Sounds good. I'll stay. Thanks."

During dinner, Jeannette carried on a conversation with Shelly trying to make friends. It consisted mostly about her new job and what she did at the warehouse — nothing of substance. Jeannette was trying to show her she was willing to have a relationship if she wanted one. Time would tell if Shelly picked up on it.

9

Over the next several months, Shelly and Jeannette got along better, and she was invited to their home often. Usually, for Sunday dinner, when Jeannette was in town. Otherwise, it was random times. Nonetheless, they were all getting along more like a family. Things were looking up, Robert thought.

Shelly was now making too much money to live in low-income housing but wasn't making enough by herself to afford another apartment. She found a roommate, Carol, and moved into a two-bedroom apartment.

Carol met Shelly at a bar when one of their mutual friends was having a birthday party. Carol was not a good influence. Shelly had an addictive personality and could get addicted to anything at the drop of a hat. Carol liked pot and had a supply in their apartment at all times. Needless to say, Shelly was back to smoking pot, but that wasn't all. When Shelly was too tired to go to work, Carol gave her a pill that revved her up. If she had a headache, Carol gave Shelly a pain pill. Their logic was they were helping each other. That's what good friends do. Instead, she helped Shelly become addicted to drugs.

Robert and Jeannette didn't see Shelly as often as they were before Carol came into the picture. In a way, they were relieved but concerned.

"I haven't seen or talked to Shelly lately. Have you?" Robert asked.

"No, I haven't. Shelly has a new roommate now, so they must be getting along and spending time together. That's my guess. On a new subject, we could spend Christmas in Chicago this year. Then we would be in Clark City for New Year's Eve. What do you think? You don't have to answer right this minute. It was something I was thinking about," Jeannette suggested.

"I think it is a great idea! We can wrap up some loose ends before the end of the year at your company and corporate. Sounds good, honey," Robert agreed.

"Okay, it's a date. I will get Bridgett to make the plane reservations. We can tell the boys tonight. Do you think we should offer to let them bring one friend each with us? So, they won't be bored while we're working?"

"I'm okay with it if you are. But we are going to have to be specific that Sean and Tyler's friend would have to be male. I know how boys think," Robert said.

"Absolutely. Only male. We can talk about it over dinner tonight. How does meatloaf sound?"

"How does the Blue Bucket sound?" Robert asked.

"Sounds wonderful! Then I don't have to cook. I'll meet you there at about six o'clock. I will tell the boys. I love you. Bye, honey."

The four of them had a nice dinner at their favorite place. They made plans for Christmas in Chicago.

"Boys, you are going to have to see if your friends can make the trip right away. We need to make plane reservations. I assume you are going to ask Zach, Tyler, and Sean will invite Kevin. Am I right?" Jeannette asked.

"You know us too well, Mom," Sean said, and Jeannette giggled.

They heard a familiar laugh coming from the bar. Robert and Jeannette shared the same look on their faces. They knew it was Shelly. Their table happened to be situated at just the right place, if Robert leaned to the left a little, he could see into the bar. That's what he did. There was Shelly, Carol, and several people standing at the bar laughing and drinking. Shelly happened to see Robert looking in the bar.

"There's my dad! Come on, Carol, and meet my dad," Shelly said overly loud.

Robert winced. Jeannette took his hand under the table. "Hi, Shelly," Robert said without a smile. "Fancy seeing you here."

"My friends and I are having a little party," Shelly said.

"I can see that. What's the occasion?" Robert asked.

"A birthday. Our friend turned forty. By the way, this is Carol, my roommate, and this is my dad, Robert, his wife, Jeannette, and my stepbrothers, Sean, and Tyler."

"It's nice to meet you," Robert said while the other three nodded their heads and smiled. "Looks like you two are getting along quite nicely."

"Yes, we are. We are best friends, and we share everything," Shelly said.

"Oh, this is the woman Jeff said was such a waste to humanity! And you two are his sons? You don't look like your dad. Maybe that's true too?" Carol blurted out.

"And what truth would that be?" Robert asked snidely.

"He wasn't sure if they are his," Carol said without thinking.

"Carol! We weren't supposed to say anything, remember?" Shelly said, trying to hush Carol.

Sean jumped to his feet so fast Jeannette didn't see him move. "How dare he say that about my mother! My mother wasn't the cheater! HE WAS! He is nothing but a lying piece of crap!" Sean shouted.

"Sean! That's enough! Sit!" Jeannette said sternly. Sean did as he was told. His face was red with anger. Tyler looked more hurt than mad. Fortunately there were not very many people in the restaurant to see and hear the outburst.

"Shelly, take your friend and go the hell back to the bar. Now!" Robert said, holding down his rage.

"Sure. Sorry. Come on, Carol, let's go back to the party," Shelly said, putting her arm around Carol's shoulders and leading her back to the bar.

"Tell me Shelly is not going to Chicago with us for Christmas?" Sean asked.

"Absolutely NOT!" Robert said, without hesitation. "I have lost my appetite for dessert. Let's go."

On their way out of the restaurant, they could hear Shelly's laughter coming from the bar.

As they made their way out to the car, Sean said, "Robert, I'm sorry you have a daughter like Shelly. She is nothing like you. Shelly must be more like her mother. She should be more respectful of you. I want you to know, Tyler and I respect you and we love you. You are more of a father to us than Jeff ever was."

Tears welled up in Robert's eyes. He cleared his throat and said, "Thank you, son. It means a lot to me you feel that way about me. I am proud of you and Tyler. In my eyes, you two are my sons." Robert hugged them both. They all had tears. Jeannette was no exception.

"Shelly has got to stop being so horrible to my mother. I am not going to put up with it much longer. I know she is your daughter, but enough!" Sean stated.

"I know, son. If you can figure out a way to stop her, let me know. I am almost to the point of telling you to go ahead and give her a right-cross!" Robert said and got a chuckle out of Sean.

"Let's go home. Sean, will you and Tyler drive my car home? I want to ride with Robert. Thanks," Jeannette said and handed him the keys. "So now you know how the boys feel about you. There's no doubt you are a good father. Shelly . . . Well, she's a bad seed. She takes after her mother. I will keep trying to befriend her and guide her down a better path. I won't give up on her because I love you."

Robert was on the brink of tears and couldn't talk. His heart was full, and it was because of Jeannette's love. He wondered what he did to deserve the love of a good woman and two wonderful boys. He was the luckiest man in the world.

What Carol had said about Jeff doubting he was the father of the boys, upset Tyler. Was there a question of paternity weighing on his mind? Was he serious? Impossible. If he reasoned it out, there was no way his mother cheated. But that little voice in the back of his head questioned.

When Jeannette and Robert got home, Tyler had to ask, "Mom . . ."

"I know what you are going to ask. The answer is, without any doubt, Jeff is your father. I did not cheat on him. He kept me at home all the time and under his thumb. Even in public, I was not allowed to talk to men. He controlled me. Yes, he is your father.

He says these things to try and hurt me. He is jealous of my success. He thinks it should be him that is successful. That is the long and short of it," Jeannette explained.

"I'm sorry if this has upset you. I knew you wouldn't do anything like that, but Carol put the slightest doubt in my mind, and I needed to hear it from you. I didn't know some of the things you just told me about Jeff. He shouldn't have ever treated you like that. Thank you for being my mom. I love you. Goodnight," Tyler said and went to his room after he kissed Jeannette on the cheek.

"It seems my lovely daughter and her friend have succeeded in upsetting the entire family! I am so tired of this! We go out to our favorite restaurant for a nice meal, and she destroys the evening!" Robert said in frustration.

"This is what she wants, sweetheart. We can't let her do this to us. She is trying to destroy what we have. Every time we see her, we need to show her how happy we are. Show her we are a unit that will not be divided," Jeannette said.

"Kill her with kindness kind of thing? Honestly, I don't know if I can be nice to her anymore. She turns my stomach! That is a horrible thing to say about my child, but it's true," Robert confessed.

"Well, if anybody has the right to say it, it's you. Unfortunately, Shelly is who she is. She's rude, crude, and socially unacceptable. That's Shelly in a nutshell." Jeannette shook her head and said, "Let's get off this negative conversation and go sit by the fire and cuddle. I have a good bottle of wine we can open. We can turn this evening around to a better one."

They did just that and succeeded in turning the evening around. Before going to bed, Robert and Jeannette had laughed and talked about only positive things and managed to change their moods completely.

They stayed clear of Shelly for weeks. Now the holiday season had arrived. Strangely enough, Shelly started calling her dad, 'just to talk.' He saw right through her. He had told her they were going to Chicago for Christmas. She was trying to get an invitation for the trip. Neither Robert nor Jeannette made any such offer to her. The week before leaving Shelly poured it on thick by going out of her way to be kind. Shelly took Robert to lunch, and she paid. It was quite a shock to Robert. She finally called him, and bluntly asked him if she could go to Chicago with them. When he refused her, she blew up.

"You won't take me, but you will take her boys and their friends who aren't family! You won't take your own daughter! I should be in Chicago with my family on Christmas!" Shelly yelled into the phone.

"Shelly, I know you are upset. You have brought this on yourself. You can't keep your mouth shut, you befriended Jeff, you questioned the boys' paternity, you embarrass me, and you hurt Jeannette every time you see her. Is that how family treats family? You are not going to Chicago! That's final! I will see you when I get back. Good-bye." Robert hung up before Shelly could say another word. He felt terrible, but he knew he had to do it. She would have ruined the whole trip.

Christmas in Chicago was beautiful. Greg, Tom, and their wives, along with Bridgett and her husband, came to Jeannette's apartment for Christmas Eve dinner. It was a wonderful time. They talked Jeannette into playing her guitar that Greg happened to bring from the studio. They sang Christmas carols, drank eggnog, and feasted on a dinner fit for a king.

Jeannette looked around the room and said, "This is family. You are all my family. I love you. Merry Christmas!" Glasses clinked in agreement.

The day after Christmas they flew home to not-so-good news. Shelly had been busy.

The evening they left for Chicago, she spent time in the bar at the Blue Bucket and had a few too many. She caused a disturbance and was forced to leave, but not before she shouted at the top of her lungs, "My dad is Robert, the attorney! You know him! He is going to sue you for this!" That started the snowball of a downfall for her.

The second night she went back to the same bar. This time, she joined her friends there, and they had too much of a good time again. This time Jeff was included. Shelly got sloppy drunk and was telling anyone and everyone the lies Jeff had fed her about Jeannette. Shelly added, Jeannette was a gold digger. That was why she married her dad, and Jeannette was the cause of Robert shunning her out of the family. The bartender cut her off and forced her to leave, again. Jeff went with her. It was unclear if she slept with Jeff, but they were together for at least part of the night.

The third night was more of the same. This time, the bartender threatened no service if she didn't behave. She promised, so he reluctantly served her. After four beers, Shelly was feeling pretty good. She sat at a table with someone she knew and began hassling a woman she didn't know for no apparent reason. She was sitting next to Shelly. The woman kept her cool for as long as she could. The next thing out of Shelly's mouth met with a fist to her eye with a right punch. It knocked her out of her chair and onto the floor. She got up without a word and staggered out of the bar.

The fourth night was Christmas Eve. This time, Shelly and Carol started the evening off at their apartment, smoking a little pot and drinking shots of whiskey. By the time they reached the bar, they were already drunk. The bartender refused to serve them but allowed them to stay with their friends.

Shelly's argument with the bartender was, "It's Christmas Eve! My daddy left me here alone while he took his precious stepchildren on an expensive vacation! Doesn't that deserve a drink?"

The answer: "No." So her friends bought drinks and slipped them to Shelly and Carol. Shelly drank until she was on the verge of passing out. She turned to Carol and said, "Come on, Carol, we need to go home."

They left, got in Shelly's car, and began the drive home. A policeman saw her stagger getting into the car. He pulled out behind her and watched her for one block where she almost hit a parked car. He lit up his lights and pulled her over. The officer asked for her license, registration, and insurance card. The officer saw Robert's name on the registration. He knew Robert and thought the car might be stolen, but there was no report of it. Shelly explained she was Robert's daughter, which surprised the officer. He then did a field sobriety test on her, which she failed, miserably. He put her in cuffs, had the car towed and impounded, leaving Carol to find another way home. She was charged with a DUI and spent two nights in jail. Because of Christmas, she couldn't appear before a judge until the day after.

She appeared in front of Judge Hill. She was quite a sight to behold. Shelly had a black eye, her hair was dirty and frizzed straight up, and her clothes looked like she was homeless. Even though Judge Hill knew Robert, he had to do his job and charge her. Shelly lost her license, was ordered to attend driving classes that cost six-hundred dollars she had to pay for, plus fines, towing charges, and impound charges. All totaled it was going to cost her six-thousand dollars. Shelly still couldn't keep her mouth shut.

"When my daddy gets back from Chicago, he will get me out of this! You are running a kangaroo court here! I am going to sue you! You are going to be sorry for this, Judge."

Shelly then spit toward the judge, landing saliva on the judge's desk. She was immediately charged with Contempt, which carried a sentence of thirty days in jail.

Shelly is now known as an aggressive drunk to the police, the court, the bars, and all the patrons who observed her at the bar. What was worse, she was known as Robert's daughter. She had succeeded in humiliating the family, plus put Robert's law firm in a negative light for future prospective clients. Did she plan to do this? Maybe. She never admitted anything.

What a mess for Robert and Jeannette to come home to. Their spirits were high until they got a call from Mr. Baker giving Robert all the details of Shelly's activities.

"Thanks for calling and giving me a heads up. I will see you in the office tomorrow. Bye," Robert said to Mr. Baker.

"Shit!" Robert yelled at the top of his lungs. "Shelly strikes again!"

He told Jeannette the entire story. She didn't say a word and just let him talk.

"What a position she has put me in! I am going to have to call corporate tomorrow and tell them about Shelly. Any time one of the attorneys is associated with or related to a criminal, it is an issue with corporate, so I have to give them the details. I'm not sure what they are going to do. I never thought Shelly would go this far. She was pissed off at me and decided to punish me."

"Is she in jail now?" Jeannette asked.

"Yes. Judge Hill gave her thirty days for Contempt."

"What do you plan on doing?"

Robert thought for a minute then said, "I am not going to go see her until I can undo some of what she did. I need to talk to the arresting officer and Judge Hill. I am not looking to get the charges dropped, but I need to know for sure what was said and how she acted. She is going to sit in that jail cell for the thirty days the judge handed her. I am not going to pay her bail and get her out! Shelly did this all by herself, and she has to take responsibility for it!"

"I agree, honey. I will stand by you with whatever you decide to do. I need to ask, are you going to get the car out of impound? The longer it sits, the more it will cost. My suggestion is to get it and bring it here. Add on the cost to what she owes you already. By keeping the car here, she won't be tempted to drive with a suspended license. We can lock it up in the garage," Jeannette suggested.

"I am going to do just that. I need to relax. How about we start a fire in the fire pit and have a glass of wine while we watch the flames?"

"Sounds wonderful. If you start the fire, I will pour the wine and get a blanket for our lap," Jeannette said, and Robert headed to the backyard.

While pouring the wine, both Sean and Tyler approached Jeannette.

Sean began, "We heard the whole story, Mom. How could she do this? Why is she so mean to you and such a humiliation to Robert? She is an evil unhappy woman! We don't like her at all."

"Well, she's not nice, that's for sure. Why does she do these things? I wish I had a real answer for you. One day she hates me, the next she likes me. But that's usually a ploy because she wants something. Shelly was agitated because we didn't invite her to go to Chicago with us. Shelly thought she deserved to go because of being Robert's daughter. Can you imagine what our trip would have been like if she had gone with us? I don't want to think about it. The only thing I can think of doing at this point is not to say anything about this fiasco to anyone outside our family and keep our heads up. She did this all by herself. We are not to blame," Jeannette advised.

"Thank God we are going to college out of town. Maybe no one will associate us with her. We don't have the same last name, so that's in our favor. This whole mess is awful!" Tyler said as he turned toward his room.

"Hang in there, little brother. It won't be long until we are at another college far out of town. Then we won't have to deal with all her drama and problems she creates," Sean said to encourage Tyler. "Seriously, Mom. What are we going to do? It can't go on. Now that she's in jail, will she lose her job? She hasn't shown up at work for several days. If she didn't notify them, she'll probably get fired. Then what?" Sean asked.

"Sean, we can only take one day at a time. Let's not borrow any more trouble right now," Jeannette said.

The next morning Robert spent several hours on the phone talking to corporate about the events over the last week. It was a problem, just as he suspected. Robert was instructed to downplay this as much as possible and not talk to any reporters if one should contact him. He was put on probation for ninety days to see how this was going to affect business. If business dropped, he would have a real problem to deal with.

Jeannette and Robert spent a quiet New Year's Eve at home in front of the fireplace. They thought it was the best way to keep a low profile. At the stroke of midnight, they clinked glasses, finished their wine, and went to bed.

On January 3 Robert decided, now that he had all the facts, to visit Shelly in the county lockup. Her eye was still black and green, but healing. She looked tired and especially not happy when Robert came through the visitation door.

"Hello, Daddy," Shelly said snidely. "Nice to see you made it home from your vacation while I am rotting away in here with all the criminals."

"Shelly, these are now your people. You are no better than they are because you are now a criminal! Shut up! Don't say a word! Not a word until I'm finished! First of all, you are a liar! You haven't cut back on alcohol! I have found out that you have been smoking pot and taking pills along with the booze. You have been driving high and drunk for quite a while. You finally got caught while you were driving a car registered in my name. I did some background on you. I discovered you have a record in Texas! You were arrested for possession of marijuana and for shoplifting! What else am I going to find out, Shelly?" Robert asked, just as snidely as she had. "If I dig deeper, what am I going to find?"

"Those charges in Texas were nothing." She waved her hand in the air like it was nothing. "I took some cigarettes, and I had a small amount of pot. It was no big deal. I didn't serve any time. They slapped me with fines. That's all. Big whoop."

"It is a big whoop, Shelly! You didn't pay those fines in Texas! There is a warrant out for your arrest if you go back! That's why you stayed in Oregon, isn't it? You were trying to run from your mistakes and stupidity! The running stops now! You are going to face those charges in Texas, and you are going to serve your time here, pay your fines, and take your classes. I am not going to get you out of this! I will have Mr. Baker represent you. Corporate, my bosses, want me to distance myself from this whole fiasco you caused! You have not only created a mess for yourself, but you have put my job in jeopardy! That's right! Corporate doesn't like it when their attorney's children decide to become criminals and spout off lies that put their integrity in question! You have no idea what the truth really is! You believe every word any nut job tells you! Not only do you believe others' lies, but you also tell some whoppers yourself!"

Shelly hung her head. Her father finally knew all about her, and he was ashamed of her. "Well, you aren't going to like what I have to tell you next either. I got fired because I am in jail and haven't shown up for work. Carol came by to visit and told me. Now I am unemployed. I don't know how I am going to pay for everything!"

"You can look at me with those sad eyes all you want, but I am not bailing you out or paying your fines! You created this. You are going to have to figure out a way to fix it!"

"But, Dad, how am I going to do that?"

"That's not my problem! It's yours! I'm done. You have a few more weeks left until you get out of jail. I suggest you think long and hard about what you are going to do," Robert said sternly and left the room with her sitting alone with a look of shock on her face.

Jeannette met Robert for lunch in another restaurant other than the Blue Bucket trying to keep a low profile. There he told her all about what he had found out about Shelly and their conversation at the County Jail. She was shocked but at the same time, not so much.

"We knew there was a reason why she stayed in Oregon, now we know," Jeannette said.

"To top it off, she lost her job, but we knew that was going to happen. I don't know if Carol is going to be able to afford the apartment. If she can't, then Shelly will be homeless," Robert said, rubbing his face.

"So, what are you thinking?" Jeannette asked cautiously.

"I have come up with three scenarios. The first, let Shelly be homeless and corporate will probably fire me for horrible press and a black eye for the firm. The second, get her an apartment and pay for it and all her expenses myself. That would lead to her never getting a job and having her hand out all the time holding corporate over my head for leverage. The third, I don't want to suggest. It's my least favorite. She can stay with us until she can find work and start paying all her fines. None of them are favorable for us. I hate this! You married into bad blood. I am so sorry to do this to you."

"Honey, I married you, not bad blood. I keep telling you Shelly is the bad seed. I think the only option is the third, unfortunately. We can keep a close eye on her and make sure she looks for a job and attends her classes. All alcohol will have to be locked up along with anything of value, such as my jewelry. I will be frank with you. I don't like this one bit! We are going to be uncomfortable in our own home as long as she is there. I don't know what we will do during the weeks I am in Chicago. Maybe hire a housekeeper who would be there all day?" Jeannette suggested. "I have to say it. I do not like Shelly. I have tried being nice, attempted friendship with her and everything in my power for peace. Nothing worked. I don't like her! I'm sorry for being so blunt about Shelly. We don't keep secrets, and I wanted you to know how I felt."

"I don't blame you at all. I don't like Shelly either. I am ashamed that we share the same last name," Robert confessed.

"If you don't mind, I am going to cut our lunch short. I have got to find a lockable liquor cabinet to store the alcohol and prepare for the criminal's arrival. I know I have some time, but this might help me work through some of my anger toward her. I love you, honey. See you at home."

Robert sat a little longer and pushed his food around his plate. He hated this feeling of knowing Jeannette was upset, and he felt that he caused it. Knowing there was nothing he could do about it only made it worse. Robert had run out of options with Shelly. Hopefully, jail would be a jolt of reality for her, along with all the fines she has racked up.

The day of Shelly's release, unfortunately, came quickly. Too fast for the family. They had been dreading the day when Shelly would walk through their front door to stay, for God knows how long. It was what she wanted all along: to live on this beautiful estate for free and be entitled to everything.

Sean and Tyler talked about sharing an apartment, so they wouldn't have to be around her. The cost was too high for two college kids to afford. They were all stuck with her.

"Hello, family! I'm home!" Shelly yelled as she walked in. "What? No greeting or ticker-tape parade?"

"Sorry, the store was out of confetti," Jeannette said drily. "You can put your things in the blue bedroom. It doesn't have a bathroom, but there's one down the hall. I am going to start dinner in thirty minutes. You can help. I assume Robert discussed what is expected of you while you are here?"

"Yes. I have to help around the house, do my laundry, help with the meals, and keep my room clean along with any other thing you ask of me. In other words, I am your servant," Shelly said and bowed.

"Knock it off! Don't be such a smartass!" Robert yelled. "I am going to give you one day, one day only, to get yourself together. The next day, you will come to work with me, and you will start the job search. Any money I have to pay for your classes or your personal needs, you will repay me. Are we clear? It isn't a free ride," Robert sternly informed Shelly in no uncertain terms.

"I know. You have told me how many times now? I got it! Geez, lighten up! I'll be good. The blue bedroom?" Shelly asked.

"Yes. The second door on the right. Clean sheets are sitting on your bed. I didn't make it. I left it for you to do," Jeannette said with no emotions.

"Yes, ma'am. I will obey," Shelly said.

"Oh, this is going to be fun. I am already stressed, Robert. I'm sorry I feel this way, but I can't help it," Jeannette said and blew out a puff of air.

Robert held her in his arms and stroked her back, trying to lessen the tension in her muscles.

"Keep your eyes looking forward, to the day she leaves. It won't last forever. I've been looking around for a job that she could do. I have one or two possibilities. The sooner she starts work, the sooner she moves out. I promise I am working on it."

She leaned back to look at him and said, "I know you are, sweetheart. I will deal with this the best I can. I'm just not happy about it. By the way, I have hired a housekeeper who will be here Monday through Friday, all day, every other week while I'm in Chicago. She will also make dinner for everyone each evening, but you guys are responsible for cleanup. If you decide to eat out, give her a heads up. She is coming by on Saturday to meet you, the boys, and Shelly. I told her a little bit about Shelly. Mainly, I don't trust her with alcohol."

"Thank you for handling all this. It will be over before we know it," Robert said, trying to encourage Jeannette.

"I hope so. I choose to try and look at it with a positive spin. I will only have to be around Shelly for two weeks a month. I get a break from her every other week," Jeannette said and pulled away.

Shelly helped with dinner. She acted as if she had never cooked before. Jeannette suspected it was because she didn't want to help, so she played dumb. That wasn't going to fly.

"Shelly, you know how to cook. For god's sake, you were a cook at a restaurant! You know how to chop vegetables!" Shelly shot her a glare. It was apparent to Jeannette she had pulled this dumb act a million times before and was very good at getting out of work. Not here. Not with Jeannette.

"Okay, Jeannette, don't be so grumpy. I just got out of jail. Give me a break. Where's the cutting board?"

"It's right there in front of you. There's a knife right by it I sat out for you to use. Shelly, you know where things are. Nothing has moved since the last time you stayed with us," Jeannette told her, not letting her get away with laziness.

There was silence during the preparation of the food. Dinner was tense. Conversations were attempted but ended quickly without participation. Sean and Tyler cleared the table as usual while Jeannette and Robert enjoyed a cup of coffee.

"Shelly, you can help the boys with the dishes," Jeannette said.

"Yes, ma'am. I will do my assigned chore," Shelly said as if she were a servant who had just gotten her orders.

Jeannette let out a sigh of frustration. "Robert, put her on a plane to Texas, NOW."

Robert shot a glare at Shelly and said, "When are you going to stop this? Why can't you be grateful for what we are doing for you? We are trying to help you! If you are going to stay here, you will be given chores, just like everyone else does. By the way, next week while Jeannette is in Chicago, we have a new housekeeper who will be here Monday through Friday. If she asks for help, I expect you to help her if you are home."

"Oh, I get it. You have hired a babysitter for me. You can't trust me to be left alone. This place is beginning to feel like jail," Shelly said.

"She's not a babysitter, but you can't blame us if we don't trust you! So far, you have not given us any reason to trust you. Not one reason. She is stopping by on Saturday to meet us," Robert told Shelly.

"Yes, Dad, whatever you want." Shelly went to the kitchen with the last of the dishes to help Sean and Tyler. Again, she played her dumb routine, but it didn't work with them either. Shelly was batting a thousand and realizing she was not going to get away with anything. "Yep, just like jail," she muttered.

Shelly went to work with Robert as promised, and he sent her out to find a job. Jeannette packed her lunch, so she ate it in the break room of the firm's office. After lunch, Robert put her to work shredding papers, copying files, and filing. She was not allowed to sit around and do nothing.

"I have made an appointment for an interview for a waitress job tomorrow at 9:00 a.m.," Robert told Shelly on the way home.

"A waitress? I don't want to waitress! Why don't you give me a job at your office doing what I did today?" Shelly protested.

"Because you need to start making some income immediately! Your first court-ordered class for your DUI is next week. Each time you go to one of these classes, it costs fifty dollars. You are paying for it, not me. This is your bill that you created, not me. You can use your tip money to pay for it."

"You have my life all figured out, don't you?" Shelly said while Robert was silent. Shelly went on to say, "Fine. I will go to the interview, and I will get a waitressing job. Whatever you want, Daddy," she said sassily.

"Stop with the attitude!" Robert said, loudly.

"So when do I get my license back?" she asked.

"After you have finished and passed your classes. Six months," Robert informed her. She sat quietly and watched the scenery. "Shelly, the sooner you drop the attitude and accept that we are trying to help you, the sooner things will change. It won't seem like, in your opinion, jail. It is the only way we know how to handle the situation you have put us all in. Yes, I said all. What you did affects a lot more people than just you!"

"Whatever."

"Okay, if you don't like it here, I will put you on a plane to Texas tomorrow! Is that what you want?" Robert raised his voice.

"No! I will be arrested!" Shelly raised her voice in return.

"That's right! I would make the call myself to the police and let them know what plane you are arriving on! If you are going to stay in Oregon, you are going to have to live with the choices you have made and change the attitude!"

The two walked into the house, and by the look on their faces, Jeannette knew it wasn't a good day. Shelly slammed the bedroom door, and Robert started toward the slam. Jeannette took his arm and stopped him.

"Leave her alone for now. If you start yelling at her, things will just escalate. Talk to me and tell me about your day. I have poured us a glass of wine while the stew finishes cooking," Jeannette said gently.

He blew out a breath of air and said, "That sounds like just what I need."

He told her about his day and what he had Shelly doing at the office. His face lightened a little when he told her about Shelly's interview tomorrow. It was a ray of hope for both of them.

Shelly got the job and started immediately. They put an apron on her and put her to work. When she didn't come back to the office, Robert thought it was a good sign, but had to make sure she wasn't just taking her time getting back. He called the restaurant to talk to the owner and was elated when he was told she was working at the moment. The next call was to Jeannette to tell her the good news. She sounded relieved.

Jeannette helped Shelly with budgeting her tip money and paycheck so she could pay for her classes as well as make payments to Texas and Oregon for fines that she was ordered to pay. They were witnessing a change in Shelly's attitude. She was becoming a kinder, more helpful person and taking Jeannette's advice. The tension was starting to ease in their household.

Six months went by, and Shelly got her license back, and her fines were about halfway paid. Things were looking up, so they thought. Jeannette was in Chicago when the housekeeper called her. She told her that she stripped Shelly's bed to wash her bedding. A small plastic bag fell out of a pillowcase. She was pretty sure it was marijuana. Jeannette told her to hold on to it and not say anything to Shelly about it.

"Give the bag to Robert when he gets home. I will let him know about this, and he will take care of it," Jeannette told her.

"Things were going so well!" Robert exclaimed. "Okay, honey, I will take care of it this evening." He asked the boys to eat in town so he could talk to Shelly so it would be just the two of them.

"Hi, Dad. Is it just you and me tonight?" Shelly asked when she arrived home.

"Come over here and sit down. I want to talk to you," Robert said. When she had sat next to him, he asked, "What can you tell me about this?" He held up the bag for Shelly to see.

"It's not mine!" she protested.

Robert hung his head and sighed. "Shelly, I thought the lying was over. It's yours." He held up a hand before she said anything, then continued, "Don't tell me it's not yours. The housekeeper was changing your bed sheets, and it fell out of a pillowcase. Now, do you want to try again? What can you tell me about this?"

"Okay, you're right. It's mine. I have been under a lot of stress with working and paying these fines that I needed something to help me relax. I'm sorry, Dad. I let you down, again," Shelly said and hung her head.

"To be honest, yes, you did. I thought you were past this. Stress is a part of life. Everyone has stress daily, and we deal with it without the aid of pot. Do you realize that if they drug-tested you right now, they would fire you? So why are you taking such a big chance?"

"I guess I backslid into some of my old ways. Give me another chance. It was just this one time, and it will never happen again, I promise," Shelly said, pleading.

"This might not be one of my better decisions, but, fine. One more chance. Please don't let me down again? There will be no more chances," Robert told her in a quiet tone.

"Thanks, Dad. I won't. How about I fix us grilled cheese sandwiches and tomato soup?" He shook his head, yes and Shelly went into the kitchen.

Robert started thinking while waiting for his sandwich, "Now I have to tell Jeannette that I was soft on Shelly. I don't think she is going to be pleased with my decision. Well, no use putting it off." He picked up the phone and dialed. Jeannette answered right away. He told her about their talk and his decision.

"If she hadn't been doing so well, I would not have given it a second thought. She would have been out the door. If she screws up again, that's it. Do you think I made the wrong call?" Robert asked.

"I think it was the right one. You have shown Shelly that we have a little trust in her, and I think she needs that to keep her moving forward. I'm not upset with you. I would have done the same thing. She and I are getting along really well. I am hoping she is taking at least some of my advice. The budgeting is working, as long as she's telling me the truth. I'm okay she is staying," Jeannette said.

Depression was Robert's normal state these days. Jeannette could hear it in his voice.

"I will pick you up on Saturday. I love you." He hung up just in time to see Shelly with a tray walking in his direction. "Looks good. You remembered I like a slice of tomato in the middle."

"Of course, I did," Shelly said with a smile.

10

Another two months went by, and Shelly was still doing surprisingly well. Her tips were increasing, which gave her a little spending money. Jeannette decided to do something nice for her on her day off.

"Shelly, how about I take you shopping on your next day off? We can go to the new mall in Carson City?"

"Really? You want to take me shopping?" She said, looking shocked.

"I do. When is your next day off?"

"Tomorrow."

"Okay. The stores will open about 10:00 a.m., so let's leave about nine. How does that sound?" Jeannette asked.

"I was going to sleep in, but I'll give that up for shopping any day!" Shelly said with excitement.

Jeannette grinned and said, "I think on our list should be new underwear and bras, but don't worry, it won't be the only things. I have noticed you could use some new clothes. Then we can have lunch at Piers. It's a nice restaurant in Carson City. Have you ever had crème Brulé?"

"Nope. I've never heard of it. What is it?" Shelly asked.

"It's a wonderful dessert. Wait until you taste it. Well, I guess it's about time to start dinner. Will you make the salad? I think I will grill some steaks."

Shopping was fun. Jeannette never expected to end up being friends or having fun with Shelly. It was a delightful surprise. They went into every store in the mall to see if anything interested them. Shelly ended up with two bras, several pairs of underwear, three blouses, three pairs of pants, and two pairs of shoes. One pair was for work. They were starving by the time they got to Piers. After being seated and looking at a menu, Jeannette noticed the time.

"It's 1:30! No wonder we are starving. Time flies when you shop."

They each ordered soup and salad with crème Brulé for dessert. By the time the ladies reached home, they were laughing and teasing one another. When Robert got home, they were still in a good mood and cooking dinner. He could hardly believe his eyes.

"Well, it looks like you two had fun," he said, walking in the door with a grin on his face and looking pleased. "Did you buy out the stores?"

Jeannette giggled and said, "No, but we put a dent in them. Most of what we bought were necessities, but some were just because we wanted them. We had a nice time. We had lunch at Piers."

"Oh, I like that restaurant. We'll have to have dinner there one of these days. Speaking of dinner, what is for dinner?"

"Lasagna. It's in the oven and won't be ready for at least thirty minutes. Would you like a glass of wine? I will join you," Jeannette tempted.

"Well, if you are going to have a glass, being the gentleman that I am, I can't let you drink alone, so yes."

Shelly went to her room to put her new clothes away while Robert and Jeannette sat on the couch with their wine.

"We had a good time today. I think she has changed. I like this new Shelly," Jeannette said.

Robert had a smile that reached from one side of his head to the other.

"I can't tell you how good this makes me feel. I'm so glad she has you as an example. You know, you are the one that changed her. After all she did to hurt you, and you still showed her kindness. I think that might have gotten to her."

"It doesn't matter what it was. I'm just glad Shelly has changed for the better. On a new subject, can you get away next week and spend some time with me in Chicago? We would have the apartment all to ourselves. Wouldn't you like to spend some alone time with me?" Jeannette asked.

"Oh, baby, you know I want to. I will have to check my schedule. I might be able to get away on Thursday afternoon. I will work on it first thing tomorrow. There's the bell! Lasagna is done! Let's eat," Robert said.

The friendship between the two women grew. Their household started to be happy, and the tension eased. Jeannette felt she could trust Shelly, so she gradually let her guard down.

Jeannette left for Chicago, and Robert planned to join her Thursday evening. Robert was not as trusting as Jeannette was toward Shelly, but he decided to give her the benefit of the doubt and go to Chicago to see his lovely wife. They had not been alone since Shelly moved in over eight months ago. He was more than ready to have Jeannette all to himself.

It was like a second honeymoon, only shorter. Robert went with Jeannette to Windy City on Friday to look over some documents she had. He stayed the entire day with her, and wandered around the studio visiting with Greg, Bridgett, and several others. He had Greg demonstrate what it was that he did.

"Listen to this, Robert, and tell me what you think," Greg said.

After listening, he said, "Sounds good to me."

Greg pushed the button on the intercom and said, "Jeannette, would you come to the sound booth and listen to this song, please? I need your opinion."

"Yes, I will be right there. Well, there you are, honey. I wondered where you were hiding." She kissed Robert on the cheek and said, "Okay, Greg. Is it cued up? Let's hear it." She listened intently. "The sound is pretty good, but the drums are too loud. Tone them down just a little. Pick up the bass guitar more so you can really hear the beat. The harmony is a little out of sync. Tighten it up. Okay, let's hear it again." All three of them smiled. She had made it perfect like she always did.

Greg looked at Robert and said, "See? She hears things we don't. Now, this is going to be a song that will probably hit the charts because she knew how to tweak it."

"You called me here for a demonstration? I take it I passed?" Jeannette asked.

"With flying colors, boss," Greg said with a smile.

"Robert, can I interest you in taking me for an early dinner? I think I have everything wrapped up."

"Sweetheart, I would never turn down a date with you," Robert said and offered her his arm.

Saturday morning, sadly, they were on a plane back to Clark City. When they arrived home, everything seemed normal. Shelly was working, Tyler was at work, but Sean was home.

"Hi, Sean. You aren't working today?" Jeannette asked.

"I went in early so I could have some time to talk to you both."

"Oh, this doesn't sound good. What happened?" Jeannette asked.

"Damn, how do I say this? Okay. I have heard from several people Shelly is back on drugs. Not just pot, but harder stuff. Pills. I don't know if it's true, but I've heard it from several people. I don't think they can all be wrong," Sean said with a worried look. "I'm sorry to hit you with this as soon as you got home, but this was the only time I could get you both alone."

Jeannette looked at Robert with disappointment on her face before saying. "She hasn't acted any different than usual that I can tell. Do we confront her? Wait until she does something wrong? I'm at a loss."

"I'm going to go back to work. I'm sorry again to do this to you," Sean said.

"I think we should confront her. These are serious rumors, and we need to get to the bottom of them, for her sake as well as ours. Thanks for telling us, Sean. We needed to know," Robert said with sadness on his face. "I am no longer on probation with my firm. But if she pulls a stunt like she did before, I will be fired."

"You confronted her last time. I will do it this time. I think she will tell me the truth since we are getting along so well. When she gets home, I'll take her in the office so we can talk," Jeannette said with the same sadness Robert had.

An hour later, Shelly got home. "Well, hi, you two! How was Chicago?"

"Shelly, could I talk to you in the office?" They walked in together, Shelly acting like she had no idea what was going on.

"I'll get right to it. I heard some rumors you have been doing drugs as well as pot. I'm not accusing you. I'm telling you what the rumors are. This is serious, Shelly. It didn't come from just one person. It was several. Please, tell me the truth? Are the rumors true?"

"No! I have not been doing any drugs or smoking pot! I swear! If I took a pee test right now, it would be clean. I'm not lying! I don't know who is spreading these rumors, but they are all lies!" Shelly protested loudly.

"Okay, okay. I believe you. But let me warn you, if we ever find any kind of drugs in this house that belongs to you, we will kick you out. I don't mean you will have a week or two to find somewhere to go. I mean immediately. I want to be completely clear about this. Do you understand? Absolutely no drugs of any kind in this house!" Jeannette warned.

"You have made yourself crystal clear. You don't have to worry. I'm clean, and there are no drugs in this house," Shelly promised.

"Thank God. My heart fell when I heard the rumors. I am enjoying having you as a friend and a stepdaughter. Please, you have got to stay clean?" Jeannette asked.

"I will. I'm beginning to like life without drugs. I don't have to be high or drunk to have fun. Holy cow! I sound like you!"

Jeannette laughed. "I'm glad I am rubbing off on you! There's still hope for you yet," Jeannette said. They left the room together, laughing.

Jeannette sat by Robert and said, "Well, we talked. She emphatically denied the rumors. She said a pee test would come out clean right now. I don't know why, but I believe her. I told her if we ever find any kind of drugs in this house, she is gone!"

"Well, that's a relief. We have to make sure we keep your word. If any drugs are ever found here, Shelly's gone. On another subject, it's pretty warm out today. Want to take a dip in the pool?" Robert asked.

"Love to."

Things were going smoothly, and Jeannette and Shelly were getting closer all the time. Shelly even told her she was more of a mother to her than her birth mother was. It made her feel good she was teaching Shelly things, and she was beginning to show Jeannette respect. But it also made her feel bad her mother was the way she was. But Jeannette still had a nagging in the back of her mind about Shelly. Something still was not quite right about her. She thought her knowing must be wrong this time and shook it off time after time.

Sean and Tyler were always suspicious of Shelly. There was something about her they didn't trust. The boys tried to share Jeannette's outlook for Shelly, but they couldn't.

Sean graduated from community college and was looking for another college out of town to attend. He graduated with a 4.0 grade-point-average. Jeannette and Robert beamed with pride when his name was called at graduation. Sean decided to study business. It only made sense. He was interested in business, and his mother has a big company that he was hoping to be a part of in a few years.

Tyler had one more year, and then he was off to another college. Although he hadn't made his mind up about what he was going to study, yet, his grades were excellent, so there would be no problem with him getting into a good college. It was just a matter of deciding what to study. Jeannette knew he would figure it out at some point. She wasn't going to push him.

Robert's probationary period with corporate had long past, and business was doing well. He had even hired another attorney to handle a backlog of clients he and Mr. Baker didn't have enough time in the day to take on.

Windy City never stopped growing and getting more well-known all the time. Jeannette expanded into more of her building with two more meeting rooms, another office, and another sound booth with a recording room. The company was thriving and making millions with Jeannette at the helm. She never felt like she was better than anybody and was always warm and friendly to everyone she met. That was one of the things the clients were drawn to. She was real. There were a lot of fake people in the music business, and she wasn't about to be one of them.

One day Jeannette was in Clark City, and she got one of her 'knowing' feelings. She had never had one this strong before. It drew her to Robert's office. She drove immediately to his office as fast as she could. When she walked in, she knew why.

"Robert! What's wrong? You are sweating, and there's no color in your face!"

"I don't know. I think maybe I am coming down with the flu or something. I can't stop sweating, I am sick to my stomach, and I'm really dizzy," Robert gasped.

"I am calling an ambulance! I think you are having a heart attack! Mr. Baker, we need you in Robert's office! I am calling an ambulance!" Jeannette called 911, and the ambulance was there within three minutes or less. He was rushed to the hospital where Jeannette's suspicions were correct. He was having a heart attack.

"Jeannette, my sweetheart, I love you more than words can express," Robert whispered in Jeannette's ear when she leaned over to put her ear close. He stopped for a minute and then whispered, "You have shown me what love is." He paused again trying to catch his breath. "Thank you for being my wife."

He fell unconscious, and all kinds of bells and beepers went off. Nurses and doctors ran into the emergency room and started working on him. Jeannette stood just outside the curtain, watching and listening. She wasn't aware her entire body was shaking, and tears were flowing down her cheeks in a steady stream.

"Stop CPR! Let's give him a shot of adrenaline! Nothing. Okay, let's shock him! Charge to two hundred! Clear! Charge two-fifty! Clear! Come on, Robert! Give me three-fifty! Don't give up! Clear! One more time! Clear! Damn it! I'm calling it. Time of death is 4:01 p.m.," the ER doctor said. He turned to see Jeannette standing behind him.

"Are you Robert's wife?" She shook her head. "I am sorry for your loss. We did everything we could, but there was too much damage. I am so sorry you had to see that. If you want to be with him for a while, you are welcome to stay as long as you want. If you need anything, just ask one of the nurses." He did something that he never does: he hugged Jeannette and kissed the top of her head just like Robert had done so many times before.

"I apologize if I was out of line. I have never done that before. I just felt I had to."

"That was my Robert. He was saying goodbye by kissing the top of my head for the last time. It was him directing you to do it. You don't have to believe it because I do," she said through sobs.

Jeannette went to Robert's side and held his hand to her face. She kissed his hand like he had done to her so many times before. There was no consoling her. Jeannette's heart was completely and utterly broken. She could feel it in her chest, tearing apart. She collapsed to her knees and prayed for God to take this pain from her.

"You gave him to me to love. Now you take him from me. Why? I don't understand. What have I done that would make you take him from me? Please take this pain from me and give me back my Robert?"

Mr. Baker walked over to Jeannette and gently took her shoulders and helped her to stand. He turned her into his shoulder, trying to comfort her, but there was no consoling her.

"Come on, Jeannette, I'll take you home."

"What is going to happen to my Robert? I can't leave him! I have to take care of him!" Jeannette protested. She didn't want to leave him.

"They are going to take good care of him, sweetie. I have given them instructions. The doctor wants you to take one of these pills to help calm yourself when you get home. I will stay with you as long as you need me. Let's get you home," Mr. Baker said all the while holding tightly.

She turned and looked at Robert one more time and gave his hand one last kiss. One of Jeannette's tears landed on the back of his hand.

"I will always love you, big boy. No one will ever replace you. You have my heart now and forever."

She turned to leave and noticed Mr. Baker was crying. "Maybe we can share these pills?" she asked him. He gave her a nod, and they walked out, holding on to each other.

At home, Jeannette had to call Sean, Tyler, and Shelly to come home to tell them about Robert. Then she had to call Pam and Susan in Texas to give them the bad news. All the while, Mr. Baker sat with her helping her find the right words and making notes about what needed to be done. The last call needed to be to the mortuary to make an appointment for the next day to plan Robert's service. Mr. Baker took the phone and made that appointment.

Sean, Tyler, and Shelly all pulled in at the same time. They knew something horrible must be wrong. Jeannette had never called them home from work before.

Sean was the first to burst through the door, "Mom! What's wrong? What's happened?"

"You all need to sit down. I had one of my knowing feelings earlier today, that I needed to see Robert. It was so strong. I went to his office as fast as I could. When I got there, he was sweating and nauseous. He had no color in his face. I called an ambulance. They rushed him to the hospital. He had a massive heart attack. They did everything humanly possible to save him, but they couldn't. He's gone." Jeannette burst into sobs again. The boys began to cry. Shelly let out a dramatic yell that sounded more fake than not and began to cry.

"Jeannette? Why don't you take one of these pills? It will relax you," Mr. Baker suggested.

"I will take one in a little while. If I had ignored my knowing, I wouldn't have got to say goodbye to my Robert. I want to be with my kids for now. They just lost the only real dad who made a difference in their life." She took them in her arms and held them as they all cried. Shelly pushed her way into the huddle.

One by one, the three children went to their rooms to mourn. That left Mr. Baker and Jeannette alone to talk.

"Jeannette, Robert had me draw up a will for him several months ago. He must have had a feeling he would need it. I think the stress of having Shelly here was getting to him. He has left you a substantial estate. He left everything to you, with one exception. He started a college fund for Sean and Tyler to help pay for their next college after community college. He also set up an account for the boys when they are ready to get married. He did not want them to struggle as you did. When they find their special someone, give me a call, and I will release it to them. All of this stays between you and me. He didn't want Shelly to know about any of this. He left nothing to her or her sisters. He didn't feel Shelly deserved anything, and he didn't know the other two well enough to leave them anything. You were everything to him. You changed his heart and his life. You made him so very happy. His face lit up whenever you came into the room or when he spoke of you. I have never witnessed the kind of love you two shared. I wanted you to know that. Tomorrow, I will go with you to help you with making the funeral arrangements."

"Thank you, Mr. Baker, for helping me. I would be at a complete loss knowing what to do," Jeannette said with gratefulness.

"Will you be okay if I step out on the patio and call corporate? I have to inform them right away."

"I will be fine. You go ahead. I'm going to sit right here," Jeannette said.

It was a rough night for everyone. The pills the doctor gave Jeannette helped a little. Sleep still escaped her. When she closed her eyes, all she saw was Robert and the doctor working on him. She walked the halls in the house but finally ended up building a fire in the fire pit and watching the flames until the sun came up.

She brewed a pot of coffee and sat at the kitchen table with a cupful between her hands and stared into space. It wasn't long before all three of the kids were up doing the same thing, with a cup of coffee and staring at nothing.

"Mom, Mr. Baker called to let you know he will pick you up in an hour," Sean said, breaking the silence.

"I have to get dressed. Mr. Baker is going to take me to make arrangements for . . . Um . . . The service. Have each of you notified your boss and let them know you won't be in for a few days?"

Sean and Tyler shook their heads yes, and Shelly said, "I need to call mine right now."

"Mom, we are here. Whenever or whatever you need, all you have to do is ask. We loved him too. He was our dad," Sean said, and the tears began again, which set off Tyler and Jeannette.

"Thanks, boys. I love you. Now, I have to get dressed. I will have my cell phone if you need me."

At the mortuary, Mr. Baker had all the information about what Robert wanted. One of the things that surprised Jeannette was Robert chose cremation. He wanted his urn to sit on the fireplace mantle where he could watch over her.

They set a date for a week away, so Susan and Pam had time to make arrangements for Jeannette to fly them to Clark City. Cremation will be performed after the girls could say their good-byes to him.

Mr. Baker had been appointed the executor of Robert's estate by Robert. He wrote a check out of the estate to cover all the funeral expenses.

As they were in the car going to Jeannette's house, Mr. Baker said, "We can settle the estate next week after the service, and everything begins to settle down. It will be relatively easy since he left everything to you."

"Okay. Whatever you say," Jeannette said in a daze.

She thought to herself, "Nothing seems real. Did this happen? Have I been left alone, again?" It suddenly occurred to her she hadn't called Windy City to let them know. She used her cell phone and called immediately.

She told Bridgett and Greg the whole story, then said, "I won't be in next week at all, but I will be the following week and probably stay longer than a week to catch up. Only call me if there is an emergency. Thanks, Bridgett. Thanks, Greg."

Jeannette flew Susan, Pam, and their children to Oregon for the services. Their husbands stayed in Texas. She wanted to see those little ones and hold them tight. They arrived in Oregon two days later, and Jeannette took Shelly with her to meet them at the airport. Shelly drove. She didn't trust herself to drive just yet.

As soon as Pam and Susan saw Jeannette, they rushed to her with children in tow. Shelly passed her sisters and went to the children. She wanted to give her sisters a quick minute to hug Jeannette. After Shelly had talked to the little ones for a minute or two, she let them run to Grandma.

The three grandchildren ran to Jeannette bobbing and weaving through other passengers to get to her for their turn at hugs. Jeannette needed it. They were genuinely excited to see Grandma. The oldest boy let the two younger children hold Grandma's hand as they left the airport.

The women did not say much because of the children. They could wait to discuss details after they got to Grandma's house. The little ones were so excited to be in Oregon and to have flown in a big airplane. They all talked at once telling Grandma all about it. Jeannette couldn't help but smile.

Sean and Tyler were waiting in the driveway for the group to return so they could help with the luggage, and, of course, see the little ones.

The oldest boy spotted Sean and yelled, "There are the big boys! Uncle Sean and Uncle Tyler! Where's Grandpa Robert?"

Jeannette's heart felt like it had just gotten stabbed all over again. She managed to say, "He's not here. We will talk about it later and explain where he is. Is that alright? He would have been here if he possibly could. Why don't you hop out and tell the big boys about your trip on the plane?"

They jumped out of the car and ran to Sean and Tyler. Jeannette turned away from them and wiped away tears before she got out of the vehicle. She didn't want the little ones to see her crying.

Inside, all the women took a seat at the kitchen table while Sean and Tyler took the three grandchildren downstairs to the basement. They had recently turned it into a playroom with toys, games, stuffed animals, and a big play pony the little ones could sit on. When the pony was switched on, it made horse sounds and moved its head around to seem real. They loved it.

Jeannette started the conversation, "Robert wanted to be cremated and have his urn placed on the fireplace mantle. So that is what's going to happen. His body has not gone through that process yet. I had them wait so you girls could say your good-byes. I made an appointment at the mortuary for you to do that two hours from now. Then in the morning, they will take care of him. The service will be in four days." She paused long enough to pass out a piece of paper to each one outlining the service. "Is there anything on this list you want to change or leave out? I want us to agree." They read the details, and they all agreed Jeannette had made all the right choices.

Later that evening, when the girls got back from the mortuary, they all sat the grandchildren down and explained to them that Grandpa Robert had gone to heaven. It was hard for the little ones to wrap their head around what it all meant.

"I'll tell you what. Tomorrow we will go to town and buy some balloons. We will bring them home, write a note to Grandpa for each one, and attach it to the balloons. Then we will take the balloons outside in the backyard and let them fly to heaven for Grandpa Robert to read," Jeannette explained to three pairs of little eyes that were filled with sadness and confusion.

All three went to Jeannette and hugged her as if they knew she needed their consolation. "Will you still be our grandma?" the oldest asked.

"Of course, I will! I love you three munchkins! Maybe you can come to see me at Christmas? Would you like that? We have a huge tree that almost touches the ceiling with purple lights."

"Purple?" the little girl asked and curled up her lip not thinking she was going to like it. "I've never heard of purple lights before."

Jeannette gave a little giggle and said, "Wait until you see it. Then you can decide if you like it. If you don't, then we can change the lights to whatever color you want. Deal?" Jeannette held her hand out to shake.

"Deal!" they shouted and shook Jeannette's hand.

"Oh, boy! Christmas is going to be awesome!" the middle grandchild said. "I can hardly wait! How long till Christmas, Grandma?"

"Let's go look at the calendar in the kitchen," Jeannette said.

Pam, Susan, and Shelly sat silently and listened to their stepmother talking to their children. They were in awe of the patience and kindness she used with the little ones.

Pam said, "I don't know how she keeps going. They had a kind of love people only dream of having. I don't know if I could go on."

"Shelly, is she like this all the time?" Susan asked.

"Yes, this is the real Jeannette. There is nothing fake about her. What you see is what she is."

"Dad hit the jackpot when he married her. The kids love her, and I think she feels the same way," Pam continued. "I can't believe Dad is gone. After we got away from Mom, we started to get to know him." Pam noticed Shelly fidgeting and asked, "Shelly, what is wrong with you? We're all uncomfortable with this. Why can't you sit still? Is there someplace else you need to be? If that's the case, leave."

"No, there's no place I need to be. I should be at work, but they fired me because I didn't call in before my shift started the day after Dad . . . Died. I don't know how I'm going to tell Jeannette," Shelly said, looking worried. "Pam, will you tell her for me?"

"NO! You're a big girl, tell her yourself! You're the one who screwed up, again! You are old enough to know you have to call your boss if you are not going to show! Quit being so damn stupid and irresponsible!" Pam said with disgust toward Shelly.

"Okay, who screwed up?" Jeannette asked, coming back to the table. "The munchkins went down to the basement to play. Now, who screwed up so we can fix it?"

Pam and Susan looked at Shelly. "Oh, damn it!" Shelly said. "Me! I screwed up again. I didn't call into work, so they fired me. I am out of work again. I'm sorry, Jeannette. I wasn't thinking. I will find another job before my next payments are due. I promise."

"Shelly, I'm not going to get mad or upset. You know what you have to do. Figure it out, quickly. There's a current newspaper on my desk in the office. Start going through the want ads," Jeannette said without emotion.

"Now?" Shelly asked.

"Yes, now! There's no time like the present." Jeannette told her.

Shelly left to get the newspaper.

"What can we do to help, Jeannette?" Pam asked. You don't have to do this alone. We are here to help."

"Could I ask you two to please recruit Shelly, to help make dinner? That's one of her responsibilities around here, to help with the cooking. I want to lie down for a bit. I don't have any energy left."

"We would be happy to. Is there something in particular you want us to make? Or shall we wing it?" Susan asked.

"Wing it. Make whatever sounds good. There is chicken that's thawed in the refrigerator. If that doesn't suit your fancy, look in the freezer and pick something. I'm not hungry anyway," Jeannette said as she left the room.

"Let's get Shelly. She's not going to get out of this. She can help us cook," Pam said. The two walked into the office and saw Shelly searching the desk.

"Lose something? Or are you being nosey as usual?" Susan asked.

Shelly jerked her head up and looked like a deer caught in the headlights. "Um . . . I was looking for a pen."

Pam said, "What's that in your hand? It looks like a pen."

"Oh! Well, that was stupid of me. I was holding it. My brain must be mush," Shelly said and shook her head in disbelief.

"Yea, okay, Shelly. Whatever you say. Come on. You are going to help us cook. You can look at the ads later. Jeannette is lying down and asked if we would put dinner together. You're helping us," Pam said in no uncertain terms.

Shelly reluctantly went with them. While she was setting the table, Pam leaned close to Susan and asked, "Is it just me, or is Shelly acting odd?"

"You noticed it too?" Susan said. "Do you think she's using again?"

"God, I hope not. That's the last thing we need to deal with right now," Pam told her.

The next morning, they went into town, as Jeannette had promised, to buy balloons. They each picked out two in fluorescent colors. They wanted to make sure they were bright so Grandpa Robert would see them.

"Okay, let's take these home and write our notes," Jeannette said.

It was a task of love to make each note and then tape it to a balloon. Most of the messages read, I love you, Grandpa Robert. One of Jeannette's read, I love you to the moon and back.

When all the notes were attached, Jeannette said, "Okay, grab your balloons and hold on tight to them by the string. We will take them outside and turn them loose at the same time. So don't let them go until I count to three. Okay, here we go."

Everyone participated. Jeannette, Pam, Susan, Shelly, Sean, Tyler, and the three grandchildren all walked out to stand around the fire pit.

"This was Grandpa Robert's favorite spot. Okay, I am going to count to three and then let go. Does everybody understand? One, two, three! Let them go!" Jeannette yelled.

"Look, Grandma, mine is going fast! See how high it is?"

"Yes, I see it, and I am sure Grandpa does too," Jeannette said.

There was something sweet and special about sending these balloons up. They all felt love pour over them. The children stood quietly. The adults, along with Sean and Tyler, had tears rolling down their faces.

Finally, Jeannette spoke, "Sean and Tyler, do you feel like building us a fire?"

They all sat around the fire and watched the flames. Two of the grandchildren sat on Jeannette's lap, and the oldest sat on Sean's. The balloons had affected all of them.

They let the fire burn down to embers before they moved from their chairs.

"There's a bit of a chill in the air tonight," Jeannette said, breaking the silence. "Let's go in and light the big fireplace. Later, after dinner, we can roast some marshmallows for dessert." The little ones ran ahead. Pam and Susan walked on either side of Jeannette.

Pam said, "Jeannette, would you mind if Susan and I stayed a few days longer? This house makes us feel so close to Dad, and the kids would love to be with you. They adore you."

"I adore them," Jeannette said. "I would love to have you stay longer. I will get the tickets changed for you as soon as we get inside."

She went into the office to change the plane tickets. When she walked in, something didn't feel right. Someone had been in here. Some of the things on the desk were moved. She opened the top drawer to get the bottle of pills the doctor had given her. She scoured the drawer before coming to the conclusion they were gone, or she misplaced them. She decided to look for them after she got the plane tickets changed.

Her search continued. She checked her bedroom, bathroom, and the kitchen. She came up empty. She was a little worried. Jeannette thought her brain wasn't functioning as it should, so the bottle of pills could be anywhere. She was concerned about the little ones getting hold of the bottle. The pills are a narcotic, and it could be fatal if taken by the grandchildren.

"Have you girls seen the bottle of pills the doctor gave me? I have put them somewhere and can't find the bottle. I think I am losing my mind," Jeannette said and shook her head.

"That bottle has to be around here somewhere. We'll help you look," Pam said.

Shelly whispered to Jeannette quiet enough so her sisters couldn't hear, "Did you know Susan used to have a drug problem? Yep. Pills were her drug of choice. This stress we are all under may have triggered her need again."

"Well, crap! Great! Okay, let's keep an eye out for any strange activity from her. Lord! This is all I need! I'm going to take some aspirin. I could sure use one of those pills. I'll call the doctor tomorrow. Maybe he will refill it?" Jeannette wondered. "How does pizza sound for dinner?" Jeannette yelled. She could hear cheering coming from Sean, Tyler, and the three grandkids in the basement. She ordered four pizzas to be delivered.

The next day was the day before Robert's service. Jeannette had a lot of last-minute things that needed to be done and confirmed. She sent the boys into town to pick up a large, framed picture of Robert which would be on an easel surrounded by flowers for all to see at the front of the room during the service.

Shelly came out of her room, looking like she hadn't slept in three days.

"Shelly, you look awful! Are you sick?" Jeannette asked.

"No, I couldn't sleep last night. I am going back to bed for a while," Shelly said and disappeared back into the bedroom.

Working in her office, where it was quiet helped Jeannette focus on the tasks at hand, but it didn't stop her from crying. She managed to stop the tears long enough to make a call and then continue to cry after she hung up. Jeannette missed Robert desperately. She physically hurt. She talked to him every day as if he were standing next to her. Jeannette liked to believe he heard her. She told him everything, what she was thinking, what she planned for the service, how sweet the little ones were, and just things in general. She dreamt of him every night. They seemed so real, so vivid like he was there and stroking her face. Then she woke up and realized it was only another dream.

Shelly came into the office with a big smile on her face and giggling. "Well, you look ten times better than you did two hours ago!" Jeannette said with surprise.

"I had a cup of coffee and a shower. It perked me right up!" Shelly said. "What can I do to help?"

"Would you mind picking up the living room and doing the breakfast dishes? I have been in here all morning. I would appreciate it," Jeannette said.

"Sure! No problem! I'm on it," Shelly said.

Jeannette stared at the door after she left and thought, "That's weird. Now she is full of energy, and only two hours ago she couldn't keep her eyes open. Whatever. Let's see, where was I?" She blew it off. She had enough to deal with at the moment.

By dinner time Jeannette was finished preparing for tomorrow. For dinner, the group built a fire in the fire pit and roasted wieners to make hot dogs. After they had their fill of hot dogs, two grandchildren climbed up on Jeannette's lap and one on Sean's.

They watched the flames for a while until Sean broke the silence and said, "Hey, Mom, why don't you play your guitar for a while like you did when Tyler and I were little? We can teach the kids the songs you taught us."

"I will, if you go get my guitar."

When he came back to the fire with her guitar in hand, he said, "Let's sing the bullfrog song. It's a fun one! Grandma wrote this one for Tyler and me when we were little. We'll sing it first, and then we will help you with the words. Okay?" They cheered and jumped around. "First you need to clap with the beat of the song. Good! Keep clapping." Sean and Tyler began to sing the song.

The little ones picked it up fast and were singing at the top of their lungs. They were having a great time. Tyler taught them the next one about barnyard animals and Sean taught the last one about hoot owls.

"How did you like those songs? Next time you come to visit, maybe Grandma will show you how to play a chord on her guitar. She taught us when we were your age," Sean said.

"That's for another day. I see some sleepy eyes. Let's get ready for bed. Everybody pick up your mess and put the garbage in the garbage can. Great job! You three are such a big help for Grandma."

Shelly didn't stand up. She was sound asleep.

"No wonder Shelly's asleep. I have never seen her do housework as fast as she did today. Even things I didn't ask her to do! She picked up the living room, did the dishes, vacuumed, dusted, and scrubbed the bathroom until it sparkled. It was just weird. I'll take the kids inside. Why don't you two wake her up and tell her to go to bed."

Pam and Susan looked at one another. Their faces said uh oh, without a need for words.

Pam shook Shelly and yelled, "Wake up! Get up Shelly! It's time to go to bed!"

Shelly opened her eyes just enough to see Pam looking down at her with disgust. "What? I am in bed. Why do I have to get up?" Shelly groggily asked.

"You are not in your bed! You are outside in a lawn chair. Get up and go to bed!" Susan chimed in.

By the time they got Shelly in the house, Jeannette had the kids ready for bed. She tucked them in and gave them each a kiss before she left their room.

"Thanks for getting Shelly up. I'm going to bed. It's going to be a long day tomorrow. Goodnight," Jeannette said trying to smile.

Pam, Susan, Sean, and Tyler shot a game of pool before they went to bed to wind down and also for the sheer fun of the game. Afterward, Pam and Susan went to check on their children. Their beds were empty. They looked at each other. They were thinking the same thing. They peeked in Jeannette's room and saw all three little ones cuddled up to Jeannette in her bed. All four were sound asleep. It touched Pam and Susan's heart that Jeannette could love their children that much without being their biological grandmother. They eased the door shut and left the four to dream sweet dreams.

11

Jeannette had a limo pick the family up, so they didn't have to worry about driving. Sean and Tyler dressed in black suits. Jeannette was wearing a black business suit, hat to match, gloves, and dark glasses. The two grandsons insisted on dressing like Sean and Tyler in a black suit. The granddaughter wore a pink-and-white dress that had a black velvet sash she picked out. Pam, Shelly, and Susan wore black pantsuits. They were escorted into the venue through a side door by Mr. Baker, who was also going to be the main speaker at the service. The first thing Jeannette saw was Robert's urn sitting by his picture. Her legs became weak, and she wobbled. Mr. Baker was on one side of her and Sean the other. They held her steady and sat her in the front row. The family took their seats around her.

"Mom," Sean whispered. "Your mom and dad are here."

"Thanks for the heads up. I can't believe they came. Never mind. Just stay close to me and don't let me be alone with them."

The service was beautiful. Mr. Baker had some wonderful things to say about Robert, which you could tell came from the heart. There must have been twenty or more people who shared stories about Robert when the floor was opened for anyone who wanted to talk about Robert. Jeannette silently cried throughout the service. There was a reception directly following the service. Jeannette estimated there to be four hundred people in attendance. Every person there shook her hand, some hugged her, but everyone gave their condolences for her loss—except Warren and Rebecca, her parents. Sean and Tyler didn't leave her side in support just in case their grandparents decided to talk to her.

Sean spotted his grandparents walking toward Jeannette. He whispered in her ear to warn her. Jeannette looked up just in time to see them standing in front of her.

"Thanks, Mom and Dad, for coming."

"So, what happened to him?" Warren asked bluntly.

"He had a heart attack," Jeannette said flatly.

"Well, I bet he left you a rich woman. Isn't that what you wanted? His money?" Warren blatantly asked.

"That's not why I married Robert! I didn't care about his money. I loved him, and he loved me. That is what I wanted, someone to love me. I have never cared about money. Why do you insist on always saying that? I have my own. Or didn't you know I own a multi-million-dollar company in Chicago?"

"You really put on a show today. Made sure everyone knows you are rich," Warren said, looking around guessing how much everything cost.

"Warren, that is enough!" Sean said.

"I am your grandfather! Show me some respect!" Warren said with a flash of fire in his eyes.

"I'll show you respect when you show my mother respect!" Sean said, pointing his finger at Warren's face, taking a step toward him and putting Warren in his place.

Sean stood a full head taller than Warren, and he used it to intimidate him. Warren stopped talking and glared at Sean. Jeannette held Sean's hand while he led her away from the angry man. Sean was at his breaking point. He had had enough of Warren treating his mother so horribly. This was definitely NOT the place or the time for his so-called grandfather to be a jerk.

"Thank you, son, for standing up for me. I don't think I could take anything he was going to dish out, not today. Why don't you boys get something to eat? I'm going to mingle for a bit."

"Mom, you should eat something. Can I make you a plate?" Tyler asked.

"No thanks, honey. I will get something to eat in a bit."

She made sure she said hello to every person who was in attendance and let them know she appreciated them being at the service. Mr. Baker was the last to talk to Jeannette. She thanked him for the beautiful things he shared about Robert.

"Sweetheart, I spoke the truth from my heart. He was my friend, and I loved him. I hope you know you can call on me at any time for anything, and don't forget about our appointment tomorrow."

"I won't forget. Thank you, again."

Jeannette said and joined her family sitting at a table. Pam had a plate of food, waiting for her. She ate a little but had no appetite. Her little granddaughter asked to sit on her lap. Of course, she didn't deny her. Together they shared Jeannette's plate of food.

That night, Jeannette cried herself to sleep. It was final. His urn was on the mantle.

The next morning Jeannette had no reason, she thought, to get out of bed. The love of her life was gone, and she was alone. Depression had taken hold. As she laid and listened to the radio, she heard her door open slightly. Three little faces peeked in.

"Grandma? Are you up?" one of them asked.

"Yes," Jeannette answered.

"Can we come in?"

"Of course, you can!"

The oldest boy said, "We thought you might be sad, so we wanted to make you smile. Do you want to play a game?"

"I guess so. What game do you want to play?" Jeannette asked.

"How about Go Fish? I have the cards. See?"

"Will you teach me how? I haven't played this game since Sean and Tyler were little. I think I have forgotten how," Jeannette said.

"Yep! I'll teach you!" he said excitedly. He was a good teacher. They played on the bed for nearly an hour.

"Thank you, my sweet little ones, for cheering me up. You were right. I was sad. How about I make you pancakes for breakfast?"

"We already ate stupid eggs."

"Well, tomorrow I will make you pancakes and not stupid eggs. Deal?"

"Deal!" they shouted.

Jeannette shooed them out of her room so she could take a shower and dress for the day. When she walked into the kitchen, she found Shelly sound asleep in a chair. "Shelly. Shelly! Wake up!" Jeannette said as she shook her shoulder.

"What? Oh, I must have fallen asleep. I was going to straighten up the basement."

"Well, after you do that, get the newspaper out and look for a job," Jeannette told her. "It's been several days, and I haven't seen you look at the want ads once!"

"I will. I promise," Shelly said as she made her way downstairs.

Jeannette enjoyed a cup of coffee while Pam and Susan were playing tag with the kids in the backyard. Sean and Tyler went back to college earlier that morning. She heard the vacuum downstairs. She thought, "Shelly's cleaning the basement. I'm not going to stop her! It's nice having the help."

Minutes later, Shelly came bounding up the stairs carrying the vacuum.

"The Basement's clean as a whistle!" she yelled. "I'm going to clean out the fireplace before I look at the want ads. I'm on a roll! Don't stop me!"

"I certainly won't stop you!" Jeannette said, then wandered outside to sit in the sun. Pam and Susan sat beside her. "Shelly sure is acting odd. I found her asleep in a chair. I woke her up, and the next thing I knew, she was buzzing around vacuuming and cleaning out the fireplace. The same thing happened the other day. I've never seen anything like it. On another subject, I never have found that bottle of pills. I called the doctor. He is refilling it. I can't find the box of jewelry I had in my office either. That is, I thought I had the box in the office. The last piece of jewelry your dad gave me was in it. I wanted to wear it to the service yesterday but couldn't find it. I don't know what I did with it. My brain must be out to lunch."

Pam and Susan shot each other an 'uh-oh' look.

Jeannette went on to say, "You girls should do a little shopping while you're here. You can take my car and Shelly with you. The kids will be fine with me."

"Jeannette, while we're gone, you need to look around Shelly's room. We think she might be back on drugs," Pam said. "The way she is acting are signs of being on drugs, speed to be exact. Look everywhere. Between the mattresses, in pockets of clothes, any piece of foil or a piece of paper. Drug addicts are good at hiding their next fix."

Jeannette's face drained of color. "This can't be happening. Do you think so? She told me she suspected Susan might have taken my pills. Oh, Lord. Robert, why have you left me to deal with by myself?" She leaned forward and put her face in her hands. "I have eighty dollars in my pocket," she said as she fumbled with the pocket. "Lunch is my treat. My pocket is empty! There was eighty dollars in this pocket the other day! I paid for the balloons with a hundred dollar bill and that was the change! So now, my medication, money, and my jewelry are missing! Oh God, please let it be that I have misplaced these things. I will get you some money out of my purse for lunch."

"Where's your purse?" Pam asked.

"In the office, where I usually keep it."

Jeannette hurried to her office. She opened her purse to find a smaller wallet. There should be five hundred dollars in it. The little bag was open and empty. Her heart fell. She had a one-hundred-dollar bill in her regular wallet she handed to the girls and began to cry. She was sick to her stomach.

"Shelly strikes again! I think I'm going to throw up!" Jeannette announced holding her stomach.

"Take some deep breaths and lean forward. Susan, get a wet washcloth. Just relax. That's it. We are here to help you. You're not alone," Pam reassured. "Let's get Shelly out of here so she can search. Shelly! Hey, Shelly! Do you want to go shopping with us?"

Shelly walked in the office all smiles and dressed nicely.

"One of my friends called and wants to go to lunch, so no. Have fun. I'll be back later!" she yelled as she walked out the front door.

"New plan. We will keep an eye on Shelly, so she doesn't come back in the middle of your searching. Let's go, Susan!"

"My car keys are hanging by the door," Jeannette said as they left.

Jeannette checked on the grandchildren before starting her search. They were playing and oblivious to Grandma.

The search began. Jeannette looked in every pocket, corner, crack, drawer, purse, bag, between the mattresses and found nothing. She had spent forty-five minutes looking and putting everything back where it was when she began. Nothing. She found nothing. She let out a sigh of relief, thinking she was home free, and no drugs were in her home. By this time, the grandkids wanted a sandwich. They helped grandma make peanut butter and jelly sandwiches, their favorite. Jeannette made herself a sandwich of another kind. They took their lunch and juice boxes to the basement and made believe they were having a picnic.

Lunch was finished. Jeannette was watching the kids build some kind of structure with blocks. Something caught her eye behind the toy pony. It was Shelly's drug bag.

"Why am I dealing with this stepdaughter alone?" Jeannette asked herself. "Shelly is a bad seed. I have worked and worked with her only to have her steal my medication, money, and probably jewelry. Shelly had become my friend, I thought. I was growing to love her. Not now. Now I am going to be a stepmother in a very negative way. I have got to call her sisters."

"Pam, I need you and Susan here right now! I am not sure what I am looking at! I found it downstairs!"

"We are on our way!" Pam said and grabbed Susan's arm and rushed out of the store.

Shelly's sisters Pam and Susan were on the other side of town and would take about ten minutes to drive to Jeannette's house. The girls' minds raced with possibilities of what Jeannette had found, although they had a strong suspicion of what it was.

Pam and Susan had been concerned about their sister, Shelly, for some time. Jeannette had mentioned some strange behavior by Shelly a few days before. One minute Shelly looked like she had been on a three-day drunk and the next, she was bouncing off the walls with energy to spare. The girls arrived to see Jeannette pacing the floor and wringing her hands with worry.

"What's wrong? What did you find?" Pam asked nervously.

"This bag." Jeannette held it out for Pam to inspect. "Tell me what this is. I have never seen anything like this before. I want to make sure it's what I think it is."

Pam took the bag from Jeannette's hand and opened it. The color drained from her face. "This is her drug stash," Pam told her.

Inside were all the things Shelly would need to get her fix—syringes, cotton balls, three bottles of pills, a bent spoon, a lighter, a pill crusher, and a rubber hose to tie off her arm.

"These pills are why she has been acting strangely. She has been shooting up. Where did you say you found it?" Pam asked.

"Downstairs under the tail of the toy horse. Oh Lord, if my little grandbabies had gotten hold of this—I don't want to think about it! I don't know what to do. I have never had to deal with anything like this before." Jeannette's voice cracked, as she paced. "I am going to call one of the police officers at the P.D. I am acquainted and ask him what I should do with this . . . garbage."

"Well? What did he say?" Susan asked.

"He said to bring the bag to the P.D.," Jeannette replied looking stunned, still holding the phone.

Pam took the phone from Jeannette and finished the conversation with the officer. He gave her instructions.

Jeannette wanted Pam and Susan present for support when she confronted Shelly and possibly for physical support if things took a wrong turn.

Shelly walked through the front door and announced she was home. Pam and Susan took a seat. Jeannette stood to face Shelly.

Looking directly into Shelly's eyes, Jeannette confronted her. "I found your stash. DO NOT ROLL YOUR EYES AT ME! Don't give me that look like you don't know what I am talking about, and don't try to deny the fact that this is your bag."

Shelly was caught. She tilted her head down, and her eyes darted back and forth as she tried to come up with a response—an excuse—a lie.

"I . . . I . . . had left over . . . I," she sputtered.

"No! Stop it! I told you, if I found any drugs of any kind in this house you would be gone. I found this, your bag, where my grandchildren play. For God's sake, Shelly! If one of them had gotten hold of this, it could have been disastrous! What were you thinking?"

"Let me explain," Shelly begged.

"There is no explaining. This is your drug bag, plain and simple. It has everything you need to shoot up. There is not just one bottle of pills but three! This is not going to take place in my home. Anyone of my grandchildren, your niece and nephews, could have picked this up. I have loved you and treated you as my own. I have tried to be your mother and your friend. I have supported you. Your father and I withstood the lies you had spread throughout the community about us. The humiliation you caused us when we were in Chicago almost cost him his job. But we still took you in after you were released from jail and allowed you to enjoy our home until you could get on your feet. I have made sure you had a car to drive, your car insurance was paid, and all your personal needs were taken care of. What did you do in return? You broke my trust and betrayed me. You stole my medication, which you blamed on your sister to take the suspicion away from yourself. Then you stole money from my coat pockets and my purse. But that wasn't enough. You stole a box of jewelry with the last piece of jewelry your father gave me. Don't deny it. Stop with excuses and lies. I know you have probably sold my jewelry by now to support your habit. How could you do this to me after everything I have done for you?"

Jeannette stood looking at Shelly with her arms crossed and refusing to cry. She was not about to shed tears over Shelly's bad choices.

"I have been upset about losing my job and . . ."

"Stop. It was your choice to get involved with drugs! Your boss fired you because of your drug use and you didn't show up for work. You told me you wanted to get clean. So, I paid for you to detox. That program didn't help because you went right back to doing the same thing with the same group of friends. I don't know when you started shooting up, after jail or before jail, nor do I want to know. I thought your drug of choice was pot, but I see you have graduated to harder stuff. What do you expect me to do? If you were going to stay here, you had to be clean. You knew that. I made it very clear. Your father told you the same thing. You agreed and promised. I will not allow drugs in my home."

Shelly did not say a word. Jeannette threw her arms in the air. She was at her wit's end.

"If your father were here, he would be doing the same thing I am. He would be just as disappointed in you as I am. We tried our best to help you. You told me what you thought I wanted to hear so that I would believe you. You are a liar and a thief."

"I don't want to be clean. It's too hard. I like the feeling of being high. I don't have to think, and I don't have to feel," Shelly attempted an explanation, trying to get sympathy as she looked at her sisters who were quietly sitting across the room.

"You have to get clean, Shelly," Pam urged and crossed the room to hold Shelly's hands.

"No, I don't!" Shelly shouted and shoved Pam away.

Pam landed unbalanced in a chair and almost fell to the floor. Shock and sympathy flashed across Pam's face. Jeannette had to end this now before it got out of hand.

"Well, then that's it. Get your things and get out. I don't want you in my house or on my property ever again. I don't want to have anything to do with you. I don't want to ever see you again. You are no longer welcome at family functions or holidays we celebrate here or anywhere else. If you step foot on this property, you will be arrested for trespassing. I'm done with you, Shelly. You are no longer a part of my family. I am sorry I ever met you," Jeannette stated without sadness. There were no tears, and she did not raise her voice. Jeannette stood straight with her head up.

Shelly walked to the bedroom she had been living in. They could hear her walk around the bedroom packing. Jeannette paced, Pam chewed her fingernails, and Susan sat silently, not moving. There was only silence. It took just a few minutes when Jeannette heard the front door close. Shelly was gone.

Jeannette stopped pacing, unclenched her fists, and turned to Pam.

"Well, that's that. She's gone. Please, someone, tell me I did the right thing?" she pleaded and broke into tears.

Pam and Susan rushed to Jeannette and threw their arms around her for comfort.

Pam said in a low voice in Jeanette's ear as she patted her back in a soothing way, "Yes, of course you did the right thing. You had to do this. She has to hit rock bottom. You were not mean about it. You stood your ground and with authority, told her how it had to be. If dad were here, he would have done the same thing, only louder. This is your home. It's okay. She has to find her way now. You did everything you could for her. Now it is up to Shelly."

Jeannette crumpled in Pam's arms and sobbed.

"Oh, God, I hope I did the right thing. This tough love is excruciating! It hurts so badly! I trusted her. I loved her. But at the same time, I hated her, but I am worried about her, and yet I am relieved she is no longer under my roof. So many emotions! I had to keep everything under lock and key so she wouldn't steal anything. It was a horrible way to live. I couldn't sleep all the while wondering what she was doing. Always worried. The mistrust. My stomach was always tied in knots." Jeannette pulled away from Pam and asked, "What did the police say when you talked to him?"

"The officer said there was nothing the police could do. You found the drugs in your home, but it was an invasion of her privacy, so she cannot be arrested or charged for possession of illegal substances."

"But this is my home! How can it be an invasion of her privacy? What rights do I have? NONE! The only thing I agreed to was to allow her to stay here until she got a job. Not make this her place to get high and stash her drugs! If this house had been searched by the police, I would have been arrested because drugs were found in my home. Shelly would have got off free as a bird and I would pay the price for her stupidity. I wonder if that was her plan," Jeannette pondered and began to pace.

"This is so much crap!" She threw her arms in the air then sighed as they fell to her side. "I didn't want her to be arrested or see her in jail. I wanted her to get some help. Would you please take the drugs and her paraphernalia to the police department and turn it in for me? They already know the situation and have talked to you about it. I will call the officer back and let him know you are on your way. I don't want that stuff in my house any longer. Before you go, we need to be in agreement no one will take her in. She is on her own." They agreed.

Pam grabbed Shelly's drug bag and went out the door. Susan followed close behind.

"Shelly certainly couldn't go back to Texas. There is a warrant out for her arrest, so Pam and Susan are off the hook," Jeannette thought before making a quick call to the police officer. He was very understanding and told her he was sorry this had happened.

"Shelly is a bad seed. I have worked and worked with her only to have her steal my medication, money, and probably jewelry. Shelly had become my friend, I thought. I was growing to love her. Not now." Jeannette told herself. I hate her! God, please forgive me for hating her? I don't know if I will ever forgive her for everything she has done to this family. Now she is out of our lives forever."

The house was silent, and Jeannette was alone with her feelings. She curled up in a corner and sobbed uncontrollably from the heartache Shelly caused.

"What led to this point? How did I get to this place in my life?" She thought. "Over and over I have cared for others and I paid a price with a broken heart. What did I do that was so wrong? Oh, God! Where are you?"

The tears flowed freely down her cheeks and landed on her blouse. Depression, sorrow, and the release from years of built-up stress were so intense her entire body shook. She wrapped her arms around herself as tightly as she could and rocked back and forth as if it would somehow take the pain from her.

Jeannette looked to the sky with her fist raised and shouted, "I tried to teach that girl how to be a responsible adult and treated her as my own! Is this the price I pay for trying to be the best parent I could be? I grew to love her, took her in when she needed a place to live. Bought her clothes. I made sure she needed nothing. She had a car which I finished paying for and handed her the title. What did she do in return? Stole everything she could get her hands on! You let her get away with it, God! The last piece of jewelry my Robert gave me is gone! You let her take it! Where were you, God? You allowed this! Why? Am I being punished? Is this supposed to teach me something? If it is, I am missing the point. Am I not supposed to love? Not care for others? I love with my whole heart. Now my heart bleeds from being broken repeatedly."

She dropped her fist to her side and her head to her chest. She let out a loud cry that came from deep within her soul. It was a sound made from complete heartbreak.

"I can't take any more of this!" Jeannette's fist was raised to the sky again, and then let them drop as she said, "God, you know my heart. I love and care for others with no thought of myself. Is that the lesson? Stop caring for others? Stop giving? Stop being who I am? What? What is the reason or lesson for me to learn? Why are you allowing this to happen to me?"

As the old saying goes, 'this was the straw that broke the camel's back.'

So that brings me where I began my journey into my memories, to the present.

Through those memories, I have seen my life hasn't always been bad, but it was not always good either. There have been some wonderful times, along with not-so-wonderful times. Losing Robert was the absolute worst thing that happened. I relive his death over and over every single day. The pain of it is just as fresh today as it was the minute he was gone.

Shelly had me blindly fooled. I thought I could trust her. We had become good friends, I thought. Then everything went in the toilet. She was using me. Thank God her sisters were here. I made sure I had them as witnesses when I confronted her so that she couldn't lie about what happened. She was good at making herself look like the victim, just like Jeff.

Shelly and Jeff were masters of manipulation and convincing others they were victims. What I learned from both of these people are, they turn the tables from them to you and make everything your fault. Now they look like the victim and they get away with everything they do without consequence. They do not feel guilty, or regret about what they have done or to whom they have done it to. In their warped mind, they have done nothing wrong.

Everybody else is to blame. They do not take responsibility for their actions. Narcissists. Both of them.

Every action and decision we make in our lives does not affect only ourselves. It always affects our family, our friends, and countless others we will probably never know about. An example of that would be spreading lies. How many will it affect besides yourself? It has a ripple effect.

The truth of this is no matter what, you and you alone are accountable for every choice and decision you make. There is no one to blame for anything you do, except yourself.

It is anybody's guess if people like Warren, Shelly, or Jeff will ever learn this in their lifetime. I choose to have hope they will. Although, I know Warren did not. It was too late for him.

I have also learned, never trust a person that has let you down more than two times. The first time is a warning. The second time is a lesson, but anything more than twice they are merely taking advantage of you. They will use you as long as they can until you put a stop to it!

The lesson that took me the longest to realize was emotional and verbal abuse. I didn't know I was being abused. I had never heard of verbal or emotional abuse. I grew up experiencing physical, verbal and emotional abuse on a daily basis, and it carried on into my adult life. I did not know any better. I chose a man who was both mentally and verbally abusive. Things turned around when I was able to recognize there are other forms of abuse, not just physical.

The biggest thing I learned is: **I HAVE WORTH!**

These are the things I will recognize and send up red flags of warning:

Constant Criticism — Repeatedly pointing out mistakes
Put-downs disguised as jokes — Yelling
A threat of physical harm — Making you feel worthless
Blame Shifting — Indifference
Hostile Looks — Snide Remarks
Lashing Out — Public Shaming
Belittling — Spiteful comments
Ridicule — Lieing

Withholding affection & emotional support

Refusing to talk or listen — Dismissing ideas and opinions
Rejection — Betrayal

Isolation from supportive family & friends

Making you believe you will never be good enough for anything or anybody

When I see a person with these traits treating another person the way I was, it angers me. **NO ONE SHOULD EVER HAVE CONTROL OVER ANOTHER PERSON!** The control gives them POWER. That is what they want. Power makes them feel important. They will use you until they have used you up, then cast you aside.

Here are some ways I believe I can take care of myself and not fall into the trap of a control freak again:

1. Do not be a people pleaser. It is okay to say no or have an opinion.

2. Never speak negatively about yourself. Focus on the good.

3. Never give up on your dreams. They could happen tomorrow.

4. Be kind to yourself.

5. Let go of a bad situation. It will only get worse.

6. Do not take on the guilt of another person.

What Now? How am I supposed to live without my Robert?

12

Shelly was completely out of Jeannette's life. Shelly caused Robert the most significant stress in his last years. Could Jeannette relieved some of Robert's stress somehow? Did she do enough to help Robert? These are questions she will always be asking herself.

Jeannette felt like a failure when it came to Shelly. She wondered if she had done enough to try and reach her. When it came to drugs, Jeannette was oblivious. She didn't understand the appeal of drugs or knew anything about addiction. It was now up to Shelly to live with the choices she has made. Jeannette was done.

The house was quiet. Susan, Pam, and the three grandchildren had gone back home, and Sean and Tyler were back at college. Jeannette was alone. It was real. Robert was gone. She will never feel his soft touch, sip a glass of wine together at the end of the day or cuddle under his arm at night. What now? What is she going to do?

Jeannette walked to the fire pit and sat in Robert's chair. She sobbed and cried out to God, "Please, take this pain from me? What did I do that I am being punished for so severely? Why don't you answer me? You allowed me to experience love and happiness, and then you took it away. I can't live without Robert. Please take my life? Please? Take me away from this world. I do not have any reason to live. My love is gone. If it is your will, please take my life? I offer it to you."

The sun came up, and Jeannette was still in Robert's chair by the fire pit. She had cried herself to sleep. Jeannette rose from the chair and walked to the kitchen to make a pot of coffee. Sitting at the table with a coffee mug between her hands, she looked up and spotted the urn on the fireplace mantle. Once more, she burst into tears.

"Okay. I have got to pull myself together somehow. Robert would not want me to be crying all the time. I need a shower then I will go into town and pick up the rest of Robert's things at his office. Then I am going to pack my bags and go to Chicago. I have to get out of here." She told herself.

Mr. Baker met Jeannette in Robert's office. "Hello, Jeannette. You didn't have to come to pick up Robert's things. I could have had them sent to your house."

"It's alright. I wanted to get out of the house, and I needed to finish boxing Robert's things. I have decided I am going to close up the estate for a few months and stay in Chicago. It's too quiet at home. I found each of the boys an inexpensive apartment close to the college that I am paying for until summer. It's just as hard on them as it is on me in our home without Robert. When the boys come home for the summer, I will have Irma, my housekeeper, open it back up again. Right now, it is more than I can bear to be there alone. If you need me for anything, you have my number at the office and my cell."

Mr. Baker took her in his arms and hugged her.

"You are going to get through this, Jeannette. It is just going to take time. Always remember Robert loved you more than life itself. He will always be with you."

"Thank you for saying that. I know Robert loved me. I wish Shelly hadn't caused him so much trouble in his last days, but that's over now. Shelly is not my problem anymore. If you haven't heard, I kicked her out of my house. She is never to set foot on my property again. I found her drug stash. If she causes any problems around town, she will have to figure it out, because I have washed my hands of her. If she comes to you asking for help, do not let her sweet talk you into anything. She is a master manipulator. Robert would tell you the same thing," Jeannette said with a cracking voice. She was doing her best not to start crying again.

"Okay, sweetheart. I think staying in Chicago is a good idea. Windy City will keep you busy. I will make sure the county sheriff's department does a drive-by of the estate every day," Mr. Baker told Jeannette.

"Thank you. I have changed the locks so Shelly can't get in. Okay, I think this box is the last of Robert's things. Thank you again for all your help with the arrangements. I could not have done any of it without your help. I will stop by when I get back from Chicago. Bye."

Jeannette packed her bags before calling Irma to let her know to close up the estate, but, to go back each week and make sure it doesn't get dusty. Sean and Tyler understood why their mother needed to be away from home. They felt the same way. Everything reminded them of Robert, and it hurt.

The next morning Jeannette flew to Chicago. It felt good to be back with all the hustle and bustle of the big city, and Jeannette did not have time to think of anything other than work.

"Good morning, Bridgett," Jeannette greeted without emotion. "Is my schedule on my desk? Thank you."

Bridgett followed Jeannette into her office and said, "I didn't expect you back so soon. May I hug you? You look like you could use one." Jeannette nodded her head, and Bridgett scooped her up in a bear hug. "Oh, Jeannette, I am so sorry about Robert." Bridgett began to cry.

There was a quiet tap on Jeannette's office door. It was Greg.

"I thought I heard your voice. Why are you here? Why aren't you in Oregon?" Greg took his turn hugging Jeannette.

"Because I couldn't stand the quiet and everywhere I turned was some memory of Robert," Jeannette explained and began to cry. "How am I supposed to live without him? I had to deal with one of his children before and after the service. It's a bit of a long story, but I will try to hit the high points. To start with, his daughter made friends with Jeff."

"Your ex-husband?" Greg asked in shock.

"Yes. Jeff told her a bunch of lies about me, and she repeated the lies all over town. But that wasn't the worst thing she did. (By the way, her name is Shelly.) Shelly spent a month in jail. She kept getting fired from job after job. Shelly is a drunk and a drug addict. She stole money from me, a prescription the doctor gave me after I lost Robert and a box of jewelry. The kicker was, I warned her no drugs in my house. Robert had told her the same thing before he . . . passed. If I found any, she was gone. I found her stash under one of the grandkids toys. I confronted her and kicked her out with her sisters as witnesses to what I said and did. I told her she was no longer allowed on my property or family functions ever again. If she steps on my property, I will have her arrested. I washed my hands of her, and then I cried."

Greg and Bridgett shared a look of surprise before Greg said, "Oh, Jeannette! I am so proud of you for standing your ground and making her leave. I am shocked he had a daughter like Shelly."

"I had no idea until we got back from Ireland. She decided to stay in Oregon because she liked it better than Texas. Well, there was a reason she did not want to go back. Robert did some checking on her when she was in jail and found out she had warrants for her arrest in Texas. I have never seen Robert as furious as he was with her. The last few years of his life Shelly caused him an unbelievable amount of stress. I hate to say it, but I think Shelly is the main cause of his heart attack. Robert was so ashamed of her. When they threw her in jail, Corporate was not happy that one of their lawyers had a criminal for a daughter. They gave him probation for ninety days. He kept his thumb on Shelly that whole time. We let her live with us because she lost her apartment and her job. The story goes on, and I am tired of remembering."

Jeannette sniffed and wiped her eyes then continued, "I changed the locks on the estate and Irma is closing it up for me. I needed a few months away, so maybe I can begin to heal. Mr. Baker is arranging for the police to drive by from time to time and check on the estate. Before the boys come home for the summer, Irma will open it again."

"Oh, Jeannette, I don't blame you for getting away," Bridgett patted her hand, trying to comfort her. "We are here for you and we will take care of you. You are with family, and we love you. Why don't you splash your face with some cold water, and I will get you a fresh cup of coffee and maybe a bagel?"

"Just the coffee, thank you, Bridgett. Before I splash my face, Greg, how has business been?"

"Business is good, but it is always better when you are here," Greg told her. "When you get a minute I need you to listen to a couple tapes. They might need to be tweaked."

"Give me ten minutes," Jeannette told Greg.

Jeannette was glad to be back at work. Music was a cure-all in her book. She worked through lunch and into the afternoon. She got a break when Bridgett buzzed her on the intercom, "Jeannette you have a visitor. May I send him in?" That turned out to be a warning, not a question. Clay walked into her office without knocking with Bridgett right behind him.

"Hello, pretty lady!" Clay's voice boomed.

"I am sorry Jeannette, I couldn't stop him!" Bridgett apologized.

"It is okay. Clay knows I always have time for him," Jeannette said with a smile and her arms stretched out for a hug.

"How are you doing? I wanted to be at the service, but The Band and I were in concert. I am so sorry for your loss. Amy sends her love," Clay said with a sad voice while he held Jeannette in a tight hug.

"Thanks, Clay, but if you don't let me go, I will start crying again. Work is the best medicine for me right now. Speaking of work, I have been out of the loop for a few weeks, how was the tour? Did you get a good response from the audiences?" Jeannette inquired.

"We sure did! They always love the songs you write. Do you have any more on hand? I brought my checkbook." Clay asked with a wink trying to get a rise out of her for negotiating a price for a new song.

"I don't have any right now. I cannot bring myself to pick up a pencil or my guitar. I feel empty inside since Robert . . ."

"I know. You know I will be the first in line for the next one you write. Hey, why don't you go to dinner tonight with Amy and me? We are only in town for a couple of days and then back on the road," Clay asked.

"Thank you for the invitation, but I am going to stay in tonight. I will pick something up on my way home for dinner. I would not be an excellent conversationalist tonight. I need more time.

13

It has been several years since Robert passed. Jeannette felt like she was on autopilot for those years. Life could be worse, but right now, Jeannette did not think it was possible. Her heart was still grieving over Robert, the man who held her heart. It seemed like yesterday she watched him die. That horrible day replayed in her mind on a loop, day in and day out. They had shared a special kind of love she never knew existed. Living was just not happy without him.

Jeannette had not been happy since she became a widow. It was time to find happiness once again. This time it would be without him. She decided somehow her life was going to be happy again.

She had spent a week at her home in Oregon. It was always beautiful and she appreciated being home for a while, but it was time to go back to work.

The plane landed in Chicago mid-afternoon on Sunday. She was looking forward to coming back to a typical day of work at Windy City Publishing and Recording. Her driver, David, greeted her with a smile and a tip of his hat.

"Good afternoon, Jeannette. How was your flight?" David asked.

"It was a nice flight with hardly any turbulence," Jeannette replied, sliding onto the backseat. "David, I would like to go to the office for a bit after we drop off my bag at the apartment."

"Yes, ma'am. Did you enjoy your week in Oregon?"

"It was nice, but it would be better if my boys were at home. Sean is in Eugene, Oregon, at the University of Oregon, and Tyler is attending college at Oregon State University in Corvallis, Oregon."

It was a short drive to her office, and she usually would be chatting with David. Today that was not the case.

"Jeannette, you are not your normal self. Is everything all right?" David asked.

"Yes, I am fine. I need to get out of this funk I'm in. At the same time, I don't feel like trying. Does that make sense?"

"We have all noticed how down you have been since Robert passed. How can I help?"

"Thank you for the offer, David. I wish you could help. I am the one that has to do it. Well, here we are at Windy City. Will you pick me up in two hours please?"

"I will be here. Don't work too hard. Leave something for tomorrow," David said with a smile.

"It depends on how much is on my desk. Bridgett is good at giving me plenty to work on."

It was almost time for David to arrive. She sat at her desk, staring off into space. The memory loop of Robert's passing began to play in her mind. She thought, "Robert, why did you leave me? I am so alone and depressed. I would do anything to feel your arms around me again." She stopped suddenly. Something was not right. Her intuition had kicked in. What was it? It was unclear, just a feeling. It did not matter what it was. She did not like it. She looked at the clock and said, "Oh, David should be here!"

She gathered her things and went to the door at the front of the building. David was standing there.

"Hello, David. You didn't need to meet me at the door. I am capable of walking to the car alone. You are parked, maybe fifteen or twenty feet away."

"I understand, but I saw a man trying the door to see if it was locked. He didn't belong around here. He was dirty and not a businessperson who worked in this area. It made me nervous for you. Maybe you should give Max, head of your security, a call?"

"How long did the man stick around?"

"Not long. After finding the doors to be locked, the man left," David said as he slid behind the steering wheel.

"As soon as I get home, I will give Max a call. Thank you for keeping an eye out for me," she added.

"What time do you want me to pick you up in the morning?"

"Seven-thirty sounds good," Jeannette answered.

"Okay. Would you like to stop by your favorite restaurant to get something to go before I take you home?" David asked.

"Good idea." Ten minutes later, she returned with two large bags.

"Oh my, Jeannette! You must be hungry!" David exclaimed.

"I am, but not this hungry. I ordered extra food for you and your wife," Jeannette explained.

"Jeannette, that was not necessary, but it was very nice of you. Thanks," David said with gratitude.

"David, I did it because I appreciate you. There are so many odd times I call you to drive me places. I know it is your job. The food is a token of my appreciation. If memory serves me correctly, you and your wife's favorite is a club sandwich, extra fries, a small salad, and a piece of cheesecake for dessert. Correct?" Jeannette asked.

"Yes! Thank you and your memory!"

"No worries. By the way, what is your wife's name? Lately, I have had a little problem remembering names."

"Raelene," David reminded her.

"How could I forget that pretty name? I will do my best to remember. One of these evenings, we will have to go to dinner," Jeannette suggested.

"Here we are, Jeannette, at home safely once again," David said.

"That was quick. I must have been talking too much. Enjoy your meal. I will see you in the morning," Jeannette announced.

Something changed. That uneasy feeling swept over Jeannette as she walked to the doorman.

"Good evening, Miss Jeannette. Nice to see you back. Will you need help with your bag?" Sid asked.

"No thank you, Sid. I can handle it."

Sid opened the door and tipped his hat as Jeannette entered the building. Although she felt better inside a safe place, something was . . . Off.

Later that evening, Sean called. "Hello? Sean, what's wrong? What happened? Are you alright?" she asked nervously.

"Mom! Mom, I'm fine. Nothing is wrong. I should be asking you what is wrong," Sean argued.

"Nothing, honey. I'm fine. You just caught me off guard. Is there a reason you called, or did you call just to talk to your old mom?" Jeannette questioned.

"Yes, there is a reason. I wanted to ask if we could have a family week. It is almost spring break, and there is someone I would like to bring home for you to meet," Sean began.

All Sean heard was silence. It was deafening until Jeannette spoke, "You have a special girl you want me to meet. She is the one you want to marry."

"Mom, how do you always know? The answer is, yes. Her name is Tia. She is beautiful, funny, caring, smart, trustworthy..."

"She sounds like a Boy Scout," Jeannette teased with a chuckle.

"Not funny. I want you to know Tia is a good person," Sean warned.

"Son, if you feel this strongly about her, there is no doubt in my mind that she is a good person. I would love to meet her. Bring her home. Have you talked to Tyler? Is he coming home?" Jeannette questioned.

"Yes. Tyler should be home about the same time on Saturday. I think he has made some plans with Zach and a few friends," Sean answered.

"Wonderful! A family week is just what I need. I will see all of you this weekend!" She hung the phone up and thought, "Sean has never brought a girl home before. Well, there was Patty when he was in high school, but this is different. Sean loves Tia. When did he get old enough to think about getting married? Hum, this is not what is making me uneasy. I need to call Max, at Windy City, to tell him about the dirty man David saw."

"He didn't belong? What do you mean?" Max asked.

"He was dirty. He looked like he lives on the street. David said he was not a businessman from that part of the city. He was looking for something. Fortunately, I locked the door behind me," Jeannette explained.

"Ok. I will alert my guards. Would you like me to place one at your door tonight?"

"No, I don't think so. My building is secure," Jeannette reassured Max.

"Alright. Rest assured my staff will be watching. Have a good evening."

"Thank you, Max."

She paced most of the night and finally went to bed at 2:00 a.m. The alarm went off at six sharp, which made Jeannette sit straight up in bed. "Dang it! I should have gone to bed earlier," she said out loud and hit the off button to stop the constant ringing. "Thank God, my coffee pot is on a timer. A cup of coffee is just what I need," she thought. It was at that moment, the pleasant aroma of roasted coffee beans filled the air.

After the first cup, her eyes were brighter. She took a second cup with her to shower. The warm water that flowed over her body felt so good she stood under the stream a little longer than she should have.

"Crap! David will be here in twenty minutes!" It was a race to get herself ready for work. She finished in twenty-three minutes.

"Jeannette! I was starting to get concerned. You are never late," David said.

"I am truly sorry to keep you waiting. I was running behind this morning." Her uneasy feeling from the night before was better this morning but was still at the back of her mind.

"I am going to work through lunch today. If I need you before five o'clock, I will have Bridgett call," Jeannette promised David.

She kept her nose buried in paperwork until a tap at her office door interrupted her train of thought.

"Jeannette, I am sorry to disturb you, but there is a client who is demanding to see you." Bridgett barely got that out of her mouth when Clay came bursting through the door.

"Hello, pretty lady!" Clay went around the desk and gave Jeannette a big hug. "How are you doing?" he asked.

She smiled at him and said, "I am doing alright. Busy morning. How about you? It has been a while since we have talked. Have a seat," she offered.

"I know. I have been worried about you. Since Robert passed away, I have not seen your normal happy face or that big smile you used to have," Clay said with concern.

"That smile faded when I lost Robert. My 'happiness' is lost. Honestly, I am trying to get it back, but I don't know how," Jeannette replied, rubbing her face.

"Sweetheart, everyone has noticed how depressed you are. Your clients come here because of you and your upbeat attitude. It makes them feel like you care about them and their music. They love working with you, but if you keep going like this, you will lose business," Clay cautioned.

"Oh, Clay. I do care about them. Every one of them!" Jeannette said and burst into tears. "I am trying to move on without

Robert. I cannot stop reliving his last day. I feel guilty for living or trying to enjoy life when he isn't here."

"That is called survivor's guilt. If you are not able to pull yourself out of this funk, I am afraid of the impact it will have on Windy City. I say this out of love for you, sweetheart," Clay said with genuine concern.

"I know. You have always told me just like you see it. I will get some help, I promise."

"That's my girl. Now down to business. I was thinking about another album. Are you interested?" Clay asked.

"I might be," Jeannette said. "What are you thinking?"

"Well, there's a catch. I want you to write me at least two new songs. Without your music, it just isn't an album," Clay proclaimed.

"Oh, I don't know, Clay. I haven't written anything since I lost Robert. I don't know if I have any more in me," she said sadly.

"I believe you have a lot more. You just need to get them out. You don't have to answer me now. Think about it. How about Amy and I take you to dinner tonight? She gave me instructions not to leave without a yes," he informed her.

"Well, I guess if I am going to get any work done, I will have to accept your invitation. Yes, I would love to join you and Amy this evening. What restaurant so I can tell David?" she asked.

"You get yourself all dressed up, and I will give the information to Bridgett. It's a surprise," Clay declared.

"A surprise? This sounds interesting. What time?"

"Seven," Clay answered.

"Seven it is. I will clear time in the booth for you in five weeks," Jeannette said. "Is that enough time for you to prepare?"

"If you write me a couple of songs in the next few weeks it will be. Thanks, Pretty Lady. Remember, two songs," Clay said and left before she could get a word out.

Jeannette dialed the sound booth. "Greg, do you have a minute? I want to talk to you about the sound booth schedule. Thank you."

"Hi, boss," Greg said, sitting in a chair across from Jeannette.

"Clay was just here. He wants to make another album. Will there be some time in the booth for him and The Band in about five weeks?" she inquired.

"Yes, we have some openings. I will pencil Clay in. Could we talk for a few minutes as friends and not employee to the boss?" Greg asked.

"Of course! You know we can always talk about whatever is on your mind," Jeannette reminded him.

"I'm not sure how to say this, so I will just come out with it. The clients have noticed your mood. One of the big reasons they come here is because of you and how you relate to them. Always smiling, a friendly and caring attitude," Greg cited.

Again, the tears ran down her cheeks. "Clay just said the same thing to me. I know it has been a few years since Robert passed, but he was my heart, my life, my happiness. I know I need to move on, so I am calling a counselor right away," Jeannette promised.

"You know I say it out of love and concern for you and Windy City, right?" he asked.

"Of course, I do! Thank you for being concerned. Bridgett, get me Dr. Lamb's office on the phone, please," Jeannette ordered. She made an appointment for the following morning to start getting her life back.

"I need to get back to work. I am glad you are going to be our old Jeannette soon."

"Bridgett, would you step into my office with my schedule? Thank you. Have a seat. Tomorrow I have an appointment at ten with Dr. Lamb. What does that do to my schedule?"

"How long will you be gone?" Bridgett questioned.

Jeannette thought and answered, "Probably until eleven-thirty."

"You had one appointment. I can push that one to twelve," Bridgette said.

"Good. Would you call Dr. Lamb's office back and make another appointment for two weeks from now? Make it a week from now. I want my life back," Jeannette said sternly.

"I am so glad to hear that, Jeannette!" Bridgett exclaimed.

"Matter of fact, I am going to do something I have not done in far too long. Wait a minute. Do I have anything scheduled for this afternoon?" Jeannette inquired.

"You have a meeting in fifteen minutes. After that, your afternoon is clear," Bridgett assured her.

"Call David for me and have him pick me up in an hour. I am having dinner with Clay and Amy tonight, and I need a new dress," Jeannette said.

As soon as her meeting was over, she left the office.

"David, I need to buy a new dress for dinner tonight. I am going to call Judy and ask if she wants to shop with me, so let's head in her direction while I call her." David nodded. "Judy, this is Jeannette. Yes, it's been a while. I need a new dress. Do you want to do a little shopping with me?"

"When?" Judy asked excitedly.

"I am on my way to your house right now. We should be there in fifteen minutes," Jeannette announced.

"Oh! Yes, I want to go! I have to run a comb through my hair, change my clothes . . . I will be ready!" Judy hung up abruptly.

"Keep going, David. She is coming with me," Jeannette instructed.

Judy was standing on the sidewalk, waiting, when the car pulled up. She did not wait for David to open the door for her. Judy was inside sitting next to Jeannette before he could open his own door. She reached over and grabbed Jeannette to hug her tightly.

"I am so excited! I don't remember the last time we did this!" Judy shouted.

"It has been too long. David, let's go to the boutique where we like to shop. Do you remember the one I am talking about?" she proposed.

"Yes. We will be there in twenty minutes." He smiled at the giddy women in the rearview mirror.

"What have you been doing for fun? Tell me everything," Judy inquired excitedly.

"To tell the truth, this is the first thing I have done for fun. I have been working and taking care of the estate in Oregon. I have decided it is time I find some happiness in my life. Right now, is the beginning," she stated.

"You bet it is! We are going to shop until we drop, get back up, and shop some more!" Judy declared.

"Judy, you are crazy! I love it! Listen, I need a dress to go to dinner tonight with Clay and Amy. He told me to get dressed up. I have no idea where we are going," Jeannette explained.

"Sounds mysterious. Have no fear. We will pick out the perfect dress. Oh! Here we are!" Judy said, surprised they had arrived so quickly.

David opened the door for the thrilled women who were in shopping mode.

"Will you pick us up in two hours?" Jeannette requested.

"Yes, Jeannette. Have fun," he said with a wink.

"This store has no idea who has come to shop," Judy said and threw open the doors.

They tried on so many outfits they lost track and tried one on for a second time. A few jokes and laughs directed at several articles of clothing that were (in their opinion) ugly, gave the clerks cause to shoot them disapproving glances. It only made them snicker and giggle harder.

Jeannette decided on a dress and two other outfits. Judy came away with only one. She was having too much fun watching Jeannette try on clothes while she critiqued.

"Oh! David should be here. Right on time. We have to go," Jeannette told Judy.

"Hello, ladies. It looks like you were successful," David said.

"We were. Let's go to our favorite place where we usually drink wine with lunch," Jeannette suggested. "We have a little time to kill before we need to take you home, Judy."

"I'm in! David, to the wine place!" Judy shouted.

"Right away, ladies," David replied with a chuckle and a smile.

One full bottle of wine had only a drop left. Between Judy and Jeannette, they drank it all before David arrived in the town car. He opened the door, and the two giggling women glided onto the backseat.

David pulled away from the curb then looked at Jeannette in the mirror with a huge grin on his face and said, "It is nice to hear you laugh again."

"It feels good. You should have seen the clerks stare at us in the store. Once we started laughing, we couldn't stop. Everything was funny," Jeannette said and massaged her cheeks trying to make the pain stop.

"You have to admit some of those outfits were god-awful," Judy proclaimed.

"Who would wear those things?" Jeannette asked. They looked at each other and started laughing all over again.

"Looks like I'm home. Thank you for the fun afternoon. Keep laughing, my friend," Judy suggested.

Jeannette was quiet on the way home. "Are you okay back there?" David asked.

"Yes. I am feeling a little guilty for having fun, but it was so good to laugh. I keep telling myself Robert would want me to be happy. Then I feel bad again. It is a vicious circle. Did Bridgett give you the address of the restaurant?" Jeannette asked.

"She did," David replied.

"What is the name of it? I forgot." Jeannette asked, slyly.

"It is a surprise, and you know I am sworn to secrecy," David said. "Nice try."

"I gave it a shot. If you pick me up at six forty-five, will that be enough time to arrive at seven?"

"That would be plenty of time to get you there. Would you like me to carry your bags in for you?" David asked.

"No, thank you."

The dress Jeannette bought was royal blue velvet, floor-length, with an empire waist. It was gathered slightly just below the bust with three rows of rhinestones emphasizing her slender figure. It was straight with a slit up the right leg that stopped three inches above her knee. Her shoulders were bare except for tiny straps attached to the dress. For accessories, she wore a simple necklace of one diamond with earrings to match. On her wrist was a small gold watch. A royal blue shawl was added to the ensemble to make sure she didn't get chilled. For shoes, she chose a beige pair of heels.

Jeannette stood before the mirror, staring at herself, being pleased with what she chose to wear.

"I hope I am dressed correctly for the restaurant. Clay said, to get dressed up. Ready or not, it's time to go."

"Good evening, Jeannette. You look stunning," David said.

"Have I dressed appropriately for the restaurant?" she asked.

"Perfectly," David assured her.

A few minutes later Jeannette was walking in the door of My City Restaurant. It opened into a dimly lit waiting area that was as big as a small restaurant. It had a desk for the headwaiter, a bar area with tall tables where patrons were standing enjoying a drink while waiting for their dining room table. Several overstuffed chairs awaited patrons in an area for others who were chatting with friends standing next to more tall tables with their drinks. There were bouquets on shelves with grapes hanging from them. Beautiful paintings of children playing and others of mountain scenes hung strategically in the waiting area.

"What name is your reservation under, madam?" the headwaiter asked.

"Clay," she replied.

"Your party is already here. I will show you to the gentleman's table."

Jeannette followed the waiter and looked around the room. It was a huge dining area. The tables had white linen tablecloths, a small bouquet of assorted fresh flowers with a tall slender candle shooting up from the middle, wine glasses, water glasses, a place setting of assorted silverware, white with gold-rimmed plates, linen napkins, and a wine list. There was a dance floor the tables encircled. Just beyond that was a stage with a live band playing soft big band music behind a sheer curtain. Across the room were huge windows which looked out over the city showing off the splendor of lights the city offered. It took her breath away. She had never been to such a beautiful restaurant.

"Jeannette! You are gorgeous this evening," Clay said. He greeted her with a hug and a kiss on the cheek.

"Clay, you are very handsome in a suit. Amy, your red dress is beautiful. That is a great color on you," Jeannette complimented.

Clay politely dismissed the waiter and held a chair for Jeannette himself. "May I pour you a glass of wine?" Clay asked.

"Yes, please. Clay, this place is phenomenal. I have never heard of My City. How did you find it?" Jeannette questioned.

"The owner is an old friend of Amy's. She gave him a call and asked if he had an open table this evening. It's usually a long wait to get a reservation," Clay told her.

"Thank you, Amy, for arranging this evening," Jeannette began. "It is beautiful. The live band is a very nice touch. The way this room is set up reminds me of the old movies from the thirties and forties that took place in nightclubs. There was dancing to big bands playing and a floor show during and after dining. I always wished there were places like those old night clubs. I even daydreamed of opening one someday. Now I can say one exists and I love it!" She tried to take it all in, but there was so much to see, it was difficult.

Clay looked up from his wine and beyond Jeannette to see the owner, Mark. Clay lifted his glass to Mark as a symbol of thanks.

Clay stood to greet him and said, "Mark! Thank you for finding us a table this evening. We brought a special friend with us this evening. Jeannette, this is Mark, the owner of this gorgeous establishment. Mark, this is Jeannette, owner of Windy City Publishing and Recording."

"So, this is the Jeannette I have heard about. You are more beautiful than Clay and Amy had told me."

Mark took her hand in his and gently kissed it. A spark of some kind radiated through her. He looked into Jeannette's eyes and stopped, not able to look away. She wondered if he had felt the same pang she had. Clay cleared his throat and brought Mark's attention back to the noise of the room.

"Well . . . It is lovely to meet you, Jeannette. I hope you enjoy the evening with us tonight. If there is anything I can get you, please let me or your waiter know. Clay, Amy, it is good to see you as always. Enjoy your dinner," Mark said and gave Clay a wink before leaving the table.

Jeannette watched as he walked away. "He seems like a very nice man and handsome too. I should have asked him what he recommended for dinner." She stopped and looked at Clay and Amy. They sat there with grins staring at Jeannette. "Wait a minute! Did you arrange to have dinner here to introduce me to Mark?"

"He is a very nice man, single, and you can tell he has good taste," Amy said.

"I should have known you had an ulterior motive, Clay," Jeannette said sternly.

"Now, sweetheart, I just wanted you to meet. That's all. If something more comes about, that's up to you. I just wanted to put the ball in your court," Clay said.

"I don't know if I am ready for the ball, or if I want to be ready. I will let you know after the evening is over if I want to thank you. What do you suggest for dinner?" she asked.

The evening was lovely, and the dinner was delicious. The conversation never lagged. Jeannette's wine glass never emptied. A waiter kept pouring wine throughout the evening until Jeannette finally said, "No more for me, thank you." Following dessert, they enjoyed a cup of coffee. It was just what she needed after drinking so much wine.

She leaned back in her chair, feeling content. She saw Clay looking toward the door with a larger-than-life grin. She turned to see what had sparked his smile this time. It was The Band, Clay's band. He waved them to the table. The waiter gathered chairs for the group to sit and enjoy a cup of coffee with Jeannette, Clay, and Amy.

Suddenly, from the stage, they heard Mark's voice on the microphone.

"Good evening, ladies and gentlemen. It is nice to see so many of you here tonight. I have a guest here this evening who I would like to introduce. Clay, would you please come to the stage?" Clay wiped his mouth with his linen and walked to the stage. "Clay is a good friend of mine, and I am going to ask a favor of him. I saw your band came along with you this evening. Would you mind playing one song for us tonight?"

"Band? What do you say? Do you feel like one song?" Clay asked. The band immediately stood and made their way to the stage. The audience broke into applause. "Mark, I had a suspicion you might ask us to play, so we brought our instruments along. While the band is getting ready, if it is alright with you, Mark, I would like to ask a special and very talented friend to join us. She wrote the song we are about to perform, and it is not right if she doesn't help us out. She writes music and owns Windy City Publishing and Recording. Ladies and gentlemen, I would like to introduce Jeannette. Would you please join us?"

Jeannette could not move, and her jaw gaped open. She felt her face drain of blood. At first, she shook her head no, then the audience erupted into applause. Amy gave her a wink and shook her head, yes for encouragement. Reluctantly Jeannette made her way through the tables and to the stage where Mark took her hand to help her up three steps to the stage.

She stood beside Clay and whispered, "I don't have my guitar."

She heard a voice from behind her say, "Jeannette, I believe this is yours." Mark said and handed the guitar to her before leaving the stage.

She strapped on her guitar. Once again, she whispered to Clay, "You had this planned. We are going to have a serious conversation about this." He chuckled at her. "What are we playing?"

"The first song you wrote. Do you remember that one?" Clay said and gave her a wink. Without hesitation, after Clay counted them down, The Band began the intro. He gave Jeannette a nod, and she began to sing.

The song ended. All over the room, men and women stood to their feet to applaud in appreciation. Jeannette unstrapped her guitar to return to her seat with Amy.

To her surprise, Clay took the microphone and said, "Don't get in a hurry, Pretty Lady. If it is okay with Mark and these lovely people, we can do one more song. This time we will rock this place!" Mark gave him the okay, and the audience applauded one more time. She re-strapped her guitar and waited for Clay.

"This next song is another one written by Jeannette."

Clay broke into a solo on his guitar as a challenge to Jeannette halfway through the song. The drummer kept the beat, the bass and rhythm guitar chimed in, and the piano came in with chords to round out the music. Clay turned to Jeannette. She knew it was her turn to answer his dare. The audience disappeared, and it was only the music, her guitar, and Clay. Nothing else existed. She blew him away with his guitar challenge and ended the song.

The music was silent, but not the audience. Mark walked to the microphone. "That was wonderful! What did you think, ladies and gentlemen?"

Every person rose to their feet as they showed their appreciation. Clay, The Band, and Jeannette took several bows before leaving the stage. Mark helped Jeannette with her guitar and walked her off stage.

"Jeannette, before you go back to your table, may I ask you if I could take you out to a show or dinner sometime?" Mark inquired.

The question took her by complete surprise. "I . . . I . . . I think that would be nice. Give me a call at Windy City. I am there every other week. This week I will be in my office through Friday. Saturday I am flying to Oregon."

"Thank you. I will call you," Mark said.

She walked back to the table and gave Clay a look of 'you are in trouble.' Clay laughed at her and Amy joined in.

"Hey, Pretty Lady, I saw Mark talking to you. Everything okay?"

"Yes, I think. Mark asked if I would like to go to a show or dinner with him sometime."

"What did you say?" Amy asked with excitement.

"I don't know why, but I said yes. What have I done?" Jeannette began to panic. "Amy! Why did I say, yes? He is going to call me. Am I ready for this?"

Amy was simply giddy. "You said yes, so I believe you are. Oh, Jeannette, that's wonderful! He is a good man. You two will make a very handsome couple."

Jeannette started fanning herself, trying to cool her hot cheeks.

One by one The Band joined them at the table for another cup of coffee.

The drummer said, "Clay, she took you down! Jeannette won that war!"

"Now, I don't know about that. Jeannette's pretty good, but I do a fine job too. I think it was a draw," Clay countered.

The bass player chimed in, "No, no, Clay. She smoked you!"

"Maybe that will teach you to surprise a girl," Jeannette said, enjoying getting a jab in.

"Okay, okay, I will give it to Jeannette. I concede," Clay said, holding his hands up in defeat. They all laughed after humbling Clay.

"Oh, I need to call David to let him know I will be taking a cab home. I don't want him to have to take me home this late at night."

"Isn't that his job?" Clay asked.

"Yes, but that does not mean I should be inconsiderate. Excuse me. I will be right back," Jeannette answered.

Clay shook his head and said, "She is one of a kind. It is no wonder her employees love her. I don't think anyone has ever quit their job at Windy City since she took over."

Mark put a hand on Clay's shoulder and asked, "Did Jeannette leave already?"

"No. Jeannette needed to call David, her driver. She decided to take a taxi home," Amy said, hoping she had planted a seed in Mark's mind about taking Jeannette home. "Here she comes."

Mark hurried to greet her before she returned to the table. "I understand you require a way home. I am available to see you home safely. I would be honored to drive you."

"I cannot take you away from your restaurant just to take me home. It is not necessary. I will take a taxi," Jeannette replied.

"It may not be necessary, but I would enjoy accompanying you to your door," Mark said.

"Um, we just met. I don't know you."

"I assure you I will be a gentleman," Mark promised.

"I might accept your offer after I check you out with Clay and Amy." That made Mark laugh out loud. He shook his head yes and pulled her chair out.

"What was all that? He wasn't bothering you, was he?" Clay asked with a stern look on his face. The Band followed suit.

"No. Mark was not bothering me. He asked if he could drive me home. I told him I might accept his offer after I checked him out with you and Amy." The table broke into laughter.

"I assure you, Pretty Lady, he is a good man. He will treat you with respect as a lady should be, or I would have never introduced the two of you. What do you think, Amy?" Clay asked.

"I agree with Clay. Let him take you home. If you get to know him a little better this evening, your first date will not be as awkward."

"Let me ask you something, Amy. Are you already planning my wedding to Mark?" Jeannette asked.

"Did I hear my name?" Mark asked, making her jump.

"Yes, you did. I was checking with Clay and Amy to see what they thought of you. I told you I would check you out. One more question. Are you an ax murderer?" Jeannette asked.

Mark threw his head back and laughed, then said, "No, I have not murdered anyone with an ax or with anything else. Did I meet with your approval?"

"I am sitting on the fence, but I think I will take a chance and allow you to take me home."

Mark's face lit up and broke into a smile from ear to ear. "Are you ready to leave?" Mark asked.

"Yes. It is getting late, and I need to be in the office early."

"Give me five minutes, Jeannette. I need to let my manager know I will be leaving for a little while. Do not leave! I will be right back," Mark said and hurried off.

"Well, I didn't scare him off. He might be alright after all," Jeannette commented.

He was back in three minutes. "I did not want you to wait or sneak out without me. I am happy to see you are still here. Are you ready?"

"Yes. Clay, Amy, thank you for an interesting evening. Clay, you and I are going to talk," Jeannette said, pointing at him. "Goodnight, everyone."

Mark put her shawl around her shoulders before they left the restaurant. He whispered something to the valet that had him scurrying off.

His car pulled up as they walked out the door. It was a jet-black sports car. She was not sure of the make, but it was beautiful. The lines were sleek, it had shiny silver rims, and the body of the car glistened in the night lights. Through the opened sunroof, sounds of soft music played on the stereo and filled the night air. Mark opened the door for Jeannette. A strong whiff of leather danced in her nostrils. She slipped onto the passenger seat that felt like pure luxury had enveloped her.

After settling behind the wheel, Mark asked, "Where do you live?"

"Oregon," Jeannette said with a straight face.

"Excuse me?"

"Every other week or so, I live in Chicago in an apartment, but my home is in Oregon," she answered.

"Oh. Let me be more precise. What is your address in Chicago?" Mark inquired, appreciating her dry humor. Jeannette smiled and gave him the address. "That is not far from here. I was hoping it would take a little longer so we could get to know each other."

"Well, if you can be away from the restaurant for a little while, maybe we could take a drive by the lake?" Jeannette suggested.

"Would you mind?" he asked.

"Not at all, but if you are a murderer, you need to take me home now," she retorted.

"I promise I am not a murderer. I love your sense of humor. You play and sing wonderfully. I enjoyed both of your songs. Did I tell you I think you are beautiful? Inside and out?" Jeannette blushed and looked down at her hands. "Are you blushing? I didn't think women blushed anymore."

"Maybe not. I don't mean to, it just happens. I didn't have a lot of compliments growing up or in my young adult life. I get embarrassed because I do not know how to react."

"When you are around me, you will have to get used to it," he said with conviction. "Lakeshore Drive is so beautiful at night. It is so clear this evening the moon is glistening off the lake," Mark observed.

Jeannette sat back, comfortable in her seat, watching the view of the lake. Without realizing it, she had kicked off her shoes and was completely relaxed.

A memory was beginning to develop until Mark brought her back to reality. "Jeannette? Jeannette, is everything all right?"

"Huh? Oh, yes! Sorry. I was enjoying the scenery, and my mind drifted. I did not mean to be rude."

"You are anything but rude. I would say you are feeling quite comfortable right now. Were your shoes hurting your feet?" Mark questioned.

"What? My shoes?" Jeannette asked in confusion.

"You kicked off your shoes a few minutes ago," Mark said and pointed to her feet.

Jeannette looked down to see her bare feet. With a beet-red face, she said, "Oh! I did not realize I did that! It is time you took me home."

"There is no reason for you to be embarrassed. It makes me feel good you are so comfortable with me that you let me see your naked feet," Mark said giving her a sly look as if she had shown him something that should have stayed hidden. They both burst out laughing.

Mark walked her to the door of her apartment building to make sure she was delivered home safely. Sid, the doorman, opened the door, tipped his hat, and smiled at Mark.

"Thank you for seeing me home, Mark. You have a lovely restaurant. I will certainly visit there again."

"I hope you do. Call me any time you would like to have dinner at My City, and I will make sure you have a table. Here is my card. Goodnight." He took her hand and gently kissed it. Jeannette felt a shiver up her spine. "Are you cold? You are shaking."

To cover up her real feelings, she said, "A little. Goodnight." She turned and stepped into the elevator. Mark watched as the doors closed with his hands in his pockets. A sudden pang of loneliness grabbed his heart.

"She is a sweet woman," Sid said. "A special woman."

"I am beginning to see that," Mark replied. "Goodnight." One more time, Sid tipped his hat to Mark.

The next morning David picked up Jeannette to take her to the office. He could see she was preoccupied but started to chat anyway.

"Did you enjoy the restaurant last night?"

"Huh? Oh, yes. It was beautiful. Did you know Clay was going to get me on stage?" she questioned.

"No! My job was to get you there. Did you perform with Clay?" David asked.

"I could hardly say no in front of all those people," Jeannette said, trying to hold back a smile. She enjoyed herself tremendously once she started to play, and the nervousness was gone. "That was the first time I had played on stage since before Robert passed. I didn't think I would ever pick up my guitar again. Do you know what, David? I loved it! I had a great time."

"Good for you! It shows on your face. Is there something else you have on your mind? You are not your usual chatty self," he asked.

"Since I got back to Chicago, I have had an uneasy feeling about something, and I can't put my finger on it. Maybe I can shake it off at work. Oh! That reminds me. I have an appointment at ten, so I need you to pick me up at 9:30. Thanks, David."

She went through her usual routine, unlock the door, relock the door, make coffee in her office, open the file cabinet, get out files, turn on the computer, and start to work while the coffee pot did its job.

Sitting back in her chair, she looked to the ceiling and said, "Robert, what is going on with me? What should I know? This feeling isn't normal for me to be uneasy this long and not know what is happening. Can you give me any hints?" She paused, hoping for a sign. "I guess not."

The coffee pot dinged signaling the end of brewing. With coffee in hand, she dug into paperwork until it was time to leave for her appointment with Dr. Lamb.

"Bridgett, I am leaving for my appointment with Dr. Lamb. I should be back in a couple of hours."

"Okay, Jeannette."

Jeannette walked out to meet David at the car and said, "I have an appointment with Dr. Lamb. Do you remember where his office is?"

"Yes, I do." He shut her door and hurried around the car to the driver's side. He slid behind the wheel and reached for the shifter when suddenly Jeannette's door flew open, and a strange man forced his way into the car. He hit her with a tackle maneuver that threw her to the other side of the vehicle. Her head hit hard against the glass and jammed her shoulder against the door. She saw stars as she crumpled in the seat. David turned as fast as he could in the seat, trying to help Jeannette, but it was too late. He met with the blade of a knife that was at least ten inches long and stuck in his face.

The strange man said through clenched teeth, "Don't you dare try anything, or I will cut her and then you! Drive!" he shouted.

"Where?"

"Drive! I will tell you when to stop!" the dirty man demanded.

"Jeannette? Jeannette, are you alright?" David asked with panic in his voice.

"I . . . Um . . . I think so," she said through grogginess.

"Shut up! You owe me money. You over-privileged, good-for-nothing bitch! You are going to pay me what Jeff owes me!"

"Who are you? I don't owe you anything! Get out of this car!" Jeannette demanded.

He wielded his knife close to Jeannette's face, so there was no mistaking that he meant business.

"You owe me a lot of money! Jeff told me to collect it from you. He said you had plenty of money! You are rich!"

"First of all, I have not been married to Jeff in years. Whatever bill you are trying to collect is his responsibility, not mine. Now get out!" Jeannette screamed and tried to give him a kick to no avail.

David made a sharp turn to the left, hoping it would get the stranger away from Jeannette. Unfortunately, he managed to recover quickly and take a swipe at Jeannette. The knife met with a slashing movement to the sleeve of her coat. The blade cut through the sleeve of her jacket and gashed her arm down to the bone. Jeannette screamed in pain.

"I told you, pretty boy, I would cut her! Do that again, and next time it will be a lot worse for both of you! Let's get down to business. Let me jog your memory. Do you remember that business lunch you had with Jerry and a client? You came to the desk to pay? The clerk called you by name?"

"That was you! Certainly, a lot cleaner at that time than you are now. You smell!" Jeannette yelled and curled up her nose.

"Shut up! Jeff hired me to watch you and report everything back to him. I did my job. He didn't pay me for my work. So, YOU owe me!" the furious man yelled.

"You are out of your mind if you think I am going to pay you one dime for stalking me! You are out of your mind! Get off me!" Jeannette yelled and gave him a kick in the leg as hard as she could. He screamed in agony. She pulled herself up to a sitting position in the seat.

"I warned you!"

In the blink of an eye, he stabbed her in the arm that was already bleeding with great force. Jeannette screamed. There was blood everywhere. David slammed on the brakes sending the madman into the back of the front seat, landing him on the floorboard. It rattled him enough that it took him a few seconds to recover. His hand had relaxed sufficient enough and Jeannette grabbed the knife from him and kicked him in the face. It did not knock him out but stunned him enough for her to get the upper hand.

"David! Find a cop! Do something to get their attention!" Jeannette dug her foot into his shoulder and held on to his left arm, pulling as hard as she could to hold him in place while David drove like a maniac to get attention. It worked. A siren blared, and lights flashed behind the car. He pulled to the curb and stopped abruptly.

David jumped out of the car and ran to the police cruiser. "Help her! Please! Help her! He's got a knife! She needs an ambulance!"

"Calm down, buddy. What's the problem?" the police officer asked as he slowly got out of the patrol car.

"Please, in the car, hurry!" David yelled and threw open Jeannette's door.

She had the knife in her hand, her foot planted hard on the dirty man's shoulder, still pulling on his arm, rendering him motionless. Even though his face was pressed against the seat, it did not stop him from screaming profanities at the top of his lungs.

The officer and his partner saw the knife and drew their guns. "Drop the knife!" Jeannette did as she was told.

"She is the one the man attacked! HE is the one who stabbed HER!" David yelled and pointed to the crumpled up, screaming man.

The officers cautiously approached the car on either side. "Are you the driver?"

"Yes! Help her!" David yelled, frantically.

One officer opened the opposite door and found a crazy man balled up on the floor, howling in pain. Jeannette had no intention of letting go until the officer was in control.

"You can let him go now, miss. Let him go. I have him," the officer said. She let go and leaned back.

Her face turned white, and her breathing was labored. "David. Help me," Jeannette said.

He rushed to her side. "Jeannette! You have lost a lot of blood! She needs an ambulance!"

"One is on the way. I need you to tell me what happened," the officer said.

"That man attacked her and stabbed her!" David pointed at the dirty guy who was now in custody. "Jeannette, stay awake. I am going to put pressure on your arm to stop the bleeding until the ambulance gets here. I am sorry that hurts, Sweetie."

"Are you okay? Did he hurt you, David?" Jeannette asked.

"No. I am fine. Not a scratch. It should have been me that got hurt," David confessed.

"Well, that's just crazy talk. The man didn't want you. He wanted me," Jeannette said.

"Cuff him and put him in the back of the car. We will hold him until we can sort all this out," the officer said. "We will have to get him checked out by the EMTs after the female is taken care of."

The ambulance arrived within a few minutes but seemed like a short lifetime.

"Over here! She has a stab wound on her right arm! Help her!" David shouted frantically.

"Step back, sir. Let me get to her. It looks like you have been in a fight, miss. Who won?" the EMT asked.

"I did, of course. The man smelled bad," Jeannette said and passed out.

"Let's get her to the hospital. She has several lacerations," the EMT said to his partner.

"Where are you taking her?" David asked as he trotted alongside the gurney.

"Legacy. I need to know her name," the EMT demanded.

"Jeannette. Her name is Jeannette. Here is one of her cards. I will meet you at the hospital as soon as I make a call to notify her assistant," David said. The ambulance sped off with the siren blaring and Jeannette inside.

"Sir, I am going to need a written statement from you and the lady. For now, tell me what happened," the officer asked.

David recounted the attack as quickly as possible so he could get to the hospital. The officers took the attacker to the precinct to hold him until they had a written statement from both David and Jeannette. Before he left for the hospital, David called Windy City from the car to provide them with the news about Jeannette.

After explaining what happened, he asked, "Bridgett, Jeannette had an appointment that we didn't make. Will you call them for her? Thanks. I will keep you posted," David promised.

David arrived at the hospital in time to see Jeannette on a gurney and being quickly wheeled down a hall. "Excuse me! Hey! Where are you taking her?"

"Are you a relative, sir?" a nurse asked.

"No. I am Jeannette's driver. I was in the car when all this happened. Where are you taking her?"

"We are taking her to surgery to repair the damage to her arm. We need to hurry. She has lost a lot of blood, and she could lose the use of her arm if we don't repair it right away. Someone will tell you when she is out of surgery. Wait in the waiting room down the hall," the nurse ordered.

The next hour was spent on the phone talking to Sean, Tyler, and Bridgett.

"Is there someone here for Jeannette?" a nurse in scrubs asked.

David hurried to her and said, "Yes, I am. How is she?"

"She is holding her own. She might need a transfusion. We need permission from a family member. Are you family?"

"No, but I can get one of her sons on the phone for you," David said and dialed the phone. "Sean, I am going to give the phone to a nurse. She needs your permission to give Jeannette a transfusion if she needs it."

"Hello. Is this a relative of Jeannette's? To whom am I speaking? Good. Do you give us permission for a transfusion if she needs it? Thank you." She handed the phone back to David and started to leave the room.

"Wait! How much longer will she be in surgery?" David asked.

"This is a very intricate and delicate repair the neurosurgeon is performing. It could take, at the very least, a couple more hours. We will let you know when it is over," the nurse said and left.

"Did you hear all that, Sean? Yes, she is holding her own. She has the best surgeon working on her. I know she will be fine. Will you call Tyler for me? I need to make more calls. Thanks." David paced as he talked on the phone. "Bridgett, I just talked to the nurse. Jeannette is holding her own but expected to be in surgery another couple of hours."

"Clay was in to see Jeannette about thirty minutes ago," Bridgett said. "I told him what happened. He should be arriving at the hospital any minute. After we close, I will be headed in your direction also. Do you need anything?"

"I could use some aspirin and a beer," David said.

Bridgett let out a little nervous chuckle and said, "I can take care of the aspirin, but the beer will have to wait. I should be there by the time she is out of surgery."

"Thanks. Bye." It suddenly occurred to David he forgot to call his wife. "Oh, no! She is not going to be happy with me. Hi, honey. Listen, I have got a story to tell you. Sit down and listen." He told the story once again.

"David! Are you alright? Did you get hurt? How is Jeannette? Should I come to the hospital?" Raelene shouted into the phone.

"Raelene! Honey. I am fine, not a scratch on me. Jeannette is in surgery and will be for a couple more hours. You do not need to come to the hospital, but I will not stop you if you want to. If you do, smuggle me in a beer, will you? My nerves are shot. Thanks, honey. I love you. Bye."

David finally sat down just in time to stand back up to greet Clay.

"Where is Jeannette?" Clay asked, holding David by the shoulders.

"She is still in surgery. A neurosurgeon is repairing the damage done to her right arm. She lost a lot of blood and might need a transfusion. A little while ago, a nurse told me it would be another two hours or so, and she was holding her own."

"My Lord! What happened?" David went through the entire story again, explaining how Jeannette hit and held the intruder down until the police got there.

"What a woman!" Clay roared with a big smile. "Excuse me a minute. I need to make a couple of calls. I will be right back."

David nodded and sat in the nearest chair. His stomach was about to get rid of everything he had consumed earlier in the day when Raelene walked in. She rushed to him and threw her arms around him. David relaxed for the first time since the incident.

"Raelene, you didn't have to come, but I am so glad you did," David said with relief in his voice.

"Guess what I have in my purse? I poured a beer in your metal to-go coffee cup," Raelene giggled.

"Is there a David here?" a man in a suit inquired standing in the doorway to the waiting room.

"I am David."

"David, I am Detective Ben Alto. I am here to take your statement about the stabbing earlier today. You did a great job holding him until the officers got there. He is a wanted man. He has been assaulting women all over the city. We have been trying to catch him. Thanks for the assist."

"Detective, you have the wrong information. I was there, but I was not the one who held him down. Jeannette did. She is in surgery right now. I was driving and could not do anything to help her. The only thing I could think of after he stabbed her was hit the brakes and get him away from her before he kills her. His head hit the back of the seat and rattled his brain enough that Jeannette managed to grab the knife, held him down with her foot, and with a death grip from her good arm, stretched his arm as far as she could so he couldn't move while blood oozed from her wounds. She is the one to thank," David confessed.

"Really? That is quite a woman. Where did she learn that?" the detective asked.

"I have no idea," David said, shaking his head.

"I need you to write everything down for me and sign it. Here is a tablet. Take your time. I need to talk to Jeannette also. Do you know how much longer it will be before I can talk to her?"

"According to the nurse, she should be out of surgery in about"—David stopped and looked at his watch— "any time." He looked up, and there was the nurse he had talked to earlier.

David rushed to her and with urgency asked, "Nurse, is Jeannette out of surgery? How is she?"

"She is out of surgery. Everything went very well. The surgeon will be in to talk to you in a few minutes."

"Thank you," David said with relief.

Clay came rushing in, "What did she say?"

"She is fine. The doctor will be in shortly to talk to us," David told him. "I think this is him now."

"Are you here for Jeannette?" David nodded his head.

"We all are Doc. How is she?" Clay asked.

"How do you do? I am Dr. Earl. She is doing very well. A transfusion was not needed. I have repaired the damage, but she is going to need physical therapy to regain movement and strength. She also has a bad concussion and severe bruising on her face and left shoulder. It looks like Jeannette took quite a hit. She will need all of you, not just for making sure she gets to therapy, but emotionally too. I was told this woman went through a very traumatic experience. I do not know the whole story, but she must have feared for her life. That has a profound effect on a person. She might be able to go home in a couple of days, maybe longer. It depends on how she progresses. I want to keep an eye on her. Does she have someone at home who can help her?"

David spoke up, "No, but we will take care of that. Probably hire a nurse to stay with her until her sons can get here."

"Thanks, Doc. We appreciate all you have done," Clay said and shook his hand. "When can we see her?"

"She will be in recovery for at least another hour, then taken to a room. A nurse will give you her room number after she is settled. She will still be a little groggy when you see her due to the effects of anesthesia, plus I have given her pain medication to keep her comfortable. She is not to go back to work for at least ten days. No work, only rest. I want to see her in my office in a week. Do not worry if you forget these instructions. It will be in her release papers along with an appointment time and a prescription for pain medicine."

"Will she be able to play the guitar again?" Clay asked with great concern.

"If she follows my instructions and does her physical therapy, she should be able to do everything she did before, including playing the guitar," Dr. Earl told them. David vigorously shook the hand of Dr. Earl in gratitude before he left the group with a smile on his face.

"Thank God!" David exclaimed. He turned to Raelene and said, "I felt so helpless. He kept threatening me if I did anything wrong, he was going to, in his words, 'cut her and then me.' At one point, I tried making a sharp turn to get him away from her. He retaliated by slashing her arm through her coat! I was so scared for her. Then when he stabbed her, she screamed, and I reacted by slamming on the brakes. That was when Jeannette grabbed the knife and held him down while I got the attention of a patrol car. You know the rest," David said and hung his head.

There was a brief moment of silence before Clay said, "David, you can't blame yourself. You acted responsibly and did what you could in that situation. You and Jeannette worked as a team in that car. Sit down. It's all over. She is going to be fine. I am concerned about you at the moment. You are shaking like a leaf. I can't imagine what a horrible experience you both suffered. Try to relax until we get to see her."

"Detective, here is my written statement. Raelene, did you bring aspirin and my coffee mug?" David asked.

"Here it is, honey. Take these and put your head back. Close your eyes. I will be right here." She gently caressed his face to help calm his nerves.

It wasn't long before the waiting room was filled to capacity with Windy City employees with flowers in hand. David told the story again. He received a hug from each one in support. He was so relieved they did not blame him for Jeannette's injury. There was a low murmur amongst the small, crowded waiting room until the nurse came in.

She took a step back and said, "Are you all here for Jeannette?"

In unison, they all said, "Yes!"

"Whoa! She is in room 248. Down the hall to the elevator. On the second floor, when you get off the elevator, turn right. Her room will be halfway down the hall on the right. I will only allow five at a time in her room for five minutes. No more! Does everyone understand? She needs her rest. Follow me to the elevator."

Thirty people filed down the hall behind the nurse. The elevator made three trips to get them all to the second floor. Clay and David were in the first group to see her. Everyone else was standing in the doorway, watching and waiting their turn to talk to her and touch her.

"Oh, honey, I am so sorry about this. You were awesome! You handled that guy like you did that sort of thing every day!" Clay exclaimed.

David stood back looking sheepish. Jeannette focused as well as she could and saw him.

"David." She held her left arm out to hold his hand. "Thank you for saving me. If you had not hit the brakes, I would probably be dead, so thank you."

"I couldn't help you!" David broke down and cried.

"You did help me. That was the only thing you could do in that situation. You did it well and have nothing to feel guilty about or be ashamed of." She squeezed his hand.

"Do you still want me to be your driver?" David asked.

"Of course! I trust you, David. Not only do you drive me, but you are also my friend. I expect you to drive me home when I get out of here. Of course, if you still want the job?"

"I will be here. I will never let this happen again! It looks like our time is up. It is the next group's turn. I will see you tomorrow," David promised.

"If there is anything you need, Pretty Lady, Amy and I are only a phone call away," Clay said and kissed her on the forehead.

By the time everyone from Windy City had left, Jeannette was exhausted. One more person walked in to stand by her bed, holding two dozen red roses. She looked at him and attempted to focus on who he was.

"Mark?" Jeannette asked.

"Yes. Clay called me. I had to see if you were alright. Are you in a lot of pain?"

"Not much. The doctor gave me some great painkillers. I feel goofy," she admitted.

"As soon as you are not goofy and feeling better, I want to take you to dinner. How does that sound?" Mark asked.

"I think it would be better if you kissed me. You are handsome. You have a cute butt. Did you feel that spark? Have I kissed you? Where are you from? Are you real?" Jeannette asked, not consciously knowing what she was saying and slurring her words before falling asleep.

"You are so out of it. I like it. You told me what I wanted to know. Rest and get better so we can have that date," Mark said with a smile. He bent down and kissed her forehead before he left.

During the early hours of the morning, she woke up abruptly, not knowing where she was. "Hello!" she yelled. "Hello! Is anyone there?"

A nurse came running in and said, "Hello, Jeannette. Are you in pain? What can I do for you? My name is Anna. Do you know where you are?"

It took her a moment to familiarize her surroundings. "I am in a hospital," she said. Her heart was pounding, and her breathing was labored.

"That's right. Do you know why?"

She looked at her arm and saw all the bandages, "Oh. I was stabbed. That man really stunk. Whew!"

Anna giggled and said, "I am your nurse tonight. On a scale from one to ten, what is your pain level? Ten being the worst pain in your life."

"That must have been what woke me up. About a six and climbing," Jeannette said.

"I will get you something for the pain. I will be right back," Anna said. Jeannette slipped in and out of consciousness until the nurse returned with a shot in her hand.

"I am going to put this in your IV. You are going to get sleepy. It will not take long. If you need me, press this button." She put the call button in Jeannette's hand. Anna stayed by her side until the medicine kicked in.

Anna was right. She was out like a light for the next four hours. It was morning when Jeannette opened her eyes. The first thing she saw was the red roses sitting on the tray table in front of her. She pushed the call button.

"Good morning. My name is Justine. I will be your nurse for the day. I understand you met Anna last night. She will be back this evening. What can I do for you?"

"I am hungry, I think. Could I get some fruit, toast, and coffee? Before you go, is there a card with the roses on the tray?" Jeanette asked.

Justine pulled out a card and handed it to Jeannette. "Here it is. Those are beautiful. You have a lot of flowers. Do you want all the cards?"

"Not right now, thank you. Could you read this card for me? I can't seem to focus."

"Sure. It says,"

For you Jeannette,

Get well so I can take you on that date.

Mark

"You have an admirer who has great taste in flowers," Justine said.

"I guess so," Jeannette said, looking a little confused.

"Before I get you something to eat, what is your pain level?"

Jeannette thought for a second and said, "It is tolerable for now. Probably a four. I don't want to go to sleep for a while. That pain medicine really knocks me out."

"It is supposed to so you can relax and heal without suffering through so much agony. I will be back in a jiffy with your food. Here is the TV remote."

She thought to herself, "Hum. Red roses. I just met him. Let's see what the news is this morning."

The TV came on with a female news anchor for Around Town announcing, "Yesterday there was a frightening event involving Chicago's Windy City Publishing and Recording Company's CEO. The complete details are not known at this time. It is reported that an assailant stabbed her. The wounds are not life-threatening, and she is resting comfortably after surgery. The assailant has been apprehended. We will have more updates as the story unfolds."

"Well, that's just wonderful. I made the news," Jeannette said out loud and shut off the TV. There was a knock on her door even though it was open.

"Jeannette? I don't know if you remember me. I am Detective Alto. We spoke briefly last night."

"You look familiar. I am sorry. I don't remember much."

"That's okay. We have your attacker in jail. He has been assaulting women all over town. We have been trying to catch him. You did us a great service by holding him until the officers arrived on the scene. Do you feel up to giving me a statement? I brought a tape recorder. I can see you are not able to write."

"Yes, I guess. I will tell you what I remember."

Jeannette had a difficult time remembering every detail due to the concussion. The harder she tried putting all the pieces together, the more frustrated she grew, and so did her headache.

Nurse Justine came into the room with a tray of breakfast for Jeannette as promised. "Sir! Can you not see you are upsetting her? She is not ready for this! Leave! Come back later. She needs her rest!"

"I am Detective Alto. I need a statement from her. That's all."

"I don't care who you are. You will have to come back later. Jeannette is not up to answering your questions. Can you NOT see she has a concussion? I will not allow you to upset my patient! Out!" Justine yelled and pointed to the door.

"But this is important," Detective Alto said.

"Her health is more important. Now leave, or I will call security to escort you out," Justine demanded with her hands on her hips. The detective was not happy when he left.

"If I had known that detective was here, he would not have gotten in the door. How is your head feeling? Do you have a headache?"

"I didn't until I tried to remember details of yesterday. Now I do. My head is pounding," Jeannette complained.

"You have a concussion. Working your brain right now is not good for you. It needs to rest, just like your entire body does. Try to calm yourself and eat a little. After that I will give you something for the pain," Justine said.

"A concussion? Really? Ouch! Dang, it! My left arm hurts too. Did I get stabbed in that arm too?" Jeannette asked.

"Let's have a look. No stab wounds, but some really bad bruising. How did you get these?" the nurse asked.

Jeannette wrinkled up her face trying to remember when she heard a familiar voice. "Good morning. How is the patient?" David asked.

"I don't think she should have any visitors right now. Maybe . . ."

"Justine, please let him in. David is my driver and friend who was in the car with me yesterday. David, come over here and let me make sure you were not hurt. Okay, you look fine. Can you tell me how I got a concussion and this bruising? I can't seem to remember," Jeannette questioned.

"When that evil man forced his way in the car, he tackled you like a football player. He struck you so hard your head bounced off the window behind me. Your head cracked the window and your shoulder hit below the window. I think you were unconscious for a brief time." David's face faded from a smile to a frown remembering the sound her head made when it hit the window.

"Oh," was all Jeannette had to say.

"I will let you stay for a short time. Do not upset her. She needs to rest. Jeannette, I will be back in ten minutes with your medication," Justine said and left the room.

"Raelene sends her love. How are you feeling?" David asked.

"In about a week, I will feel much better. Right now? I feel pretty rough. How is the car?"

"The window your head hit is cracked, and there is a lot of blood in the backseat. It will need some repairs," David reported.

"I do not want to be in that car again! It is time for a new one. I will call my accountant today and have him arrange it and give you a call when it is ready. My boys! Did anyone call my boys? We were supposed to have a family week in Oregon! I need to talk to them. Ouch, my head!"

"Don't worry. I have called the boys and told them everything," David reassured her. "Of course, they are worried. I have a suggestion for you. If you ask Bridgett, she could arrange for the boys to fly to Chicago. Then they could take care of you. The doctor said you need someone to stay with you because you will need help. He does not want you to be left alone. It is either the boys, or we hire a nurse. What will it be?" David asked with authority.

"Dial Bridgett for me," Jeannette said, not looking happy while David smiled. "Hi, Bridgett, this is Jeannette. Yes, I am doing okay. I need you to do something for me. I want to fly my boys to Chicago to help me. You already did? You are a jewel.

Sean has a girl he was . . . Yes, Tia. Did you get her a ticket also? You are way ahead of me! Call Tyler and let him know he can bring one friend also. Who is he bringing? Zach? That's who I thought. I am glad one of us is on top of these things. Thank you for doing that. When will they be here? Friday? Red-Eye? Good. I need to hang up for now. Before I go, call the accountant, and tell him to trade my car in and get a new one. Then give David the details. Bye."

David said with concern in his eyes, "Jeannette, you are always taking care of us. It is our turn to take care of you. Raelene has volunteered to stay with you until Sean and Tyler get here Saturday morning. I am picking them up at the airport. See? You do not need to worry about the details. You probably need to call the boys. They want to talk to you."

"In a minute," Jeannette stopped talking to think. When she had gathered her thoughts, she said, "This has taught me something. From this experience, I have learned I have a spark of fire inside me that flares red hot when I need it. It gives me the strength to face any situation. I had no idea I was that strong or knew how to hold that guy down. I amazed myself."

"We all knew you were strong, inside, and out. Now call your boys," David said with a comforting smile.

Justine walked into the room with a shot in her hand. "She can make whatever calls she needs to when she wakes up. She will be asleep in short order. I suggest you say good-bye."

"If it is all right with you, I will stay until she falls asleep," David said.

Jeannette fell asleep, holding David's hand.

14

Three days later on Friday morning, Jeannette was released from the hospital. Clay met David at the hospital to help gather all the flowers and take them to her apartment.

Jeannette grabbed David's arm and said, "Do we have a new car? You better have a new car out there."

"Yes, ma'am! It is a sight to behold."

Justine pushed her in a wheelchair and helped her into the car.

"Remember, Jeannette, do not try to use that arm. Let others help you." Justine looked at David and asked, "There will be someone to help her, right?"

"Yes. My wife Raelene will be with her, and I will check in from time to time."

"Did you get her pain meds from the hospital pharmacy?" David shook his head yes then looked away so he could roll his eyes. "Looks like you are ready to go, Jeannette. Drive as gently as you can. Do not shake her up. You will open up her stitches." David tipped his hat as he walked to the driver's side.

"Are you ready to go home?" David asked Jeannette.

"I am more than ready. By the way, I like the new car."

On the way home, they talked about the new car and its features. David was more excited than she was. Jeannette listened with a smile.

"From now on, I have a separate fob that I will carry with me at all times. That's this thing. When I shut your door, I push a button, and it locks you safely inside. When I get to the driver's side, I will unlock only my door with this button. As soon as I am inside, we are locked in. Does that make you feel safe?"

"Yes, it does. Thank you."

"Max will be sending over one of his team members to stay outside your door tonight. He will post a guard for as long as you want. Are you getting tired? We are almost home. Right around the corner, and here we are. Here comes Sid to help you."

"Miss Jeannette! Let me help you. Easy now," Sid said. Jeannette tried not to flinch when Sid took her left arm to steady the wobbling woman. "Oh! Did I hurt you? I am so sorry."

"It is okay, Sid. I have bruises everywhere. I need to lie down. David, is Raelene here?"

"If you look toward the door, you will see her smiling little face waiting for you," David told her. "Sid, would you mind giving Clay and I a hand with the flowers? There are more bouquets than two men can carry. Thanks."

Raelene was the epitome of help. She cooked lunch and dinner, made sure Jeannette was comfortable at all times, gave her the prescribed medications, helped her with a shower, and getting dressed.

"I do not know what I would do without you. I need to find someone who will help me for a few days with showering and dressing. Those are things my boys will not be doing. I'll call Bridgett," Jeannette said.

"That is not necessary. I would be happy to come over and help you every day with personal things. It would only be a few hours each day. It would be no problem. If you still want someone to come in and help you next week, then you can hire someone, but for now, please let me help?" Raelene asked.

"Are you sure? I will be paying you for your time, and I will not take no for an answer. It is settled. I will accept your help with pay." Raelene opened her mouth to protest, but Jeannette held her hand up to silence her. "You are my paid helper," Jeannette said with authority. "Why don't you invite David over this evening to watch a movie with us? I have popcorn in the cupboard and a stack of movies. You get to choose. There is an extra bedroom down the hall you will be sleeping in so he can spend the night too, if he wants."

"Jeannette," Raelene's voice got quiet as she said, "you don't want to be alone, do you? It is okay and understandable. You are safe. One of your security officers is right outside your door, the building is secure, and I am here with you. Sid is standing guard at the door and will not allow anyone to enter who does not belong in the building. The man that did this to you is in jail. He is not going anywhere. Why don't we make you comfortable on the couch? I will call David and invite him to movie night."

"Thank you for understanding," Jeannette said.

"I just talked to David. He is on his way over. He is even going to stop and get a pizza for us. Popcorn, pizza, and a movie. It doesn't get better than that," Raelene said with a big smile.

"It would be better with beer," Jeannette said with a giggle.

"No doubt, he will bring beer. I know my David."

David chose a comedy from a stack of movies Jeannette had accumulated. Laughing felt wonderful but tiring, and painful. After the movie was over, it was all Jeannette could do to keep her eyes open. Raelene gave her a pain pill and helped her dress for bed. Sleep came quickly.

David was up and gone early the next morning to pick up the young people at the airport. After disembarking the plane, the four were so concerned about getting to Jeannette they almost sprinted across the airport to the awaiting David.

Slightly winded, Sean asked, "How is Mom? Is someone with her? Has she been in a lot of pain? The jerk that did this to her is still in jail, right? If he isn't, I am going to put him in the hospital!"

"Calm down. Your mom is doing well. The pain comes and goes. She handles it very well with pain meds. My wife is with her, and one of her security officers is standing outside the door to her apartment. Yes, the jerk is still in jail. Did I answer all your questions?" David asked.

"Yes, you did. Let's go. I need to see Mom," Tyler said.

"Do not be concerned when I lock you in as I go around to the driver's side. New protocol. It will make it safe for everyone," David explained.

As they drove to Jeannette's apartment, introductions were made to David for Tia and Zach. David explained how their mother did not want to be left alone and to be gentle with her. This event could have a lasting effect on her. Only time will tell.

"I need to warn you, she might look a little rough from bruising, but she is healing," David told them.

The car came to a stop in front of the apartment building. David had never seen anyone exit a vehicle as fast as they did.

"Your bags! You forgot your bags!" David shouted.

The closer they got to seeing Jeannette, the more nervous they grew. The elevator took forever.

"Why do these things go so slow? Come on!" Sean said impatiently.

After being checked out by security, which seemed like it took forever, they were allowed into her apartment. "Mom! Mom! Where are you?" Sean shouted.

"I am right here," Jeannette said, sitting at the kitchen table with a cup of coffee.

Shock set in when they saw Jeannette. Tyler hurried to her and got on his knees. He looked up at her with tears in his eyes.

"Mom, you look so much worse than I thought you would. The side of your face is black-and-blue, your eye is almost swollen shut, your arm is all bandaged and, in a sling, your fingers are swollen, but here you sit smiling." He stopped and looked sideways at her and asked, "Are you on drugs? You can tell me, Mom." That made Jeannette laugh and shake her head yes.

"I want a hug from all of you! A very gentle hug, and don't make me laugh. It hurts my face," she stressed.

Jeannette made introductions around the room for Raelene, and the four took a chair at the table with Jeannette.

"That guy is lucky he is in jail because I would hunt him down and kill him!" Sean announced.

"No, you would not, Sean. I will heal, and he will go to prison. The detective said they needed me to testify at his trial. They are also trying to convince some of his other victims to testify. You look surprised. From what I understand, he has assaulted several other women around town. Though nothing like what he did to me.

He had a grudge. The police thanked me for holding him until an officer cuffed him," Jeannette informed them.

"David said you were a badass!" Zach told Jeannette.

"I don't know, maybe I was. Now you know to never get on my bad side," Jeannette said. Everyone laughed.

"We already knew that Mom. You said he had a grudge. What did you mean? Did you know him?" Tyler asked.

"Sit down. All of you, sit down. Not personally. I think you are old enough now to know what I am about to tell you." She took a breath and began.

"Before Jeff and I divorced, and you two were very young, Jeff hired this guy to stalk me, report back to him every move I made and every person I had contact with. He wanted to know everything." Sean opened his mouth to say something. Jeannette stopped him by saying, "Sean. Stop. Let me finish. Your father was very insecure. He thought I would find someone better and run off with him. Jeff told me that one night when he was drunk and does not remember saying it. He would not allow me to talk to other men or go to home parties at women's houses selling plastic wares and such. The only time he allowed me to play in Clay's band, he had to go with me to keep his eye on me. I lived in fear all the time. He kept me that way on purpose. Jeff made sure he kept me away from everyone, except you two," Jeannette explained and smiled at Sean and Tyler. She took a drink of water and carried on with her story.

"Clay offered me a position in the band. I wanted it so badly! But your father would not allow it. The way he kept me under control after that night was with a threat. If I joined the band, he would take you boys from me, and I would never see you again." They all gasped, including Raelene and David. "I knew his threat held truth. There was no doubt in my mind he would do it just to spite me. He wanted to hurt me."

"I remember the night we saw Clay and The band on TV. Dad told us you played with them once and you were offered a position in the band. He made sure you saw them playing on TV, too. When I asked why you didn't accept Clay's offer, you told us it was not the right time, and your place was at home with us. I heard you crying that night," Tyler said.

"I cried all the way home the night I played with the band. Jeff crushed my dream. I know he enjoyed hurting me. You should have seen the evil smile Jeff gave me that night Clay was on TV. I think he wanted to see if I would tell you about his threat. I kept it to myself because he was your father, and I did not want you to see him in a bad light right then. To get to the end of this old tale, Jeff skipped to Oregon without paying this guy for stalking me. Jeff told him I was rich and to get the money from me. That brings you up to date," Jeannette said with a sigh.

"Why did you let him treat you like that? I knew he was mean to you, but I did not know the extent! You should have told us a long time ago!" Sean said in a raised voice.

"Now what good would that have done? It served no purpose. I knew someday he would show his true colors, and he did. The best thing he ever did for me, for us, was leave. He had me under his thumb for so many years I could not think on my own. He broke me. After he left, I found my old self, partially. Every day is a struggle to stand my ground when I face him. Think about it. If I had not applied for the job at Windy City, where would we be now? I would not own the company or be my own woman. God had a plan. I needed to go through what I did so I would be ready for what was to come. Bitterness was not going to be part of my personality. That emotion takes too much energy. I went through all of the bad stuff to become the woman who attracted Robert. Do you understand? Even though the years have been rough on me, I would not trade them for anything. They made me who I am today," Jeannette explained.

Sean, Tyler, Zach, and Tia stood to put their arms around Jeannette.

"Sean told me you were 'supermom.' I thought he was exaggerating. I was wrong," Tia said, standing to her feet. "I already love and respect you."

Jeannette smiled with a tear in her eye. "Okay, enough of the mushy stuff. Is anyone hungry? Did you eat on the plane?" Jeannette asked.

"I'm starved!" Tyler announced. "Can we order a pizza? We can tell you all about college while we eat."

"Pizza it is, and salad. I want a salad," Jeannette added.

While they ate, there was plenty of laughter and teasing. After a couple of hours, the pain had set in again. She whispered to Raelene, "Is it time for a pain pill?" She shook her head yes and handed her a pill.

"Ladies and gentlemen, I am going to lie down for a while. Don't be alarmed. All this fun has made me tired. I will be up in about an hour. Please enjoy yourselves. You are on vacation."

Tia saw Raelene helping Jeannette walk out of the room. She hurried to the women and said, "Raelene, let me help Jeannette. Please? I want to do this for her."

Raelene looked at Jeannette to see if she was okay with it. Jeannette gave her a nod of approval. She then left and rejoined the group still devouring pizza.

"Tia, now that you are helping to spoil me sit by my bed and tell me about yourself."

"Okay, let's see. I was born and raised in Portland, Oregon. My mother is a physical therapist, and my father is a landscaper. Both still live in Portland. They divorced when I was ten. I spent most of my time with Dad. Mom was always at the hospital, working with the disabled and surgery patients. She did not have much time for me. As soon as I graduated, I went to Eugene to study business law. That is where Sean and I met. We have been together ever since."

Jeannette looked at her and said, "You are a pretty young lady, educated, smart, and from what I have seen, caring. You love my son, don't you?"

"Yes, I do. With all my heart. How did you know that? I have only been here for a few hours," Tia said.

"Sweetheart, it is written all over your face. You glow. I watched you two together. He loves you just as much. What are your plans?" Jeannette said, getting personal.

"Plans? Oh, you mean with Sean. We have not discussed it, but I can tell you I never want to be without him. I cannot imagine my life, minus Sean. No plans yet," Tia said.

"Tia, I am getting groggy, and I am about to fall asleep. Thank you for talking to me." After Jeannette said that she closed her eyes to give into sleep.

Tia slipped quietly out of the room. Sean greeted her, took her by the hand, led her to a quiet area, and said, "Thank you for helping mom. Is she comfortable?"

"She is sleeping. She is a remarkable woman, Sean. Everything you told me about her is true."

"Of course, it is! I don't lie!" That raised a giggle from Tia. "I am worried about her. The things she told us. How can anyone treat another person like Jeff did? I had no idea. Mom gave up her dream for Tyler and me. It makes me feel awful we held her back."

"You should never feel that way! She loved you and Tyler more than music. To her, there was no choice. You guys are the most important things in her life. Look where she is today! She has a company, still writes music, and you told me she played with Clay's band on stage last week. She made the right decision to be your mother. God honored her decision. He did not forget the talent he gave her. Because of what she did, music came back around to her more than tenfold! Your life would have been a lot different not having a loving, strong mother like Jeannette to raise you. You would not have had a happy one, I am sure!" Tia scolded.

"I know you are right. Mom gave up so much for us. It's hard not to feel a little guilty."

"Stop it! If I had children, I would have done the same thing," Tia told Sean.

"I know you are right. I will work on it. I love you, Tia. Let's check on Paul, the guard at the door. We can give him a piece of pizza if Zach and Tyler haven't eaten it all."

Jeannette awoke to a living room full of young adults sleeping. One on a lounge chair, one on the floor, and two cuddled together on the couch.

"How long have they been like this?" Jeannette asked Raelene quietly.

"Not long. Do you want me to stay longer? If not, David and I will leave, and you can enjoy the quiet while you can."

"Could you come by about eight in the morning to help me with a shower?"

"Of course," Raelene answered.

"There is a spare key in the drawer. Take it with you. Thank you so much for all your help."

While the brood napped, Jeannette attempted typing on the computer with only her left hand. It was a challenge and took four times longer than usual. It gave her a headache and made her left arm ache.

"There! One contract is done. How many more to go? Bridgett and I are going to have to put our heads together and come up with a plan to get this work done," Jeannette thought. Suddenly she heard a noise. "What was that? It must be Paul. He is standing watch. I'm okay. I'm okay." She heard it again. "Nope, I am not okay."

She grabbed a stapler from her desk. It was the heaviest thing she had. She held it slightly over her head and crept to the door. Sean stepped in the door, and Jeannette swung. He caught her hand before she connected with his jaw.

"Sean! You scared me! I forgot you were here. Thank God!" Her heart was pounding.

"Mom! What did you think you were going to do with a stapler? Sit down. You don't have any color on your face. You were scared," Sean said, looking unsure at his mother. "You are not alone. We are all here for you."

"I know you are. I was working on a contract and forgot you were here," Jeannette said and paused. "This will not get the better of me! I will not feel like a victim! I am better than this. I will overcome this fear like every bad situation I have ever experienced. I will overcome, learn, and move on. That is life. I refuse to hide or be afraid of my own shadow. I have to face this head-on! This is just another challenge in my life and will make me stronger," she said with her head held high, and her chin squared in defiance while tears escaped her eyes.

"Would you feel a little better if we checked on Paul? We could offer him something to drink. You will see he is securing your apartment, but most of all, you," Sean reassured.

"When did you grow up and get so smart? I must have done something right in raising you. You are a good son. Let's say hi to Paul."

One by one, the group woke up. They all agreed they were starving, again, but the group could not decide what they wanted.

"I have an idea," Jeannette said. "Let me make two phone calls. Will someone help me down the hall? Thanks. I will be right back." Five minutes later, she returned with a smile and an answer to the dilemma of dinner.

"We are going to a very nice restaurant, a few blocks from here. A table is reserved for us. We need to be there in one hour. You all need to dress up a bit. David will pick us up in forty-five minutes. Shake a tail feather! Tia, would you mind helping me dress? We also need to put on some thick makeup to hide these bruises."

"Jeannette, I did not bring anything appropriate to wear to a nice restaurant," Tia gasped.

"You and I are about the same size. You can pick whatever you like from my closet. Sound good?"

"Sounds wonderful!"

"Boys, you should have something in your closets. You do not need a sport coat or jacket. Dress shirt and slacks, not jeans and a t-shirt, will be fine."

It took Tia and Jeannette longer to prepare for a night out than it did the young gentlemen waiting for them.

Tia made an entrance first. Sean lost his breath, and his jaw dropped. She was stunning. Tia chose a red evening length dress with a slightly flared skirt, a square neckline trimmed in crystals, short sleeves, with matching shoes.

Sean's knees were weak at the sight of her.

"You look beautiful. Now I am going to have to keep my eye out for others guys."

"I only have eyes for you, Sean," Tia said.

"Gross! Come on! We are going to dinner. You two are making me sick," Tyler said and made Zach laugh.

"Shut up, Tyler," Sean said without taking his eyes off Tia.

Jeannette walked in, wearing an elegant, evening business suit. It was navy blue and trimmed in satin and crystals. Her shoes were flats and matched the outfit. Her jacket hid her arm and sling. That was the main reason she chose to wear it.

"Is everyone ready? Let's go. There are too many of us to fit in the town car, so David should be downstairs with a limo. Tyler, will you please give me your arm to steady me?" Paul was standing at his post when they walked out. "Paul, you can take a couple of hours off while we are at dinner. Just make sure you clear the apartment before we get back."

"Yes, ma'am. Thank you," Paul said and escorted them down the elevator to the awaiting limo.

Entering the restaurant, the headwaiter recognized Jeannette immediately and seated her group right away.

"Excuse me. Is Mark here tonight? Would you mind asking him to stop by our table if he has a chance? Thank you." She turned her attention back to her group and asked, "What do you think of My City? I was up on that stage less than a week ago singing and playing with Clay and The Band. We rocked the house," Jeannette said with a huge smile.

"Jeannette! I was very pleased you took me up on my offer. How are you doing?" Mark asked as he hesitantly kissed her left hand.

"It was very generous of you to reserve us a table. I am slowly healing. Mark, I would like to introduce you to my sons, Sean and Tyler. Next to Sean is Tia, Sean's girlfriend, and this is Zach, a good friend of Tyler's, and one of the family. They are here from Oregon to help me. Everyone, this is Mark, the owner of this beautiful restaurant."

"Gentlemen, miss, it is very nice to meet you," Mark said and turned his attention to Jeannette. He took her left hand and kissed it again. She felt the same spark as the first time.

"What may I have the chef prepare for you?"

"I have not looked at the menu yet. Do you have a suggestion?" Jeannette asked.

"I do. It is a special dish the chef created for My City. Would you like to try it?" Mark asked.

"Yes. I will give it a go. Thank you," Jeannette accepted.

Mark held up his arm and snapped his fingers. A waiter immediately appeared at their table.

"Anton, the lady will have the Chef Special. I believe the others are ready to order." He took their order without writing one thing down.

Zach and Tyler quietly discussed if the waiter would be able to get their order correct. It ended with a bet of twenty dollars between them.

"It's a bet! I say he gets it right. You, on the other hand, do not have any faith," Tyler said with a grin and a handshake.

A discussion ensued around the table about college and some of their humorous experiences. It kept Jeannette occupied, somewhat. Her mind would turn to Mark if there was a lull in the conversation.

"Madam, may I serve?" Anton asked.

"Yes, of course. Thank you."

Anton served their meal without one error.

"I told you! Pay up," Tyler told Zach.

"Man, that guy is good. I didn't remember what I ordered. He is impressive," Zach said.

After consuming dinner and dessert, Jeannette was getting tired. "Sean, would you call David and let him know we are ready to go home? His number is in my phone."

Mark was subtle as he walked to their table.

"Was everything to your liking?" Mark spoke to Jeannette only.

"It was wonderful. Please give the chef my compliments. We were getting ready to leave. I am glad you stopped by before we did. I wanted to thank you again for the table and the wonderful meal," Jeannette said.

"You are most welcome," Mark said and took her hand once again to kiss it. Bending to her, he asked quietly, "May I call you when you are feeling up to having an evening with me?"

She had momentarily lost her breath but regained control quickly to say, "I would like that."

They were not fooling anyone about their feelings for one another. Sean and Tyler shared a look at each other of approval.

"Excuse me, Mom, I do not want to interrupt, but David is outside," Sean said.

"I will walk you out," Mark said and pulled Jeannette's chair out. She wobbled slightly. He gently, with strength, steadied her. That simple gesture made her feel secure and protected. It was wonderful. She had not possessed that feeling since Robert.

Little did the group know, someone had recognized Jeannette and called the Chicago Town News. A photographer and a reporter were waiting outside, hoping for a picture and a statement.

"Miss Jeannette! Jeannette! Do you have a minute to give me a statement? Please? Our readers want to know what happened and how you are dealing with the incident."

Mark let go of Jeannette's arm, ready to force the reporter and photographer to leave.

She caught Mark's arm and said, "It is okay, Mark, I will give them a statement. It is time I did."

She turned to the reporter and said, "I was attacked several days ago by a stranger. He forced his way into my car and demanded money. I refused. After taking a swipe at me with a huge knife, something rose inside me, and I refused to act like a victim. I had had enough. I managed to turn the tables on him and held him down until the police got there. I took control of the situation. Life is not perfect. The pitfalls we experience exist for a reason, to teach us things we need to learn. Afterward, I picked myself up to move forward. I refuse to dwell on the attack. Life lessons make me stronger every day. This incident is no different. You look at me right now and what you see is a wounded woman. I am, physically, but let me reassure you I am a strong woman and I will heal. I was not born strong. I was carved from each challenge I faced, mentally, and physically. I can move forward with my head held high with a strength that no one can contradict. Yes, there was a crime committed against me last week, and the man will spend the rest of his life behind bars. The way I look at it, I can either be bitter, or I can be better. I will not allow this event to tear me down. The choice is mine. I will be better and stronger." The reporter was silent as Jeannette walked away.

"That statement was perfect!" Mark said. "You make me proud to say, I know you."

Jeannette's face turned red with embarrassment. He helped her into the limo and said goodbye.

"That was great, Mom. You left the reporter with nothing to say. I have never seen that happen before," Sean said and stopped to chuckle. "By the way, this Mark guy. How did you meet him? What do you know about him?"

"Clay and Amy introduced us the night before . . . The incident. We went to My City. It was the night I played and sang with Clay and The Band. I don't know much about him, yet. He drove me home after dinner," Jeannette said. "Clay and Amy speak very highly of him."

"You got in a car with him, and you just met him? That was not very smart. He might be a serial killer!" Tyler said with a raised voice.

"He's not. I asked him if he was. He said he wasn't," Jeannette replied. She turned her head away from their shocked looks and tried not to laugh.

"Of course, he said he wasn't! Do you think he would tell you the truth?" Sean shouted.

"Put the brakes on, son. Do you remember my superpower? I felt completely at ease with him. I knew he was a normal person. Thank God, we are home! Thank you, David. I have a doctor's appointment on Wednesday. I forgot the time. I will let you know. Goodnight."

Tia helped Jeannette get ready for bed. As she was hanging the dresses in the closet, Jeannette said, "Tia, come sit by me. I want to talk to you. Tell me more about yourself and your parents."

"As I said, my mother is a physical therapist, and my father is a landscaper. Both are still living in Portland. Mom was always at the hospital. She could not bring me with her to work, but my dad could. Sometimes he would give me a job to do, like planting flowers. I liked going to work with him. Mom never remarried. Dad has had the same girlfriend for years. They bought a house together but have not married. His girlfriend is a secretary for a business downtown. As soon as I graduated from high school, I headed for Eugene, got a job, a tiny apartment, and applied to the University of Oregon. I have been on my own since I was eighteen," Tia paused. "I apologize if I shared too much."

"Not at all. I want to get to know you better," Jeannette said and yawned. "Have you and Sean made plans for after college? That is only three months away."

"We have talked a little about it, but nothing concrete. Why do you ask?"

"I am nosy." That made Tia laugh. "Would you excuse me, sweetie? My pain pill has kicked in," Jeannette said.

"See you in the morning," Tia said.

There was one day left before the young ones were flying home to Oregon. Jeannette sat at the kitchen table, sipping a cup of coffee, when Sean came in to talk to her.

"How are you feeling this morning, Mom?"

"I am feeling better. Honestly, I am. It has been ten days, so I should be by now," Jeannette said impatiently.

"You don't look like you feel better."

"I am a little depressed. I just realized you are all leaving tomorrow. I love having all of you around. It probably hasn't been a lot of fun taking care of me this week. You could have had more fun in Oregon. Thank you for being here. I appreciate the four of you so much. I was thinking. How about this evening you all go out on the town and have some fun? It will be my treat."

"Mom, first of all, we have enjoyed being here with you. We went to dinner a couple of times, Tia and I went sightseeing, Zach and Tyler did whatever it is they do, we had a movie night and a game night. It has been a nice time," Sean paused for a moment and then said, "I wanted to ask you what you thought of Tia. Give me your honest opinion."

"The only opinion I would give you is an honest one," Jeannette told him. "I like her. She is smart, educated, down-to-earth, caring, and she loves you. I know you love her just as much. Even a blind person could see that. You want my approval to marry her, don't you?"

"Why did I not see this coming? You knew already," Sean said, shaking his head.

Jeannette smiled and said, "Of course I knew. Sweetheart, you have blessed my heart by asking me about Tia."

"It is important to me. You are important to me. Without you giving me the okay, I would not ask her," Sean said, looking worried about what his mother would say.

"Son, I believe you have chosen just the right girl for you. You complement each other. As far as I can tell, you get along very well — no fighting or bickering. I see young couples all the time who cannot say one nice word to each other but are planning their wedding," Jeannette shook her head. "It is sad."

Sean let out a big sigh. "Now, I need to ask her. Do you think she will say yes?"

"There is no doubt in my mind, son."

"I have been trying to put away money to buy her a ring, but working part-time and going to school, I haven't been able to save much. That is what is holding me back. Any suggestions about how I can earn extra money?"

"I do. Let's go to my desk in the other room. We have a phone call to make. Sit down. I am going to call Mr. Baker. You remember him, don't you? He and Robert worked together. Good morning, Mr. Baker. This is Jeannette. I am calling about the accounts Robert set up for Sean and Tyler. Yes. He has found her and needs to buy a ring. Yes, he is right here. I will put him on. Sean, Mr. Baker, would like to speak to you." She handed him the phone and left the room.

Fifteen minutes later, Sean emerged from the office. He looked to be in shock. "I cannot believe this! Robert put money aside for Tyler and me? Neither one of you said a word about it."

"Robert loved you and your brother as his own. He did not want you to struggle like I did when you were growing up. He wanted to give you a solid foundation to start with when you found your bride. That money is for the wedding, a ring, a honeymoon, and to set up a household. I assume there was enough?"

"More than enough! Seventy-five thousand dollars is a huge amount!" He ran his hand through his hair in disbelief. "He has already called the bank and given them instructions to release the money. It should be in my account right now."

"Why don't we check that out? Do you bank online?" Jeannette asked.

"Of course. Is there another way?" Sean said and Jeannette grinned. "What is my password? Focus. I Got it. It's there! Look! Look at my account!" He threw his arms around his mom and hugged too tight. Jeannette let out a yelp. "Oh no! I am sorry! I didn't mean to hurt you! I am just so excited!"

"I am fine. It just pinched a little. You need to keep your voice down unless you want everyone to come in here asking what is going on. Please do not tell Tyler about this money. His time will come. I think you might want to get her a ring."

"Where do I go? I have never been to a jewelry store in Chicago," Sean questioned.

"Would you rather wait until you get back to Oregon?" Jeannette asked, even though she knew the answer.

"No! Will you help me pick it out?"

"I would love to, son. Let's go right away while everyone is sleeping. We can leave them a note. I'll call David." Determined to get dressed by herself, she struggled until she had succeeded. "I did not realize getting dressed could be this strenuous. Whew!" she said to herself.

Jeannette heard a light tap at her door.

Sean said, "Are you ready, Mom? Do you need help?" She opened the door and blew a stray hair out of her face. "Whoa, you are sweaty."

"Watch it, young man! If you want my help, keep your comments to yourself. I am ready." She grabbed a hat to cover up her hair. She did not want to comb it again. "David should be waiting." They walked out the door and saw Paul faithfully standing at his post. "Good morning, Paul. I am relieving you of your duty by my door. It is time you went back to Windy City. Tell Max I said it was time, and I will give him a call later today. Thank you for watching over me. You can take the elevator with us." Paul nodded and stepped onto the elevator.

Jeannette and Sean got in the backseat and heard the doors lock. "David, we are looking for a jewelry store. Do you know of a good one that is not terribly expensive?" Jeannette asked.

"Matter of fact I do. I bought my wife's ring there. It is about twenty minutes from here. Are you going to pop the question?" David asked.

Sean was trembling with excitement or fear. Maybe both. He did not sound sure when he said, "Uh, yes. I want to, I think. Yes. I definitely want to."

David looked in the rearview mirror at Sean who, by now, was shaking.

With a big smile, he said, "Don't worry, she will say yes. Take a deep breath. That's right. Remember to breathe. I was nervous when I asked Raelene too. Every man is. It is the biggest decision in our life. From what I have observed, there is no doubt Tia loves you. If you need some advice from a male, just ask."

"Thanks. I've got this," Sean replied.

"If you are like your mother, I know you do," David said. "Here we are, Scott's Fine Jewelry. Give me a call when you are finished."

"Are you ready?" Jeannette asked her ashen-toned son. "Remember to breathe. Here we go."

It was not long before he had found the perfect ring. It was made of white gold with a round one carat diamond in the center and a sapphire on either side. The wedding band was a simple white gold band. It was stunning.

As they walked out of the store, Sean said, "A perfect ring for a perfect girl."

Jeannette's eyes welled up, thinking her baby will soon be a married man.

"Oh! How are you going to propose?" She asked. "Do you want me to call Mark at My City? I'll bet he has private rooms looking out over the city or at least a table by the big windows to set a romantic mood."

"Perfect," Sean agreed.

Mark was pleased to hear from Jeannette. He graciously agreed to her request for eight o'clock that evening.

"You are all set. Dinner is at eight. David will pick up all four of you at 7:30. He will take you and Tia to My City first. Tyler and

Zach will probably go to a club somewhere people their age like to frequent. When you are ready to come home, give David a call. Tyler and Zach will take a taxi home. Now all you have to do is propose."

"What would I do without you, Mom? I hope Tia will grow to be half the woman you are, and I wish someday I can be half the man Robert was. Together you and Robert have helped me build a wonderful life I never asked for nor expected. I love you so much," Sean gushed with gratitude.

"We did it out of love. A parent always wants their children to have a better life than they did. We don't want you to struggle with hardships. Most of all, we want you to be happy. With Tia as your wife, I believe you will be a happy couple who will give me grandchildren I can play with," Jeannette said.

"You have to teach them how to make shake chick," Sean demanded.

"Of course, I will! Well, we are jumping the gun, don't you think?" Jeannette asked. "First, get the ring on her finger. Then we will go from there."

"There you are!" Tia said, walking into the room. "What are you whispering about? Should I leave or may I join in?"

"Tia, Sean and I were talking about having a family weekend in Oregon in a few weeks. Would you like to see Clark City? I have plenty of room at my house. There is a pool too. It will be a mini vacation. I will use any excuse I can to get my boys home," Jeannette said, covering up the real conversation.

"I would love that."

"Tonight, is our last night in Chicago," Sean started, "I would like to take you to dinner at My City. Mark has a table at eight waiting for us. What do you say? Would you like to have dinner with me?"

"Oh, Sean, I would love to, but I don't have anything to wear, unless I can borrow something from Jeannette," Tia said, looking a little disappointed.

"You and I can take care of that, Tia," Jeannette said. "We can go to my favorite store I shop at and buy you a new dress. Before you protest, you took care of me this last week, which I am very grateful for, so let me do this for you in return. Let's buy you a new dress."

Tia's face lit up with excitement. "Are you sure you are feeling up to it?"

"I still have pain pills if I need one. We need a little girl time that does not include dressing me," Jeannette said and rolled her eyes. "I apologize for taking up your spring break and having to play nursemaid to me."

"I was happy to help. When do you want to go shopping?" Tia asked excitedly.

"How about an hour? I need to relax for a bit," Jeannette told her. Tia nodded anxiously.

The afternoon went by fast. It always does when women shop. Jeannette sat in a comfortable chair at the boutique while Tia modeled dresses for her approval. They came away with an evening-length black dress with long sleeves. It was simple and accentuated her slender figure.

Later that evening Sean, Tyler, Zach, and Jeannette sat at the kitchen table talking while Tia readied herself for a dinner she will never forget.

"What are your plans for this evening?" Jeannette asked Tyler and Zach. "Sean and Tia are having dinner. Are you two going to a club?"

Tyler spoke up and said, "I thought we could ask David. He knows where everything is."

"Don't forget, you are taking a taxi home. Oh dear! I almost forgot! I have money for you three. My promise was that the evening was going to be on me. I meant it." She handed each one several hundred dollars. "This may seem like a lot of money, but it really isn't in Chicago."

Tia walked into the room without Sean hearing her. Jeannette grinned as she looked over Sean's shoulder to see her. He turned around and fumbled standing up when he saw her. She looked so elegant. He stuttered, trying to find the words to tell her just how beautiful she looked.

Tia walked to him and took his hands, "Well? How do I look? Did Jeannette and I pick out the right dress for dinner?"

"Um, yes, I mean, wow. You are gorgeous," Sean managed to say.

Tyler and Zach moaned. "Come on, you two. I think I am going to throw up," Tyler whined. "Let's get out of here."

On their way out the door for their evening adventures, Jeannette kissed each one on the cheek and gave them a one-armed hug. For her dinner, she made a grilled cheese sandwich and tomato soup that she consumed in front of the TV while watching a sitcom.

Jeannette was asleep on the couch when they all returned. Sean woke her up to tell her Tia said yes.

The next morning was hard for Jeannette to say good-bye to her children.

"Thanks to all of you for staying with me and taking care of me. I love you so much. My apartment is going to be very quiet without you. Tia, you are glowing. I am excited to have you as a daughter. Call me anytime, especially when you set a date for the wedding. I would love to have it at my estate in Clark City. Of course, that will be up to you. When you come to see me in Clark City in a few weeks, I will give you the grand tour. You can bring Sean too," She chuckled. "We can have a real family weekend, not cooped up in an apartment. Tyler, Zach, I will expect you too. Just give me a few more weeks to heal. It is hard to believe my baby is getting married," Jeannette said. Tears appeared in her eyes.

"Aw, you are not going to cry, are you?" Tyler said with an eye roll and a sigh.

"You hush up! I will do the same when you get married."

"Then I am never getting married," Tyler announced making Jeannette spin around in surprise. Tyler stood looking at her with a grin so big it was as wide as his face.

"Not nice, Tyler. Just for that, when you find the right one, I am going to tell her about every embarrassing thing you have ever done," Jeannette said pointing her finger at him, which only made the four laugh.

"Seriously, kids, let me know when we can have a family weekend. Now scoot! David should be waiting downstairs. Call me as soon as you are in Oregon and safe."

She gave each one a kiss and a hug. Jeannette watched them get on the elevator and the doors closed. They were gone. "What now?" Jeannette thought.

Lesson learned: Giving up my dream when I did, was the right choice. It gave me the opportunity to give my children love, attention, and teach them the good things about life. When I needed it most, what I had given, came back to me tenfold. I have raised wonderful children.

15

The phone rang. "Hello?" Jeannette answered.

"Jeannette, this is Mark. How are you doing?"

"I am glad you called. Thank you for making my son's proposal so romantic. It was perfect, from what they told me."

"It was my pleasure. Tell me, how are you feeling? When you were here the other day, you looked a bit tired and pale. Are you getting better?" Mark questioned, genuinely concerned.

"Thank you for noticing my tired face. Blame it on the pound of makeup covering the bruises," Jeannette said jokingly with a little giggle. "I am slowly healing. This week I start physical therapy."

"Wonderful! Are you feeling up to taking a drive with me this evening? I promise I will not keep you out too late."

"It just so happens my calendar is open this evening. I would love to," Jeannette said.

"I will pick you up at seven if that is a good time for you?"

"It's a date. I will meet you downstairs. Bye." Jeannette said and hung the phone up. "A date? Did I say date? Am I going on a date? What was I thinking? It must be the concussion. Whatever the reason, I said yes. I can't back out now! That would be rude. I could use my arm as an excuse. That would be a lie. Get it together, Jeannette. Why do I feel like I am cheating on Robert?" She sat down in a comfy chair, put her feet up, and dozed off.

She began to dream: There was a big pond with swans swimming two by two, enjoying the sun and gliding through the calm water. She sat beside the body of water wearing a white dress, a wide-brimmed hat with a long pink ribbon that fell to the side. She kicked off her white sandals to put her feet in the water. The shade she enjoyed that protected her from the hot sun was from a substantial weeping willow — one of the many that outlined the pond.

"Hello, sweetheart. You look beautiful. May I sit beside you?" Robert asked.

"Of course, my love," Jeannette said.

"Why are you sitting here alone?"

"I have been waiting for you. You hold my heart, Robert."

"But I am gone. We are in two different worlds. Why have you not moved on? I watch over you. I know you are unhappy. I miss your smile. Isn't it time you accept the fact I died? You need to live. You need to find happiness again."

"I am starting forward, a little at a time. I still love you. No one can compare to you."

"Do not compare others to me. We are all different. You need love in your life. Everyone needs love, Jeannette. Love is waiting for you. Let me go," Robert said and held his hands out to her. He was holding a pretty gold box with a red ribbon tied around it. "You said I hold your heart. I am giving it back to you. Fill it with love, one more time." He sat the box beside her and disappeared.

"Robert!" she called out, but there was no answer. He was gone. Jeannette held the box tightly in her arms.

She woke with her left arm holding on to the wounded arm. She whispered, "Robert is gone. My brain tells me he is gone, but my heart has not accepted it until now. There is no reason for guilt. He has set me free to love again."

No tears were shed by Jeannette this time. There was a heaviness that lifted. She began looking forward to going for a drive with Mark.

"Mark! What time is it? Six o'clock! I have to change. I will never be ready on time!"

It was hard work changing her clothes with one arm. "Ouch! Dang, it! Stupid arm. I will be glad to start therapy so I can move it again. Baby steps, I guess. This time last week, I was unable to get myself dressed without help. I am improving. I am finally dressed. Now to tackle my hair after I wash the sweat off my face, put on extra deodorant, and one more squirt of perfume." She was ready with ten minutes to spare. Just long enough to sit and rest for a few minutes. "Whew! That pooped me out! Time to go downstairs."

She reached for the doorknob and thought, "Paul is not out there, but you live in a secure building. Sid will not let anyone in that does not belong in the building. You can do this. Open the door far enough so you can see down the hall. Okay, the hall is empty. All clear. Step into the hall. Lock the door. Hurry to the elevator." Jeannette gave herself instructions. She nervously pushed the call button for the elevator several times. "Come on! What is taking so long?" She pushed the button one more time for good measure.

"Jeannette! Good to see you," her neighbor, Jack said. She spun around with wide eyes and froze against the wall. "Whoa. I did not mean to scare you. I do not blame you for being jumpy after being attacked. Next time I will make more noise."

"No, no. It's fine. My mind was focused on the elevator. You surprised me, that's all."

"I am going down also. Do you mind if I ride with you?" Jeannette shook her head no. "That was a very well-written article about you in the Chicago Town News. I am glad to see they locked that guy away," Jack said. "He needs to be off the streets forever. Thanks for sharing the elevator. Have a nice evening." Jack told her and left.

Jeannette cautiously stepped off the elevator. She saw Sid and relaxed a little. Mark saw her through the glass wall of the building. He walked faster than usual to meet her.

"Hello, Sid. I am here to take Jeannette for a drive," Mark explained.

"Excellent, sir. She just stepped off the elevator," Sid said. "Miss Jeannette. It is a lovely evening for a drive. Enjoy."

"Thank you, Sid. Mark, you are right on time," Jeannette said, trying her best to sound healthy and not scared to death.

"You are shaking. We can do this another night if you are not up to it," Mark suggested.

"Heavens, no! I need to get out of my apartment for a while," Jeannette said with a slight smile.

As they walked to the car, Mark said, "I am taking you to my favorite spot in the whole city. I think you will like it." He shut her door and heard the lock from the car door click. He said to himself, "She is scared. I should have known. I wonder if this is her first time out alone." Mark settled in behind the wheel.

"You are safe with me. Sit back and relax while I take you to a wonderful place."

"I am relaxed. My neighbor frightened me while waiting for the elevator. I did not see him until he said my name. I jumped. He apologized. We chatted on the way down. I am fine."

"Did he hurt you? I saw his face. Say the word, and I will take care of him," Mark promised.

"No. My neighbor did not hurt me. He just surprised me. The hall was empty when I left my apartment. I didn't expect someone to say my name."

"Is this your first time out alone?"

"Yes. It was harder than I thought it was going to be. I told Paul, my security guard, to go back to Windy City, that I no longer needed him guarding my door. I think I jumped the gun. I had to do it sometime, though. My fears the mugger gave me must be faced. I will not allow him to take away my freedom or peace of mind. I refuse to act like a victim. There is a difference between throwing in the towel to give up and knowing when you have had enough. I have reached the point of enough. Sometimes it takes time to overcome obstacles in our way. I will stay positive, be patient, and I will get better. Then once I defeat these demons, I will be a stronger woman because of it. Sorry, that was more than you asked for," Jeannette explained.

"If you get any stronger, I am heading for the hills, lady," Mark said and made Jeannette laugh. "I love it when you laugh. Your face becomes a beacon of light." He paused a moment while debating if he should ask her about remembering him being at the hospital.

"I have a question. Do you remember me visiting you in the hospital after surgery?"

Her brows furrowed together as she tried to remember. "No, I don't. Did you visit me? Did I talk to you?"

Mark chuckled and said, "Yes, we had quite a conversation. I learned a lot about what you think of me."

"Excuse me? You are Lying!" Jeannette raised her voice.

"I am not! It's the truth! Do you want me to tell you what you said about my butt?"

"Oh, my lord, no! Whatever I said, please forgive me? It was the drugs. I was high. Whatever I said, I will make it up to you. Please don't hold it against me?" Jeannette begged.

"No . . . I don't think I want you to make it up to me," Mark enjoyed stretching out the story and making her squirm. "You said I had a cute butt. That was a compliment. Thank you for noticing."

Jeannette cringed and put her hand over her face. "I . . . I don't know what to say. Please, give me the courtesy of accepting my apology?" She dropped her hand in her lap and looked at Mark with a very red face.

Mark was smiling as he said, "They gave you truth serum. Now I know what you think of me and my butt. You also thought you had kissed me," Mark said and paused to look at Jeannette's expression. "I forgive you. It was cute. You told me what I wanted to know. You like me, you have thought of me, and watched me walk away."

She stared at Mark with shock and realized he was enjoying her embarrassment.

She sat up straight, squared her shoulders to say, "I am so happy I entertained you while being on drugs. Now you know the truth. Yes, I like your butt, it is cute. Yes, I have thought about kissing you. Each time you kiss my hand, I get a spark. The kind of spark that makes me want to jump in your arms and passionately kiss you. Now you know all of the truth. How does that make you feel?"

"Give me a minute. We are almost there."

Mark brought the car to a stop and got out to open Jeannette's door. He reached inside to help her stand up.

"This is how I feel."

He bent to her face, put one hand on her cheek and the other around her waist. Their lips met gently, at first, then deepened. Sparks flew from both of them. He pulled back to see her eyes flutter open.

"From the moment I saw you at My City, I have wanted to kiss more than your hand. Remind me to buy Clay and Amy dinner for introducing us."

Jeannette gave a slight giggle and said, "I want to tell you, that you are the first man I have kissed or wanted to kiss since I became a widow. You are special, handsome, and a gentleman and . . . and . . ."

"Hush up and kiss me," Mark said.

She pulled back to look at his face, then said, "I thought you brought me here to show me something. Was it your lips?"

"Turn around and walk with me. Now, look. I come up here to look at the lights of the city, the hustle and bustle, while everything here is quiet. What do you think?"

"I love it here! It is beautiful." Mark stood at her back with his arms around her waist. "The best part is having your strong arms around me," she said.

They stood in silence and watched the world moving without them. Mark put his cheek next to hers in a loving gesture. Time did not seem to exist until she got a chill from the night air.

"You are shivering. Time to get you home, but first, one more kiss." It was a sweet, soft kiss that left her wanting more. "Forgive me for saying this, but I will be glad when you get your sling off. Then I can pull you in close to me and kiss you like I want to," Mark said.

They walked at a slow pace to the car. Jeannette turned to Mark and said, "Thank you for bringing me here. If you don't mind, I would like to call it 'our place.' We shared our first kiss here."

"I dub this spot 'our place.' Done. Now let's get you in the car."

As Mark drove, he held her hand. From time to time, he raised it to his lips and kissed it, making Jeannette's eyes roll. Mark loved it. She made him feel glad he is a man.

Jeannette was enjoying the ride so much she had not noticed the car had stopped. She was home. The evening was over, and Mark was opening her door.

"I would like to take you to your door if you will allow me? I want you to feel safe."

"Yes, I would like that. Good evening, Sid. Mark is going to see me to my door," Jeannette told him.

"Yes, miss," Sid said with a big smile and a tip of his hat.

"This is my door. Would you mind operating the key for me? I am a little awkward with it."

He took the key from her and opened the door. "May I kiss you one more time? Then I will leave. I promise." He leaned in close and kissed her one last time. "Goodnight, Jeannette. I will call you tomorrow."

"I am going into the office for a while tomorrow morning. You can reach me there. It was a lovely evening. Thank you again. Goodnight."

It was a little easier to walk down the hall to the elevator alone the next morning. She was starting to feel more like her usual self, but she was still going to make an appointment with Dr. Lamb.

David arrived for Jeannette at 9:00 a.m.

"Good morning. You look happy. It is a great look for you," David said and shut her door. She heard the click of the lock before he walked away. Another click and David was behind the wheel.

"Thank you. I am feeling a lot better. I am not sure how long I will be at the office. I will have Bridgett call you. I see you looking at me in the rearview mirror with a grin like you know something. What is going on with you?" Jeannette asked.

"Nothing. I am just in a good mood, like you are," David replied.

"Uh-huh. Okay, if that's your story."

Max helped Jeannette from the car and said, "Welcome back, Jeannette! Everyone is anxious to see you."

"I have been anxious to get back. Oh, David, I almost forgot. I have physical therapy tomorrow. I will have Bridgett call you with the time." She turned to Max and asked, "How is life at Windy City?"

"Normal. Busy. Lots of phone calls wishing you a speedy recovery. There is a greeting set up for you in the conference room. Do not try to protest. The staff is just trying to show you how much they care," Max said. He ushered her into the conference room, where the room erupted in applause. Jeannette's face turned red with humility. Her feelings slipped from her eyes and rolled down her cheeks.

When the persistent loudness of the room died to silence, Jeannette said, "I am grateful to every one of you for your support. I felt your prayers. It is my understanding that all of you came to the hospital. My time in the hospital is very vague in my memory. I apologize for that. There is no way I know of, to demonstrate how much I love and appreciate all of you. There are some hurdles I need to overcome over the next few weeks. The doctor is very hopeful I will regain all use of my arm, most importantly, play my guitar again." Applause and cheers filled the room. "Windy City would not be what it is today without all of your hard work. Thank you from the bottom of my heart for making this a wonderful place of business. You are my family." Her voice cracked with emotion as she held out her arm to show they were all included. "Now I think we should get back to work as soon as the donuts and coffee is devoured!"

Jeannette struggled with a cup of coffee and a donut. Bridgett immediately came to her rescue.

"Let me get that for you. Would you like to take this to your office?"

"If you wouldn't mind, yes. It is going to be interesting to see how I am going to manage to type. I am not able to write, for now. I am learning one-handed computer skills. I can do it," Jeannette said out loud what she was thinking by mistake.

Bridgett snickered. "That is why I am here, to assist. We will tackle the job together. There are a few contracts on your desk that I need you to look over. No typing required. If anything needs to be corrected, I will do it. I know you can't make notes, so tell me, and I will get it done. Is there anything else I can do for you?" Bridgett asked.

"No, thank you. It is good to get back to some normalcy."

"The world seems right with you at your desk. You have a smile today. It is wonderful to see, and I do not need to know why. Whatever has changed, I support it," Bridgett said.

Before she shut the office door, Jeannette said, "One more thing! Would you call Dr. Lamb and make an appointment for me this week, please? Look at my schedule and set up a time. My first physical therapy session is tomorrow. I have forgotten the time. David needs to know. That was two things. Sorry."

"I will take care of it." Minutes later, Bridgett buzzed Jeannette, "Mark is on line two. Do you want to take the call?"

Without sounding excited, Jeannette said, "Yes, I will take the call. Put him through." She needed to be professional when answering, "This is Jeannette. How may I help you?"

"You can help me by kissing me and letting me hold you in my arms," Mark answered.

She could hear him grinning, if that is possible to hear through the phone.

"That is so sweet, you silly man. Unless you have extremely long arms, you are out of luck, for now."

"May I take you to lunch?" Mark asked.

"It would have to be a late lunch around two," Jeannette said.

"I have stock coming in at that time. How about dinner? Only one catch. Dinner would have to be at My City. I have a new waiter. I need to keep an eye on him for the first few shifts," Mark said.

"That would be wonderful. I love your restaurant. Two reasons come to mind, you are there, and the food is delicious. Besides, there is a possibility you might have something to take care of, and I can watch you walk away." Jeannette's face lit up with a smile as she said that, and a giggle slipped out.

"I will make sure of it! I will pick you up at eight. Bye," Mark said and hung up.

Jeannette thought, "Now how am I supposed to concentrate? My mind is wandering." She looked to the ceiling and said, "Robert, you had something to do with me meeting Mark, didn't you? Thank you."

Dinner with Mark was nice. He had to excuse himself several times to keep his restaurant running smooth.

"Next time I take you to dinner it will be somewhere else without interruption," he promised.

"You don't have to worry about me. I had plenty to watch when you left the table," Jeannette said with a sly look on her face, which made Mark smile back.

The days remaining in the week were impossible for either one of them to spend time together. By the weekend, Jeannette was exhausted. Between work, Dr. Lamb, and physical therapy, all she wanted was rest. On Saturday, Jeannette decided it would be pajama day. She ordered lunch to be delivered and ate it in front of the TV. Shortly afterward, she became restless. Her phone rang.

"Hello?"

"Hello, my lovely. Are you resting after your first week back to work?" Mark asked.

"I have been all day. My arm has stopped throbbing, I had lunch delivered, watched TV, and now I am bored. It's crazy because I am still tired!" Jeannette exclaimed.

"Well, how about I take you to the theater. There is a musical play performing tonight. It is supposed to be a comedy. We can laugh and maybe even sing along if we know the songs. What do you think? Is it a date?" Mark asked.

"It is a date! It is a good thing you called me this early. It will give me plenty of time to get ready, I think. What time?"

"Seven. It starts at eight. It will take us about thirty minutes to get there."

"It sounds wonderful. I get to go to a real theater and watch a live play with music! I am excited. I have never been to the theater. It is a new adventure!" Jeannette said in her head.

Precisely at seven, Jeannette heard a knock at her door. It caught her off guard. Her stomach tightened, her breath caught but she managed to say, "Who is it?"

"Mark. It is safe to open the door," Mark said with compassion. She opened the door after giving her cheeks a pinch to put color back in her face. "If you were expecting another date, I will tell him to leave. It is our night," Mark said teasingly.

"I already called and canceled," Jeannette said, teasing back.

"You look lovely. These calla lilies are for you. Elegant, like you. I have waited all week to kiss you." He tipped her chin with his hand to meet his lips. "That was worth the wait. Do you want to put those in water before we leave?"

"Yes. Come in," Jeannette said.

Mark walked around her apartment, looking at the view of Chicago while Jeannette put the flowers in a vase. "You have a great view of the city. Instead of driving to our place next time, we could sit in comfortable chairs and watch the world go by from here."

"It is not the same without the stars or the darkness making the lights from the city dance. I am ready if you are," Jeannette said.

"Let's be on our way. I hope you did not mind that I came to your door. It doesn't seem right for you to come to me like I am a teenage boy who pulls up in front of a girl's house, revs the engine, and honks the horn for her to come out."

"I have gotten so used to meeting my car at the curb, it gave me a bit of a surprise when you knocked, but a nice surprise. It was enjoyable opening the door to the smiling face of a man holding flowers," Jeannette said.

Mark veered through traffic skillfully to arrive in plenty of time before the curtain rose.

The theater was still in fashion of the era it was built, in the 1940s. Each chair was overstuffed with red velvet covering. The floor had the original carpet in rose-design that had been kept clean and vibrant. Chandeliers hung from the ceiling that dimly lit the auditorium. Jeannette looked up to see a balcony filled with patrons fanning themselves while catching glimpses of those coming to see the play. The stage was raised at least four feet above the front row with an orchestra pit against the stage. A small portion of the flooring on stage was visible under the heavy red velvet curtains that matched the chairs. Jeannette was in awe. It looked exactly like something out of the old movies she loved to watch.

"Jeannette? Sweetheart, here are our seats," Mark said, noticing how she tried to take in everything. "Have you not been to the theater before?"

"No, I haven't. The theatre is a new experience. Am I wearing the correct attire for the evening?" Jeannette questioned.

"You are perfect. I am the envy of every man here," Mark said and made Jeannette blush.

It was not long before the music began to play, and the curtains opened. Jeannette's heartbeat quickened with excitement. She squeezed Mark's hand with anticipation. He looked at her with a smile and love in his heart. She was like a child experiencing something for the first time and enjoying every second.

When the play was over, the actors took a bow to a standing ovation. Jeannette had not realized how long the performance had lasted. Three hours had flown by, and she was disappointed it was over.

"Oh, Mark! It was a wonderful night! The play was hilarious, and the actors were perfect. I enjoyed it so much! Could we come again sometime?"

"Of course! We can see whatever play you like. Are you feeling alright? Tired?"

"I am fine. The play kept me so entertained I forgot all about my arm. It doesn't hurt at all. I don't know when I have enjoyed an evening more! Thank you for introducing me to the theater."

"It is my pleasure. My enjoyment came from watching you. Are you hungry? We could stop by My City for a light dinner. The chef will prepare something special. I promise I will not be leaving the table," Mark aked.

"That sounds like a perfect ending to a perfect date." Jeannette beamed with happiness.

Having been out later than usual, the next morning she stayed in bed longer for some much-needed rest. It was Sunday, a day of comfy slippers, a cozy robe, sipping coffee, and reading the Chicago Town News. Brunch sounded nice, but then she would have to get dressed, so that was not going to happen. Breakfast consisted of toast, bacon, and coffee.

Jeannette thought, "I hope Mark calls today. I love the theater! Who knew? Mark is very handsome. I like him a lot. I wonder if he feels the same about me." The phone rang. She jumped, almost spilling her coffee.

"Hello?"

"Good morning. Sleep well? You must have been exhausted after all the laughing last night," Mark said.

"Good morning to you too. You were on my mind. I confess I slept longer than normal. I was tired in a good way. My cheeks are sore. You gave me an evening I will never forget. Anytime you want someone to accompany you to the theater, I'm your gal."

"Gal? Is that Oregon talk?" Mark teased.

"Yes. After all, I am a country girl or gal. Whichever you prefer," Jeannette said, and Mark chuckled.

"Would you be interested in going to brunch?"

"I . . . Uh. . . I," Jeannette stammered. "I'm not dressed for a public appearance."

"How about I bring brunch to you? Will you be presentable in an hour?"

"That is pushing it, but for you, I will give it my best shot. See you in an hour." It took her the full hour to make herself presentable.

Brunch was great. The food was delicious, and the conversation was exciting and full of laughter. Jeannette and Mark talked as if they had known each other for years.

"Would you answer a question for me?" Jeannette asked.

"If I know the answer, sure. Ask away," Mark said.

"Why are you not married? Have you ever been married? Or engaged? Have you always been a bachelor?"

"Slow down!" Mark exclaimed and held his hand up. "That was a lot more than one question. Why have I not married? For one reason, I have not found the right woman. Another reason is that I have concentrated on my restaurant. I poured my life into it. I was never married. I lived with a woman for about a year and almost asked her to marry me. Before I had a chance to propose, I came home early one day and found her in bed with another man. She blamed me for never wanting to spend time with her, and I was always at the restaurant. Besides the cheating, she did not see my vision or support me. Those are the reasons why the relationship ended."

"Bachelor? Since I have had several relationships that lasted over a year each and lived with someone who I almost married, that is not the definition of a bachelor. I am not a man who looks for a new partner every night. Instead, I am a man who wants a special kind of woman to settle down with, and I was beginning to think that woman did not exist." He stopped and smiled.

"I have answered all your questions, so I am going to change the subject. What did the doctor say about your arm?"

"I might get the sling off this week. It depends on how physical therapy goes."

"You talk about living in Oregon, and your sons are going to college in Oregon, but you live and work in Chicago. How does that work?" Mark asked.

"It is a long story. Let's see if I can condense it. Originally, I am from Oregon. I married a man right out of high school who was from Chicago and wanted to move back here, so we did, three days after we were married. Later our family grew with the birth of my two boys. My husband had two failed businesses, and I took in ironing to help support the family. We divorced for many reasons. After he left me, I got a job at Windy City as a temporary receptionist. Jerry, the owner at the time, noticed I had an ear for tweaking songs to make them better. When the receptionist came back from maternity leave, Jerry offered me a job in the sound booth. I held that job for a couple of years. Jerry and Clay convinced me to sell Clay a song I had written. I wanted to move back to Oregon, so I sold Clay another song and moved my boys and me across the country. I consulted for Windy City from Oregon."

"Jerry suddenly died. The company flew me to Chicago for the funeral and to drop the bomb on me that I was now a business owner and worth millions. He left everything to me in his will. I had no idea he planned on doing that. He saw something in me I never knew was there. I have never been to college or taken any business classes. It just came naturally. What I didn't know I learned on the job. My boys and I had discussions about moving back to Chicago, but they are happy in Oregon. They have made a lot of good friends and did not want to move. Being teenagers, they were old enough to be left at home for a week at a time, so I rotated every other week. One week in Oregon, the other in Chicago. We were living in an apartment at the time. I met Robert on a plane. He was headed to Chicago as well. We visited during the flight and discovered we were living in the same town in Oregon. Skipping ahead, just before we were married, he was offered a deal to purchase a gorgeous estate for ten percent of its value. It was a surprise gift for me. That is my home, then and now. Then Robert died suddenly. I still go back and forth between Chicago and Oregon, but not as much as I used to. My boys and I will always call it home. It is where we have been the happiest. We will have family time as soon as I can fly to Oregon. We have a wedding to plan. Now you know the condensed story."

"Wow! That is quite a story. Mine is very boring compared to yours," Mark said and ran his hands through his hair.

"I'll let you know if it is boring as soon as you tell me where you are from and details about your life. The condensed version," Jeannette said.

"Let's see, where do I begin? It was a stormy day in September when a remarkable baby was born . . ."

"Come on!" Jeannette groaned. "Condensed version, not from birth."

"Okay. I was born just outside of Chicago in Miller, Indiana. I have one sister, Skylar, who is two years older than I am. We were a happy family, for the most part. Skylar went to design school then studied in Paris for a while. I went to a business school here in Chicago. I knew I wanted a business. I just wasn't sure what kind of business. After I got my degree, I was watching an old musical on TV only because there was nothing else on at the time. I fell in love with the old night club design. That is when I decided that was what I wanted to do, open a restaurant that was designed in the fashion of the old night clubs. I was going to need a lot of money to make this a reality. My family is considered middle income, so there was no money I could borrow from them."

"I started working in Chicago at restaurants to learn how they operated. I educated myself on the business of the food industry inside and out. For several years I worked three jobs. I was a waiter, a line cook, and supply clerk. I rarely had a day off. One day I was a waiter for a man and his son. He struck up a conversation with me about always having to eat out, how the food was, etc. He asked me if I liked my job. I told him I did, and I had two other jobs as well. He looked amazed. After that, he came in daily for a month, always sitting in my section, always striking up a conversation asking me questions to get to know me better. At the end of that month, he asked why I worked all those jobs. I explained what my plan was. He was impressed. He made me an offer. He had a space that was perfect for what I wanted to do."

"The deal was he would rent it to me with the rent to start in one year, to give me time to remodel, get approval from the health department, and set up for the opening. Then he shocked me. He offered to put up all the money I needed to get my restaurant off the ground. He had two restrictions. The first, after I started making a profit, I had to pay him back. The second, he always had a table every night for dinner and never pay for his meal. I agreed."

"That was eight years ago. I have paid him back, and I am purchasing the square footage my restaurant operates in currently. Not the building, just the space. I hope to have it paid off in ten years or less." There was a pause. Mark went on to say, "See? Not exciting at all."

"You are wrong. You were impressive to that man. Someone was watching over you to put you in the right place at the right time to meet him and become friends. When he made you the offer, it excited you, I am sure. Your excitement is what makes your story interesting. It was what you felt. Do not downplay your work ethic, the goals you set, your vision, and the knowledge. You worked for it, and you had a personality this man trusted. Everything you did throughout your life led up to that point and prepared you to meet him. In turn, he was ready to meet you. He knew a good risk when he saw one. Chances are he hoped to see what he saw in you in his son. Does he still come in every evening?"

"Matter of fact, he does come in for dinner. Next time you are at the restaurant, I will introduce you. He is a very nice man. His son, well, I think you are spot on about him. I don't think he has much ambition. Probably one of those spoiled rich kids."

"I am usually right," Jeannette said and grinned. Mark reciprocated.

Mark looked at his watch and said, "I hate to break up this conversation, but I am going to have to get back to the restaurant. Would you have lunch with me sometime this week?"

"Yes, I would love to. Before we make a date, I will need to check my schedule," Jeannette said.

"May I kiss you before I leave?" Mark asked. Jeannette nodded, yes.

The week proved to be a very busy one for both of them. Windy City had new clients with contracts to discuss and sign and others to discuss advertising strategy. Mark was doing some remodeling at My City that would enable him to have a bigger dance floor, expand the stage by several feet without losing tables, and more space in the kitchen for his chef.

Dr. Earl took off Jeannette's sling after physical therapy that week. The healing process was coming along nicely. Little by little, she was able to write. It was such a small thing for most people, but for her, it was a milestone. The doctor told her she could try playing the guitar in two weeks as long as she did everything she was supposed to.

16

She was coming to the end of a hectic week and looking forward to sleeping in on Saturday until she got a phone call.

"Hello. This is Jeannette."

"Hello. It is Rose, your sister."

"I know who you are, Rose. Why are you calling?"

"Dad, you call him Warren, is in the hospital and not expected to live. He is in a coma. The doctor said he would probably not wake up. He is suffering from several things, hardening of the arteries, old age, and something else about his stomach. Anyway, I wanted to give you a call to let you know. If you want to say good-bye, you need to do it soon."

"Thanks for calling. I will think about it," Jeannette said.

"I know you two never got along, but he is your father, so think hard about it. Good-bye." Rose hung up.

Jeannette leaned back in her chair and let out a big breath of air. She thought, "I don't want to go see him! He hates me. I feel the same toward him. If I don't go, I will never hear the end of it and possibly feel guilty later on. I should go to make sure he is dying. That wasn't nice, but true. Dang, it!" She wrestled with the decision for several minutes then rang Bridgett.

"Bridgett, I need a flight to Oregon. Make it for Sunday. I will be in Oregon all of next week. Is that going to be a big problem with my schedule? Good. Please call physical therapy and have them send over some exercises I can do while I'm there. I got a phone call that Warren, sorry, my father is not expected to live. Thanks, but I am fine with it. Let me know what time my flight is. Would you also call Irma, my housekeeper in Oregon, and tell her I am coming home? Thank you."

She made a conference call to Sean and Tyler about their grandfather. Warren never got to know her boys. They saw how he treated their mother, so no effort for friendship or otherwise was made on either end.

"Do you want me there? I will be there for support if you need me," Sean told her. "You know how I felt about Warren. The rest of your family is not much better."

"I feel the same way. I will be there to support you, Mom," Tyler said.

"Thank you, but it will not be necessary. I am leaving on Sunday. We'll see if he lives that long. If not, oh well. I apologize, that was not nice of me to say. As soon as he passes, we will have to make arrangements for the funeral. For now, stay at school. I will let you know when he is gone."

"Okay. If it gets rough dealing with your family, give me a call," Sean told her.

"Me too," Tyler chimed in.

"Thanks, boys, I love you. Bye." She hung up and dialed Mark. "Hi, Mark. Did I catch you at a bad time?"

"No. I just sat down to have a cup of coffee. I hear something in your voice. What is wrong?"

"I have to fly to Oregon on Sunday. My father is dying," Jeannette said.

"Oh, sweetheart, I am so sorry."

"Don't be. I am fine with it. That may sound cold since you have such a good relationship with your parents. Mine was not like yours. I will tell you about it sometime. Depending on when he dies and the day decided for the funeral, I hope to be back a week from tomorrow."

"I can't get away right now, or I would ask if I could accompany you," Mark said with frustration.

"It is not a problem. I will be fine. By the way, I got my sling off."

"Oh, sure! Tell me that then run away to Oregon! What a tease. I would like to see you, if possible before you leave," Mark said.

"When will My City be open?" Jeannette asked.

"We will open tomorrow. Would you have time to have dinner with me tomorrow? I will need to be here at the restaurant. I want to make sure everything goes smoothly for the unveiling."

"I need to eat, so, yes, I would love to. No need to pick me up. I will meet you there."

"I am looking forward to seeing you minus the sling. Bye, for now," Mark said.

Jeannette entered the newly remodeled restaurant the evening of the unveiling. She had no idea it could be more beautiful than it was. Mark had proven her wrong. Where did he get such excellent taste?

The paintings on the walls in the waiting area changed to flowers and pictures of Chicago's elite night clubs from the thirties. The lighting in the bar was replaced. Each table had one lone small lamp with a white shade. The bulbs gave off a dim amount of light to create a warm atmosphere. As she walked to her table, her eyes darted around the room, taking in as much as she could without gawking. A red velvet curtain hung at the back of the stage, keeping with the era of the night clubs. Each band member had a music stand that resembled a desk with the letters MC on the front (for My City), again staying with the era theme. The wood floor on the stage had been sanded and polished, so it shone brightly. The dance floor had a new light-colored marble covering. The linen tablecloths were now red with a lamp sitting in the middle, like the bar, only slightly bigger. It was beautifully elegant. It was a place where she had dreamt of going.

Mark met her at the table and said with a big smile, "What do you think?"

"It is wonderful! You did such a marvelous job! It is just like those night clubs in the movies!"

"That was the look I was going for. I would show you the kitchen, but you didn't see it before. Let's say it made my chef happy. He is preparing us a special meal," Mark informed Jeannette, pulling out a chair for her.

"It looks like the customers approve of your changes. I heard a lot of chatter in the waiting area — all compliments. Being closed for a week certainly did not cost you any patrons. You have a full house. Nice job. Before I forget, is your Mr. Regular here?"

"He is sitting at the table right behind me." Mark stood and said, "Sam, how is your dinner this evening?"

The man looked up, dabbed his mouth with a linen napkin, and answered, "Very delicious, as usual. Don't let that chef get away. You did a beautiful job with the new design. May I ask who the lovely lady is?"

"Please excuse my manners. Jeannette, this is Sam. Sam, I would like you to meet Jeannette." She rose from the table and stepped to Sam to gently shake his hand. Sam stood to his feet to greet her.

"It is a pleasure meeting you, Jeannette. Mark speaks very highly of you. Oh! I know who you are. You played with Clay and The Band here one night. If memory serves me, you were excellent," Sam said, making Jeannette blush.

"Your memory is correct," Mark said. "She is an amazing woman. We will let you get back to your dinner."

"It was very nice to meet you, Sam," Jeannette told him.

"The pleasure was all mine, Jeannette," Sam said and winked at Mark.

Throughout the evening, many people stopped at their table or asked for Mark to stop by theirs, to compliment him on the new look. They barely had the opportunity to eat the lovely meal the chef had prepared.

"Mark, it is getting late, and I have some things to finish before I go to bed. I am going to have to excuse myself and go home," Jeannette said with sadness in her voice.

"Come with me." She followed him through the kitchen to a room she assumed was his office. "I am going to get that kiss before you leave," Mark said and locked the door behind them. "No one will come in here. We can be alone for a few minutes. Let me show you how I have waited to kiss you." He took her carefully in his arms, drew her close, and kissed her.

"That was well worth the wait," Jeannette admitted. "I think I just melted. What a man."

"Be careful. You might not leave tonight," Mark threatened.

"Now who is teasing?" Jeannette said, smiling. "I need to leave, sweetie. I should be back in a week. Assuming Warren dies this week. If he doesn't, I will stay until the end. You are going to be extremely busy this week anyway. Especially when word gets out how beautiful the restaurant is."

"Thank you. I hope you are right," Mark said and kissed her one more time. There was a knock on the door.

"Mark, excuse me. Table twenty is asking for you," a voice came from outside the door.

"I will be right there!" he shouted. "The price I pay for having a successful business. Be safe traveling. Do not talk to strangers. Call me when you land in Oregon."

"Really? I am a big girl who can take care of herself, remember?" She held her arm out to remind him of the mugger.

"I know you are. I worry. I do not want anything more to happen to you."

"The only thing that will happen to me in Oregon is arguing with my siblings and getting dirty looks from Rebecca, sorry, my mother. I can hold my own. I have had lots of experience," Jeannette said with a half-smile. "You are wanted at table twenty, and I need to go. I will talk to you soon. I promise."

"I will miss you a lot. Let me walk you at least partway to the door." Mark opened the door and walked Jeannette as far as he could with his hand placed at the small of her back as a sign of protection. She was his.

The flight to Oregon was a turbulent one. All passengers had to remain in their seats with seat belts buckled the entire way. Nevertheless, they landed safely six hours later. She thought, "Is this a sign of what's coming this week? If it is, I want to go back to Chicago, NOW!"

She waited to call Mark until she walked through the front door of her home. "Yes, I am home safe and sound. The flight was rougher than I have ever experienced, but it all turned out fine. How is the—"

"Miss Jeannette!" Irma yelled, catching her by surprise.

Jeannette screamed, the phone went flying, and the color drained from her face in a split second.

"Oh! Irma! Dang, it! You scared me to death!" Jeannette said breathlessly. She sat in the nearest chair and put her head down, attempting to regain her faculties. She could hear a muffled voice coming from the floor.

"Mark! I am so sorry. Irma scared me, and I threw the phone. Everything is fine. I will call you later. Bye."

"I am so sorry, Miss. I did not mean to scare you. I am excited to see you!"

"Apology accepted. From now on make some noise or quietly say something to me, so I know you are close. My experience a few weeks ago is still fresh in my mind. The house looks very nice. Thanks for sprucing it up before I got home. What is that wonderful smell?"

"I baked crusty bread for soup bowls. I have homemade clam chowder for the filling. Are you hungry?" Irma asked.

"Even if I weren't, I would say yes to that. Let's eat. Join me, and I will tell you all about the last several weeks. Before I forget, I might need a reminder about exercising my arm," Jeannette warned.

For the next couple of hours, they sat at the table eating soup out of a bread bowl while Jeannette recounted the whole ordeal with the mugger and Irma caught her up on the local gossip.

"Well, Irma. I guess I have put off going to the hospital long enough." She rose from the table but was stopped by Irma.

"The hospital? Are you sick?"

"No. Bridgett did not tell you?" Irma looked puzzled. "My father is dying. I need to pay my respects. How do you do that for someone you don't respect? Humph. I guess I will find out."

"I am so sorry to hear that. Is there anything I can do? Something you need?" Irma asked.

"Thank you for asking, but no one can do this for me. I do not know when I will be back. I will pick up something to go from The Blue Bucket for dinner. The soup and bread were great. Thanks," Jeannette said and left for the hospital.

Upon arrival at Warren's room, she saw her siblings, Beth, Leroy, and Rose, positioned around the room with Rebecca standing next to Warren. Sitting on the empty bed across the room was her niece, Laiklyn. She was concentrating on coloring. Therefore, she did not hear Jeannette come in.

"Well, here we are, gathered by Warren's side. Did he wake up yet?" Jeannette asked without feeling.

"Aunt Jeannette!" Laiklyn yelled and jumped off the bed to run to her.

"Are you Laiklyn? You are too big to be her. Are you sure you are Laiklyn?" Jeannette teased.

"Yes, Auntie! I got bigger since I saw you last time. Do you like my dress? Grandma bought it for me. I like it because it has big pink flowers all over it."

"It is beautiful. You are beautiful too. Are you taking pretty pills?" Jeannette asked Laiklyn.

"Silly Auntie. There is no such thing as pretty pills. I just grew this way." Laiklyn held her arms out wide to show how she had grown.

"I am impressed! I see you are coloring. Why don't you color a pretty picture for me?"

Laiklyn jumped out of Jeannette's only strong arm and onto the bed to look through the coloring book to find just the right picture.

No one had said a word to Jeannette. The silence was deafening.

Somebody had to say something first, so Jeannette broke the silence, again, "Has the doctor been in today?"

Beth answered, "Yes, about an hour ago. He said it could be anytime. It is up to Dad."

"How long have you been here?" Jeannette asked.

"About three or four hours," Leroy said.

"Jeannette, would you mind staying with Dad for a while? Leroy needs to check on the other children who are playing at a friend's house, Beth has some errands to take care of, and Mom and I need to get some groceries," Rose explained.

"Are you all staying with Rebecca? I mean Mom?" Jeannette asked. Rebecca shot her a disapproving look.

"Yes, we are," Rose said.

"Okay. I will stay. Do whatever you need to, and I will hold the vigil, but first put your number in my cell phone, Rose. I will call if there is any change," Jeannette promised.

"We will be back in a while," Beth said. "Thanks for staying. Come on, Laiklyn, you can finish the picture later."

"Okay. Bye, Auntie!"

"Good-bye, beautiful," Jeannette said.

After the room emptied, she spotted a chair across the room to sit on. With a TV remote control in her hand, she sat looking at Warren. The only movement he made was from breathing. She thought to herself, "I should whisper in his ear that he was a horrible father and I am glad he is dying, but if I did that, his eyes would probably fly open and haunt me the rest of my life. So, I will NOT be doing that. I shouldn't be like this. He is my father. Well, he is the man who lived in the same house. I wanted so badly to have a loving, caring, and fun dad like my friends. Instead, I got the complete opposite. He was mean, showed no affection toward me, liked to whip me, verbally abused me, and purposely degraded and humiliated me to his friends to make them think I was a bad seed for the eighteen years I lived under his roof. By his example, I knew what kind of parent I did not want to be."

Jeannette had watched two hours of sitcoms waiting for her family to return. She had held the vigil long enough. It was time for her to leave whether they come back or not. She walked to the door, turned toward Warren and said, "Bye."

The next day, after making several calls to Windy City and Mark, she argued with herself about going to the hospital. She knew she had to, or she would feel guilty down the road. It was the right thing to do. She performed the exercises for her arm before driving to the hospital.

The same sight from yesterday greeted her when she stepped in the doorway of Warren's hospital room.

"I see we all made it back," Jeannette commented.

"Auntie!" Laiklyn shouted. "I finished a picture for you! Isn't it pretty? It has flowers like my dress!"

"Oh, it is a masterpiece! You should hang this on Grandma's refrigerator."

"No! I colored it for you, Auntie!" Laiklyn shouted.

"You did? I love it! Thank you, my little munchkin. Hug me. That's my girl. I will put it on my refrigerator as soon as I get home," Jeannette promised.

"Really?" Laiklyn asked.

"Of course! When Sean and Tyler come home, this will be the first thing they see. Can you write your name on it? Great."

"Auntie? Why didn't you eat with us yesterday? We had a big dinner. Everyone was there except you. Grandma said her church gave us all the food. There was chocolate cake! I ate two pieces. Do you like chocolate cake?" Laiklyn innocently asked.

"Dinner? Yes, I like chocolate cake." After answering Laiklyn, she looked at each face in the room. Guilt was written all over them.

"So, you had a big family dinner?" It was clear they had every intention of keeping it from Jeannette. They had not expected Laiklyn to spill the beans.

"We were going to invite you, but we didn't think you would come," Rebecca said.

"Don't you think I should have had the option? The church brought food?" Jeannette asked.

"We have a small cake left. I will give it to you, if you want it," Rebecca offered.

Jeannette's heart squeezed with the pain of isolation from her family once again. She was not going to let them see they hurt her, again. "No, thank you. You can keep the cake."

"You should have seen the planes we went to see!" Laiklyn added about the activities of the day before. "I saw pictures of Grandpa on the wall. Grandma said he helped build the place where all the airplanes are."

"Laiklyn, would you please stop talking and color in your book?" Beth said, trying to hush Laiklyn.

"You took a field trip to the airport too, huh? Was there anything else you did while I sat here watching Warren breathe? Were these your errands you had to run?" The room was silent as Jeannette scanned the guilty faces. "Let me know when he is gone. Rose has my number."

Jeannette turned to leave when Laiklyn shouted, "Auntie, your picture! Don't forget your picture! Will you come to eat with us sometime? I like to play with you. We can eat chocolate cake!"

"That's what makes you so pretty! It's the chocolate cake!" Jeannette told Laiklyn, making her giggle. "I will see you next time we get together. Okay?"

"You are silly, Auntie. Why do you have water in your eyes?"

"I have allergies. I need to go home and take some medicine before I start sneezing," Jeannette lied. "Give me a hug and a kiss. I love you, munchkin. Bye." She left with her head up and shoulders squared. She would not allow tears.

She sat in her car in front of her house and sobbed. She thought, "Why do I let them get to me? They always find a creative way to hurt me. I should be used to it by now and see it coming! I guess I still held out hope I would be accepted for who I am and a part of their family. Not anymore! I will not allow them to hurt me any longer! It is infuriating that I keep letting this happen! It stops now!"

Lesson Learned: It does not matter what my family thinks of me. I am who I am. I have my boys, my family at Windy City, Clay, The Band, and my best friend Judy, who loves me no matter what. I have not and will not allow bitterness or resentment to rule my life. I have overcome a lot and came out on top. I know who I am, and I can say with conviction, I love myself.

Her thoughts were interrupted by the ringing of her cell phone. "Hello? Mark! I am glad you called. I needed a friendly voice."

"Jeannette, what is wrong? Did your father pass?"

"No. Not yet. Warren is still hanging on. What's wrong is dealing with my family. It's always a nightmare for me. I will tell you all about it when I get back to Chicago."

They talked about the restaurant, her arm, Oregon, and they missed each other. She hung up in a better mood. Mark succeeded in making her feel good about herself once again. The possibility of bringing Mark to Oregon played on her mind. It would be a big step. They had not been intimate, yet. She was not sure if she was ready for that. Although she would love to show him the estate she loved so much, it was going to take more thought.

That evening she sat at her desk paying bills. A tune kept playing in her head, over and over. She stopped working on paperwork to hum the tune. Where had she heard that tune? "It would be beautiful on the guitar. The doctor said I was not supposed to try playing my guitar for another week. I can't stand it any longer. I have to try," she told herself.

At first, it felt awkward trying to strum her guitar. Jeannette's hand was so gentle on the strings that it was difficult to hear if there was music coming from the guitar at all. Her arm was stiff and sore. After a few minutes, she gave up.

"I am giving up for now. Tomorrow is another day. Before I go back to Chicago, I will play that guitar," she said with determination.

At noon on Tuesday, Rose called Jeannette to inform her Warren had passed earlier that morning.

"We are getting together with the preacher this afternoon to plan the funeral. You are welcome to join us if you want. We are meeting at Moms'. I wasn't sure if you wanted to drive to Stokes Landing."

"What time?" Jeannette asked Rose.

"Let me see. I wrote it down. The preacher will be here at four o'clock."

"I will be there. Thanks for calling." Jeannette hung up. "He finally died. I am free — no more glares, sarcastic remarks, arguments, disapproval, degradation, and judgments. I will never have to see him again. I need to call Sean and Tyler," Jeannette thought out loud.

She made a conference call to the boys. "Hello. Can both of you hear me? Good. Is that Tia I hear? Put me on speaker so she can hear. Your grandfather passed away this morning. He never woke up. We are meeting with the preacher this afternoon to plan the funeral."

"When do you think it will be?" Tyler asked.

"I am guessing Saturday. I hope so, and then I can fly back to Chicago on Sunday or maybe take a red-eye Saturday."

"Jeannette, we will be there for you," Tia said.

"Thank you, sweetheart, but it is not necessary. Warren never knew you guys. I don't think you boys ever wanted to know him either. It would be a waste of gas and time for you to come here. I would rather you all wait to come to Clark City for family time in a couple of weeks."

"Mom, are you sure you will be alright with the rest of your family? They never treat you with any respect or kindness, it's awful," Sean said.

"I can hold my own with them. I just wanted to let you know Warren is finally gone. Tia, I am sorry if this sounds cold coming from a daughter. Sean can fill you in later. I am going to say good-bye for now. I need to change before I go to Stokes Landing. I love you. Bye."

Jeannette drove to Stoke's Landing. She pulled up in front of Rebecca's house and could hear voices coming from inside. She opened the front door to her family home and followed the noise. She found everyone in the living room, including the preacher all talking at once.

"Hello," Jeannette said. The talking stopped. "I am right on time. It is four o'clock. When did you start?"

Beth spoke up, "About ten minutes ago. Everyone was here, so we started."

"Everyone, huh? Typical," Jeannette said under her breath. "Please, go on. I will catch up."

Rebecca sat quietly allowing her children to take care of the arrangements. She no longer had anyone telling her what to do. Warren's death had rendered her helpless. He always barked out orders, she obeyed without thought. She did not know how to take care of anything. Warren did not let her or teach her how to handle everyday tasks. A checking account was a total mystery to her. Pay bills? She did not know what they were or how much income she had.

Beth spoke up, "We have decided on Saturday for the funeral. Do you agree with that, Jeannette?"

"That is fine with me. I assume in the afternoon?" Jeannette asked so she could make a reservation for the first flight to Chicago.

"Yes, one o'clock," Rose answered.

"What music do you want?" the preacher asked.

Beth took the lead and said, "Dad liked the old hymns. His favorites were 'The Old Rugged Cross' and 'Amazing Grace.' Leroy, you are going to speak about what it was like being Warren's only son, right?"

"I don't know if I will be able to, Beth. I might not be able to get through it," Leroy said with his head hanging down.

"Of course, you will! Put it on note cards or something. Rose, here is a poem to read during the service. At the end, read these three scriptures. Jeannette, here's another poem to be read," Beth barked out orders.

"Beth, I'm telling you, I won't make it through a speech!" Leroy protested.

"Why are there two poems? Are you sure about the music?" Rose asked.

"Just a minute!" Jeannette raised her voice slightly to get everyone's attention. "Leroy, write out what you want to say. If you cannot do it, one of us will read it for you. Why don't we skip one of the poems? Choose the best and toss the other. Rose, read the scripture at the end. Is that all right with the group? Good. Beth, I assume you are giving a speech. Okay. The music will be "The Old Rugged Cross," and "Amazing Grace." The service is planned. The next question to be answered is, who is paying for this? Did he have insurance, or are we all going to have to split up the bill?"

"I can answer that," Preacher Dave said. "Warren had insurance for this. It is paid in full. You need not worry about the cost." Everyone let out a sigh of relief except for Jeannette.

"We need to open up the floor so others can tell a story or comment about Dad's life," Beth said.

"This is how I see the service going," Jeannette interrupted. "Preacher Dave will say a prayer to open the service and read the obituary. Then he will introduce Beth to give her speech. 'The Old Rugged Cross' is sung by the congregation. Leroy either gives his speech, or one of us reads it for him, then we open the floor for comments and stories. Everyone sings, 'Amazing Grace.' I read a poem, and then Rose will read her scripture. Preacher Dave says a prayer then he announces to everyone about the potluck dinner. I am assuming the church will be having a potluck for the family as always?" Jeannette asked.

Preacher Dave shook his head yes while Beth was quietly angry. Her temper was humming under her skin.

"Jeannette? Is that your name?" Preacher Dave asked. "I think that sounds like a perfect service. Does anyone have any more suggestions or changes? Then it is settled."

Beth sat across the room with her arms folded across her chest with a look of anger directed at Jeannette for taking over the lead. Leroy had his head down, looking sad. Rose had no expression. Rebecca sat in the corner and rocked in her chair. The room was silent.

It took less than ten minutes after Jeannette arrived to have the service planned. Jeannette decided it was time for her to leave. She stood to exit but preacher Dave stopped her.

"That was awesome. It took you five minutes to come up with a plan while we had been at it for probably fifteen or twenty minutes and we were not even close to having a plan. What do you do for a living?"

"I am the CEO and owner of Windy City Publishing and Recording in Chicago."

"You own that company?" Preacher Dave asked.

"Yes, I do," Jeannette said proudly. She happened to see Beth roll her eyes and look away.

"Did you start it? Or did you buy it?" he asked.

"Neither." The preacher looked confused. "It is a long story. Here are the highlights. I worked for Windy City for several years. The owner at the time, Jerry, became a good friend of mine. I started as a temporary receptionist. Then I worked in the sound booth recording music and producing songs and albums. I wrote a few songs, which I sold to a friend and client to record on an album I was helping produce. I gave up my job to move to Oregon. I stayed with Windy City as a consultant even though I lived in Oregon. One day I got a call Jerry had a heart attack and died. He was the owner and founder of Windy City. The company flew me to Chicago to help keep the company running and assist with arrangements for the funeral. That is what I thought, anyway. I loved the business and was familiar with contracts and all of Jerry's business dealings, and clients. After I arrived, an attorney was waiting for me to go over Jerry's will. He left everything to me: the company, the money, the building, everything. I was in shock. I had no idea he had this in mind. From that day I have built the company into an even bigger and more successful business than it was before."

"Wow. That is quite a story," Preacher Dave said. "What college did you attend to prepare you for such a position?"

"I did not have the opportunity to go to college," Jeannette said and glanced at Rebecca. "What I do is by instinct and common sense."

"God is with you. You know that, right? Forgive me for saying this, but you should have fallen flat on your face, given the circumstances. You are blessed. Always give thanks," Preacher Dave said, giving her advice. "It was nice meeting you."

Jeannette shook his hand as he was leaving. Thinking, she said to herself, "Blessed? I never thought about it that way. I guess all the years of suffering and sadness were worth it for a greater blessing. There was a plan afoot I never imagined in my wildest dreams. I am thankful. I promise to give thanks every day."

It was time to confront Beth.

"I saw you roll your eyes. You don't think I deserve to have a company that is worth millions, or anything else for that matter. You have no idea what my life has been like, what I have lived through, and the horrendous experiences I have endured. I have fought for everything I have, except Windy City. It was a gift. One that I did not ask for or expected. Nonetheless, God saw fit to bless me with it. Your jealousy of me will not get you anywhere. It takes up too much energy. As long as you hold on to this negative emotion toward me, you will only attract more negativity into your life. The scowl on your face tells me you are not happy and have not been for a long time. Stop trying to find reasons to be unhappy. Instead, turn your mind to what you have, and the many reasons you have to be happy. Be thankful. Only you can make yourself light-hearted. I have done nothing to deserve what you are dishing out. Choose to be happy instead of angry like Warren always was. If you change your attitude, you will change your life. If not, then I feel sorry for you. See you on Saturday."

Jeannette's monologue hit home. Beth was furious, but had no words to retaliate, because every word was correct. Her face turned red as she watched her younger sister leave.

The drive home to Clark City seemed shorter than usual. She felt lighter after confronting Beth. It was a difficult step forward to have said what she was thinking. Saturday might turn out to be an interesting day.

"Miss Jeannette, how did things go with your family?" Irma asked Jeannette when she came through the door.

"It is never easy or fun when it comes to my family. I finally put my older sister in her place, as nicely as I could. I gave her some advice I hope she takes to heart and implements. The funeral is on Saturday at one. I will be flying to Chicago Saturday after the service."

"It makes me sad to know your family is a contradiction to who you are. How did you turn out to be a compassionate woman with a big heart?" Irma asked.

"That is a very nice compliment, Irma. I appreciate it," Jeannette said with a smile.

"Do you need me for anything else this evening?"

"Not tonight, Irma. As a matter of fact, take tomorrow off with pay. If you don't mind, I could use some time to myself. I will see you on Thursday."

"Of course, Jeannette, and thank you. Goodnight."

Each day Jeannette attempted to play her guitar. She could see improvement, just not enough to make music. It became exasperating to try so hard, and not a sound would come out. "Patience," her mind kept saying.

Saturday rolled around, and Jeannette was ready to get on with the funeral, then straight to the airport. She arrived at the church an hour early to help with anything that her siblings needed. It so happened she was not assigned anything. She gave herself the job of greeter, just up her alley, to stay occupied. Beth had not said a word or even glanced at her. Rose and Leroy were busy and had nothing to say. Rebecca stood about five feet to Jeannette's left oblivious to what she should or should not do. The guests were gracious to give her their condolences.

During the service, the floor was opened for comments and stories as planned.

Rose leaned to Jeannette to whisper, "I thought the church would be full. There are only about fifty to seventy-five people here if that many and that number includes all of us!"

Jeannette bit her tongue. Nothing good would come from a catty remark. She patted Rose's hand and smiled at her. Leroy was too broken up to read his speech. Beth read it. The things he said about Warren made the man sound like he was a saint. Jeannette was shocked and wondered if they were in the same family. She had to remind herself Leroy was not like her. He and Warren had a different relationship. No one offered a story for an excruciating several minutes. Just when Preacher Dave rose to move on with the service, a gentleman stood up and told a hunting story. Beth released a breath of air she was holding; thankful someone had a story. At the finish of his story, Preacher Dave continued with the service. Several grueling minutes later it was over. Now for the potluck.

She made sure Rebecca had a plate of food before serving herself. Jeannette visited for an allotted amount of time before she decided to leave. She said goodbye to Rebecca and made her exit. One last thing she wanted, needed, to do.

Jeannette went back to the church, stood by a broad picture of Warren, and said, "You were not the father I wished I had. You treated me horribly. You hated me. I hated you. Although I detested the experiences and treatment you put me through, it helped shape me, by my choice, into a good woman. Who knows? You might have been proud of me if you had tried to know the real me." She paused. "I tried over the years to understand the anger within you that made you take it out on me. There were times I felt sorry for you until your mouth opened, and your sharp tongue emerged to humiliate, degrade, or lie to me. Or your hand rose in the air to hit me. I don't want to carry the hate anymore. The hurt is over. Today, I forgive you." As soon as the words came out of her mouth, she was truly free. Peace washed over her. She turned and walked out.

While driving to the airport, in her mind, the day repeated itself. The words she said to Warren's picture were on a loop. "I should have forgiven him a long time ago. I could not imagine saying those words to him. He made my life a living hell. So many times, I wished him dead. Oh, God, forgive me for that! Years ago, in my reasoning, his tirades of abuse verbally and physically justified my wish of his death. If he was alive, would I have told him I forgive him? No, I don't think so. I know he can no longer hurt me and it gave me the courage to forgive him, but to have said it to his face . . . probably not. I will never know. My belief is, his spirit heard me where ever he is."

Lesson Learned: Good people can bring you joy. Negative or angry people can give you experience if they do not rub off on you. Let the meanness run off your back. From the worst people, observe them and allow yourself to learn lessons. The underlying logic is, there is a purpose for these people to be in your life. In my time of existence, I have learned lessons from experiences that I will NEVER have to learn again. The resolution is to determine the lesson the first time and learn it so you do not have to repeat it.

17

It was good to be in Chicago after spending a not so happy week in Oregon. Jeannette's plane landed at 3:00 a.m. It was too early to call Mark or David to pick her up. Her choice would have to be a taxi. By 4:00 a.m., Jeannette was in a comfy bed sound to sleep.

Mid-morning the cell phone by her bed, woke her to the tune of 'I Finally Found Someone.' That was Mark's assigned ringtone.

She answered, groggy from sleep. "Good morning, Mark."

"Good morning, beautiful. Are you in Chicago?"

"Yes, I am. My plane landed at three."

"You could have called me to pick you up," Mark said.

"There was no way I was going to wake you at that time of the morning. How is the restaurant? Still going strong?" Jeannette asked.

"It has been packed since we reopened. You were right. It was probably a good thing you were in Oregon. My time was limited," Mark was pleased to report.

"I am delighted your restaurant is doing so well! You have worked hard at making a success of My City. You are very deserving. Will you be able to get away sometime this week? I would like to see you," Jeannette asked.

"Nothing could keep me away from you! Another new thing we are implementing for a trial period is brunch on Sundays. We open at eleven. Would you like to have brunch with me?"

"I would love to. What time is it? Never mind, it's ten-thirty. How about noon? I want to take a long steaming shower," Jeannette said.

"Noon it is. Do not make me wait one minute longer. Please? It has been too long since I kissed you," Mark said with a touch of whine in his voice.

"It is a promise. I will be there at noon. Let me hang up so I can call David. Bye for now."

The realization of how tense she was in Oregon had come to light. Her muscles gave it away. She was sore from head to toe. The hot water of the shower helped her relax. Steam rose to the ceiling and filled the air like a dense fog. The water began to cool down signaling time to get out of the shower and on with her day.

"Jeannette! You look so much better without a sling," David said as he shut the car door. When she heard the click of the lock, she loosened her grip on the door handle. "I am sorry about your father. He did something right by raising a wonderful woman like you."

She thought for a moment then said, "Hum. I guess you could say that but give ME some credit. It was my choice to be a good woman. I could have been a bitter old woman with frown lines and a chip on my shoulder because of the curveball always thrown at me. No one treated me like a princess — just the opposite. I didn't even have a nickname. Wait a minute. That is not true. Once he called me the devil, but it didn't stick." She laughed at David's shocked look.

"What?" David said.

Jeannette could not stop laughing. She regained her composure and said, "It is a long story, David, but he did call me the devil. Maybe I will tell it to you someday, but for now, I can tell you I have no hatred any more for my father. I carried hatred for too many years. That will make sense when I tell you the story, sometime. Oh, good, we are at My City. I am starving. David, did you know Mark is trying out brunch on Sunday? Today is the first day. If he decides to stick with it, one of these Sundays, I will treat you and Raelene to brunch."

"That would be wonderful! Enjoy your meal. Call when you are ready to leave," David instructed.

Jeannette disappeared into the building. Mark was waiting at the headwaiter's station. When he saw her, he rushed to her, took her left hand, and kissed it. Her eyes rolled with pleasure, which made him feel masculine. He offered his arm. She gladly accepted and put her arm through his. They walked at a slow pace to a table Mark had prepared.

"Before we sit, would you mind coming to my office?" Mark asked. As the door shut behind them, he could wait no longer. He scooped her into his arms and kissed her passionately. His breathing had changed, along with the pounding of his heart.

He pulled back to look into Jeannette's eyes. "I have missed you more than I have ever missed anyone. I am in love with you, Jeannette."

He rendered her speechless for a moment. "Ahem," she cleared her throat before she could respond. "Give me a second to find my legs. That was a wonderful kiss." Her face beamed. "I have been waiting to hear you say those words. I love you too."

"I do not think I have the words to enunciate how happy you have made me! I wish I could make love to you this very minute!"

"Cool your jets; for now, it is not the time or place. Sex is the icing on the cake. Love's basis is respect, honesty, and in my opinion the biggest one of all, trust. The intimacy will come. I need a little more time. Please? Be patient a little longer? We only get to have the 'first time' once. I want it to be unique and special. An experience we will never forget. Like our first kiss. Am I making sense?"

"You are. I will give you all the time you need. I want you to be sure." He kissed her again before they left Mark's office.

A young waiter stepped to the table and introduced himself, "Good afternoon. My name is Seth, and I will be your waiter. Would you like me to escort you to our brunch area, or would you prefer to order something special from our menu?"

She could see the young waiter was nervous waiting on his boss. She tried to make it a little less stressful for him. "I believe I am in the mood for eggs Benedict with coffee and a mimosa."

"Make it two," Mark said. He noticed a bead of sweat roll down the side of Seth's face. Mark had picked this table on purpose to see how his new waiter would handle the pressure. "Before you go, Seth, we would like our mimosas right away and coffee with our food. We will need cream with the coffee."

"Yes, sir," Seth said with a slight bow then quickly left.

"Are you trying to rattle that young man?" Jeannette asked.

"Yes, I confess I am," Mark said with a smile. "He is a new waiter, and I want to see how he does under pressure."

Seth arrived at the table with mimosas on a tray. "For the lady." He picked up the champagne flute to serve Jeannette. He hit the stem of the fluted glass on a water glass sitting in front of her, sending both upside-down on the table. Water and mimosa spilled across the table and onto her lap, making Jeannette gasp from the cold liquid. Seth's face turned white, then a beautiful shade of red.

"I am so sorry for my clumsiness! Please allow me." He quickly took the towel from his arm and started to dab Jeannette's lap.

"Excuse me, Seth, but I can do that myself," Jeannette said.

Mark quickly got to his feet. In a scolding whisper close to Seth's face, Mark said, "It is inappropriate to touch a woman's lap. Offer her the towel and let her clean it herself. Now take the wet tablecloth, silver, plates, and glasses away. Reset the table. Offer the lady a pastry with her breakfast at no charge for the mishap."

Seth looked terrified. "Please accept my apology for the mess. I will have this cleaned up in a jiffy. May I offer you a pastry at no extra charge for my clumsiness?"

"That would be very nice, Seth. Thank you. Excuse me, Mark I will be right back," Jeannette said.

Mark sat patiently and quietly watched, while Seth prepared the table, which in turn only flustered the young waiter. Being the boss, Mark could not let him see the smile that threatened to appear out of enjoyment at making him sweat.

Jeannette returned. Mark pulled her chair out and whispered in her ear, "He is sweating."

"Thank you for your patience. Your table is now ready," Seth said.

"Thank you, Seth. Let's try the mimosas again," Mark said with a straight face.

"Right away, sir," Seth nodded.

"You are enjoying this, aren't you?" Jeannette asked.

"I admit it, I am. It is hard not to smile. Here comes Seth with our meal," Mark warned as he watched his new employee's every move.

Seth served their plates of food with ease. "I will be right back with coffee and cream."

"Thank you," Jeannette said. "He is doing better this time around. Not quite so nervous."

"Look at you! Your right hand is working!" Mark exclaimed.

"How about that? I can feed myself! I tried my guitar, but I still cannot play. Changing the subject, I want to tell you about what happened in Oregon. I have not told you about my father, have I? Let me finish eating, and I will tell you the whole saga. I will need another mimosa for this story."

Jeannette persevered through the story of her childhood. Mark looked saddened at what she had to endure. He held her hand without saying a word.

"I did not tell you all of this to get sympathy. I told you because of what happened while I was in Oregon. You needed some background to understand."

After I arrived in Oregon, I tried putting off going to see Warren in the hospital. I finally gave in and went. My family was all accounted for and holding the vigil waiting for Warren to die. Not a word was said when I walked in. I broke the ice and tried to chit chat. My niece Laiklyn was there coloring. When she saw me, she jumped in my arms, well my left one, and hugged me. I asked Leroy how long he had been there. He told me about four hours. One of my sisters spoke up and said mom and one of the girls needed to get groceries, Leroy needed to check on the rest of the kids at a friend's house and one needed to run errands, I think. Rose asked if I would stay with dad while they left. I said yes. They all left. I sat across the room and watched a couple of hours of sitcoms and decided it was time to leave.

The next day I took my time going back to the hospital. I was greeted with silence except for Laiklyn. She was excited to see me.

"Auntie, why didn't you eat with us last night? We had lots of food the church brought to us. I ate chocolate cake! Do you like chocolate cake, Auntie?" Laiklyn asked innocently.

"Yes, I do. So, you had a big dinner?" Jeannette said and looked around the room to see guilty faces trying not to make eye contact. They didn't think about Laiklyn spilling the beans.

"We went to see planes and saw pictures of Grandpa on the wall. Grandma said he helped build the airport."

One of my sisters told her to go back to coloring and stop talking. She did what she was told.

I said, "So you had a dinner?"

One of them said, "There is a small chocolate cake left. You can have that."

I told them they could keep the cake and to let me know when Warren is gone. I was left out again and I let it get to me. It hurt, but I did not let them see me cry. I waited until I pulled into my driveway and sobbed. That is when you called me. Warren died the next morning, so the funeral needed to be planned. When Rose called to tell me about Warren, she said they were all getting together at 4:00 o'clock with Preacher Dave at Mom's if I wanted to come to Stoke's Landing. I told her I would be there. I arrived right on time.

"The first thing to set the tone of planning Warren's funeral, I walked into my mother's home and the meeting with the preacher was already under way. They told me everyone was already there, so they started. After the silence of seeing me, the planning commenced. It was chaos. So, my CEO skills kicked in. Five minutes after I started, the plan for the ceremony was finished. Beth was really upset with me because I took over. The preacher was surprised and impressed I could do that in short order. He asked me what I did for a living, so I told him. I could see Beth, my older sister, behind him rolling her eyes. I decided it was time to tell Beth she needed to stop being jealous and angry with me for whatever reason. I had done nothing to warrant it. I told her she needed to do what makes her happy, and being mad at me was not the answer."

"How did she take it?" Mark asked.

"Just like you would expect. She was furious. I hit a nerve. She did not say anything, but I thought her head might explode. She had a very large vein sticking out on her forehead. After I said my piece, there was total silence in the room. I left."

"After the funeral and potluck, I went into the church alone. Standing next to Warren's picture, I told him he was a terrible father, that I knew he hated me, and the feeling was mutual. I went on to say I felt sorry for him over the years until he spoke to me just to hurt me with his sharp tongue. The next thing that came out of my mouth was a shock. It was not planned or expected. I told Warren I forgave him. It came from my heart. I meant it! I realized that if I had hate in me, how could I love completely? My heart was in two pieces. One was hate, the other love. To love someone halfway is unacceptable. As soon as I forgave my father, I felt lighter. A weight lifted from me. I felt happy. That is when I knew that I loved you. I have never been able to sleep on a plane. I fell asleep for the first two hours of the flight. I was exhausted from emotion. Now I am not saying that I love Warren. I just forgave him."

"Holy cow, Jeannette! You are a better person than me! I salute you. It would be impossible for me to forgive him for the abuse he dished out. I know physical abuse heals after a while, but how do you heal the mind from verbal abuse and the heart from emotional abuse?"

"I wish I had a clear answer for you. The only thing I know what to do is keep moving forward and leave the past in the past. There have been times the past has reared its ugly head, and I had to beat it down. I would tell myself to stop focusing or giving attention to whatever was trying to defeat me. It gave the past too much power over me. That helped for a long time, but it did not fix the problem. When I gave forgiveness, I was sent free. Did you notice when I told you all about growing up, I did not shed one tear? That would not have been the case a week ago. I would have sobbed, which would spur the nightmares again." Jeannette paused and took a deep breath before she went on.

"There is one other person I need to forgive: Jeff, my ex-husband. He picked up where Warren left off. He never hit me, he controlled me by threatening, and with verbal and emotional abuse. He belittled me in front of his friends and made me ashamed of myself to keep me in line. Jeff is a toxic person. If he remotely thought his control was slipping, he tried to control how others saw me. When his paint store failed, he told his friends, and whoever would listen, that it was my fault. I had my hand in his till, which was a total lie. I knew if I left it alone, the truth of who he is would come to light someday," Jeannette explained.

"I know a little about your ex-husband. Clay told me a few things. Now I really hate him! He is a jerk! If I ever see him . . . I might give him a right cross to his jaw!" Mark promised.

"No, you won't. Jeff did not do anything to you. I know you want to protect me, but it is over. He will never hurt me again. I will not be his victim again. That said, I want you to know I plan on calling him this evening," Jeannette informed Mark.

"That is NOT a good idea! If you insist on doing this, I will be there when you do," Mark demanded.

"Will you let me do the talking, stay in the background, and let me handle it? I need to do this. My heart is telling me I need to. I want to be free to give you all of my heart, not just a piece of it," Jeannette explained.

Mark put his head down while holding tightly to her hands. After he had thought for a moment, he raised his head, looked at Jeannette, and said, "I trust that you are following your heart. I promise I will not say anything while you talk to him, but only if Jeff does not get out of hand. If he starts badgering you, I will take over. Do we have a deal?"

"Deal," Jeannette agreed. "The sooner, the better. If we could go to your office, I will make the call now and get it over with."

She sat in a chair across from Mark sitting at his desk. Her heart started to pound, her stomach was getting tight, and her hands began to shake.

"This is silly for me to act like this! He is over two thousand miles away in Oregon!" Mark watched as she settled herself by taking deep breaths with her eyes closed. "Okay. I am ready. I will put him on speaker so you can hear." She said with intent and dialed.

"Jeff? This is Jeannette."

"What do you want? Did you have a visit from a friend of mine?" He laughed. It was an evil-sounding laugh.

Robert looked like he was going to pounce on the phone he was so mad. He realized that Jeff was guilty of trying to have

Jeannette killed. He just admitted it. Jeannette looked at him and held a hand up so he would not take the phone. She needed to finish the call.

"Yes, he visited me. He tried to kill me. He failed. I took him down, and he is now in jail. That is not why I called you. When we were married, you controlled me, didn't you?"

"Yes, I did. I am very good at that. I had you under my thumb but good! My friend helped. Too bad he didn't finish the job," Jeff said snidely.

"You verbally abused me, didn't you?"

"Speak English! What are you talking about?" Jeff yelled into the phone. Mark moved toward the telephone. Jeannette held her hand up, again to stop him.

"You degraded me every day, demanded that I do whatever you told me to, called me names, and embarrassed me in front of your friends. That is called verbal abuse."

"Yep. I had you right where I wanted you, until Judy messed it up. I hated her. Is she still alive?" Jeff asked.

"Yes, she is alive," Jeannette shook her head in disgust at his question. "The reason I called is to tell you I forgive you. I do not want to hate anymore. I want to be clear. We will never be friends, but I forgive you for everything you did and said to me." Jeff said nothing. Breaking the silence, Jeannette said, "Jeff? Jeff? Are you there?" She heard a sniff. Her mouth dropped. She looked at Mark in shock.

"I'm here. Why would you forgive me?" Jeff asked.

"Because I don't want to carry the hate directed at you anymore. It takes too much energy, and I want to have a whole heart. The only way I know how to do that is to forgive you. Do not mistake this as I want to be your friend. That is something we will never be. That is all I wanted to say. Good-bye." Jeannette hung up and sat back in the chair, shaking all over. "I did it! I am free! I can feel it!"

Mark had a look of amazement when he said, "Did he sniff? Was he crying?"

"I think he was. See what I mean about the power of forgiveness?"

"I witnessed a miracle!" Mark exclaimed. He took Jeannette in his arms and kissed her hard. He let go when she winced. "Did I hurt you? I did not mean to! I forgot about your arm! How is it possible for me to be more in love with you now than I was ten minutes ago?"

"It only hurt for a second. No worries," Jeannette said as tears streamed down her cheeks.

"You ARE hurt! Do we need to go to the hospital? Let me get my keys," Mark asked frantically.

"No, no. It is not my arm that has made me cry. It is an emotion of cleansing. There is no more hate in my heart for Jeff. I have forgiven. Whatever Jeff is feeling toward me is not my problem. He is the reason I got attacked. He just confirmed that." Mark's face went red with anger. "Let me finish. This is how I look at why my father and Jeff treated me so terribly. My father was an unhappy man, my father's father was on the crazy side, and his mother was a mean woman who also did not like me. The feeling was mutual. He grew up poor in a big family of nine children. I think he was angry because he never had enough of anything. He only had a fifth-grade education. When the Great Depression hit, the children had to quit school to work in the fields to help the family. He was mad at the world for the hand he was dealt.

Therefore, he needed an outlet for his hatred, so he chose me to take it out on. I also think I scared him. I have the gift of intuition. I call it a 'knowing.' Because of that, he thought I was the devil. He went so far as to call me that once."

"A devil?"

"Yes. As far as Jeff goes, he didn't talk very much about his family and his childhood. The only thing I know is that his mother was married several times. He barely knew his father. He has several half-brothers and sisters, and I don't think it was a happy household. My guess is, he felt the need to have control over something. He was insecure about everything, except himself. It was like he was born rebellious. Of course, this is my opinion. He saw in me a girl that was controlled by her father so it would be easy for him to step in and take control. I was already broken. The only way for him to feel good about himself was to lash out at me in anger to make sure he had the upper hand. He was a control freak, a narcissist. No one was going to have any notoriety but him. After a while, he got bored with me. A young girl flirted with him making him feel young, desired, and good about himself, so he tossed me aside. In my opinion, that was a gift. If he had not left me, I would probably still be with him. I would have never been where I am today or be the woman I have become. I believe that God rewarded me for all the misery. It was he who put the ability to forgive in my heart," Jeannette explained. "Whether I am right or wrong, this is how I look at it."

Mark remained quiet for a few minutes while he thought about what she had just told him.

"That is a lot to take in," Mark said, running his hands through his hair. "You are an amazing woman. I am having trouble knowing Jeff is the reason for your injury. I want to hunt him down and beat the crap out of him!"

"Think about it. What good would that do? It already happened, the man is in jail, and I survived," Jeannette said.

"It would make me feel better, that's for sure!" Mark exclaimed.

"I know you think so. I love that you want to protect me and make me feel secure. You already do, sweetheart. Remember this, sometimes bad things happen. Those bad things can put us on the path to the best things of our lives. All these events have led to you. Let the anger go. It is all in the past, and you cannot change it. Live in the now and look to the future."

"How did you get so smart?" Mark asked. He held her with gentleness. "I want to introduce you to my family."

"Okay. When?" Jeanette asked.

"I will talk to them to find out what evening works for them. I have a private room that we can use."

"Sounds wonderful. I will do my best to make a good impression. That reminds me. In a few weeks, I am going to have family time in Oregon at my home. Would you consider accompanying me? I have plenty of room. I would like you to get to know my boys and my soon-to-be daughter-in-law. I will introduce you to the young people who stop by who are my boys' friends and my adopted children. You will be under the microscope, again," she cautioned.

"Man, oh, man! There are a lot of people in your life that I have to impress! I should be able to get away in a few weeks. I am anxious to see Oregon, but I am more anxious to spend special time with you," Mark said with a big smile.

"Time for David to bring the car. I should be home doing my exercises, paperwork I did not finish, and checking my e-mail. I am sure there are several from Bridgett. No more procrastinating," Jeannette told him.

"It is just as well. My new waiter needs to be checked on. Hopefully, he has not spilled anything more. When will I see you again?" Mark said with a pout.

"Don't pout. It is not a good look for you. There is no telling what Bridgett has on my schedule for the week. I will check it first thing in the morning and call you. By the way, I am ready for our first time." Jeannette kissed Mark tenderly before she left.

Mark groaned, "You tell me that and leave? Woman don't tease me. I am likely to explode!"

Jeannette smiled with pleasure and left.

That night Jeannette slept better than she ever had. She woke up with a smile on her face and free of pain. She stretched and said, "What a wonderful day! No more black cloud hanging over my head."

Her phone rang. She answered with a cheery, "Hello."

"Am I Speaking with Jeannette?"

"Yes, this is she. Who am I speaking to?"

"This is Detective Alto. I wanted to let you know the date of the trial. Originally it was set for July, but it is now going to start on May 15. That is five weeks from now. The DA thinks the trial will last for two to three days but plan on all week. We have several other witnesses who are willing to testify against him. Are you still willing to testify?"

"Absolutely. By the way, what is his name?" Jeannette asked.

"Jim Westcock. The DA will be contacting you from now on about the case. Do not be surprised if you are served with a subpoena. It is just a legal document that makes sure you will testify at the trial," the detective explained.

"Nothing will stop me. Jim Westcock needs to be in jail. Thank you for the call, Detective," Jeannette said calmly.

The first thing she did upon arriving at Windy City was sit down with Bridgett to go over her schedule for the week and have her block out the week of May 15 for the trial.

"My condolences for your father," Bridgett said.

"Thank you. My father is gone. I am okay with it. Look at it this way. When there is an ending, God will give you a new beginning. My new beginning is Mark," Jeannette confessed with a pink face.

"Mark? I wondered why your face glowed, and you have a smile that won't quit," Bridgett said.

"The restaurant Clay surprised me at a couple of months ago? That is where I met him. He owns My City restaurant."

"That is wonderful! When do we get to meet him? He has to have our approval. You know that, right?" Bridgett asked.

"Maybe this week. We will have to see how Mark and my schedules work out," Jeannette said.

"Wednesday! Wednesday is a light workday. He could come by at our closing time," Bridgett suggested.

"Hum. I am not sure if Mark wants to be evaluated and scrutinized by all of you. If it were me, I would be overwhelmed," Jeannette confessed.

"We will be on our best behavior, I promise," Bridgett said with a smile.

"I will ask him, but no guarantees," Jeannette warned.

She picked up the phone and dialed Mark before Bridgett shut the door. "Hello. Is this the handsome man I like to kiss?"

"If this is a beautiful blonde that I am in love with, then yes, this is he. How are you, Sweetheart?"

"I am wonderful! I slept like a baby — no more nightmares. I did not feel fearful at all this morning leaving my apartment. That is a big improvement. That reminds me, Detective Alto called this morning. The trial starts on May 15. I promised to testify. The guy's name is Jim Westcock," Jeannette said very calmly.

"I will be there with you," Mark said with certainty.

"Now, on to a better subject. Everyone at Windy City would like to meet you. As Bridgett put it, you need to have their approval. So before you agree, you know you will be under a microscope with my family at Windy City? With that said, how does Wednesday sound?" Jeannette asked.

"Wednesday looks pretty good. I can be there at five o'clock. Afterward, I will take you to dinner somewhere other than my restaurant. On the way home we can take a drive to our place," Mark suggested.

"It sounds like a very nice date. Bye. Bridgett, will you come in here, please? Have a seat. Mark is stopping by on Wednesday at five. Can we make that work?" Jeannette asked.

"I thought that maybe we could host a meet and greet in the conference room. We always lock the door at five anyway. There might be a client or two still working on putting tracks down, but they could join us. I could order finger food and champagne. We have all been working pretty hard, so this would be like a bonus!" Bridgett said excitedly.

"You started planning this the minute you left my office, didn't you? That is why you are my assistant. You have brilliant ideas. Okay, set it up. Thank you."

It was Wednesday before she knew it. Closing time was almost upon them. Jeannette walked to the conference room to see what Bridgett did. It indeed was more than she had expected. The room was rearranged with a party-like atmosphere. Little tables sprinkled around the room with two red roses jutting up from small vases. There was one long table on the far side of the area where the food was arranged buffet style, and alongside was a table set with champagne.

Bridgett spotted Jeannette and hurried to her. "What do you think? Does it look like a party? I didn't hire waiters. Everyone can serve themselves. It's buffet style. That makes it more comfortable. Like family."

"I think you have done a fine job and just in time. Mark will be here in fifteen minutes. I will stop by the sound booth and remind Greg he has a party to attend," she informed Bridgett.

Jeannette was almost at her office when she heard Max say, "Good evening. You must be Mark. My name is Max. I am head of security."

"It is nice to meet you, Max. Will you point me in the direction of Jeannette's office?" Mark asked.

"No need for pointing. I am standing behind you," Jeannette said with a larger-than-life smile.

"Hello, beautiful. I think I am a few minutes early. I could not wait another minute to see you."

"Would you escort me to my office before we go to the conference room? I need to grab something. Max, will you lock the door? Bridgett has her hands full. Thank you. How do you like my office? It is a little bigger than yours, and the decor is not as manly.”

Mark closed the door. He had a growing need to hold Jeannette in his arms. “Sure, your office is nice. Kiss me, please? I cannot hold out any longer,” he said hastily.

“One kiss then we have to—”

Mark closed his mouth over hers cutting off her sentence.

“That was a nice way to shut me up. We need to go to the conference room. It should be full by now. I need to grab these envelopes. Shall we?”

The conference room burst with applause as the couple walked in. Mark gave a parade wave while Jeannette giggled at him.

“You act like this is a normal thing for you to receive applause,” Jeannette whispered in his ear.

“Well, I am a special kind of guy, so yes, this is normal,” he bragged.

“Liar,” Jeannette said and held a hand up to quiet the room.

“Hello, everyone, employees, and talent. I want to introduce Mark. He is a restaurateur. My City Restaurant is his creation. If you get a chance, try it out. It is an amazing place, and the food is wonderful. While I have you all here, I would like to say a few words. Don’t worry. I will keep it short. In the last few months, we have had some, let’s say, challenges to overcome, and business has picked up. I know how hard all of you have been working. I saw a team getting the job done and helping each other. Thank you, talent, for sticking with us. I am thankful for each one of you that works at Windy City. To show my appreciation, I have an envelope for each one of you with a little bonus. Thank you, family, I love you. See Bridgett. She will give you an envelope. Now back to eating and drinking! Enjoy yourselves!"

"Mark? My name is Greg. I run the sound booth. So, you own a restaurant? Do you know anything about the music business?"

"Nice to meet you, Greg. No, I do not know anything about the music business, but I am willing to learn. It is Jeannette's baby, and I will support her 100 percent. Just so you know, I am not a serial killer, a cop has never arrested me, and I will never hurt Jeannette."

The answer Mark gave Greg astonished him. With surprise in his voice, Greg said, "Okay. Thanks for answering my questions. Come by the booth anytime. Enjoy yourself."

"Well, look who's here! Mark!" Clay said in his usual loud voice.

"Hello, Clay. Jeannette is showing me off. I am her arm candy," Mark said proudly.

"Excuse me? You are what? Did you say arm candy?" Jeannette asked in a slightly high voice and rolled her eyes. "Oh, my goodness. You are quite the comedian tonight! Hello, Clay. What brings you here this evening?"

"I was talking to Greg about scheduling time in the booth. I am getting ready for the next album. By the way, how is your arm?"

"Healing, slowly. I tried playing. I couldn't get a sound out, yet. I am getting close. In a couple more weeks I should be able to work on the songs you wanted. I have one that has been rattling around in my head," Jeannette told Clay.

"Hot dog! Then you agree to write a couple of songs for me? Is that what I am hearing?"

"Yes, Clay, but the price might go up. Now that I am in demand, I can ask for more money," Jeannette said with a straight face for as long as she could, then burst out laughing. "Oh, Clay, I'm just kidding. Same price as always."

"Thank God. Little lady, you had my heart pounding," Clay said.

"Mark, would you like a quick tour around the building? Clay, come with us. Together we can show him both the sound room and sound booth where you make all that beautiful music," Jeannette suggested.

During the tour, Mark took it all in and listened to every word Jeannette said. He could see the love she had for her company. He was amazed at what a wonderful, caring boss she is by observing how every person displayed love and respect for her. Actions always tell the truth. All he had to do was pay attention. It made Mark wonder how his employees felt about him.

The evening was lovely. The couple's date ended at Mark and Jeannette's special place overlooking the city. They stood as they had the first time, he brought her to this peaceful place. He leaned against her back with his arms wrapped around her, and his head leaned against hers in silence.

An unexpected car pulled next to theirs. The engine quieted. One person got out of the vehicle. Mark guardedly moved in front of Jeannette. A figure walked toward them. His muscles tightened, preparing to protect his love, if necessary.

"What do you want?" Mark shouted. There was no reply. The figure kept moving closer. "Who are you, and what do you want?" Mark shouted

"Hello. I see you have found the most romantic spot in the entire city," a faint voice said.

"What do you want?" Mark asked again.

The figure emerged from the shadows to reveal an older lady, small in stature, gray hair, with a sad look on her slightly wrinkled face.

"I want nothing from you. I came here to capture memories. My husband, Henry, brought me here to propose fifty years ago. The bushes and trees are bigger, but this place is just as I remembered it." She stepped closer. "My name is Irene. I apologize if I frightened you. You see, I lost my Henry a few days ago. I left his memorial service to come here to remember how our life together began. We were so much in love. He put a ring on my finger, and I thought my heart would burst. See, this is the ring," she said, holding her hand up to show them. "I am sure after all these years it doesn't look very special to you, but to me, it is the most beautiful and most precious thing in the world. It is the most valuable thing I own." Irene dabbed at her eyes with a cloth handkerchief.

Jeannette stepped from behind Mark to say, "Irene, this is Mark, and I am Jeannette. Please, come join us."

She put her hand out to welcome Irene. She stood close to Jeannette holding her hand. Mark stood behind them with an arm on either of the ladies' shoulders, clutching both close. Irene cried softly, feeling as if Henry was once again with her. The three stood content and still as long as Irene needed.

Irene turned to the couple and said, "Thank you for being so kind and helping me with memories of my beloved Henry and the love we shared. I am waiting for the day I join him in heaven. Well,

I have taken enough of your time. Your marriage will be long and happy. Your love is as strong as ours was. God bless you."

Either she disappeared into thin air, or Mark and Jeannette lost time in their shock at what she said. Irene said marriage. It had never been uttered between them. They had only been dating for a few months. Although Jeannette had believed she would be with Mark for the rest of her life. But marriage had not occurred to her. Maybe this was a message sent from above?

Mark regained his senses, clearing his voice, then said, "Ahem. Well, I guess we should be going. It is getting late."

Jeannette felt a sense of coldness coming from him. "Mark? Did Irene say something to make you uncomfortable? Was it that she mentioned marriage? Was it because she assumed we were married or getting married?" Jeannette asked with concern in her voice.

"No!" he said nervously, lying, almost shouting. Marriage was not in his plan. It was written all over his face. He loved Jeannette, but marry her? Whoa! The last time he thought about marriage, it did not turn out well.

He put his hands in his pockets with his head down, trying to mask what he was thinking and said, "She disappeared. I didn't hear or see her leave. Don't you find that a little spooky?"

Jeannette knew he was lying and skirting around the issue. He wanted to get her mind off of what Irene had said. Although she had not consciously thought about marrying Mark, it had been at the back of her mind. Irene brought it to the front. Since they started dating, she could not imagine her life without Mark. At that moment she thought, "He does not want to spend the rest of our lives together. He doesn't love me. Why did he tell me he loved me? Why waste time with me? Does he want to get me into bed, then be done with me? Her stomach was sick and tied in knots. I opened my heart only to have it broken by a man who alone lives in the here and now and his satisfaction. Mark only cares about what he wants. She was married to a man like that once before. Never again! What now? Is it over? Was this just a game to him?"

"Spooky? Maybe. I don't know. Please, take me home? I suddenly got a chill." The chill came from Mark, not the weather.

The drive home was quiet. Their minds were spinning with questions, at least Jeannette had things whirling in her head. Maybe he was planning to dump her? She was doubtful if she wanted to see him again.

Mark was terrified at the thought of marriage. "Do I want to commit? Do I want to give up my freedom? I thought I wanted to be married once before. What if Jeannette cheated on me? It would kill me inside. Do I want to take that chance? What is wrong with what we have now?"

The car came to a halt in front of her apartment building. Jeannette quickly got out of the vehicle before Mark had a chance to open the car door.

Jeannette said without looking at him, "Goodnight, Mark. Thank you for a lovely evening."

"Jeannette, let me see you to your door, please?"

"Not tonight, thanks. I can find my way. Good evening, Sid," she said, sweeping through the door leading to the elevator. Jeannette hurried by Sid so quickly he barely had time to tip his hat. Sid turned to see Mark leaning against the car with hands in his pockets, and his head hung low. Something happened that upset them both, but it was none of his business to feign concern. Mark gave a wave to Sid then pulled into traffic.

It was apparent there was something wrong with her when she arrived at work the next morning. There was whispering among the employees about Mark. Jeannette had Bridgett reserve a seat on the red-eye leaving on Friday night for Oregon. She needed as much distance as possible from Mark so she could reflect on their relationship if that was what they had. The one question that plagued her was, "Is Mark like Jeff? Tell me he loves me then turns into a monster? If that is the case, I will kick him to the curb! No one will ever treat me like that again!"

Throughout the day, Greg was talking about visiting My City to have a chat with the owner.

"Something has happened between them. Mark has hurt her. If this is the kind of man Mark is, breaking women's hearts, I will tell him to stay away from Jeannette in no uncertain terms! She doesn't need that jerk!" Greg said with certainty.

"Jeannette, Mark is on line two," Bridgett said over the intercom.

"Tell him I am in a meeting," Jeannette replied.

Bridgett delivered the message and was tempted to ask Mark what happened between them, but she held her tongue. When the moment was right, she would broach the subject with Jeannette.

Over the next two days, Jeannette buried herself in work not coming out of her office until it was time to go home. She only took calls that were important for business. Otherwise, Bridgett took a message. Her suitcase was left in the car on Friday morning so David could take her straight to the airport from the office.

Friday evening, Jeannette emerged from her office ready to leave for the airport. Before she went, she gave strict instructions to her assistant.

"Bridgett do not give out my home phone number to anyone. Is that clear? I know that is company policy. I just felt the need to say it. Of course, as always, if you need me, call. I will see you in ten days."

Jeannette was off to the airport. Just after she left, Mark called Windy City. "May I speak with Jeannette, please?"

"I am sorry she is not available. Jeannette has left for the day. May I take a message?"

"This is Mark. Where is she? At home? Dinner? Where?" he asked frantically.

"I am not at liberty to say. Would you like to leave a message?" Bridgett asked again.

"No! I need to talk to her! Please tell me where I can find her? I need to talk to her," Mark pleaded.

"I am sorry, Mark. She is unavailable. She is not here," Bridgett said sternly trying to keep her professionalism in check.

Greg overheard Bridgett say the name, Mark.

"Are you talking to Mark? Give me the phone! Mark? Greg. I don't know what game you are playing, or what you have done to Jeannette, but it ends now! Stay away from her! Jerk!" Greg slammed the phone onto its cradle. "If he calls again, let me know. I will pay him a visit. One more thing, call the answering service and tell them not to put any calls from Mark through to her even if he says it is an emergency. They are not to tell him where she is."

"I am way ahead of you. I already took care of it," Bridgett told Greg.

Jeannette turned her phone off as she left the building, assuring herself that no one could reach her. Mark had already called at least ten times over the last couple of days. It upset her just seeing his name on her phone, so she put it on silent and chucked it into a desk drawer while she was at work.

"Is everything alright back there?" David asked, looking at Jeannette via the rearview mirror.

"I have a lot on my mind. David, if Mark sees you and asks where I am, do not tell him. I need an uninterrupted week. I thought I loved him, but . . . Well, I don't think he is the right man. Sorry, David. I am a little down in the dumps."

"Not to worry. We all have those days. Oregon is just what you need, I think," he said cheerily. "I have never seen the state, but I hear it is beautiful."

"David, I don't mean to be rude, but I need quiet," Jeannette said as nicely as she could for David to stop talking.

"Yes, miss," David said.

He wanted to get her mind on something other than Mark and failed. There was silence on the way to the airport. Upon arrival, David popped the trunk to retrieve her bag before opening her door. He knew she did not want to feel vulnerable standing by the car alone.

"I hope your time in Oregon is peaceful," David told her as he tipped his hat.

"Good-bye. Thank you for understanding, David. I promise when I get back, I will smile more," Jeannette assured him.

It felt good to be home. Irma kept the house sparkling clean in Jeannette's absence and always had something prepared for her to eat when she arrived.

"Hello, Irma. What smells so good?"

"I have made a ham and cheese quiche."

"Sounds wonderful. Is there any coffee? Thanks. Join me. I want to hear all the gossip."

Irma told her everything she had heard at the beauty salon. Who was having a baby, who got arrested, what couple split up along with other miscellaneous topics. When the one-sided conversation finally died to silence, Irma observed Jeannette had not said a word.

"What's wrong, Sweetie? Your heart is hurting. Tell me about it. Get it off your chest. You can talk to old Irma. I never repeat anything you tell me. Your secrets are safe." She put her hand on Jeannette's in a bond of compassion.

"Yes, my heart is hurting. I fell in love with a man. He said he loved me and then, well, he suddenly turned into someone cold. I was stupid! How could I let myself fall for him? Thank God I did not sleep with him! He does not want to commit, even though he said he loved me. I will not be with another man who is like Jeff. It scares me with the thought he might be. I have not spoken to him since Wednesday night. He keeps calling. I hit ignore. His name is Mark. If by some miracle he gets my home phone number, tell him I am not here. I apologize for complaining. I let my thoughts become vocal. I think I will take a short nap. I have a hard time sleeping in-flight. I will be up in a couple of hours. You don't need to stay for the rest of the day if you do not want to. It is your choice. I will be fine."

Irma watched Jeannette drag a suitcase behind her like a child with a favorite blanket. Her heart ached for Jeannette.

Mumbling to herself as she cleaned the dishes, Irma said, "Men! Good for nothing! That woman has been through enough! What is wrong with him? She is a good woman. It is smart not getting involved with a man like Jeff. If this . . . Mark was here, I would give him a good tongue lashing he would not soon forget! Good riddance to Mark! What a jerk!"

Irma heard low whimpering coming from Jeannette's room. She hesitated for a moment, then tapped on the door.

"May I come in? Please?" Irma pleaded.

"Come in," she answered.

She rushed to Jeannette, scooped the sobbing woman into her arms, and rocked, attempting to soothe her broken heart.

"That's it. Get it all out. Irma's here. He is not good enough for you. It will all work out for the best. I promise. There are lots of people who truly love you. For now, find comfort in knowing that. Oh, sweetheart, I wish I could make this all go away."

Up to this point, she had not shed a tear for Mark. She could not hold them in any longer. Eventually, Jeannette grew tired and fell asleep. Two hours later, she woke, feeling drained with puffy eyes.

"There's my sweet girl," Irma greeted. "Did you have a good rest?"

"Yes, I did, but I feel like I have been drug through knotholes. This is ridiculous. Why did I let myself get so wrapped up with Mark?" Jeannette said, beating herself up. "I am trying to be upset with him. Instead, I wonder what he is doing and if he is alright. Crap! I wish I could play my guitar! Humph. Might as well try. I feel stronger. Irma, will you be making dinner, or should I plan on ordering in?"

"I have a nice pot of stew simmering on the stove. Comfort food, there is nothing better than a big bowl of stew with a thick slice of crusty bread," Irma said with a smile.

"I need comfort food. That sounds wonderful. I will be in my office if you need me. Oh! I forgot to turn my phone back on! If Sean or Tyler tried calling, they will be freaking out. I didn't tell them I was coming home. I had better give them a call right now."

The conversation with her sons was short and to the point. She told them about Mark. Neither was happy with him. Jeannette reassured them she was okay and was glad it happened now instead of later.

In her office, the beat-up old guitar stood in the corner waiting to be picked up. Jeannette stared at it. She was hesitant to try the soundless strings from her last attempt. Alas, she put her pessimism aside and picked it up.

"Okay, old friend, let's give you a try." The first down stroke did not make a sound. "Stupid thumb! You are stronger than that!" she yelled at her thumb in frustration. She tried again. This time she could faintly hear a chord. It was not loud but evident. She tried again. The sound was music to her ears in more ways than one. There was no mistaking the sound of a full chord. Her happiness rained down her cheeks in the form of small drops of saltwater.

Irma was listening outside the door, wiping her hands on the apron she wore. Her heart swelled hearing the chord.

"Thank you, my God in heaven, for giving the gift of music back to Jeannette. You have blessed her with a beautiful talent. Thank you," Irma prayed.

Jeannette laughed out loud with each chord. It was like a child with a new toy that made noise. The perseverance had paid off. It would be a gradual process to be able to play as she did before the incident. Right now, it was impossible to play for more than five minutes. It made her arm ache. She sat the scruffy-looking guitar back in the corner, for now.

Yelling to the ceiling, "I'm back! Do you hear that, Jim Westcock? You cannot stop me from making music! Thank you, God!"

It took until Wednesday for her to feel the depression starting to ease. She turned her mind to graduation as well as Sean's wedding. Tia was thinking August, but Jeannette was lobbying for Labor Day weekend in September. One point of Jeannette's argument was more people would be able to attend and have an extra day for travel. The decision was ultimately up to Sean and Tia.

Jeannette and Tia were becoming very close. They talked several times a day. Sometimes it was about nothing in particular, other times it was the wedding, more recently it was about graduation. The date was confirmed, June 13 Sean and Tia would receive their diplomas and Sean would deliver the valedictorian address. A reservation at a hotel close to the campus was made right away for June 12 and 13. The next item on the agenda was what to give them for graduation? That was going to take some thought for another day.

She spent the week lounging by the pool when the weather cooperated, exercising her arm and playing her guitar. Mark called her cell phone twice every day. Ignore was always her response.

One of her favorite places in the evening was sitting by the fire pit, watching the fire dance. There she talked to Robert, drank a glass of wine, played the guitar, or prayed. This night was for praying.

"Heavenly Father, I know you are looking after me. Sometimes it is hard for me to have faith that you are. Forgive me for that. I am human. I do not know what your plan is for my life. I wish I did. My belief is, you put in my heart that I needed to forgive my father and Jeff. I did. I felt the black cloud lift from my shoulders. So why does it feel like punishment? I do not want to harden my heart or put-up walls to protect myself. I opened my heart, and now it is broken because of Mark. Please heal my heart and stop the pain? What do you want me to do? No matter how hard I try to forget, Mark is at the forefront of my brain. He is impossible to forget. How do I forgive him? Does my life always have to be about forgiveness for being mistreated by men? Robert treated me wonderfully, but you wanted him in heaven. Now there is Mark. Is he a monster like Jeff? Does he really and truly love me or just saying that so I could be another one of his conquests? Is he the one you picked for me? Is all this in my mind? How do I go back to Chicago knowing that I will see him at some point? Oh, God, I need answers to all these questions! My mind will not shut off. Please give me a sign of what you want me to do? Thank you. Amen."

Friday came too quickly. Saturday she would be flying to Chicago. The facade of being over Mark was far from the truth. The tight ball in the pit of her stomach told the truth. The time was quickly coming to face him and hear what he has to say. She hoped it would be evident if he were telling the truth when they talked face-to-face.

Jeannette's cell phone rang late Friday evening. It was from Mark. She thought, "I should probably answer and talk to him over the phone to get it done. He has waited long enough."

"Hello?"

"Jeannette? Is it really you? I have been frantic and lost without you!" Mark exclaimed.

"Okay, Mark. Before we go any further with this conversation, tell me why you turned so cold toward me the night we met Irene? Tell me the truth," she said without emotion.

"The thought of marriage had me shaking in my boots. I was enjoying what we had. I was scared."

"You told me over, and over that you loved me. Is that the truth? Or just a lie to get me in bed?"

"Jeannette, please believe me. I love you with all my heart!" His voice cracked with emotion, but he continued, "Making love to you would be the icing on the cake. Just like you said. That was not my intention. I swear it! I intended to get to know you. I thought you were stunning, sweet, and nothing like anyone I have ever known. I told you at the beginning that I am not someone who is looking for a one-night stand."

"Yes, you said that. Anybody can say that. You showed me you are someone who can turn love off and on when it suits you. You were cold as ice to me. You hurt me. It felt like whatever we had was a lie. I will not give any man my heart that is going to stomp on it!" Jeannette said, raising her voice.

"I know I hurt you. I am so, so very sorry. I promised you I would never hurt you, and I did. If I could take it back, I would. I am so sorry. Please, let me see you? I am a mess without you. Bridgett refused to give me a number where I could reach you. Your answering service said the same thing. I have been so scared I lost the best woman I have ever known to my stupidity! Please let me see you? Please?" Mark pleaded.

"I am not sure this is smart on my part, but I will agree to see you tomorrow night. I will meet you at our place at eight o'clock. If I want to shout at you, I can without anyone hearing me."

"Can't I see you tonight? Jeannette, please do not make me wait another day?" Mark begged.

"No. Tomorrow night. Good-bye." She ended the conversation.

She laid on the bed, going over what he had said. "His voice sounded panic-stricken. That was good. He missed her. It didn't occur to him I was in Oregon. He said he was scared he lost me. Hum. He sounded sincerely upset. It might not have been an act. I should be able to tell when I see him in person. My employees did their job. He couldn't find me. Bridgett deserves flowers. Enough of this. My suitcase is not going to pack itself."

Jeannette landed in Chicago at five o'clock. David, as usual, was there to pick her up.

"Hello! How was your flight?" David asked.

"Good. Will you take me by my favorite restaurant to pick up something to go, please?"

"Of course. You look like you feel better," David said.

"I do, but later tonight I will know for sure. I have agreed to meet Mark. He needs to grovel. I caved and took his call last night. When I last saw him, a woman we were talking to mentioned the word marriage. He immediately treated me like I was the black plague. I was not the one that put the idea of marriage in his head! I have never mentioned marriage! I hadn't even thought about it! A switch flipped inside him, and Mark became cold as ice toward me. I have been questioning if he, in truth, loves me as he said or if he is playing me for a fool."

"Oh, I see," David said. "We have all been guessing at what happened. From what I understand, Greg is fit to be tied. He called Mark a jerk over the phone. If Mark remains in your life, he has a lot of fences to mend, and apologies to make. It will not be easy."

"Way to go Greg! He's got my back!" That put a smile on Jeannette's face.

"We all do, Jeannette. How is your arm? It looks like you can move it a little easier," David observed.

"It is much better. I played my guitar! I could only manage five minutes at a time. Those five minutes were a godsend. It made the world feel right again."

"I am so happy for you! Things are looking up!" David said, relieved to know she would play again.

"I need you to drive me to my meeting with Mark. I will have to show you how to get there. Pick me up at seven-thirty?"

"Yes, ma'am."

After eating dinner, Jeannette took a quick shower and put on a pair of slacks and a crisp, pink cotton blouse. She brought along a jacket to stave off any chill from the night air, or ice from Mark.

"This is odd. You are giving me directions from the back seat. Does that make you a backseat driver?" David asked, jokingly.

"Funny, but yes it does. Take the next exit. Turn right at the next signal. Now follow this road for a mile or two. I will tell you when we are close," Jeannette instructed.

"I assume you want me to wait for you in case the need arises for you to leave?" David asked.

"Yes, please. I am not sure how this is going to end. I am nervous. We are almost to the turn. At the red mailbox turn right. It is not a very good road. This is the way it is in the country. In Oregon, this would not be considered the country. In some places it would be considered downtown," Jeannette said, getting a laugh out of David. "There he is, straight ahead. Park in the wider area on the left. Okay, here I go."

Mark stood, looking sheepish, with his hands in his pockets. His face was anything but happy. He had dark circles under his eyes like he had not slept in days. He forced himself not to run to her. She looked so beautiful an angel would pale to her.

"Jeannette! I am so glad to see you!" He made a gesture as if he was going to hug her. She took half a step back. "Okay, I will keep my distance until you are comfortable."

"Well, here we are. What do you want to say?"

"Now that you are here, the speech I had prepared to ask for your forgiveness doesn't cut it. I should never have reacted like I did. Up to that moment, I pictured us growing old together, playing with grandchildren, and enjoying every moment together. I guess what I was imagining was marriage, but I had not heard the word out loud. It scared me. I told you about the woman I was engaged to, and what happened with her. I had a flashback. It would kill me if it happened with you."

"You mean to tell me you do not trust me? Do you know me at all? You think I would do something like that?" Her voice was getting louder. "I have been cheated on too! I would never cause pain like that to anyone!" She calmed herself as much as she could. "If true and complete love exists between two people, there is no desire to look for love or sex elsewhere. You are content with each other. You trust each other. Trust is a small word, but it is the all-important one in a relationship. Look me in the eyes and tell me how you really feel about me, and DO NOT LIE!"

"Jeannette, you take my breath away. When I am away from you, my chest tightens to the point of strangulation. My heart compresses and causes such pain I want to curl up and die. All I can think about is you. My business has taken a back seat to you. I want to be with you every minute. I want to be your protector, and your partner. I love you more than life itself. The days we spent apart almost killed me. I lost ten pounds because of worry. I never want to be without you again! I love you with all my heart. Please, please, I am begging you, forgive me? I will get on my knees and beg if you want me to," Mark said with tears welling up.

"No, I don't want you to beg, grovel maybe. Give me a minute. I will be right back."

She went to David and said something to him that made him leave. She once again joined Mark.

"You are telling me the truth. I can see it, I feel it. Let me make this crystal clear. I am not trying to trap you or force you into marrying me! I love you. It is that simple. If you ever have a trust issue with me again, talk to me. Don't clam up! I was terrified you were turning into Jeff! One minute you said you loved me, and the next you made me feel like I had the black plague! That was one of the ways Jeff used to control me. I had a flashback from hell! You cut me to the quick. I couldn't make the pain stop. I openly gave you my heart, and you handed it back, broken. I thought you did not want me any longer. If I forgive you, Mark, you have to promise me that your love is true and my heart is safe in your hands, and you better be telling me the truth! If not . . ."

He took a long stride to be close to her. He wanted desperately to touch her but held back until she gave him the go-ahead.

He said, "Sweetheart, I promise to love you until the day I die. There is no one I want, but you. I will take your heart and protect it. I love you with every ounce of my being. That is the truth."

She looked in his eyes and thought for a minute before saying, "I forgive you, Mark." In a split second, she was in his arms with his lips crushing hers.

He pulled away from the kiss. Jeannette saw tears glistening in the moonlight that spilled onto his cheeks.

"I promise I will never break your heart again. You feel so good in my arms. I don't want to ever let you go," he said. Mark was not embarrassed that he was crying. His worry was over. He was forgiven. She loves him.

They stood holding each other until the headlights from a car interrupted them. "Is David back?" Mark asked.

"He shouldn't be. I sent him home. Oh, look! I think it is Irene. Is that you, Irene?" Jeannette called out.

"Yes, it is Irene. I was hoping you would be here. The two of you have been on my mind. I need to deliver a message. I believe it is from God. It just came to my mind, and I knew I had to deliver it to you. Here it is," she said. "Your love was made in heaven. Both of you had things that needed to be learned and experienced before you were ready for each other. Do you understand? All the bad and all the good shaped you into who you are today. Jeannette, you are a gift and were made for Mark. Mark, you are a gift and was sent to Jeannette. Your hearts are a gift to each other."

"Irene! You were sent from God! I know it! I asked for a sign, and you delivered it." Jeannette hugged Irene and sobbed into her shoulder.

"Sweetheart, you are loved more than you can imagine. You should be holding Mark, not me. Love him," Irene whispered in her ear. Jeannette let Irene go to be held by the awaiting arms of her love.

"Jeannette, I love you so much that it physically hurts," Mark told her.

"I feel the same way. Irene, how can we thank you?" Jeannette said as she turned to Irene. She was gone. "Mark, did you see Irene leave? Did you see her headlights or hear the engine start?"

"I did not see or hear anything. Just like last time, Irene disappeared," Mark said.

"I think she was an angel!" Jeannette looked to the night sky and said, "Wow, God! You are awesome! Thanks!" Looking at Mark, she asked, "Do you believe Irene is an angel?"

"I will believe whatever you want me to believe. It got you in my arms. Irene very well might have been an angel. She was an answer to prayer!"

They stayed a little longer wrapped in each other's arms — their hearts were beating as one.

Lesson Learned: Communication is the key to a successful relationship. Express what you feel. Do not let things fester. It becomes a cancer of sorts and will destroy the base on which your relationship stands.

Trust is the almighty word that makes or breaks a relationship. If you lose trust, you lose the connection.

I have a lot to be thankful for. The most important is love, real love.

What Now? There are things that I am going to change in my life. I chose to get the negativity out of my life, even when it meant breaking my heart by kicking Shelly out. I have faced problems head-on and not turned tail and run from them. Because of that, I am a stronger woman. It is okay if someone does not like me. I am not perfect, and neither are they. I like myself for who I am. I am real. What you see is who I am — nothing more, nothing less. Fake people, in my opinion, have personality issues or issues they are hiding. They are probably people who are not suitable for me to have in my life.

I will change my mind to have a more positive outlook, and I will be thankful for what I have, the lessons I have learned, and who I am. I am going to work on myself by going ***Full Steam Ahead.***

Jeannette has a court case against Jim Westcock coming up. Will she be able to face him without fear?

Will Mark and Jeannette get married?

Will Jeannette eventually move back to Chicago?

Is Irene an angel?

Jeannette and her family have a lot more living to do. For all the answers, coming out soon is the final book about Jeannette: "Full Steam Ahead".